The new Zebra Regency Romance logo that you see on the cover is a photograph of an actual regency "tuzzy-muzzy." The fashionable regency lady often wore a tuzzy-muzzy tied with a satin or velvet riband around her wrist to carry a fragrant nosegay. Usually made of gold or silver, tuzzy-muzzies varied in design from the elegantly simple to the exquisitely ornate. The Zebra Regency Romance tuzzy-muzzy is made of alabaster with a silver filigree edging.

A HEADY COMBINATION

"Don't let's quarrel. Have another glass of champagne," said Jason hastily.

Her mood changing, Araminta laughed, saying, "No, thank you. You'll have me foxed if I take another drop." She eyed him quizzically. "Perhaps that's what you had in mind?"

Jason recoiled in mock distress. "Miss Smith! How could you even think such a thing? No, don't go," he added as she rose to leave. "The evening is still young, and we could get to know each other much better."

"Oh, I think we know each other quite well enough."

Catching her hand as she went by, Jason swung her around to face him. "I'd hoped that you enjoyed my company."

"I do. Very much. But I must go." Even to her own ears, Araminta sounded breathless.

"Well, then, why are we wasting time?" Jason murmured. Placing his hands on her shoulders, he pulled her close to him, bending his head to brush his lips across her eyes and her cheeks.

Shivers of electric excitement raced through Araminta's body, and she had an almost irresistible ~~~~~~~~~ her arms tightly around h~~~~~~~~~~~~~~~~~~ am foxed . . .

THE BEST OF REGENCY ROMANCES

AN IMPROPER COMPANION   (2691, $3.95)
by Karla Hocker
At the closing of Miss Venable's Seminary for Young
Ladies school, mistress Kate Elliott welcomed the invitation to be Liza Ashcroft's chaperone for the Season at
Bath. Little did she know that Miss Ashcroft's father, the
handsome widower Damien Ashcroft would also enter her
life. And not as a passive bystander or dutiful dad.

WAGER ON LOVE   (2693, $2.95)
by Prudence Martin
Only a rogue like Nicholas Ruxart would choose a bride on
the basis of a careless wager. And only a rakehell like Nicholas would then fall in love with his betrothed's grey-eyed
sister! The cynical viscount had always thought one blushing miss would suit as well as another, but the unattainable
Jane Sommers soon proved him wrong.

LOVE AND FOLLY   (2715, $3.95)
by Sheila Simonson
To the dismay of her more sensible twin Margaret, Lady
Jean proceeded to fall hopelessly in love with the silver-
tongued, seditious poet, Owen Davies—and catapult her
entire family into social ruin . . . Margaret was used to
gentlemen falling in love with vivacious Jean rather than
with her—even the handsome Johnny Dyott whom she secretly adored. And when Jean's foolishness led her into the
arms of the notorious Owen Davies, Margaret knew she
could count on Dyott to avert scandal. What she didn't
know, however was that her sweet sensibility was exerting a
charm all its own.

*Available wherever paperbacks are sold, or order direct from the
Publisher. Send cover price plus 50¢ per copy for mailing and
handling to Zebra Books, Dept. 3347, 475 Park Avenue South,
New York, N.Y. 10016. Residents of New York, New Jersey and
Pennsylvania must include sales tax. DO NOT SEND CASH.*

An Independent Lady

Lois Stewart

ZEBRA BOOKS
KENSINGTON PUBLISHING CORP.

For my daughters
Alice, Monica and Claire

ZEBRA BOOKS

are published by

Kensington Publishing Corp.
475 Park Avenue South
New York, NY 10016

First printing: March, 1991

Printed in the United States of America

Chapter One

As the heavy traveling coach lumbered to a stop in the courtyard of the inn, Lady Araminta Beresford poked her companion in the ribs. "Odile, wake up."

"I'm not asleep," came the long-suffering reply in mournful French. "But if I open my eyes, even a crack, I know I'll be sick. Never again will I set foot aboard a ship. *Jamais, jamais.* It will kill me."

"Nonsense. The Channel crossing *was* a bit rough, but you'll soon recover after a rest and a good meal. I'm told that the Ship is one of the best inns in Dover." Araminta motioned to the thin, middle-aged servant sitting opposite them. "Jessie and I will help you to your bed and in no time at all you'll be feeling quite yourself again. And please, Odile, do try to practice your English now that we've arrived in England."

A stableboy opened the carriage door and let down the steps. As Araminta reached for the lad's extended hand, she paused at the sudden sound of an angry altercation. "Good God, that's Hassan's voice."

Araminta scurried down the steps and raced to the rear of the coach, where a sinewy dark-complexioned youth dressed in a flowing headdress and a long striped gown had fastened his hands in a death lock around the throat of one of the hostlers. The latter's fellow stable hands swarmed around the dark youth, striking him on the head and attempting to pull him off his prey, but they failed to break his

5

grip. Meanwhile, the unfortunate victim was turning blue.

"Hassan, release that man at once," Araminta called out in rapid Arabic. But Hassan in his blind rage was beyond hearing. She ran up to him, pushing aside the hostlers and repeating her command as she tried desperately to pull Hassan's hands away from the hostler's throat.

It was useless. Hassan was past reason, past feeling. Araminta had turned away, looking about her for a heavy object that she could use, with luck, to stun Hassan into insensibility without killing him, when a curricle drawn by two magnificent matched grays swung into the courtyard of the inn behind the coach. Almost without thinking, Araminta took two long steps and snatched the whip from the hand of the surprised driver of the curricle. Swinging around, she raised her arm and slashed the whip with a stinging crack around Hassan's midriff. A fractional moment later Hassan relaxed his hold on the throat of the now insensible hostler. Clutching his sides, he turned toward Araminta with a dazed, questioning look. "But why, lady, why did you strike your servant?" he asked in Arabic.

"Why on earth were you trying to kill the hostler?" Araminta countered. "If you'd succeeded, his friends would have torn you to pieces."

"The infidel dared to lay his filthy hands on the horses, lady, and then when I pushed him away, he pointed his finger at me, at my clothing, and laughed at me." Hassan, his eyes smoldering again into anger, moved protectively closer to the two beautiful horses that were beginning to shy nervously as they were surrounded by a swarm of inn servants and spectators.

Araminta sighed. "I'm sure the hostler meant no harm, Hassan. Your appearance was strange to him, that was all. Do try to hold your temper in future."

"I'll have a word with him, my lady," said her elderly coachman, who had come up beside her to transfix Hassan with a disapproving stare. "If I may say so, the sooner he learns some English and gets rid of those heathen clothes, the better off he'll be. And I think I'd best give a shilling or two to that stableboy he almost strangled. To mend the lad's feelings, if you take my meaning. We don't want any trouble."

"A good idea, Ben. Make it a sovereign. That should speed the boy's recovery." As the somewhat chastened Hassan went off to the stables with the horses, Araminta glanced down at her hand, observing with a slight surprise that she still held the borrowed whip. She walked over to the curricle, the owner of which was standing beside his vehicle, eyeing the scene with an air of quiet amusement.

"I must apologize for snatching your property away so rudely, sir," said Araminta, handing the whip to the man. "As you may have noticed, I was faced with a sudden emergency."

"An emergency you handled with uncommon finesse, ma'am. I was about to come to your assistance when I realized you had no need of my help. Permit me to congratulate you." There was an easy smile on the man's lips, but his eyes, beneath the well-brushed beaver hat, were keen as he studied Araminta.

This was no miss fresh out of the schoolroom, he thought. Twenty-one, perhaps twenty-two years of age. Obviously a gentlewoman of some means, judging by her entourage, but he was a little puzzled to note that her clothing, though becoming and quietly expensive, was somewhat out-of-date; her leghorn bonnet, especially, with its flat crown and wide brim, had not been in the mode for several years. She was only of medium height, though she looked taller because of the grace of her slender, erect figure. Even if she had not been a strikingly pretty girl, her extraordinary coloring — titian hair and green eyes — would have given the illusion of beauty. But what most struck him about this girl was not her remarkable good looks but her air of complete self-possession. Never in his thirty-five years had he observed such poise in so young a woman.

"Thank you," said Araminta with a cool nod as she turned to go back to her carriage.

"If you would give me just a moment, ma'am . . ."

7

Araminta paused. "Yes?"

"I was admiring your horses. I wonder if you could tell me something about them. They're Arabians, I presume?"

"Yes. A mare and a stallion of the Anazeh stock."

"But a little larger, I think, than your average Arabian. Fifteen hands?"

"The mare, yes. The stallion is fifteen and a half."

"My hobby is horse-racing. Would you be interested in selling your horses to me?"

Araminta broke into a chuckle. "I would not, sir. I plan to race those horses myself. Perhaps I'll see you at the—what would you say is the most prestigious race?—the Derby?"

"Er—quite." It was clear that he was thoroughly taken aback, unable to conceal how nonplussed he felt.

A plaintive wail caught the attention of both of them. *"Miladi, ou êtes-vous? Je suis malade."*

"Je viens, Odile." Araminta walked quickly to the open door of the coach. Odile, a small figure dressed in deepest black, sat huddled against the bony shoulder of the abigail, who had removed the Frenchwoman's heavily veiled black bonnet. "Madame suddenly felt faint," explained the servant, vigorously fanning Odile, whose pertly pretty face, normally so enlivened by a pair of sparkling black eyes, looked wan and miserable.

The gentleman of the curricle strolled over to stand beside Araminta. "Your friend seems unwell, ma'am. May I be of any help? Perhaps I could carry the lady to her bedchamber?" He broke off as Odile, opening her eyes to find a strange man gazing at her, gave a little shriek and reached for her bonnet, jamming it on her head and pulling the veil over her face.

"I beg your pardon, ma'am," said the gentleman stiffly. To Araminta he said, "I had no intention of intruding. I was unaware that the lady is a widow. A very recent bereavement, I presume."

"Yes, very recent," agreed Araminta solemnly. "I thank you for your offer of assistance, sir, but my coachman will do what is necessary." She beckoned to the hovering coachman. "Ben, please help Madame to her bedchamber." She tossed the gentleman of the curricle a cool, friendly smile, bowed slightly, and followed her servants into the inn, leaving the gentleman to stare after her with a curiously dissatisfied expression.

"Well, Odile, you certainly made a cake of yourself," exclaimed Araminta. Ben had left the bedchamber and she and the abigail were helping Odile out of her widow's weeds. "You looked a perfect fool, screaming at that gentleman and then cramming your head into that ridiculous bonnet."

"But I was unveiled, and he was staring at me," Odile replied indignantly. A little color had returned to her cheeks and some of the liveliness to her dark eyes. "And you know, *ma chère,* fully as well as I do, how fatal it would be if I were recognized."

Araminta threw up her hands. "How often must I tell you, now you've arrived in England, that you're perfectly safe? Not a soul in this country will recognize you. And even if someone *did* recognize you, what harm could it do? Actually, you've been in no danger for several weeks, and so I've told you until I weary of hearing myself say it."

"It's all very well for you to talk, *ma mie,* but *you* are not running for your very life," said Odile stubbornly.

Araminta exchanged a resigned glance with Jessie the abigail, who, though she could speak only a few words of French, could follow the conversation reasonably well.

"Very well, Odile, if you wish to wallow in your fears, do so, with my blessing." Araminta crossed to the bell. "I'm ferociously hungry. We'll have supper served here in your bedchamber. What do you fancy to eat?"

"Eat? Eat?" Odile shuddered. "The very thought of food sickens me."

"I'm sorry to hear that. Perhaps Jessie can go down to the kitchens and prepare you a *tisane.* As for me, if I'm not to have the pleasure of your company, I think I'll order

9

supper served to me in the landlord's best parlor."

The Ship deserved its reputation, thought Araminta, as she poured herself a second glass of a very decent Chambertin. She studied the label, recalling idly that she had once heard that Chambertin was the favorite wine of Napoleon. Then, picking up her fork, she eyed with pleasure a plate laden with a slice of boiled ham, a portion of goose pie, and an enormous piece of roast beef. Not only did the landlord have an excellent cellar, but he also set a very good table, although it had taken Araminta, accustomed of late to more exotic fare, several minutes to acclimate her eyes and her palate to plain and robust English cookery.

A little later, she put down her knife and fork with a satisfied sigh and leaned back in her chair, dreamily watching the cheerful flickering of the log fire. She stirred as a knock sounded at the door. "Come," she called, expecting the arrival of the maidservant to clear the table.

"Good evening. May I come in?" Coolly anticipating Araminta's consent, the gentleman of the curricle advanced into the room. "The landlord told me you were dining alone, so I thought, why not join forces? Why shouldn't we keep each other company to while away a lonely evening?"

Caught between surprise and annoyance, Araminta studied her uninvited visitor in silence for several moments. He was a handsome dark-haired man in his middle thirties, tall and well built, his broad shoulders and slim hips admirably displayed by a superbly cut coat of blue superfine and gray pantaloons that fit without a wrinkle. He had bright, intent blue eyes, a well-modeled and somewhat sensual mouth, and a deep cleft in his chin. From one hand dangled a bottle of champagne and from the other a pair of glasses.

Araminta flicked a glance at the bottle and a slow smile curved her lips. "Is that a Nuits-St-Georges? If so, it would be heresy not to share it. Do sit down, sir. No, not beside me," she added, as the man, first depositing the bottle and glasses on the table, shoved an armchair next to hers. "On

10

the other side of the table, please."

The man paused, his confident smile fading. "But I thought—"

"You thought I was a lightskirt, open to dalliance," replied Araminta calmly. "On the contrary, I'm a respectable gentlewoman, perfectly aware that a lady of quality does not accept casual invitations from strange gentlemen. However, I've lived in out-of-the-way places for the past several years, places not under the sway of English or European social conventions, and I'm inclined to think that the laws of etiquette—unlike the Ten Commandments!—can occasionally be broken. So, since my traveling companion is feeling unwell, and since this is my first evening in England in many years, I'd be happy to share a glass of wine and a few minutes of conversation with you." Her eyes danced with a wicked merriment as she added, "Provided, of course, it's understood that nothing of a more intimate nature is contemplated."

Her companion's expression was a study in mixed emotions, in which chagrin and disappointment finally yielded to a rueful amusement. "Agreed. Half a loaf is certainly better than nothing," he said, smiling. He removed the cork from the bottle and poured the wine. Lifting his glass, he added, "Shall we drink a toast to our new acquaintance, Miss—?"

"Oh, I don't think it's necessary for us to exchange names, do you? We're not likely to meet again, but, should we do so—"

"Should we do so, you might not care to acknowledge the acquaintance?" The man narrowed his eyes. "I could always find out your name, you know. The landlord—"

Araminta chuckled. "The landlord won't be very helpful, sir. My friend and I are traveling as Miss and Mrs. Smith."

The man threw up his hands in mild exasperation. "I'm dashed if I've ever met a female quite like you before," he said feelingly. "Are you really going to insist that I call you Miss Smith for the entire evening?"

11

"Not at all. You may call me Jane," replied Araminta calmly.

Her companion cocked a sardonic eye at her. "Jane Smith. What an unusual name."

"Isn't it, though?" Araminta reached for a glass of champagne. Peering at him over the rim as she sipped, she said, "And what am I to call you, sir? How about 'Sir Galahad'? After all, you *did* offer to come to my assistance in the inn yard."

After a startled pause, the man burst into laughter. "No, not Sir Galahad, perish the thought. I'm the—my Christian name is Jason."

"How do you do, Jason. What brings you to Dover? Have you just made a Channel crossing?"

"No, I've been visiting friends near St. Margaret's at Cliffe. I'm on my way back to London, but I left my friends' home later than I had planned, so I decided to break the journey in Dover." Jason reached across the table to replenish Araminta's glass. "Now it's my turn to ask questions. You said you had just returned to England after many years. Where have you been living abroad? From your groom's appearance, I'd guess that you've spent some time in the East."

"Quite right. My friend Odile and I sailed from Beirut a little over a month ago for Marseilles."

"Beirut. Syria. Did you buy those beautiful horses there? And will you change your mind about selling them to me?"

"Certainly not," replied Araminta, laughing. "I told you I intend to race my horses."

"I thought you were bamming me, of course," said Jason, lifting an amused eyebrow. "What could a female know about racing?"

"This female is quite knowledgeable, as it happens. During my stay in Syria, I lived among the Bedouins for a time. The tribesmen are among the finest horsemen in the world, as I'm sure you know, and they adore racing. I learned a great deal from my hosts about the finer points of the art and I've ridden my stallion, Selim, in a number of races."

Araminta sighed. "I suppose I must bow to convention here in England, however, and put my groom Hassan up on Selim instead of riding him myself."

Jason looked at her warily. "Own up. You're trying to gammon me, aren't you? You say that you lived among the Bedouins. Don't you mean that you visited them in the company of your father, or your brother, or perhaps a male guardian? As for taking part in a race, I'm prepared to believe that you may have beaten out that same father or brother or guardian in a friendly ride in the park, but—"

"You're quite abroad, Jason," said Araminta good-naturedly. "I meant just what I said. I was unaccompanied when I visited among the Bedouins—except for my servants, of course—and I took part in several races that, while not comparable to the Derby, were certainly not regarded by the tribesmen as mere 'friendly rides.'"

Jason's face was a study in bemusement. He said cautiously, "You don't think it was somewhat unwise for a young woman to travel alone in such an unsettled part of the world?"

Jason's question gave Araminta pause as she reached for her third glass of champagne. She'd also consumed several glasses of Chambertin at dinner, she reminded herself. Had the wine loosened her tongue? For the first time she felt a slight misgiving about talking so freely to a complete stranger. During the past six years she'd grown accustomed to speaking and acting very much as she pleased. But this was England, and though it was unlikely she would ever see Jason again, perhaps it behooved her to be more discreet.

Orphaned at sixteen, Araminta had gone to live with her godfather, who was also her guardian. Thanks to a large private income, "Uncle Will" had been able to indulge a lifelong passion for botany and had traveled all through Europe looking for rare plants. At the time Araminta came to live with him, the war with Napoleon having put many countries out of his reach, he was concentrating his studies on the Mediterranean. He and his niece had lived for some years in Greece, where he discovered more than a hundred new species, and later in Egypt and Syria. A year ago, when Araminta turned twenty-one, her uncle had died, leaving her his entire estate.

"Oh, I haven't really been traveling alone very much," she said easily. "I lived with an uncle for a number of years. He died just as we were planning another trip to Syria, so I decided to carry on with our original plans. I think he'd have liked that."

"I see." Jason sounded as befuddled as he felt. Though she looked and spoke like a lady of quality, he thought, it was clear that "Jane Smith" was either unaware of the impropriety of her way of life, or was willfully disregarding it. He shrugged. It was nothing to him how she chose to live. However, he did regret the girl's prudishness, which seemed out of character in so unconventional a person, and which was certainly preventing him from fully enjoying his unusual evening with this beautiful young woman. Unless, of course, the prudishness was a pose? There could be no harm in trying for a mood of romantic intimacy, surely?

"You interest me extremely," Jason said with an encouraging smile. "Tell me more about your travels in Syria. How did you chance to become so friendly with the Bedouins? They're a race who look down on females, or so I've heard."

"On the contrary, the Bedouins regard women very highly, as well they should. The women do all the work! They pitch the tents, grind the wheat, carry the water. I first met the Bedouins when I hired some tribesmen to escort me on my journey to Palmyra—or Tadmor, as the Arabs call it. It's necessary to engage an escort of local Arabs for these desert trips as a protection against bandit raids by other tribes in the desert. During the course of this journey, I became very friendly with the wife of the sheik, who later invited me to stay with his tribe. I encountered only one real problem with the Bedouins: they have a superstition that fair hair attracts the Evil Eye."

"And what did you do about that?" asked a fascinated Jason, looking with admiration at Araminta's luxuriant red-gold hair, swept to the back of her head and terminating in ringlets.

"Why, I covered up my hair, of course," replied Araminta with an air of faint surprise.

"Of course. A simple but perfect solution. Well, then, you made a pilgrimage to Palmyra, and you stayed among the Bedouins. What other adventures did you have in Syria?"

"Let me see. I made a short expedition to the Jordan area, where I bought my horses, Selim and the mare Balkis. Later I decided to visit Aleppo . . ." Araminta broke off as one of the maidservants pushed open the door and rushed breathlessly into the parlor. "I'm sorry to disturb ye, ma'am, but yer friend, that Mrs. Smith, she's acting fair dicked in the nob, screaming and crying and carrying on—"

"Good God," said Araminta blankly. Hesitating only an instant, she jumped up from her chair and dashed out of the room and up the stairs, followed by Jason and, after him, the wide-eyed maidservant. As Araminta reached the head of the stairs, Odile emerged from her bedchamber. She was wailing loudly and making an ineffectual effort to fasten her dressing gown as she ran blindly down the corridor toward the stairs.

"Mon Dieu, Odile, what is the matter with you?"

"Please help me, *chère,* don't let them take me away," shrieked Odile, throwing herself into Araminta's arms.

"Stop this instantly. You're acting like a caper-witted ninny," said Araminta coolly, disengaging herself from Odile's frantic grasp. She led the girl back to her bedchamber and firmly closed the door in the face of Jason and the curious maidservant. "Now then, what's sent you into such a state? When I left you, over an hour ago, you were sound asleep."

"I remember feeling relaxed and drowsy," said Odile slowly. Her voice was calmer, and the dazed expression was leaving her eyes. "The next thing I knew, I was being gagged and bound and carried away by Mirhan's men. I woke up screaming, and for a minute or two I really believed that I was being kidnapped. I soon realized it was only a dream,

15

however, and I got out of bed and was putting on my dressing gown, with the idea of going to your bedchamber, Araminta, when I chanced to look out the window into the courtyard below. There — *quelle horreur* — I spotted an Arab wearing a *kaffiyeh* and a striped tunic, and I thought, it *wasn't* a nightmare! Mirhan's men really have come for me. I began screaming again, and the maidservant came in and tried to calm me, but it was no use. And when I discovered that you weren't in your bedchamber, I was even more frightened, and I came looking for you . . ."

"*Quelle sottise,* Odile," said Araminta in good-natured resignation. "As I've told you so often, Mirhan's men are all in Syria where they belong. That must have been Hassan you saw in the courtyard. So far as I know, there's not another Arab within thousands of miles of here! Come now, let me tuck you back into bed."

Several minutes later, observing Odile's eyes beginning to close, Araminta said, "Are you feeling more the thing, *petite?*"

"Oh, yes, I'm fine now," replied Odile drowsily. "You must go get yourself some rest, *ma mie.*"

Araminta tiptoed out of the bedchamber, pausing in surprise outside the door at the sight of Jason, lounging against the wall of the corridor.

"I was concerned about your friend," Jason explained at Araminta's look of polite inquiry. "How is — er — Mrs. Smith?"

"Very well, I thank you. It was kind of you to ask about her. Good night, sir."

As Araminta moved to pass him, Jason put out a detaining hand, placing it lightly on her arm. "Do you think you're being quite fair, Jane Smith? Our pleasant tête-à-tête was interrupted by those bloodcurdling screams and general carryings-on. Surely you're not going to leave me in a limbo of ignorance, eaten up with curiosity? And besides, I've ordered another bottle of champagne."

Araminta looked up into Jason's face. He certainly was a handsome, charming man, and that mouth of his above the sensual cleft in his chin . . . She did not allow herself to dwell on Jason's cleft chin. She was not in the least sleepy, however, and it *had* been a very pleasant evening before Odile's nightmare had interrupted it. She smiled, saying, "Well, I daresay another glass of champagne would do me no harm, and perhaps I do owe you an explanation of sorts."

Sitting relaxed once again in the cozy parlor, Araminta took a sip from the glass of champagne that Jason had just handed to her, saying, "Let me see, now, how can I best explain Odile's predicament without going into too many embarrassing personal details? I first met her in Athens. She was living with an uncle, a moderately successful merchant dealing in antiquities. After I left Greece, I never really expected to see her again. Several months ago, however, during that visit to Aleppo that I was telling you about, I did meet Odile again under very shocking circumstances."

Araminta shook her head, as though she were still not quite able to believe what had happened. "In the interval since I'd last seen her, Napoleon had been overthrown and her uncle had decided to return to France. He and Odile took ship in Piraeus for Marseilles; midway into their voyage the ship was captured by Algerian pirates. Odile's uncle was killed in the fight to take the ship, and she was sold into slavery, ending up in the harem of Mir—of a Turkish official in the *vilayet,* or province, of Aleppo. This official is only a pasha of two tails, but he rules an important *sanjak,* or department, of the province, and is reported to be a very wealthy man."

As Araminta paused to take another sip of champagne, Jason whistled softly, saying, "What an incredible tale in this day and age! How did you chance to meet your friend Odile again, if she was held captive in a Turkish harem?"

"Oh, the harem ladies do leave their homes, you know, though when they go out on the street, they're heavily veiled and guarded by eunuchs. I came upon Odile in the women's baths in Aleppo. Later I visited her in the harem. The pasha was perfectly willing to allow Odile visits by another European lady. We were careful to conceal from him, of course, that Odile and I were old friends. After a time, I bribed the eunuch who was escorting Odile to the baths to agree to a pretended abduction, and I managed to spirit her on board a ship sailing for the western Mediterranean."

Jason had been listening to Araminta with absorbed interest. "Good God, the story becomes more fascinating with every word you say," he exclaimed. "So Odile—er, 'Mrs. Smith'—is wearing a widow's veil to avoid being recognized by the pasha's men? Is there any real danger of such a pursuit, do you think?"

"Oh, I suppose there was some danger, during the first few days of our voyage, that Mir—the pasha—might have tried to overtake us by ship, although it wouldn't have done him much good. We were traveling on a British frigate as far as Malta, thanks to a friendship struck up by my uncle with the frigate's captain during our stay in Egypt. Anyway, as I've repeatedly told Odile, she's been as safe as safe could be for weeks now. Not even in the most exotic flight of fancy could one imagine the power of the Ottoman Empire reaching out for a victim traveling under the protection of the Royal Navy!"

"I understand why your friend is so apprehensive, after the harrowing experiences she's undergone," said Jason sympathetically. "After visiting here in England with you, will she be returning to France?"

"No, now that her uncle is dead, there's no reason for Odile to return to France. She was his niece by marriage, not a blood relation, and whatever small estate he left would go to his own family." Araminta hesitated. "I suppose I shouldn't say anything about this, but—you see, while she was living in Athens, Odile became betrothed to a young English naval officer, who was staying with the British consul there while recuperating from a bout of fever. Rog—the officer was to join Odile for their wedding at her uncle's home in France after his next tour of duty. So, now that we're back in England, I hope to contact Lieutenant—the young man—and reunite him with Odile, unless . . ."

Araminta paused, frowning.

"Unless the young man considers that Miss Odile was somehow soiled and made unfit for marriage by her stay in the harem?"

"That thought did cross my mind," snapped Araminta, her eyes shooting angry sparks. "Men! They pride themselves on their logical minds, and yet they refuse to admit the injustice of a double standard of conduct for men and women!"

Jason looked mildly astounded. "I won't say that I've read deeply into the feminist writings of Mary Wollstonecraft Godwin, but you sound very much like one of that lady's disciples."

"Godwin? I don't think I know—oh, wasn't she some relation to the poet Shelley? No matter." Araminta dismissed the subject. "I'm nobody's disciple. I just happen to believe that fair is fair, and one human being is as good as another, male or female."

Seeing the possibility of an amorous interlude disappearing down the drain of Araminta's sudden belligerent feminism, Jason said hastily, "Don't let's quarrel. I hope as fervently as you do that Odile's young man comes up to the mark. Have another glass of champagne."

Her mood changing, Araminta laughed, saying, "No, thank you. You'll have me foxed if I take another drop." She eyed him quizzically. "Perhaps that's what you had in mind?"

Jason recoiled in mock distress. "Miss Smith! How could you even think such a thing? No, don't go," he added, as she rose to leave. "The evening is still young, and we could get to know each other much better."

Araminta laughed again. "Oh, I think we know each other quite well enough. Good night, Jason."

Catching her hand as she went by, Jason swung her around to face him. "I'd hoped that you enjoyed my company."

"I do. Very much. But I must go." Even to her own ears, Araminta sounded breathless. It was disconcerting to stand

19

so near to him, feeling the fine strength beneath those elegant clothes, even though their bodies were not actually touching.

"Well, then, why are we wasting time?" Jason murmured. Placing his hands on her shoulders, he pulled her closer to him, bending his head to brush his lips across her eyes and her cheeks.

Shivers of electric excitement raced through Araminta's body, and she had an almost irresistible urge to clasp her arms tightly around him. Good God, I *am* foxed, she thought rather incoherently. Much more of this and I'll be seduced, like any kitchen maid. Calling on her willpower, she wrenched herself out of his grasp and walked to the door, waving a jaunty farewell. "Jane—Miss Smith—whatever your name is, wait! I must see you again. Where can I reach you?" Jason called, racing to the door. But Araminta was already halfway up the stairs. At the landing she turned, smiling mischievously, and threw him a kiss.

Chapter Two

"Araminta? *Araminta?* Is it really you? I could scarcely credit my ears when the butler told me that you'd arrived."

Araminta laughed outright at the sight of her half sister Henrietta's excited face and the sound of her breathless voice. The sisters had not met for six years, but Araminta remembered Lady Middleton as a sedate, very proper lady whose sense of decorum would never have allowed her to make such a whirlwind entrance into the elegant drawing room of her house in Bruton Street. "Of course it's me, you goose," Araminta exclaimed, rushing to embrace her sister.

"Let me have a good look at you," said Lady Middleton a moment later, holding Araminta at arm's length and scrutinizing her closely. "You've grown up," Henrietta added with a tinge of disbelief. "In fact, you've become a remarkably beautiful woman. No thanks to those." Henrietta flicked a dismissive glance at Araminta's out-of-date gown and nondescript bonnet. "We'll visit my dressmaker immediately, before anyone sees you in those impossible clothes. I presume that the rest of your wardrobe is equally dowdy?"

"I fear so. It's been several years since I bought any new clothes. There aren't many fashionable modistes in the Upper Nile or the Syrian desert, you know. In any case, I never had your sense of style, Henrietta."

Lady Middleton accepted the compliment with a complete lack of self-consciousness. The daughter of the late Earl of Edenbridge and his first wife, Henrietta was fifteen

21

years older than Araminta, the Earl's child by his second wife. The half sisters were relative strangers, having seen little of each other after Henrietta had been married at eighteen to Richard, Baron Middleton, and had gone off to live on her husband's estates in Lincolnshire. She had been a very pretty girl, with a fair delicate beauty and an unerring taste in dress, although her mind had always been rather shallow and she had never had any interests that did not revolve around her husband, her home, and her position in society. But now, at the age of thirty-seven, Henrietta's looks had faded, Araminta thought a little sadly. Henrietta looked older than her years, and her face, when not animated in conversation, wore a vaguely careworn expression that probably reflected the burden of family responsibilities assumed after the death of her husband just over a year ago.

"Come sit down," said Henrietta, motioning Araminta to a settee, "and we'll catch up on each other's news. But first, where is your luggage? Simpson tells me that you arrived without any."

"I'm staying at Stephen's Hotel. I couldn't descend on you with my mountain of possessions."

"Nonsense. I insist that you stay with me. What would people think if I allowed my only sister to live in a hotel rather than in my home? And besides, I want to see something of you after our long separation, my dear."

"Well, there is just one thing. I'm not alone. I arrived in London with a friend, a widow, Madame Lacoste."

"A French widow?" said Henrietta rather doubtfully, as if being French somehow altered the state of widowhood. "How did you happen to meet her? I thought you and Sir Wilfrid were living in Greece."

"That's where I met Odile." Fortunately Araminta had given some thought to inventing a story that would explain Odile's presence in London without revealing any detail of the harem experience that would surely shock Henrietta and cause her to brand Odile as a loose woman. "Her uncle was a French merchant in Athens. Her

22

husband worked for the uncle."

"The husband and the uncle were in trade?" said Henrietta, even more doubtfully.

"The uncle, yes. Odile's husband came from a distinguished *émigré* family in Aquitaine," Araminta improvised quickly. Henrietta's eyes brightened at this upgrading of Odile's status. "Poor Armand, he died so young, so tragically," Araminta sighed, making a mental note to remind Odile of these facts about her imaginary husband.

"Oh. Madame Lacoste is quite young, then?" There was an oddly hopeful note in Henrietta's voice that puzzled Araminta.

"Why, yes. Odile is a little younger than I am. About twenty, I would say. Why do you ask?"

Henrietta shook her head. "It's of no importance. I merely thought . . . since you've been traveling alone, it might have been more seemly if your chaperone had been an older lady. Of course, your friend is very welcome to stay here too." She changed the subject. "Why didn't you write to say you were coming, Araminta? For that matter, why didn't you write oftener during all those years that you were gone?"

"Oh, I'm no great letter writer, as you know better than anyone! In any event, it's rather difficult to post a letter from the wilds of Thessaly. But I *was* remiss. I should have written to you more frequently, especially after Richard died."

Henrietta's eyes moistened. "Thank you for the beautiful letter you wrote when you learned of Richard's death. I was so comforted by it. But then you know how hard it is to lose someone dear to you. It's strange, isn't it, that Richard and your guardian died within a month of each other?" Her expression altered. "My dear, far be it from me to speak ill of the dead, but I never did approve of your journeying about the world with Sir Wilfrid. It was no way for a gently reared female to spend the years when she should have been preparing to enter society and find a suitable husband. You should have come to live with me after

23

Papa and my stepmother died."

"You had your hands full with a family of young children. And I enjoyed my life with Uncle Will. While he lived, I had no desire to return to England."

"But now that you *are* here, you'll want to settle down, meet the right people . . ."

"And meet the right husband?" Araminta finished, smiling.

"Well, yes. Provided that . . ." Henrietta paused, groping for words. "If only there aren't any nasty rumors . . ." She paused again, looking acutely uncomfortable.

"Really, Henrietta, if I didn't know better, I'd say that you were a little dicked in the nob," exclaimed Araminta, exasperated. "There's obviously something embarrassing you think you should tell me, so out with it. Now, what's this about rumors? I don't know a soul in England except you and your family. I haven't even *been* in London for six years, so how could there be rumors about me?"

Her eyes downcast, Henrietta fidgeted for several moments with the fringes of her Paisley shawl. Finally she raised her head, saying, "There's nothing for it but to speak plainly. Several months ago a very old family friend, Lord Henry Minton, came to see me. He'd just returned from a journey to the Holy Land. On his way home, he'd stopped off in Syria to visit a place he called—let me see, now—oh, yes, Palmyra."

"Yes, I believe I did hear last year that some high born Englishman was making the pilgrimage to Palmyra," interjected Araminta. "But what has Lord Henry to do with me?"

"Araminta, he told me that while he was in Syria he heard stories about some beautiful young Englishwoman who had been wandering about the Levant alone, without a respectable chaperon, or an escort of any kind. The young woman was traveling as Miss Smith or some such thing, but Lord Henry said it was commonly believed that she came from a titled and wealthy aristocratic family."

"So?" said Araminta, looking at her sister with an air

24

of limpid innocence.

"Well—Sir Wilfrid had been dead for almost a year at that point, and you hadn't returned to England, so it did cross my mind that perhaps you were 'Miss Smith.' Oh, I know it was a ridiculous thought," Henrietta added hastily. "Lord Henry said that the young Englishwoman was unchaperoned and unescorted, and of course I *knew* that your governess had accompanied you when you left England to join Sir Wilfrid, but . . ."

Araminta cleared her throat. "Well, actually, Miss Gillespie hasn't been with me for several years. For that matter, I didn't need a governess once I had joined Uncle Will. He was the best teacher I could have had. Miss Gillespie always disliked intensely the discomforts of travel in primitive countries, so two years ago, with my best wishes, she accepted a post as governess to an English family in Athens."

"Oh, Araminta, surely you haven't been living and traveling alone since Sir Wilfrid died?" asked Henrietta apprehensively.

"Not exactly. Only if you omit any reference to my abigail, my coachman, my groom, and a sizable escort of Bedouin tribesmen," Araminta replied drily. "I certainly haven't been living loosely, however, if that's what you're implying."

"Araminta! Of course I don't believe for a moment that you're a—a lightskirt! But in all innocence, you've been playing ducks and drakes with your reputation. If the prattle boxes should get wind of this—but no, I don't see how that could happen. Lord Henry himself didn't have a notion that my sister and this scandalous Englishwoman were one and the same person. He was simply repeating interesting gossip he'd picked up during his travels." Henrietta's face brightened. "I have it. We'll just allow people to assume that Miss Gillespie stayed on with you after Sir Wilfrid died. That should take care of the matter."

Araminta stiffened. "I thank you, but there's no need for you to protect my reputation," she said coldly. "I'm of age, I have an independent income, and I see no reason why I shouldn't live my life as I see fit without causing public scandal to anyone. I have no plans, I assure you, to engage in an illicit affair, or to rob His Majesty's Mails, or even to walk down St. James's Street in broad daylight or to attend a masked ball at the Pantheon. In short, I have every intention of leading a blameless life here in London."

"Oh, Araminta, I didn't mean to make you so angry," wailed Henrietta. "It's just that an unmarried female must be careful to avoid even the suggestion of being fast."

After a moment, Araminta's mobile face assumed its normally sunny expression, and she smiled, saying, "I know you have only my best interests at heart. If it will make you feel better, I'll suppress my usual truthful instincts and tell your friends a real bouncer about Miss Gillespie. I'll say that she left my employ just before I took ship for Malta. And I certainly won't mention a word about my travels in Syria! There, I think that's enough about my reputation. Tell me about the children. Let me think: Damaris must be—good God, can she be eighteen years old?"

"Indeed she is," said Henrietta proudly. "And a real beauty. She looks a good deal like me at the same age, but much prettier. Gillian, who is still in the schoolroom, of course, is sixteen, and Philip, who is at Eton, is twelve."

"I'm eager to see them all again. I presume that Damaris will soon be in the midst of her first London season. As pretty as she is, and so well connected, I daresay she'll take London by storm. As her mother did."

"I suppose so." Henrietta did not smile at Araminta's joking compliment, and there was an oddly doubtful tone in her voice. "Yes, Damaris will enjoy her season immensely, I'm sure, but . . ."

"But? Is there something wrong?"

"No. Oh, no. What I meant was—well, normally a family has one main interest in launching a daughter into society . . ."

"To catch a husband, you mean."

"I wouldn't put it so baldly, but yes. In Damaris's case, however, there is no need for her to attract

26

an eligible suitor."

"Is Damaris already affianced, then?" asked Araminta in surprise.

"Yes." Henrietta's eyes glowed with pride. "Mind, you mustn't breathe a word of this to anyone, but yes. At the ball I'll be giving for Damaris in June I'll announce her betrothal to Harwood!"

"Harwood? The Duke of Harwood? I'm not *au courant* with the aristocracy, but I seem to remember hearing that he's one of the wealthiest men in England. An old title, too, isn't it?"

"Old! The Dukedom is very nearly as old and as prestigious as Norfolk. And the Duke is more than merely wealthy. The Windham family for generations have been the biggest landowners in Durham and Cheshire, and the present Duke's mother was the sole heiress to an estate that included coal and iron mines and fisheries, large properties in Lancashire, and most of the land underneath central London."

"Lucky Damaris. The Duke sounds like quite a catch," said Araminta lightly. "How did they chance to meet even before Damaris came out?"

"Why, the Duke is Damaris's guardian—and Gillian's and Philip's too, of course. But naturally, you wouldn't know that. During the last years of his life, my Richard worked closely with the Duke in the House of Lords, and as there were no close relatives on either side of our families, Richard asked Harwood to be the children's guardian. Why do you look so surprised?"

"Well—it's not the usual thing, surely, for a guardian to marry his ward?"

"Araminta! What a thing to say! As if anyone could suspect the Duke of marrying Damaris for her money! Why, his fortune is so large that Damaris's portion must seem a mere pittance to him. And besides—though it's not an expression one normally likes to use—this is a *love* match!"

* * *

"Must I go down to dinner, Araminta? Could I not have a little something on a tray in my bedchamber?"

"No, you may not, Odile. I won't allow you to hide behind that widow's veil any longer."

From her seat in front of the dressing table, where she had been arranging her dark curls, Odile said, drooping pathetically, "But I'm a complete stranger to your sister, even if she has invited me to stay in her house. Just as I'm a stranger in a foreign land."

Araminta suppressed a quick grin of amusement. The volatile Odile was always quick to overdramatize herself, to swing from elation to abject misery. She and Araminta had moved only that afternoon from their hotel to Henrietta's house in Bruton Street, and Odile had not yet met her hostess.

"Lady Middleton is a very friendly lady, Odile. She won't seem a stranger to you for very long. As for your being a stranger in a foreign land, you'd best start trying to feel like an Englishwoman, if you expect to marry your lieutenant!"

"Oh." Odile's eyes widened. "Yes, perhaps I must make an effort to adjust. Does *Miladi* Middleton speak French?"

"I presume she does, and her daughters, too. I'm sure they all had very accomplished governesses. Yes?" Araminta called as a knock sounded at the door.

A small, slim girl with a gamin face topped by rather tousled red-gold curls advanced shyly into the room. "Aunt Araminta?" she said doubtfully, glancing from one girl to the other.

"I'm Araminta—pray don't call me 'aunt,' it makes me feel impossibly old!—and you're either Gillian or Damaris. Shall I guess? Are you Gillian? Your mother told me that Damaris has blond hair, and yours is much more like mine, the color of grass fires in autumn!"

One look at her aunt's laughing eyes and outstretched arms made the newcomer's shyness evaporate. She rushed to kiss Araminta, saying, "Oh, yes, I'm Gillian. I'm so happy to meet you at last, Aunt—Araminta. I wanted to say hello to you before you went down to dinner, because of

28

course I'll be eating supper with my governess." She turned to Odile, speaking in careful French, *"Maman* told me that you have been recently widowed, Madame Lacoste. Please accept my condolences. I hope that your stay with us will be most happy and comfortable."

Picking up a wisp of a handkerchief, bordered in black, Odile wiped a tear from the corner of her eye. "Thank you, my child, that was most kind of you," she said with the pathetic air of one who is bravely standing up to life's misfortunes.

Resisting the urge to grab Odile by the scruff of her neck and shake her, Araminta smiled at Gillian, saying, "You've just relieved my friend's mind no end. Odile was afraid that none of you would speak French. You have a very nice accent, Gillian. Does Damaris speak French as well as you do?"

"Much, much better. But then, Damaris does everything perfectly. She's an exquisite dancer. She paints and embroiders and plays the pianoforte very well." Gillian chuckled. "Her best friend said the other day that it almost seems unfair that Damaris should be so accomplished as well as so impossibly beautiful."

"Come now, Damaris can't be *that* much of a paragon," said Araminta bracingly. "I daresay there are many things you do better than she does."

"Please, Aunt—please, Araminta, don't think that I'm jealous of Damaris," exclaimed Gillian, her face clouded with a quick concern. "I love her dearly, and I wish her every happiness in the world, but I'm glad that I'm not her—she," Gillian added conscientiously.

"Oh? Why not?"

"Well, you see, Damaris is looking forward to being the belle of her season. She wants to make a grand marriage and become a great London hostess, just as Mama has always planned for her, but I would dislike such a life excessively." Gillian's eyes sparkled. "Mama says that you've been traveling about the world for years, Araminta. *That's* what I'd like to do! Well, perhaps not to travel that much, but to live the kind of life I choose. Mama seems to think that females should have only one ambition in life, to catch a husband."

"We-l-l." Noticing with sympathy the rebellious expression on her niece's face, Araminta was very sure that her sister Henrietta would greatly disapprove of this conversation with her younger daughter. "I don't say that marriage is necessary to every female's fulfillment," she began cautiously. "Most girls do marry, however, and live quite happily, so I'm told. But tell me: if you don't wish to marry, what are your plans for the future?"

"I'd like to live in the country and write poetry and—and things," said Gillian promptly.

"Poetry! How wonderful! I like to scribble verses myself. Perhaps you'll let me see some of yours."

"Oh—of course." The animation faded from Gillian's face and her voice sounded curiously dissatisfied. She peered at the little watch attached to her bodice, saying abruptly, "It's later than I thought. I'll say good night, Araminta, Madame Lacoste. The Duke of Harwood is coming for dinner tonight, and you won't wish to be late."

"Indeed not. One doesn't knowingly antagonize a Duke!" said Araminta merrily but, watching her niece leave the room, she was a little puzzled by the subtle change in Gillian's demeanor. The girl was at that awkward, in-between stage when slights are easily imagined. Had Araminta failed to treat Gillian's poetry with the gravity the author felt it deserved?

"Tell me something about the Duke, so I'll know what to talk about when I meet him," said Araminta as she sat with Henrietta in the drawing room before dinner. Opposite them, Damaris was talking animatedly to Odile.

"Well, he's handsome, and wealthy, and charming, so much so that females have been setting their caps for him since he came down from Cambridge, but to no avail until now, of course," replied Henrietta in a low voice, trying but failing to suppress a note of triumph as she gazed proudly at Damaris.

Henrietta's pride was certainly understandable, thought Araminta. Damaris was simply too good to be true. She was beautiful, with silky pale gold hair, cornflower blue eyes, rose petal skin, and a pure Grecian profile. She wore her white muslin gown, embroidered with seed pearls, with incomparable grace. She had a lovely speaking voice and exquisite manners. She was, in short, so close to perfection that Araminta momentarily felt *démodé* in her well-worn gown. She wished suddenly that she had her sister's sure sense of fashion, or Odile's knack of always being perfectly turned out. Momentarily diverted, Araminta reflected with an inward chuckle that Odile, Frenchwoman to the core, would look fashionable in a fig leaf!

"The Duke is also very kind," Henrietta continued. "I don't know what I would have done without his help and advice this past year since Richard died. He took over all the dreadful details of the funeral, and the will, and the management of the estate. Nothing is too difficult or too insignificant for his attention."

Good God, what a paragon, thought Araminta a shade resentfully. Damaris certainly seemed to be getting the husband she deserved, but the Duke of Harwood didn't sound at all like the kind of man in whom Araminta herself could become interested. She'd always found that a touch of human frailty added a bit of spice to the human condition! Besides, the Duke sounded quite managerial, not to say domineering. "What about the rest of his family?" Araminta went on, dismissing the subject of the Duke's perfections.

"He has a younger sister, who was married several years ago, and very well, too. A charming girl. And he had a younger brother, Rupert Windham, who was killed last year at Waterloo. He was a captain in the Blues. He and his brother were very close. It took the Duke many months to get over the loss."

"Was Captain Windham married?"

"Why, no."

"So now the Duke has no heir?"

"Well, I believe the next in line for the dukedom is an elderly distant cousin," replied Henrietta, sounding mildly surprised. "Why do you ask?"

"Oh, I was wondering if the Duke has decided he must marry soon to provide an heir to the title, now that his brother is dead."

Looking ruffled, Henrietta exclaimed, "I *told* you, Araminta, this is a love match."

Damaris looked over at her mother just then to exclaim, "Mama, Madame Lacoste has been telling me the most interesting stories of her life in Athens with her husband." Turning back to Odile, Damaris said, "I admire your courage so much, Madame, in taking up your life again after your terrible loss."

"Mademoiselle is *très charmante, très sympathique,*" murmured Odile, drawing around herself a mantle of gentle grief.

Araminta suppressed an urge to giggle. Odile seemed to be rapidly convincing herself that she was indeed the patiently enduring widow of Araminta's glibly embroidered tale. She might have to be taken down a peg later, in private, but for the moment Araminta was content to allow the charade to continue. "Yes, indeed, Odile has been very brave," she was saying when the butler appeared in the door of the drawing room to announce to Henrietta, "The Duke of Harwood, my lady."

Across from Araminta, Odile drew a sharp breath as she stared at the tall man who had just entered the room. He had abundant curling dark hair and intensely blue eyes and a sensual mouth above a deeply cleft chin.

I should have known this would happen, Araminta said to herself resignedly. I've lived long enough in the Levant so that I should have sensed that Nemesis, or Fate, or *something* would bring Jason into my life again. She forced a brilliant smile to her lips as Henrietta exclaimed, "My dear Duke, I must share a wonderful surprise with you: my sister,

Lady Araminta Beresford, has arrived with her friend, Madame Lacoste, to pay us a visit."

Araminta was maliciously pleased to note that the Duke missed a stride and almost stumbled; he reddened slightly and the practiced smile slipped from his handsome face. Quickly recovering, he bowed, saying, "Madame, Lady Araminta, I'm enchanted to meet you." He sat down beside Damaris, engaging her in a brief conversation that left her smiling and dimpling, before walking over to sit with Henrietta and Araminta.

"I knew, of course, that Lady Middleton had a younger sister," he remarked to Araminta with a hard glint in his eye, "but I thought you were living with your guardian in Greece."

Henrietta clapped her hand to her mouth. "Oh, Araminta, I do hope you'll forgive me," she said guiltily. "I suddenly remembered that I never put the notice of Sir Wilfrid's death in the *Times*." She explained to the Duke, "My Richard had just passed away when I received Araminta's letter telling me of her guardian's death. It was such a terrible time, it's a wonder I could recall my own name. I must have forgotten to inform you, too, Duke, about Sir Wilfrid's death."

"It's certainly understandable, Lady Middleton. You had so many things on your mind," the Duke assured her.

To Araminta he said politely, "So you finally decided to return to England. Did you tire of living in Greece?"

"Oh no, not at all, but I thought it was time to come home," replied Araminta blandly. "Then, too, my friend, Madame Lacoste, lost her husband recently. I wanted to take her mind off her grief by bringing her to meet my family in England."

Jason tossed a quick glance at Odile and promptly fell into a fit of coughing. Araminta knew his mind must be full of Syrian harems and Turkish Pashas. "I daresay Madame Lacoste is fully appreciative of your kindness," he said drily when he had recovered his breath. There was a touch of malice in his voice as he added, "Tell me, Lady Araminta, did you have the opportunity to travel elsewhere in the Levant during your stay in Greece? Did you ever go to Syria, for instance?"

Beside her, Araminta could hear Henrietta's quick intake of breath. "My guardian was a scholar, Duke. He kept pretty much to his books," she replied innocently. "We did once take a trip to Egypt." Out of the corner of her eye she could see Henrietta relax.

At the dinner table a little later, Araminta ate heartily of Henrietta's excellent dinner and allowed the others to do much of the talking. Jason, seated opposite his hostess at the end of the table, seemed perfectly at ease as the sole male in a roomful of women. To Henrietta he was deferential and attentive, to Damaris warm with controlled admiration, to Odile properly sympathetic. To Araminta he displayed a coolly detached friendliness that eventually began to grate. He's really having far too comfortable a time, she decided. As the first course was being removed, she smiled at him, saying, "I understand you have large real estate holdings in London, Duke. I'm thinking of leasing a house, or perhaps buying one. Could I ask you to help me choose a suitable place to live?"

"Suitable!" exclaimed Henrietta in horror. "Araminta, it would be highly improper for a young unmarried woman like yourself to set up her own household."

"So it might be in the normal course of events, but you forget that I have a chaperon."

"*Vraiment,* I should be so happy to help my dear friend Araminta in any way possible," said Odile bravely. "Society, *bien entendu,* is not very agreeable to me at present, but . . ."

"We-l-l, of course," said Henrietta, looking doubtfully at Odile. "But you are so young yourself, Madame Lacoste. If you were only older, it would be just the thing, but—no, it won't do." She looked toward Jason. "I'm persuaded that you must agree with me, Duke. Pray tell my sister that she must not even consider moving to her own house."

Jason cleared his throat. "Uh—Lady Middleton is quite

34

right, Lady Araminta. It would cause raised eyebrows, I fear, if two young and beautiful ladies were to set up their own household."

"You're most kind, Duke," murmured Araminta. "In future, if I should ever need your advice, I will certainly ask for it." Her smile was so sweet, her glance so appreciative, that only Jason apparently noticed the barb beneath her thanks.

Later, after only a token solitary sip of port at the dinner table, he joined the ladies in the drawing room. Suspecting he'd be seeking out an opportunity to speak to her, Araminta sat down at the pianoforte.

"I fear that I'm sadly out of practice," she said to Jason as he came up to her. "There are no pianofortes in the desert, you know."

He stood beside her in a pose of negligent ease, one hand resting on the pianoforte, but his tone was savage as he muttered under his breath, "Araminta, what deviltry are you up to?"

"Why, my lord Duke, whatever do you mean?" Araminta airily played a trill on the upper keys of the pianoforte.

"Don't play the innocent with me. I want the answers to a few questions. Why, for example, did you allow me to walk into your sister's drawing room completely unprepared to learn that you were my fiancée's — er — aunt? I never felt like such a ninnyhammer in my entire life. Couldn't you have warned me?"

"And how, pray, could I have done that? I didn't know that you were Damaris's Duke until you walked into the room. You'll recall that I knew you only as 'Jason'."

"Oh." Jason looked foolish. "Well, what about your performance at the dinner table? You deliberately goaded me into giving you advice and then you snubbed me royally for doing it. And all for no purpose, because you know quite well that you shouldn't be setting up your own household."

"I don't know anything of the sort. I have every intention of renting or buying a house."

"Don't try to bamboozle me—" He broke off, looking

past Araminta with a hunted expression. "Damaris is coming over here," he said urgently. "Quick, are you going to tell her and Lady Middleton that we met at Dover?"

"I see no reason why I should embarrass you—or myself, for that matter—by telling them."

"Good," said the Duke with considerable relief. "Look, Araminta, I must talk to you privately. Will you meet me in Hyde Park tomorrow morning? Rotten Row, at eight o'clock. And don't tell anyone you plan to ride with me."

"Your wish is my command," said Araminta as she turned to greet Damaris.

Chapter Three

Ahead of her as she neared the entrance to Hyde Park at the southern end of Park Lane, Araminta could see Jason waiting for her. Mounted on a superb bay stallion, he was the picture of lounging elegance in his double-breasted black coat with brass buttons, leather breeches, Hessian boots, and beaver hat. Araminta glanced down at her own rather shabby habit and vowed to visit Henrietta's dressmaker that very day.

"Lady Araminta." Jason tipped his hat and bowed from the saddle. "Prompt to the minute." His eyes kindled as he looked at the two Arabians. Araminta was riding Selim, and Hassan, exotic in his Bedouin garb, was astride the mare, Balkis. "By Jove, those horses are even more beautiful than I remembered them," said Jason enviously. "My offer to buy them still holds."

"As does my refusal to sell," Araminta replied with a laugh. "Shall we have a little gallop? Selim and Balkis are dying for exercise."

She touched her heel lightly to Selim's side and the horse leaped forward. Before the bemused Duke could collect his wits, Hassan had taken off after his mistress and the two horses and their riders were well down the scant mile of the sandy riding track. Gritting his teeth,

Jason spurred his mount into a headlong pursuit of Araminta and Hassan, who reached the eastern end of Rotten Row a half-dozen lengths ahead of him. As Jason reined in his horse, Araminta was giving instructions to Hassan in rapid Arabic. The groom turned Balkis and slowly cantered away on the riding path toward the park entrance.

"I do hope Hassan's Arab dress doesn't attract too much attention while he's waiting for me at the gate," Araminta observed. "I'd hate to see a repetition of the incident at Dover where he almost strangled the stable-boy. All Bedouins are fiercely proud, of course, but I think Hassan has a thinner skin than most. Perhaps I shouldn't allow him to ride with me on the streets of London until I can get him into proper English clothes."

"I'd outfit him as soon as possible," agreed Jason. "The London cockney doesn't take kindly to foreigners in skirts. Shall we ride north beside the Ring?" A few minutes later, as they neared the bridge over the Serpentine, he remarked, "You're a superb horsewoman. There aren't many female riders who could control a horse as strong and nervous as Selim."

"Thank you. I wish I didn't have to use a sidesaddle, however." Araminta flashed Jason a mischievous glance. "If I'd been riding astride, I would have beaten you by at least ten lengths."

Jason refused to be baited. "I doubt it," he said calmly. "You surprised me with your start, or I might well have beaten you to the finish line. In any case, it's academic. Despite your feminist beliefs, you know very well that English ladies don't ride astride, in public or otherwise."

"Alas," sighed Araminta. "There are so many things that English ladies don't do. My new life in England promises to be very dull."

Ignoring Araminta's provocations, Jason said, "I'm glad you don't intend to tell your sister that we met in

Dover. Lady Middleton might not—she might misinterpret the incident."

"Indeed, yes. Henrietta is perfectly aware that gentlemen often indulge in private peccadillos—I believe that even Richard strayed occasionally—but she certainly wouldn't care to hear that her future son-in-law had been casting out lures to a respectable unmarried female, and her own sister to boot!"

"I resent very much your imputation that I plan to be unfaithful to your niece after our marriage," said Jason angrily. He clamped his lips tightly together, and after a moment he said, "Must we continue this skirmishing? Can't we agree to forget that we started our acquaintance off on the wrong foot and be friends?"

Shaking her head, Araminta said ruefully, "I beg your pardon. I have a runaway tongue, and I do like to tease, but you're quite right, I *have* been baiting you and it was most ungenerous of me." She reined in, leaning across her saddle to hold out a hand to the Duke. "There, shall we shake hands on a new friendship? Or rather, a new relationship? After all, I'm about to become your aunt by marriage!"

"My favorite, and certainly my youngest, aunt, I daresay! Thank you, Araminta. That was handsome of you." Jason clasped her hand warmly, his lips above that cleft in his chin curving into a smile that Araminta found too beguiling for comfort.

They rode on amicably for several minutes, with Jason pointing out monuments and other objects of interest in the park. "Did you know that Rotten Row is a corruption of *route du roi?* Back in the seventeenth century the park was plagued by highwaymen, so when William III took up residence in Kensington Palace, he had three hundred lanterns hung from the trees along the *route du roi* in the hope that he might have a safe route between the palace and St. James's. It was the first road in England to be lit at night!"

"Well, I'm very glad indeed that there are no more highwaymen in Hyde Park," Araminta declared. "Some people may think of them as romantic, but I assure you it's not in the least bit romantic to be accosted by 'knights of the road.' Uncle Will and I were very nearly abducted by brigands in Macedonia. The Greeks call them 'Pallikari.' Most of them are descended from patriots who retreated to the mountains during the centuries of foreign occupation to conduct guerrilla warfare against the Turks, although they're little more than bandits today. Many Greeks tolerate or even admire the Pallikari for their opposition to the Turks, but they're no less brutal for that. Uncle Will had to pay a small ransom for our release."

"Good God, is there no end to your adventures?" Jason exclaimed. He looked amused, but Araminta thought that she detected an undertone of disapproval in his voice.

"I suppose my experience with the Pallikari is another subject you'd rather I didn't mention?" she said challengingly.

"Not at all. It would liven up the conversation in Lady Middleton's drawing room." Jason's cheerful grin put Araminta into checkmate. He went on, "Now that we've become—or are about to become—friendly relations, I'd like to give you some proof of my friendship. Since the identity of Odile—I beg your pardon, Madame Lacoste—is no longer a secret from me, won't you let me help her to discover the whereabouts of her lieutenant? I have good contacts in the Admiralty. What is the young man's name and the name of his ship?"

"That's very kind of you. Odile and I would be delighted to accept your help. Her fiancé's name is Roger Craddock. He's a lieutenant on *HMS Bellerophon* in the Mediterranean fleet. Odile last saw Roger in December, just before she embarked for France and was captured by pirates. At that time, Roger expected that his tour of duty on *Bellerophon* would last until midsummer."

"I'll begin inquiries immediately. It shouldn't be difficult to learn the location of the *Bellerophon*. I'll pull a string or two, and with luck, we may soon have Lieutenant Craddock back in the bosom of his loved ones." Jason's eyes lit up with mischief. "I believe you said that he was recovering from fever when he first met Madame Lacoste in Athens. Perhaps the Navy surgeons will decide that he needs additional time to recuperate from his illness here in England."

Araminta beamed. "The very thing! I fancy Lieutenant Craddock might well require—oh, three months or more—to recuperate from the effects of his fever. Long enough to introduce Odile to his family, make arrangements for the wedding, and find her a suitable place to stay when he goes to sea again." She paused, looking at Jason thoughtfully. "It seems to me that you'll be putting yourself to a great deal of trouble to help Odile. I wonder why? You scarcely know her, after all."

"I told you, I wanted to give you some proof of my friendship. I'm also sorry for the young woman, and I'd like to help her. By the way, have you told your sister about Lieutenant Craddock?"

"No. Since Odile is dramatizing herself as a grieving widow, it didn't seem appropriate to mention Roger."

"Good. I suggest you continue your silence until I've informed him by letter about Madame Lacoste's harem experiences. As I hinted to you in Dover, the lieutenant may not wish to marry her once he knows what happened to her in Syria."

"And as I told *you* in Dover, that would be an infamous application of the double standard—" Araminta broke off, her angry expression fading. "I'm sorry. I shouldn't have bitten your head off. I know you mean well." After a thoughtful pause she said, "Perhaps you're right. Roger was so much in love with Odile that I'm positive he won't hold her kidnapping against her. If I'm wrong, though, he won't want to see her once he learns the truth, and then we'd be faced with the problem of explaining to Henrietta why Odile's great love wasn't her love after all. Very well, we'll keep Roger a deep dark secret until he actually appears on Henrietta's doorstep panting to marry Odile."

The Duke nodded approvingly. "That would be best. Now then, Araminta, I'd like to talk to you about something else. Surely you weren't serious last night when you announced your intention to set up your own establishment. Weren't you simply trying to bait me?"

"Well, that was part of it," admitted Araminta with a grin. "But I do plan to set up my own household. I'm no green girl. I've been independent for the past year. For longer than that, really, because Uncle Will didn't believe in keeping me in leading strings. After being my own mistress, I don't think I could settle down quietly in another woman's household. Henrietta is kind and loving, but she can never quite forget that she's considerably older than I am, and therefore entitled to give me sisterly advice."

Jason's face turned grim. "Set up your own household? That's quite out of the question," he snapped. "I absolutely forbid it."

"Forbid?" A stupefied Araminta reined in her mount and glared at Jason. "What right have you—" She paused, her eyes narrowing. "I see it now. What a slowtop I've been. You were trying to turn me up sweet with your invitation to ride in the park and your vows of friendship. You didn't offer to help Odile out of the kindness of your heart. You wanted to get rid of her. If she were reunited with Roger, I wouldn't be able to establish my own household because I'd no longer have a chaperon. Why are you doing this? Why are you attempting to interfere in my life in this high-handed way?"

"Damnation, girl, I'm trying to help you," exploded Jason. "Yes, I was trying to get your Odile out of the way. If only you'll consider the matter calmly, I'm persuaded you'll agree with me that setting up a household with Madame Lacoste as your chaperon would be a catastrophe. What if the gossips should learn that your companion wasn't a respectable widow but just another concubine from a Turkish seraglio? She'd be barred from every polite drawing room in London, and your own reputation would be in shreds."

"My reputation is quite secure," said Araminta, tossing her head. "I'm not in the least concerned about gossip."

"Well, you should be," Jason shot back. "I remember quite clearly those stories you told me at the inn in Dover. If society should learn that you've been traipsing about the Middle East unescorted, engaging in public horse races with Bedouin sheiks, visiting Turkish seraglios, you'd run the risk of being considered a demirep. That risk would only be intensified if you insist on setting up your own household in the company of a woman—and I'm sorry if this offends you—a woman who, even if it was through no fault of her own, has seriously compromised her own reputation. If *you* won't take steps to protect your name, then I must, for I refuse to admit even the possibility of my future bride being linked with you as the object of scandalous gossip!"

Her eyes blazing, Araminta exclaimed, "So now we come to the crux of the matter. You're afraid that my living arrangements will somehow compromise Damaris's position in society. A kind of disgrace by contamination, no doubt! Do you have any idea how priggish and self-righteous you sound? You've been playing the tyrant with all the females in your orbit—Henrietta and Damaris and Gillian, and your own sister, probably, before she escaped your clutches by getting married—but I assure you that you won't manage *my* affairs. I plan to live my life independently, as I've always done, and if London society rejects me, then the Devil take the hindmost!"

* * *

Araminta was still fuming with righteous anger at Jason's interference in her affairs as she galloped away from him in the direction of Rotten Row, slowing to a canter when she neared the entrance gate of the park. However, she lost the leading edge of her anger when she was obliged to deal with a small crisis at the gate, where she found Hassan about to erupt in violent rage at the merciless needling of a group of grubby urchins. The youths had completely encircled Hassan, pointing at his colorful garments, emitting raucous catcalls, and clutching at their sides in helpless mirth.

Slipping from her saddle, Araminta rushed to throw her arms around Hassan as he made a lunge for his nearest tormentor. "Cease this foolishness immediately," she exclaimed urgently in Arabic, but Hassan merely struggled desperately to free himself, his face contorted with frustrated rage.

"Allow me, ma'am," came a voice over her shoulder, and a pair of strong hands seized Hassan's arms and twisted them sharply behind his shoulder blades. Uttering a screech of pain, Hassan went limp.

Araminta turned to look at the tall, fashionably dressed figure whose slender hands constrained Hassan's sinewy strength so effortlessly. The stranger was a handsome man in his mid-thirties, whose hooded eyes bespoke a jaded, ironical view of life.

"Thank you for your help, sir. You can release Hassan now. His rages never last very long." To the urchins, who had lingered to watch with fascination what would happen next, she tossed a handful of coins from the tiny reticule attached to her wrist. "Be off with you now, you rascals. If you ever bother my groom again, I'll give you a taste of this." She wagged her riding whip threateningly at them as they scattered.

"Would you really be so cruel?" the stranger asked

44

in an amused voice.

"Probably not," Araminta grinned.

The man glanced at Hassan, who was standing beside his horse in sullen silence. "Is your groom a Syrian Bedouin, by any chance?"

"Why, yes. Hassan is an Anazeh, a member of the Saba tribe. Do you know Syria, sir?"

"Not really. I served for a time in the British Embassy in Stamboul. My duties required me to make short visits to some of the outlying Turkish provinces." The man's eyes narrowed as he looked more closely at Araminta. "You seem familiar, ma'am. Have we met before?"

"Not to my knowledge, sir." Araminta had an excellent memory for faces. She was sure she would have remembered this man with his handsome face and his lounging elegance.

"I could have sworn—but here, I'm forgetting my manners, ma'am. May I introduce myself? My name is Manning, Silvanus Manning." He paused, his full lips curved in an expectant smile.

"How do you do? I'm—" Araminta checked herself. A tiny glimmer of caution held her back from giving her name. She knew very well how much Henrietta—and yes, Jason—would disapprove of this casually informal encounter. "Thank you again for coming to my assistance, sir," she went on with a politely dismissive nod, turning to mount Selim from Hassan's waiting hand. Leaving Mr. Manning to stare after her in frank disappointment, Araminta exited the Stanhope Gate.

As she headed north toward Mount Street, she found herself engaged in an unfamiliar exercise in introspection. Lurking in the back of her mind for several days now had been the suspicion that her gypsy life with Sir Wilfrid had been far more unorthodox than she had ever realized. Leaving England at the age of sixteen after a quiet and solitary childhood in the country, and never having experienced a London season, Araminta had simply been unaware that the life of a young lady of quality was so severely circumscribed by convention. Perhaps she'd overreacted to Jason's criticisms? Not, she added hastily to herself, that Jason had any right to judge her actions, and she certainly had no intention of allowing him to dictate what her conduct should be! But she was beginning to understand why both he and Henrietta wanted her to button her lips in circumspect silence about her adventures in the Levant. Those experiences were highly unlikely to make her feel welcome in the polite drawing rooms of London society!

A thoughtful frown furrowed her brow. If she wished to remain in England—and she rather thought that she would like to make her home here for a while, to become better acquainted with Henrietta and her children, her only relatives, before she started out again on her travels—why, then it might be advisable for her to conform, at least outwardly, to the social rules that had produced a paragon like her niece Damaris.

Damaris. Araminta's frown grew a little deeper. Thoughts that she had put firmly to the back of her mind now resurfaced. She could remember every word, every glance, every gesture of her meeting with Jason at the inn in Dover. She could remember especially the heady exhilaration of sparring with him in a male-female encounter that pitted them as equal opponents, and the equally heady but far different sensation that had sent her blood racing when he pulled her into his arms. Jason had shown every indication that he shared her feelings. But if he was so plainly attracted to Araminta, how could he also be drawn to the prim and decorous and dewily innocent Damaris?

A sudden rush of color heated Araminta's face. How could she have asked herself such a naive question? As she herself had intimated to Jason, a gentleman's private indiscretions bore no relationship to such important aspects of his life as marriage. Now that Araminta had

46

metamorphosed into a member of his future wife's family, Jason apparently wanted to erase any memory of their first meeting. It behooved Araminta to do the same.

Arriving at her sister's house in Bruton Street, Araminta dismounted and handed her reins to Hassan. A hackney cab rounded the corner and stopped in front of the house as Araminta climbed the steps to the entrance. Just as she raised her hand to the knocker, the door opened and an elderly woman, flushed of face and with her bonnet askew, rushed past her, turning her head momentarily to say in an agitated voice, "Oh, I beg your pardon, my lady, I'm sure." The woman hurried down the steps to the pavement and climbed into the hackney.

As Araminta entered the house, the butler emerged from the rear of the hall. "My lady," he exclaimed. "I had no idea you were at the door. How—"

"Oh, I let myself in," said Araminta cheerfully. "I was about to knock when a lady, whom I didn't recognize, opened the door and rushed past me."

"Oh, yes. That was Miss Baddeley. Miss Gillian's governess." The butler sounded faintly disapproving.

"Indeed? She seemed to be in a great hurry. I'm famished, Simpson. Is Lady Middleton coming down for breakfast, do you know? If not; perhaps you could send me up a tray."

"Her ladyship *was* down, my lady, but she—she decided to return to her bedchamber." Simpson's usually stolid face looked harassed, and Araminta tossed him a glance of mild surprise before she turned to mount the stairs.

In her bedchamber, she had removed her hat and the elderly Jessie was helping her out of her jacket when Odile entered the room after a perfunctory tap.

"Up so early, Odile? I've never known you to bestir yourself before noon unless I had sent Jessie to pull you out of bed."

"You like to tease me, but I assure you that I don't keep to my bed without a good reason. You forget that my health is delicate," replied Odile with injured dignity. She walked to the cheval glass and looked closely at her simple black dress, to which she managed, as usual, to give an air of elegance. "I was thinking. Do you suppose I might start wearing lavender, or gray? I get so tired of black. And it isn't, *bien entendu,* as if I were actually a widow. We could tell your sister's friends that my husband died some time ago. Perhaps almost a year ago. Then I could shortly begin to wear *real* colors." She sighed reminiscently. "I wore a gown in the most exquisite shade of deep rose when I first met *mon cher* Roger in Athens. I was reminded of it when the little Gillian knocked at my door a little while ago, looking for you. Her gown was in that same delicious shade of deep pink."

"Gillian was looking for me?"

"Yes. She seemed very distressed, *pauvre petite.*"

"She didn't say why she was troubled?" Araminta frowned. "No matter. I'll go to her after breakfast." A knock sounded at the door. "That will be my tray now, Jessie."

But it was not a footman with a breakfast tray who entered the room, but Damaris, fully dressed for the day, with every golden curl in place. "Aunt Araminta, Mama would like to see you in her bedchamber."

"Is something wrong? Is your mother ill?"

"Oh, no. Not ill." Damaris sounded rather subdued, but Araminta, after one keen glance, said merely, "Let me drink a cup of tea first, and I'll be with your mother directly."

A few minutes later, she entered her sister's bedchamber to find Lady Middleton lying prostrate on her bed, a vinaigrette bottle clutched in her hand. Araminta exclaimed, "Good God, Henrietta, you really are ill, then, despite what Damaris said?"

"No, I'm not ill, at least not in body," replied Henrietta weakly as she lifted the vinaigrette to her nose. "It's just that my younger daughter seems bent on breaking her mother's heart."

"Gillian? *Gillian?* What in heaven's name has the child done?"

Seemingly recovering some of her strength, Henrietta raised herself on her elbow and said in a voice quivering with indignation, "You may well ask. This morning Gillian's governess, Miss Baddeley, received an urgent message from her brother, a clergyman in the North, requesting her presence in his home to care for his infant son, whose mother had just died in childbirth."

"So that's why she was in such a hurry," said Araminta, enlightened. "Miss Baddeley almost bowled me over at the front entrance as I was returning from my ride in Hyde Park."

"Yes, she wanted to leave for Lincolnshire as soon as she possibly could. Mind, I don't resent her hasty departure, even though it leaves me in the inconvenient position of having to find another governess at a moment's notice. But scarcely had Miss Baddeley begun to pack her bags when Gillian declared that she did not want another governess. She wished, she said, to attend a school in Sussex, the headmistress of which is a notorious bluestocking, a follower of that dreadful Godwin woman, the one who used to go about preaching female emancipation!"

Araminta blinked in astonishment. "Is that all?"

"All! When I told Gillian that eligible suitors would shy away from a girl who had been educated in such a vulgar place, she declared that she did not intend to marry. Instead of breeding children, of whom she says that there are already too many in the world, she wants to write novels. Araminta, the child is only sixteen, and I have not allowed her even to *read* novels! As you'll recall, our papa always said that novels were corrupting to female morals."

"Oh, come now. I daresay there's hardly a well-bred girl in all of England who hasn't sneaked off to her bedchamber to read her mother's latest selection from the subscription library," said Araminta with a grin. "*I* used to do it. Once when my governess thought I was safely asleep, I set my bedclothes afire as I was reading *Tom Jones* by the light of a candle under my comforter."

"Well! I certainly thought to receive more understanding and sympathy from you, my own sister!"

"I *am* sympathetic, but I fail to see why you're so perturbed. For example, why shouldn't Gillian attend this school you spoke about? I confess, I shouldn't care at all for such a place, but then I'm not a bright, studious girl like Gillian."

"What? Allow her to associate with nobodies, the daughters of newly prosperous cits or insignificant country squires?"

"What harm could it do?" Araminta said reasonably. "Gillian's whole outlook might be broadened if she were exposed to the company of girls from outside her own social circle. *I* certainly learned a great deal about human nature during my travels with Uncle Will, meeting people from every walk of life."

"Yes, and you know my opinion of your life with Sir Wilfrid," retorted Henrietta. She was silent for a moment, frowning in thought. "I can settle the question of this dreadful school easily enough," she said at last. "I will simply forbid any further mention of it, and engage another governess at once. But what to do about this novel-writing notion of Gillian's? I can scarcely station a servant in her bedchamber twenty-four hours a day to ensure that she doesn't put her pen to paper!"

Araminta threw up her hands. "What flummery! First of all, it's highly unlikely that Gillian has the ability to write a publishable novel. However, if she should ever succeed in doing so, why shouldn't we be happy for her?

I understand that there are a number of famous female authors. Madame d'Arblay, for one; I loved *Evalina*. And Mrs. Radcliffe. I won't believe you if you say that you've never even skimmed *The Mysteries of Udolpho!*"

"I'll just remind you that neither of those ladies is Gillian's social equal, and that I don't care to have my daughter emulate either of them by turning herself into a middle-class bluestocking," snapped Henrietta. She bit her lip, adding, "I don't want to quarrel with you, Araminta. I know that both of us want what is best for Gillian."

Leaving Henrietta's bedchamber, Araminta walked down the corridor to Gillian's room, tapping lightly on the door. Receiving no answer, she called softly, "Gillian? It's Araminta. May I come in?"

"Please excuse me, Aunt Araminta. I'd rather not see anyone," came a muffled reply from beyond the door.

"I'd really like to talk to you, my dear."

There was a long pause, and Araminta was about to turn away when the door opened, and a wan-faced Gillian stood aside to allow Araminta to enter. "I suppose Mama asked you to come," she blurted.

"Well, yes, she did," replied Araminta calmly, settling herself comfortably into an armchair.

"Go ahead then, talk away to me, but it won't do the slightest bit of good." Gillian glared at Araminta. "I daresay that Mama can forbid me to attend Miss Elphinstone's academy, but she can't force me to accept a new governess who would be no better educated than her predecessor. Miss Baddeley didn't know any Greek or Latin—I've taught myself a little of both languages from my brother Philip's textbooks—and her Italian was quite dreadful. And Mama can't prevent me from writing novels either, even if I must write in the middle of the night."

"Just don't set fire to your bedclothes." At Gillian's uncomprehending stare, Araminta chuckled, saying,

"You goose, I'm not here to discourage you. If you become a published authoress, I'll bask in your fame! But why did you try to bamboozle me by telling me that you write poetry?"

"Because writing verse is a ladylike accomplishment," said Gillian, her expression softening. "Miss Baddeley always said that novels were common and vulgar."

"Then a good riddance to Miss Baddeley. Gillian, will you let me see something of what you've been writing?"

Gillian looked flustered. "Oh, I don't know—writing is so private. . . . But then, on the other hand, one writes for a *public,* I quite see that." She squared her shoulders and walked to her wardrobe, opening the doors and extracting a thick sheaf of paper from a shelf. "You'll give me your honest opinion, Aunt Araminta?" she said anxiously. "You won't tell me the story is good when it's quite dreadful?"

"I'll be as honest as a pillar saint. And please call me Araminta. If you say 'Aunt' once more, I'll feel myself sliding into old age."

After Araminta had returned to her bedchamber and had settled herself into an armchair with a second cup of tea close to hand, she began to read Gillian's novel. *Castle of Horrors* seemed to be the story of beautiful young Matilda, who journeys through the wild mountains of Italy in search of Sebastiano, her aged and noble father, held captive for ransom in the dungeon of a gloomy castle by the satanic Count Ugolino; when she arrives at the castle, Ugolino, desperate for money since he has lost his fortune, imprisons the wealthy heiress Matilda in a room of the castle until she will agree to marry him in exchange for the freedom of her father.

A little smile wreathed Araminta's lips as she skimmed over the first few pages of the manuscript in Gillian's neat, small handwriting. As she had more or less expected to find, the novel's extravagantly flowery language and melodramatic plot were strongly reminiscent of works by Mr. Walpole or Mrs. Radcliffe. There was no need for Henrietta to feel the smallest qualms about Gillian's aspirations to become an authoress, thought Araminta, because it seemed highly unlikely that *Castle of Horrors* would ever find a publisher.

Midway into the second chapter, however, Araminta sat up straighter in her chair, her eyes glued to the page, and soon she was racing through the manuscript with breathless interest.

". . . Creeping down the worn steps, slimy with dampness, Matilda reached the cellars of the castle. Around her, beyond the range of her candle, she could hear the furtive rustling of nameless living things, and recoiled as something slithered across her shoe. A current of freezing air caused her candle flame to flicker, and for a moment Matilda thought she would be caught in the Stygian blackness of this malodorous place of evil.

" 'Father,' she called softly. 'Are you here, dearest Father?' From a short distance away came a stifled groan of misery, and she hurried toward the sound. In the pallid light of her candle she could see massive iron bars across an opening in the wall. Again she heard that groan of boundless misery. Peering in through the bars, she could spy a figure lying on the floor of the dungeon. 'Father, oh, Father, is that you?' breathed Matilda. To her horror, the ghostlike figure struggled to its feet and stumbled painfully over to the barred door. Clad in a flowing white garment long since darkened to dirty gray, the apparition was now seen to be, not Matilda's father, but an aged female. Grasping the bars, the figure gazed at Matilda with crazed, hollow eyes and said, 'Oh, most noble Ugolino, the husband of my soul, have you come at last to have speech with me?' . . ."

* * *

Araminta did not wait for Gillian to reply to her knock. She bounded into her niece's bedchamber, exclaiming, "You've written a masterpiece, Gillian! I couldn't tear my eyes away from the manuscript until I had come to the end. You must finish the book immediately so that I can find out what happens to Matilda. What a horrible monster you've created in Ugolino, forcing poor Matilda to marry him when he has driven his first wife mad and imprisoned her in the dungeons of his castle!"

Chapter Four

"*Tiens, chère* Araminta, you're not ready yet? Madame Middleton awaits us below."

Turning her head to look at Odile, standing at the door of the bedchamber, Araminta said with a laugh, "Is it my sister who's impatient, or is it you, Odile? Henrietta said she wanted to leave at ten o'clock, and it's only a quarter of the hour. *I* think you can't wait to fix your eyes on all the new fashions in the Bond Street shops!"

The abigail, Jessie, with the freedom of an old and trusted servant, seized her mistress's shoulders, forcing her to face the mirror on the dressing table. "Drat, my lady," she grumbled, "don't keep moving your head. How I can I arrange your hair when you won't stay still?"

"I merely thought we should be prompt, since Madame Middleton is kind enough to escort us on this shopping expedition," said Odile in an injured voice, advancing into the room. "*Le Bon Dieu* knows, of course, that *I* have no expectations of making any purchases. I am accompanying you, *chère* Araminta, only because you said you wished my advice in choosing a new wardrobe. Which I agree with Madame your sister that you urgently need," she added pointedly. "That kerseymere dress you are wearing would do better as a dustcloth!"

Gazing at Odile's image in the mirror, Araminta said soothingly, "You and Henrietta are the most stylish women I know. I'm sure I'll be turned out like the Top of the Trees when the two of you finish with me! And I want you to select a new costume or two, also. As you were saying the other day, it's a dead bore for you to wear black all the time, when you're not even a widow!"

Odile's eyes brightened. "That's kind of you, *ma mie*. Something in purple, perhaps, or a deep shade of violet. In sarsenet or possibly *Soie de Londres* . . . But no, at this time of year doubtless jaconet or mull might be preferable. We'll see," she ended happily. "You will join us in the morning room, then, in—shall I tell Madame Middleton five minutes?"

Araminta exchanged an amused glance with Jessie as Odile left the room. A moment later, with only an unceremonious excuse for a knock, Gillian bounded into the bedchamber, her reddish curls in their usual state of dishevelment. "Araminta, could I talk to you?"

Nodding a dismissal to Jessie, Araminta said to Gillian, "I can give you a few moments. Your mama is waiting to take me shopping. Is something wrong?"

"Yes! Read this!"

Suppressing a smile at Gillian's dramatic tone, Araminta accepted the letter her niece handed to her. In the three brief days that she'd been living in Henrietta's house, she and Gillian had become fast friends. The shy girl had blossomed in the warmth of her aunt's sympathy and support for her writing ambitions.

Opening the letter, Araminta read the few curt lines. "My dear Gillian: Under no circumstances would I allow you to attend any school conducted by Maria Elphinstone. Harwood."

Mystified, Araminta looked up at Gillian. "But what is this? I wasn't aware that Ja—that the Duke knew you wanted to attend Miss Elphinstone's academy. Did you write to him?"

"Yes, I did," said Gillian mutinously. "He *is* my guardian, after all, but when I asked Mama to broach the subject with him, she refused, so I wrote to him myself."

Araminta read Jason's reply again. "It—it sounds a bit unfriendly," she ventured. "What did you say in your letter, Gillian?"

"The truth, only, as I saw it," Gillian said defensively. She bit her lip. "Well, perhaps I *was* a bit blunt. . . . I told the Duke that my mother had refused me her consent to attend Miss Elphinstone's academy, but that I felt I had the right, as a mature person, very nearly grown up, to have a voice in my own future. I asked the Duke to overrule Mama's decision, especially in view of the fact that you, Araminta, with so much more knowledge of the world than Mama, heartily approved of the notion."

"Oh," said Araminta hollowly. She could well imagine Jason's reaction to Gillian's letter. He must have been annoyed and embarrassed at being asked to intervene in a personal matter between Henrietta and her daughter, and he must also be nursing a hostile conviction that his ward had fallen under the influence of her newly found aunt's pernicious theories of female emancipation. Araminta groaned inwardly. Why, oh why, had she allowed herself to talk so freely to a complete stranger in that inn in Dover? Why hadn't she suspected that a man of Jason's elegance and address was a prominent member of the Ton whom she might well meet later in London?

"Araminta, will you talk to the Duke for me? He might listen to you."

Jolted out of her reverie by Gillian's question, Araminta choked back an impulse to giggle, recalling her last stormy encounter with Jason in Hyde Park. After *that* declaration of independence on Araminta's part, the Duke was hardly likely to pay much heed to any request that she might make on Gillian's behalf. Her eyes narrowed. A direct assault might fail, but what about a flank attack? Summoning up a thoughtful smile, she said, "I'd like to know more about this school before I approach the Duke. Perhaps if I wrote to Miss Elphinstone . . . What's her direction?"

"The academy is in the village of Eastwick, near Tunbridge Wells." Gillian hugged her aunt. "Thank you, Araminta. I know you won't fail me."

Araminta had her doubts about that, but she was obliged to put Gillian's scholastic problems to the back of her mind in the course of the strenuous shopping that Henrietta apparently considered necessary to enable her younger sister to appear presentable in London society. It seemed to Araminta's dazed eyes that Henrietta did not omit a visit to a single linen draper, silk mercer, haberdasher, dressmaker, milliner, or corsetier in the areas of Leicester Square and Covent Garden and Oxford Street.

Hours later, standing with Araminta and Odile outside the fashionable premises of Madame St. Aubin in Bond Street, Henrietta said with a complacent smile, "Well, now, it will take a few days, a week at most, before all your new clothes are delivered, Araminta, but I think I may say that we've done a very good morning's work!" She gazed approvingly at Araminta's new walking dress of pale green jaconet muslin, worn with a spencer in darker green *gros de Naples* and a French bonnet of silk *pluche* decorated with ostrich feathers. "How fortunate that Madame St. Aubin had this gown already made up, and such a perfect fit, too!" Henrietta nodded graciously at Odile's gown of lavender mull worn with a pelisse of deepest violet. "You look charmingly, Madame Lacoste. Araminta tells me it took considerable persuasion on her part to induce you to part with your blacks. I agree with my sister: you're far too young to dwell in the past, much as you still grieve for your husband."

"Oh, my poor Armand . . . But yes, one must get on with one's life, as *chère* Araminta is always telling me," Odile replied with a pathetic catch in her voice.

A tall gentleman walking from the direction of Brook Street paused as he came up to them, touching his hat and saying with a pleasant smile, "Lady Middleton, dare I hope that you'll remember me?"

The tiniest of frowns settled between Henrietta's eyes and she sounded unwontedly formal as she replied, "It's Lord Manning, isn't it? I believe we met some years ago. Araminta, Madame, may I present Viscount Manning? My lord, this is my sister, Lady Araminta Beresford, and her friend, Madame Lacoste."

Bowing deeply to her and Odile, Lord Manning gave no indication that he and Araminta had met previously and rather dramatically in Hyde Park. With a charming smile he said, "Do you live in London, Lady Araminta, or are you merely visiting? Or are you, perhaps, preparing to make your come out under Lady Middleton's wing?"

"Something like that," Araminta replied coolly. "I've been living abroad until recently with my guardian."

Lord Manning beamed. "That gives us something in common, then. I've just returned from a stint in our embassy at Constantinople." He turned to Henrietta. "Will you take pity on a lonely expatriate and permit me to call, Lady Middleton?"

Henrietta hesitated momentarily. "Why . . . if you wish, Lord Manning."

The Viscount ignored Henrietta's patent lack of enthusiasm. "Capital. Lady Araminta and I will be able to compare our foreign travel experiences." He bowed gracefully, taking leave with a smiling, "Until we meet again, then."

"Well!" Henrietta stared in a far from friendly fashion at Manning's retreating back. "I had no idea he was back in town."

"You don't seem very fond of him," Araminta observed.

"Oh, I really don't know Lord Manning well enough to dislike him. Actually, I haven't seen or heard of him in years," Henrietta said impatiently. "It's just . . . the fact is, I think there's bad blood between him and the Duke."

"Bad blood? My, that sounds serious," said Araminta, trying to sound suitably disapproving. But she smiled to herself as she recalled Lord Manning's handsome face and laughing, impudent eyes. She wouldn't be at all averse to knowing the man, charming rogue though she suspected him to be. She hadn't a doubt that he'd renewed a superficial acquaintance with Henrietta solely in order to wangle an introduction to Henrietta's younger sister. The introduction that Araminta had denied him in Hyde Park in an unaccustomed fit of conventionality. "What caused the bad blood between the Duke and Lord Manning?" she asked her sister after the groom had handed them into their waiting carriage and put up the steps.

"Oh, I don't know precisely," said Henrietta, sounding uncomfortable. "I shouldn't be speaking of it, because it's all rumor. Naturally, Harwood would never discuss such a subject with me."

"Come now, Henrietta," Araminta coaxed as the carriage started up. "You know you like a good gossip as well as the next one. Tell me about the feud between the terrible Lord Manning and His Grace the Duke of Harwood."

"*Really,* Araminta! The things you say," Henrietta exclaimed, red-faced and flustered.

Odile, who understood English better than she spoke it—and better than she sometimes cared to admit—said anxiously, "There is something wrong, *chère* Madame Middleton? This gentleman we just met, he is an evil person?"

"No, no, Madame Lacoste, nothing is wrong," Henrietta assured her, lapsing into French. She lowered her voice. "Well, perhaps it would be remiss in me not to at least *mention* some of the stories I've heard about Lord Manning. He did say he'd call, after all, and you should be on your guard, both of you. According to the *on dit,* Lord Manning fell madly in love with the Duke's sister Felicity, and then, when Harwood forbade the match, on the grounds that Manning was a fortune hunter, Manning persuaded Felicity to elope. She was very young then, not even out yet. Well—and please understand this is *all rumor*—the Duke caught up with the pair before they could reach Gretna Green and managed to hush up the affair. Lord Manning was posted off to the Middle East, and two years later Felicity married the Earl of Salford, the greatest catch of her year."

"I am desolated to hear this," said Odile earnestly. "This *Milord* Manning, he seemed to be such a fine gentleman, *très gentil,* would you not say so, Araminta?"

"Oh, indeed, he was quite charming. Could it be, Henrietta, that poor Lord Manning has been grossly maligned by all these rumors?" Araminta asked innocently. "Perhaps we should give him the benefit of the doubt."

* * *

The footman intercepted Araminta as she was descending the staircase to the foyer. "The woman you were expecting has arrived, my lady. I've shown her into the library."

Glancing at the little jeweled watch fastened to her bodice, Araminta said vexedly, "She's very early. Well, it can't be helped. Thank you, Beeson. Tell her I'll be with her as soon as I can. Perhaps you could bring her some tea."

Walking into the drawing room, Araminta found it was already comfortably filled with callers. Her customary clutch of admirers surrounded Damaris's golden head, and off in the corner Lord Manning was chatting animatedly with Odile. As Araminta approached them, Manning rose with his usual bow of incomparable grace.

"How pleasant to see you again, Lord Manning."

"Thank you, Lady Araminta. I'm sure you were about to add, how unexpected it is to see me, were you not?" Pulling out a chair for her, the Viscount tossed her an unabashed grin. Since their meeting five days ago in Bond Street, he had called every day at Middleton House.

"Only fancy, *chère* Araminta, *Milord* Manning has been telling me about his experiences at the Congress of Vienna," said Odile eagerly. "Oh, how I should like to see strange places and meet exciting people!"

"But, dear Madame, you are already so well traveled. You lived in Athens before your good husband died, and you were just describing to me the sights of Beirut," observed Manning.

Araminta narrowed her eyes at the Viscount. With his exquisite manners, his perfect French, his air of viewing all womanhood as gentle creatures to be cherished and coddled, he had all the gifts to captivate Odile, a romantic to her fingertips. And of course, as might have been expected, the Frenchwoman's tongue had run away with her, although Araminta had warned her repeatedly not to speak of their Levantine adventures. Suddenly Araminta remembered a snatch of conversation from her last encounter with the Duke of Harwood in Hyde Park: ". . . if the gossips should learn that your companion was not a respectable widow but just another concubine from a Turkish seraglio, she'd be barred from every polite drawing room in London, and your own reputation would be in shreds . . ."

Araminta put the unwelcome thought out of her mind. "Odile and I spent only a day or so in Beirut, waiting for our ship, so I fear we didn't see much of it," she informed Manning with an easy smile.

Manning lifted an eyebrow. "Oh, I would have thought—Madame seemed so conversant with the city . . ." He smiled at Odile. "But surely, no matter how far you traveled, nothing could compare with the beauties of your husband's home in Poitou?"

Odile looked confused, as well she might be, Araminta thought grimly. Affecting a giggle, she said to Odile, *"Pauvre petite,* you never had the most rudimentary notion of geography. Aquitaine, Odile, not Poitou. Unfortunately poor Armand was never able to take you there because of the doings of the Corsican monster, but you know very well he came from Aquitaine."

"Well, of course he did," exclaimed Odile indignantly. "Did I not say so, milord?"

"So you did, madame. My wretched memory." Manning put a languid hand to his head. "I'm not as young as I was. Perhaps premature senility is setting in?" But Araminta wasn't deceived by his smiling nonchalance. She had a shrewd idea that the Viscount's agile diplomatic mind was carefully recording every slip that Odile made. After a moment he said, "Madame has been telling me that you and she are planning to set up your own household. Have you decided in which part of London you would like to live?"

"No, not as yet. Do you have any ideas?"

Manning looked at her thoughtfully. "As a matter of fact, I myself have a house in Hanover Square. I've been renting it out since my mother died and I entered the foreign service. But only the other day my man of business informed me that my most recent tenant has died. Would you care to look at the house? It's large and well appointed—though perhaps the furniture isn't in the latest style—and the public rooms are suitable for entertaining."

"Why, yes, I'd love to see the house. But Lord Manning, now that you've returned to England, don't you wish to live in your own house?"

"Lord, no," said Manning cheerfully. "I can't afford to live there. My pockets are completely to let. You'd be doing me an enormous favor if you rented the house."

He stood up politely as Henrietta stopped by her sister's chair. "Pray excuse me, Lord Manning, Madame Lacoste. Araminta, could I have a word with you?"

Seated beside Araminta on the opposite side of the room, well away from any visitors who might overhear them, Henrietta muttered, "Really, my dear, you must put a stop to this. That man has been fairly haunting this house. To my knowledge, since he first met you, he hasn't missed a day calling on us. On you, I should say. It's obvious he doesn't come here to see *me!* You simply shouldn't encourage him."

"But Henrietta, I've merely been polite to the man," said Araminta rather absently as she peered down at her watch. It was later than she'd thought. She looked across the room. "Actually, I think Lord Manning has a *tendre* for our lovely widow," she grinned, watching the

Viscount as he resumed his conversation with Odile.

"Nonsense," snapped Henrietta. "Lord Manning is simply flirting with Madame Lacoste. It must be obvious to him that the widow of an impoverished *émigré* has no fortune. For I must tell you, Araminta, that I believe the man to be a gazetted fortune hunter."

"Because the Duke of Harwood has so labeled him?"

Henrietta bridled. "Certainly not. I told you, the Duke has never mentioned Lord Manning to me. But only yesterday I was talking to my friend, Mrs. Hendon, who told me it's known all over London that Lord Manning's in low water. His estates are rumored to be mortgaged to the hilt and he's desperately trying to sell or rent his town house. And now it's obvious he's discovered you're a wealthy heiress, and he's casting out his lures to you, hoping to fasten his interest with you before he's towed into the River Tick." Henrietta stared at her sister's unconcerned face. "You don't seem in the least shocked," she said accusingly.

"No more I am," said Araminta merrily. "Lord Manning has already informed me about the impecunious state of his finances, for one thing. For another, it wouldn't be the first time a man of good family was obliged to find a wealthy bride. It's done all the time, as you very well know, and nobody points an accusing finger at the bridegroom."

"Araminta! You can't mean—"

"I don't mean anything. I like Lord Manning very well but I haven't a case on him. I was only suggesting that not all prospective bridegrooms are as full of juice as His Grace of Harwood."

An odd look crossed Henrietta's face. She wasn't an especially perceptive woman, but it was obvious she'd caught the slight barb in Araminta's voice. She said uneasily, "Araminta, you haven't—you couldn't possibly have quarreled with the Duke?"

"I? Quarrel with the Duke?" Araminta's eyes opened wide in surprised innocence. "Henrietta, you've been present at all my meetings with him. You *know* we haven't quarreled."

"Well, of course . . ." Henrietta sounded confused. "It was foolish of me. Why on earth would you and Harwood quarrel?"

Araminta felt a twinge of discomfort. No, Henrietta wasn't very perceptive, but apparently she'd grasped intuitively that her sister's relations with the Duke of Harwood were being conducted on two separate levels. When Jason called at Middleton House, he and Araminta spoke in polite commonplaces, but beneath the surface they were conducting a skillful sparring match in which neither, so far, had given any quarter. The most innocent of remarks could turn into yet another skirmish in Araminta's continuing campaign to make Jason realize he had no authority over her life. And equally, Jason's blandest reply covered his determination not to allow Araminta to disrupt the domestic peace of Middleton House.

"Araminta! You're woolgathering." Henrietta's exasperated voice broke into her thoughts. "I asked you a question. And why do you keep looking at your watch? Oh—" Lady Middleton's voice softened with pleasure. Araminta followed her gaze to see Jason standing in the doorway of the drawing room. "There's the Duke. I wasn't sure he'd call today. He said something about the pressure of business affairs." She rose, crossing the room to Jason, who, as he stood waiting for Henrietta to join him, met Araminta's eyes and inclined his head politely, quite as if they were the bare acquaintances they always pretended to be.

Araminta felt a stab of annoyance as she acknowledged that he was the handsomest, most elegant man she had ever met. If only he weren't quite as tall and

66

graceful, or if he didn't possess that lethal cleft in his chin, it would be much easier to stay angry with him. As he moved with Henrietta to speak to Damaris, who greeted his appearance with a dazzling smile, Araminta left her chair to rejoin Odile and Lord Manning.

"I've been abroad for so long that I've had to make a real effort to keep myself *au courant* with the latest *on dit*," said the Viscount pleasantly. "Tell me, Lady Araminta, is it true what I've heard, that the Duke of Harwood is the guardian of Lady Middleton's children?"

"Why, yes."

"Ah. Then it's likely I'll encounter him often when I come calling on you?"

Araminta raised an inquiring eyebrow. "I daresay you will. The Duke takes his responsibilities *very* seriously. Does that pose a problem?"

"Not at all. His Grace of Harwood has every right to visit where he chooses, as have I," said Manning, shrugging. He rose slowly as Jason walked across the room toward them.

The Duke paused, stiffening slightly, as he became aware of Manning's identity. Then, his gaze passing over the Viscount as if he were invisible, the Duke bowed to the two women. "Lady Araminta, Madame Lacoste."

"Good afternoon, Duke," said Manning coolly. "How pleasant to renew an old acquaintance."

For several dragging moments Araminta feared that Jason would give Manning the cut direct. The noise level in the room dropped abruptly, and she realized that many of those present whose memories went back more than a few years must be aware of the old enmity between the two men. As they faced each other, Araminta noted with a tinge of surprise that superficially they were much the same type: tall, rangy, urbane, quite ridiculously good-looking, and exquisitely well-tailored. Then, to her relief, before the silence could become deadly, she saw Jason's innate good breeding come to the fore. He nodded, saying curtly, "Lord Manning." However inclined he might be to cut the Viscount in the street or in one of his clubs, he would not do so in Lady Middleton's drawing room, where it could only cause her embarrassment.

"And how is Lady Felicity?" inquired Manning. To Araminta, it sounded like an open provocation.

"My sister is in good health," Jason replied, even more curtly. "If you'll excuse me, sir, I'd like a word with Lady Araminta."

"But certainly. I was just leaving, in any event. Lady Araminta, I look forward to seeing you tomorrow."

Jason slid into Manning's vacated chair. His face expressing only a mild interest, he said politely, "Your note asked me to call. I'm quite at your disposal."

She flashed him a bright smile. "So kind, Duke. I wanted to talk to you about the possibility of Gillian's attending Miss Elphinstone's Academy."

A curtain came down over his eyes, but his voice was perfectly collected as he said, "As you're no doubt aware, I've already refused Gillian permission to attend the school."

"Well, yes, I'm aware that you've refused Gillian's request, but I don't understand why. Could you explain your reasons?"

"Certainly. In a word, Maria Elphinstone is a female dragon who is trying to turn her students into wild-eyed bluestockings!"

"I don't know about turning wild-eyed, but what would be the harm if Gillian became a bluestocking?" asked Araminta reasonably. "Some very respectable ladies have become scholars, I believe. Some of them have even written books," she finished with an air of discovery. Quickly realizing, however, that she was skirting uncomfortably close to Gillian's writing secret, she added hastily, "Are you quite sure you've given the matter enough thought? How much do you really know about Miss Elphinstone's establishment?"

"I know it by reputation." There was a definite edge now to Jason's voice.

"Well, exactly." Araminta beamed. "But you don't really *know*, do you? That's why I've invited Miss Elphinstone here today to meet you and to answer any questions you might have about her academy."

"You've *what?*" After his involuntary exclamation, Jason drew a deep, calming breath. "On more than one occasion, Lady Araminta, you've accused me, on no reasonable grounds whatever, of trying to interfere in your life. May I remind you that what is sauce for the goose is also sauce for the gander? You won't dispute, I trust, that Gillian's affairs are my responsibility?"

"No, but I think you should heed what my Uncle Will used to say."

"Which is?"

"Uncle Will had a cardinal rule: unless one has all the facts, one cannot reach a reasoned decision. I don't think you have all the facts about Miss Elphinstone. If you were to talk to her, you might find that her ideas aren't as outlandish as you think they are. However, if you don't wish to see her, I'll send her away immediately."

Not a shadow of emotion crossed the Duke's handsome face, but Araminta caught the glint of anger in his eyes. "I wouldn't dream of contradicting a dead man, especially a paragon like Uncle Will," he said coldly. "Shall we interview Miss Elphinstone together? To ensure that I give the lady a fair hearing?"

"Yes, that would be best, I think," said Araminta, ignoring the sarcasm in his voice. She rose. "Join me in the library in a few minutes. It might cause comment if we left the drawing room at the same time."

As Araminta entered the library, a tall, thin, soberly dressed woman rose from a chair beside the desk. "Lady Araminta Beresford? I am Maria Elphinstone."

"How do you do? It was so kind of you to come all the way from Tunbridge Wells. I'm sorry you were kept waiting. The Duke of Harwood was delayed. He'll be with us directly. Won't you sit down?"

Sitting opposite Miss Elphinstone, Araminta covertly studied the headmistress's severely austere features. She didn't look to be a lady who indulged in small talk. "My young niece admires your theories of education so much," Araminta began.

Miss Elphinstone inclined her head graciously. "When you spoke in your letter about the young lady's writing aspirations, I felt quite sure that my academy was the proper place for Miss Gillian to complete her education. The school isn't for just anyone, as you've doubtless gathered. I want only serious pupils."

"I'm persuaded that your students must all be real scholars," said Araminta hastily.

Jason came into the library. Nodding to Araminta, he bowed to the schoolmistress, saying, "How do you do. I'm Harwood," and sat down behind the desk. "So. Tell me about the kind of education my ward might expect to acquire at your academy," he said pleasantly. "But first, am I correct in assuming, ma'am, that you're the daughter of Baron Elphinstone of Ware?"

"Quite correct, Duke."

"And what are your father's views of your school?"

"He completely disapproves of my life's work."

"Ah. And why is that, pray?"

Miss Elphinstone gave Jason a long, considering look. "I think you already know, Duke."

"Possibly," he agreed. "However, since this is a matter

of my ward's future, I should like an answer."

Araminta felt the first faint stirrings of disquiet. It was quite obvious that Jason's knowledge of the Tunbridge Wells Female Seminary was based on more than hearsay.

Miss Elphinstone settled back in her chair. "Let me see," she began calmly. "Basically, my father objects to my fundamental belief that females are the intellectual, physical, and moral equals of men, and should be treated neither as toys nor slaves. Holding such a belief, naturally, I've tailored my curriculum accordingly."

"I see. Would you describe your curriculum?"

"I should be delighted. First as to what I do *not* teach. At my school you will find no classes in waxwork, mold work, embroidery, painting on glass, shell work or lace making, nor do I offer lessons in deportment or dancing. My pupils study literature, history, classical and foreign languages, mathematics, and the physical sciences. In other words, the same subjects that are taught in a good boys' school. I see no reason why, with the proper education, my girls could not aim for careers in medicine, law, government. I should like to see a female Prime Minister one day."

"You don't speak of your pupils as wives and mothers. What are your views on marriage, Miss Elphinstone?"

"I consider it an outmoded institution, weighed down by a false double standard of morality. For those females interested only in breeding, I presume marriage might be considered some form of protection. I would hope that my pupils would have their interests fixed on a higher plane."

"Indeed. I have one last question, ma'am. Do I understand correctly that you favor abolishing both the monarchy and the aristocracy?"

"I do. In a world in which men and women associate

71

in conditions of perfect equality, I see no reasons for the marks of privilege."

Jason stood up, saying, "Thank you for acquainting me with your views, Miss Elphinstone. I regret to inform you that under no circumstances would I entrust my ward's education into your care."

Rising in her turn, the schoolmistress said composedly, "I think we met under false assumptions on both sides, Duke." She turned to Araminta, saying with a touch of acid, "Might I suggest, Lady Araminta, that before you next set up an interview like this, you do what I require of all my pupils — your homework?" Bowing to Jason and Araminta in turn, she stalked to the doorway, throwing over her shoulder, "I'll see myself out."

Hardly had Miss Elphinstone closed the door behind her when Araminta collapsed into her chair in a fit of helpless laughter. "Marriage an outmoded institution. Abolish the aristocracy. A female Prime Minister," she gasped, reaching into her reticule for a handkerchief to wipe her eyes after she had laughed herself out. "Oh, Jason, have you ever heard the like?"

She paused, her handkerchief halfway to her face, when she observed Jason's unsmiling face.

"Yes, I'd heard the like. I investigated the Tunbridge Wells Female Seminary quite thoroughly before I refused Gillian my consent to attend it," said the Duke coldly. "If you'd taken the trouble to ask my opinion before you decided in your usual harebrained fashion to force me and that wretched bluestocking into a confrontation, we should all of us have avoided a great deal of trouble! I trust this will be your last foray into matters that don't concern you."

The laughter died out of Araminta's eyes. She'd been on the verge of offering Jason a handsome apology, of telling him he was quite right to turn thumbs down on

Maria Elphinstone's academy. The woman was an antidote and a crank and could do Gillian nothing but harm, and in future Araminta would leave Gillian's welfare to the care of her guardian. The apology died unborn on her lips.

"Not at all," Araminta snapped. "My family *are* my concern, and I'll continue to do whatever I feel is helpful to them. And at the very least, I'll do it out of love, not arrogance!"

Chapter Five

Wearing a new pelisse in pale green lustring, with a matching bonnet trimmed with a wreath of Provence roses, Araminta walked down the corridor to Odile's bedchamber and nearly collided with her abigail Jessie at the door.

"But what's this?" Araminta asked, glancing at the tray in Jessie's hands. On it reposed only a steaming pot, trimly covered with a tea cozy, and a cup and saucer. "Is Odile still abed at this hour? It's past noon. She and I have an engagement at one o'clock. And this surely can't be her idea of breakfast."

"Madame won't be stirring from her bedchamber this morning," replied Jessie grimly. "This isn't tea, nor her breakfast chocolate, neither. It's a *tisane*. Madame has one of her headaches."

Araminta sighed, pushing the door open for Jessie and following the abigail into the bedchamber. Odile was a past mistress in using imaginary maladies to create sympathy for herself, or to enable her to avoid doing what inconvenienced her, but occasionally nervous strain brought on a genuine headache that could prostrate her for the entire day.

Pouring out a cup of the strong-smelling *tisane*, Araminta brought it to Odile's bedside. "Here, *petite*.

This will make you feel better," she said briskly.

Slowly Odile unraveled herself from her cocoon of coverlets and extended a shaking hand for the *tisane*. She downed the scalding liquid and lay back against her pillows, shielding her eyes against the pale light escaping into the room through the heavily curtained windows.

"Now, then, what brought this on?" Araminta inquired. "You were merry as a grig last night when we were playing spilikins with Gillian."

"I had the most dreadful nightmare, Araminta," Odile said in a thready voice. "I dreamed that my Roger was dead. So then I woke knowing I was quite, quite alone in the world, and something that felt like a giant hammer began beating inside my skull."

"You're not alone in the world, you goose. You have me. And Roger isn't dead. He's in no danger at all, now that the war is over. It was just a dream."

"But it was so real, Araminta." Odile shivered. "How do I know my sweet Roger is safe? He could be dead. How would I know it? And the war may be over, but Roger, he is still serving on a ship. He could have drowned!"

"Well, I'm sure he's done no such thing," said Araminta, rising from her chair. "I must be going now, Odile. You stay in bed for the rest of the day. Jessie will bring you as much of that foul-tasting brew as you need, and I hope you'll be feeling more the thing by evening."

As Araminta came down the staircase to the foyer, she could hear the faint notes of a pianoforte. To the alert young footman who materialized as soon as she set foot in the foyer, she said, "Lord Manning will be calling for me in a few minutes. I'll be in the music room."

Slipping into the room so quietly that the player was unaware of her presence, Araminta sat down behind the pianoforte to listen to Damaris play. As Gillian had said on the day of Araminta's arrival at Middleton House, not only was Damaris beautiful, but she did everything superlatively well. That included playing the pianoforte. Listening to the silvery cascade of notes rippling in a lightning-fast arpeggio from her niece's flying fingers, Araminta thought that Damaris's playing must be very near professional quality.

Damaris turned, startled, when Araminta applauded softly at the end of the piece. "Oh, Aunt Araminta, I didn't realize anyone was here," she said, smiling. "Did it sound all right?"

"It sounded quite perfect to me."

"I'm glad. The first important event of the Season will be the Cathcarts' ball next Tuesday, you see, and the Duchess has asked me to play. I hope I won't disappoint her."

There wasn't a hint of toploftiness in Damaris's voice, only a shy desire to please. She never seems to put her foot wrong, thought Araminta, and this afternoon she was looking impossibly lovely in pale blue muslin, with her golden curls secured with a knot of blue ribbon. So why, then, was it so much harder to warm to her than to her untidy, impulsive younger sister?

As Damaris turned back to her instrument, her mother entered the music room, saying, "The modiste is here to make the final fitting on your ball gown, my dear. Run along, you won't want to keep her waiting."

After Damaris had obediently left the room, Araminta said pleasantly, "I enjoyed hearing Damaris play. She's very talented."

"Oh—thank you. Yes, everyone says Damaris is very accomplished." No doubt about it, Henrietta sounded distinctly cool. She hadn't been her usual amiable self since her discovery, two days ago, that Araminta had arranged for Maria Elphinstone to come to Middleton House for an interview. It was Jason's involvement in the scheme that seemed to exercise Henrietta's ire the most, although he'd brushed off the incident with a bland unconcern that Araminta was sure masked his real feelings. In any event, though Araminta had offered a pretty apology, and had even made a handsome admission that the Tunbridge Wells Female Seminary was *not* the place for Gillian, Henrietta hadn't gotten over her grievance and was obviously not yet ready to clear the air.

Glancing at Araminta's pelisse and bonnet, Henrietta said, an edge to her voice, "Watson tells me that Lord Manning has arrived to see you. Surely you aren't planning to go somewhere alone with the man?"

Araminta smiled, pulling on her gloves of York Tan. "Odile was supposed to accompany us, but I've had to scratch her. She's prostrate with one of her bilious headaches. Not that it really matters. Lord Manning was merely proposing to drive us to inspect his town house. If I find the house is suitable for renting, I can always bring Odile there later to see it."

Henrietta sat down, as if her knees had suddenly become weak. "Araminta!" she wailed. "Don't tell me you're still thinking of setting up your own household. I thought we'd agreed that, after your—your adventures in the Levant, you couldn't be too careful about your reputation, and that in any case Madame Lacoste was far too young to be your chaperon. And of course you'll recall how much the Duke disapproves of the notion . . ."

"And *you'll* recall, Henrietta, that while the Duke of Harwood may be the guardian of your children, he certainly isn't mine!" Araminta flashed, and then, at her sister's look of alarm, immediately regretted her outburst. "There's no need for you to worry about me, Henrietta," she said soothingly. Her eyes sparkling with sudden mischief, she added, "I promise on my word of honor that Odile and I will be models of propriety when

77

we settle into our new home. We won't cause a breath of scandal. We'll give such proper parties that our guests will die of boredom, and we won't set foot out of doors without at least a footman *and* an abigail in attendance."

Henrietta stood up, a spot of angry color in either cheek. "I can't prevent you from funning at my expense," she said stiffly, "but might I suggest you begin *now* to build a reputation for propriety? It was bad enough, your proposing to go to Lord Manning's house in the company of Madame Lacoste. You must know, without my telling you, that no lady of quality accepts an invitation to visit a gentleman's home without a chaperon. Especially not the home of a known libertine and fortune hunter!"

Araminta threw up her hands. "Oh, don't talk such fustian," she said impatiently. "Lord Manning may be a loose fish, but at the moment he isn't interested in plotting an assignation. Certainly not in broad daylight! He merely wants to rent me his house!" She walked to the door, pausing to wave airily to Henrietta. "I'll be back in a trice, safe and sound."

"Araminta, I absolutely forbid—" Henrietta clamped her lips tightly together as she observed, through the door that her sister had just opened, the hovering figure of one of the footmen.

Saved in the nick of time from Henrietta's interference, Araminta grinned to herself as she walked on down the hall. Not even an imminent danger to life or reputation could make Henrietta relax her rigid rules about discussing personal matters in front of the servants.

Lord Manning's expression was discontented as he stared out the window of his town chariot as it swung out of Bruton Street. "If I'd known Madame Lacoste wasn't accompanying us, I'd have escorted you in my curricle," he remarked. "I hate being driven. However, I know better than to try to crowd three people into a curricle, when two of those people are beautifully dressed young ladies. You look very handsome today, if I may say so. That color is very becoming."

"Thank you," replied Araminta, adding, "It's all due to my sister's good taste, I assure you."

He continued to look at her, his eyes narrowing. "When we met for the first time in Hyde Park, you seemed so familiar, remember? Are you sure you were never in Stamboul?"

"No, never. Lord Manning, you're not being very gallant," she chaffed him. "Surely if we'd met previously you couldn't have forgotten me?" She glanced out the window as the carriage turned into a curiously funnel-shaped street past the classic portico and Corinthian columns of an imposing church. "Fortunately you needn't suffer the discomfort of being driven for very long," she observed. "It's a very short drive from Bruton Street to Hanover Square." In a few moments the carriage drew up in front of a tall, four-storied house on the west side of the square. The house had a facade of red and gray brick, like most of its neighbors, and a pedimental doorcase.

As Lord Manning gave Araminta his hand to help her down the steps, he motioned to the opposite side of the square. "If you're a music lover, Lady Araminta, nothing could be more convenient for you than my house. Those are the Hanover Square Rooms over there. Only last week I attended a concert by the Philharmonic Society."

It took only a brief inspection to satisfy Araminta that the Manning town house would serve very well as a temporary London residence for herself and Odile. It was certainly large enough, with handsomely proportioned rooms, furnished tastefully if not in the first style of elegance. It had been well maintained by the previous occupant and there was ample stabling for her horses. "I like your house very much," she informed Lord Manning as they stood in the foyer of the mansion after their tour of the premises. "If you'll have your man of business contact my bankers, I daresay they'll have little difficulty coming to terms."

"But why complicate a simple matter?" Lord Manning said cheerfully. "Why don't we simply settle it ourselves over a glass of wine and a small nuncheon?" As she looked at him, her eyebrows raised in inquiry, he laughed, saying, "Yes, my house is unoccupied and servantless, but I can still manage to offer you some hospitality."

Taking her arm, he led her down the corridor to the morning room at the rear of the hall. She'd looked into the room only a short time before, and at that time the shutters had been tightly closed and the furniture had been swathed in holland covers. Now the sun shone brightly through the windows, the furniture was uncovered, and a small fire burned on the hearth. Bending over a large hamper, a soberly dressed manservant was arranging dishes and food on a low table set in front of a comfortable-looking settee near the fireplace.

Casting a critical look around him, Lord Manning nodded to the servant. "Excellent, Bates. You may go now. We'll serve ourselves." He turned to Araminta, holding out his hand. "Will you remove your pelisse and bonnet, Lady Araminta? The room seems quite warm."

"Indeed it is," agreed Araminta affably. "The temperature is also quite balmy out of doors today, which is where I propose to go. Will you order your carriage, please?"

Lord Manning's face fell. "Lady Araminta, won't you at least take a glass of wine? A bite of chicken? Bates has gone to a good deal of trouble—"

"Trouble he could have easily avoided if you'd consulted me beforehand about this little feast. You know as well as I do, Lord Manning, that it would be highly improper for me as a young unmarried woman to take a meal alone with you."

"But I didn't know we'd be alone when I had Bates arrange for a hamper from Gunther's," said Manning in an injured voice. "I was expecting Madame Lacoste to accompany you as your duenna. Will you look at all that food? There's enough to feed a regiment. I even had Bates order some coffee creams, because Madame Lacoste told me she was especially fond of them."

"Oh." Araminta looked at Manning, trying to refrain from giggling.

"Admit you've misjudged me," he coaxed.

"Oh, very well. I'll admit you had no intention of enticing me into a cozy luncheon *à deux* in an empty house. Doubtless, from what I've heard of your reputation, you had more interesting ideas in mind, involving two females in a luncheon *à trois* in an empty house."

"You have the tongue of an adder, Lady Araminta," complained Manning. "Not at all what I've become accustomed to in the well-brought-up young ladies of my acquaintance. Come now, be generous. We're here, and this food and wine is here. Wouldn't it be very wasteful not to at least sample it?"

Araminta gazed at the thinly sliced ham and the glazed squabs and the deep red strawberry tarts, to name a few of the delicacies that Bates had removed from the hamper. They looked delicious and she was suddenly hungry. After all, she reasoned, any harm to her reputation, so direfully predicted by Henrietta, must already have been done. She'd been closeted alone with Manning in his house for the better part of an hour. What did a few more minutes matter?

"This is really an excellent pickled salmon," she commented a little later, smiling at Manning sitting next to her on the settee.

"Yes, Gunther's has done us very well. Another glass of wine?"

"No, I thank you. Not in the middle of the day. Some of the lemonade, perhaps." Araminta put down her glass after taking one sip of the lemonade. "Now that, sir, has an interesting flavor."

"Doesn't it? My own invention. Three parts of brandy to one each of white wine and water. Oh, and half a lemon, naturally."

"Yes, the taste of the lemon was quite pronounced," said Araminta drily. She put down her fork, saying thoughtfully, "Lord Manning, should you object if I removed several of the book cases from your library in favor of some display cases? My late uncle, Sir Wilfrid Lambert, collected rare botanical specimens from all over Europe. I think he'd like to know that his collection was giving pleasure to others."

"Do whatever your fancy moves you to do with the house. It will be your home."

Araminta leaned back against the settee, a pleased smile curving her mouth. "Yes, it will be my home, won't it? I can do exactly as I like. Buy all new furnishings. Entertain when and as I wish, without consulting anyone else. It will be such a change. For so many years I've lived out of my trunks in hotels, or as a guest in other people's houses, or as my uncle's hostess . . ."

"I daresay you realize it's most unusual for such a young woman to be her own mistress," said Manning. "You're fortunate, Lady Araminta, to be able to go your own way, and to have ample means to do so."

Araminta looked at her host thoughtfully. He met her gaze with an unclouded smile, seeming perfectly at ease. Surely he realized he'd just revealed to her that he'd looked into her family background and her financial circumstances? Araminta gave a mental shrug. Of course he realized it. He'd already informed her he was in low water. He was assuming that, as a woman of the world, she was aware that men of good family often couldn't marry without some consideration for money and that she wouldn't hold his candor against him.

"Yes, I do like to manage my own affairs," Araminta told the Viscount with a laugh. "I cut my wisdoms long ago, though at times my sister seems to find it hard to believe I'm no longer in the schoolroom."

"Perhaps Lady Middleton's behavior toward you is influenced by the Duke of Harwood," said Manning as he poured himself another glass of wine. "A friendly word to the wise, Lady Araminta, since you now have a family connection of sorts with the Duke. He's a natural-born tyrant who likes nothing better than managing the affairs of everyone in his family."

"Aren't you being rather censorious?"

"Certainly," replied Manning coolly. "And it's only fair to say that Harwood and I have known each other practically from the cradle, and disliked each other for almost as long. In my opinion, he succeeded to the title when he was much too young, and it gave him delusions of grandeur."

"Well, I thank you for your warning, Lord Manning," said Araminta equally coolly, "but I assure you that I'm in no danger of being managed by anyone. I'm quite independent and intend to remain that way."

"I'm delighted to hear that," he grinned.

She put down her napkin and rose, shaking out her skirts. "This has been delightful, but as you know, all good things must come to an end. I must go."

Rising in his turn, Manning picked up her pelisse from a nearby chair and helped her into it. His hands lingering on her shoulders for a fraction of a moment longer than necessary, he murmured, "I'll let you go for now, but only if you promise to go driving with me in Hyde Park this afternoon."

Araminta turned away from him, stepping back several paces. Annoyed, she admitted to herself that Henrietta had been right. She shouldn't have come here without Odile. Lord Manning was drawing the wrong conclusions from her gesture of informality and he would have to be given a set-down.

Buttoning her pelisse, she looped her reticule around her wrist and picked up her bonnet, moving to the side of the room, where she stood looking into a mirror set above a small table against the wall. Lifting her hands to put on her bonnet, she said over her shoulder, "I'm sorry, Lord Manning, I can't go driving with you this afternoon. Or at any time in the near future, I fear. The Season will be starting next week, as I'm sure you know, and my engagement book is filling up rapidly."

She gasped in surprise when the Viscount came up behind her, grasping her shoulders to turn her around to face him. Putting his hands lightly on either side of her waist, he said cajolingly, "We were getting on so famously, Lady Araminta. Why have you turned so unfriendly all of a sudden?"

"You forget yourself, sir," she cried furiously, slapping down his hands. "You might better ask why I allowed myself to make the mistake of being friendly with you in the first place!" Snatching up her bonnet, which had fallen to the floor, she whirled, making for the door.

"Oh, come now, there's no reason to be in such high gudgeon," Manning exclaimed, reaching out a long arm to pull her into his embrace. He looked down at her with a smiling confidence. "If I've done something to offend you, I apologize. There, can't we be friends again?"

He lowered his mouth to the lips so invitingly close to

84

his, his arms tightening, when Araminta, holding her face averted, pushed with all her strength against his chest in an effort to free herself. For several moments they struggled in panting silence, and then, with one final shove, she hooked her foot around his left leg and jerked.

Sprawled on the floor, Manning looked up at her blankly, his face gradually registering a sickly chagrin. "Oh God, Lady Araminta, I don't know what came over me. Please believe I didn't mean to manhandle you like that. Can you ever forgive me . . ."

His voice trailed away as he stared at the masses of Araminta's red-gold hair that had escaped its neat chignon during their struggle. Slowly he got to his feet, still staring at her hair. "Damascus," he muttered. "I knew I'd seen you before. You're the English 'Lady Smith' who won the big race against Sheik Ibrahim in Damascus. You were wearing native dress that day, with your head and face covered, but just as you came across the finish line your *kaffiyeh* slipped off and your hair came tumbling down around your shoulders. I remember the gasps of horror from the Arabs who were standing around me. 'The Evil Eye,' they kept saying, pointing at your hair . . ."

Araminta burst into reluctant laughter. "Yes, the Arabs believe that fair hair attracts the Evil Eye. I'm beginning to think so, too. If my hair hadn't fallen down during that race, you wouldn't have recognized me today, Lord Manning. Come, shall we cultivate a mutual lack of memory? I'll forget that you behaved in a most ungentlemanlike fashion if you'll forget you saw 'Lady Smith' race in Damascus."

"Done! Believe me, I'm only too eager to forget that I forced myself on you. I must have been dicked in the nob," said Manning. "Perhaps, in a millennium or two, we might even be friends again?" He paused, frowning at the sound of a heavy, repeated knocking coming from the front of the house. "Who could that be? I'd have thought it was common knowledge that this house hasn't been occupied for a month. Well, no matter. Bates will take care of it." He bent to pick up Araminta's bonnet, which had once again fallen to the floor and which was now considerably the worse for wear, with its wreath of Provence roses hanging by a thread. He gazed at it in dismay. "Won't you allow me to replace your hat? Some years ago, before I went to our embassy in Stamboul, I was used to know a milliner in Coventry Street who turned out the most fetching confections in the first style of elegance . . ."

"I'll warrant you knew her very well," Araminta retorted. "Doubtless you were one of her best customers!"

Manning's appreciative grin faded as the door of the morning room crashed open and a tall figure strode into the room.

The Duke of Harwood shifted his hostile gaze from Araminta's tumbled hair and ruined bonnet to the Viscount's disheveled cravat and said coldly, "I observe that your travels abroad haven't improved either your manners or your morals, Manning."

Reddening, the Viscount stood his ground. "You may be the Go among the Goers—a Trump, a Trojan, up to every rig and row in town—but you've no authority to judge *my* conduct. And may I remind you that you're trespassing in my house?"

"Trespassing? That's a rum way of putting it," Jason jeered. "I was under the impression that I was rescuing a respectable young woman from the unwanted attentions of a libertine." He turned to Araminta. "I'm here to take you to Middleton House. My curricle is waiting outside the house."

Before Araminta could replay, Manning said sharply, "Coming it too strong, Harwood. I escorted Lady

Araminta here, and I'll drive her home."

Araminta judged it time to intervene. "Indeed, Duke, it's not necessary to 'rescue' me," she said hurriedly. "Lord Manning and I had—had a misunderstanding, that was all. I'm perfectly safe in his company."

Jason's eyes turned to ice. "Your pardon, Lady Araminta, but I wouldn't allow a chambermaid of my acquaintance, let alone a lady under my protection, to remain under the roof of a ramshackle court card like Manning."

Pivoting neatly on one heel as the Viscount, with an inarticulate snarl of rage, launched himself at him, fists flying, Jason delivered a crisp short blow to Manning's jaw with his left hand that sent his opponent crashing to the floor.

For several seconds the Viscount lay unmoving and insensible. Then, his eyes clearing, he scrambled to his feet, his hand wiping away a trickle of blood from his chin. "You'll answer to me for this, Harwood," he grated. "Name your second."

Araminta clenched her fists in exasperation. "Oh, don't be such a ninnyhammer, Lord Manning. Haven't you caused me enough trouble for one day? If you and the Duke were to fight a duel on my account, the story would be all over London in a matter of hours, and my reputation would be in shreds."

"Lady Araminta is quite correct, Manning," said Jason with a look of contempt. "Not content with enticing her to this house under false pretenses, you now want to compound the situation by embroiling her in scandal. But the point is moot. I've no intention of fighting you. Actually, I'm surprised you even considered issuing me a challenge. If you're no better with pistols than you are with your fives, it'd soon be bellows to mend with you. You'll have to think of some other means of getting satisfaction from me."

Manning made a sudden angry movement, quickly controlled. His lips tightened into an ugly line. "Be sure I will. Oh, be sure I will. I don't forget easily, my lord Duke."

"Oh, the devil, sir, stop enacting a Cheltenham tragedy," exclaimed Araminta. "I won't have a feud starting over a trifle like this. Look, Lord Manning, I appreciate your showing me your house, but since you seem to be considerably the worse for wear, I think it might be more sensible for me to accept the Duke's offer to escort me home."

Casting an involuntary glance at his once immaculate frilled shirt and silk waistcoat, now splotched with blood from the cut on his chin, Manning flushed a dull red. He bowed stiffly. "As you wish."

Araminta turned to Jason. "Duke?"

He looked at her critically. "May I suggest you tidy your hair and put on your bonnet before we leave? I feel sure you don't wish to occasion comment by your appearance. Doubtless you'll want to remove those roses straggling from your hat, also. They seem to be serving very little purpose in their present condition."

Giving Jason a long, hostile glance, Araminta silently pulled the wreath of roses off her hat, bundled her hair into the high crown of the bonnet, and tied the strings firmly under her chin. Still without speaking, she walked beside the Duke down the corridor to the foyer and out the door to his waiting curricle. Helping Araminta into the carriage, Jason climbed in beside her. Taking the reins, he tossed a coin to his tiger, saying curtly, "I won't need you anymore this afternoon."

As the Duke put his team in motion, Araminta said between her teeth, "How clever of you to get rid of your groom. Now you can browbeat me as much as you like."

"So I can," said the Duke grimly. "Lady Araminta, even with your lack of upbringing, you *must* have known you were risking a shocking scandal by going alone with Manning to his house. Why didn't you heed Lady Middleton's warning?"

"My lack of upbringing . . ." Araminta's voice swelled with outrage.

Jason cleared his throat. "I didn't mean that precisely—I was thinking of the years you lived abroad so informally with your uncle. I realize there was no knowledgeable lady to tell you how to go on in polite society."

Araminta was unappeased. "I'm delighted we have this opportunity to set some facts straight. First of all, I am *not* living under your protection, as you so casually mentioned to Lord Manning. I'm my own mistress and intend to remain so. Secondly, I'm quite capable of dealing with any personal situation without your help. All you accomplished by bursting in on Lord Manning and me this afternoon was to embarrass me."

"Really? I had the distinct impression, from the state of your hair and clothing, that I'd arrived in the nick of time to prevent Manning from assaulting you!"

Araminta took her reticule from her wrist and opened it. "I was never in the slightest danger from Lord Manning. You see, I always carry the ultimate persuader." She reached out to dangle a tiny pistol in front of Jason's affronted eyes.

Chapter Six

"Oh, Araminta, look," exclaimed Gillian excitedly. "The Rosetta Stone!"

Araminta stared rather blankly at the battered slab of black asphalt, covered with mysterious markings. "It looks so very ordinary. I daresay it's — it's historically significant?"

"Well, of course it is! The inscriptions on the stone may eventually help scholars decipher Egyptian hieroglyphics. Napoleon's troops found it, you know, after the capture of Alexandria. Oh, it was *such* a splendid notion to visit the British Museum today. I've *never* been anywhere half so interesting."

"I'm happy you're enjoying it," rejoined Araminta rather hollowly. She was standing with Gillian and Damaris and Odile in the Egyptian Gallery at Montagu House, after having already seen the marvels of the Great Hall, which had included a giant elephant tusk, a Red Indian canoe from North America, and a wooden model of Blackfriar's Bridge. Odile and Damaris were already looking a trifle fatigued, and Araminta privately considered the treasures of the British Museum to be somewhat insipid after having visited the great classical sites of Greece and the Levant, but Gillian seemed bent on examining every artifact in the museum.

Consulting the "synopsis of contents" that Araminta had purchased for her at the door of Montagu House for two shillings, Gillian said in tones of awe: "The guidebook says that the large tomb over there is probably the sarcophagus of Alexander the Great."

"Really? I thought he died in India or some such place." Lowering her voice, Araminta said, "I've no doubt you're planning to put some of these marvels into a book. That mummy over there—what a chilling scene you could write about that!"

Gillian chuckled. "A capital idea! But first I must finish the book I'm writing." She hadn't fallen into the dismals, Araminta had been glad to observe, by the collapse of her plans to attend Miss Elphinstone's Seminary. For one thing, Henrietta hadn't succeeded in finding a governess to replace the departed Miss Baddeley, so that Gillian, left to her own devices, was able to spend virtually every waking hour working on her novel.

Again consulting her guidebook, Gillian continued, "In the next gallery there's a fine collection of classical sculptures, the Towneley Marbles. Shall we go see them next?"

"*Chère* Gillian, could we not perhaps see these marbles another day?" inquired Odile plaintively. "I do not wish to complain, *vous savez*, but I feel a trifle weary . . ."

"Oh, Madame Lacoste, pray excuse me," said Gillian, conscience-stricken. "I was forgetting your health is delicate."

There were times when Odile's charming selfishness was quite helpful, Araminta thought with a secret grin, as she shepherded her charges down the magnificent wrought iron Grand Staircase. Leaving the museum by the stately west entrance, they were soon traveling through the streets of Bloomsbury in Henrietta's landau. It was a beautiful day in late April, so warm and spring-like that the forward half of the landau's top had been removed and the rear half had been folded back.

Araminta relaxed against the upholstery, feeling decidedly in charity with the world. In the week since her visit to Lord Manning's house in Hanover Square, nothing had happened to disturb the domestic peace at Middleton House. Fortunately, after Jason had driven her home from the Viscount's house, Araminta had managed to slip up the stairs and into her bedchamber without encountering her sister and giving herself away by her disheveled appearance. Mercifully, Henrietta remained quite ignorant of Lord Manning's botched attempt at gallantry. In any case, save for venting her feelings in a few mild reproaches, Henrietta was too busy preparing for Damaris's come-out to dwell on Araminta's escapade.

It had been helpful, too, that Lord Manning had stayed away from Bruton Street, so that Henrietta wasn't continually reminded of how much she disapproved of him. Araminta surmised that the Viscount was feeling too humiliated to face her as yet, which was just as well, in her opinion. He deserved to suffer for a bit, though she'd absolved him of any serious intention of seducing her. It was partly her own fault, after all, that she'd placed herself in a situation where he was even tempted to play the loose screw. Eventually she'd proceed with her plans to rent his house, but it might be easier to keep him in line in the future if she didn't admit him back into her good graces too quickly.

Nor had there been any further clashes with Jason, rather to Araminta's regret. She would have been quite happy to make it even clearer to him that she wouldn't brook any interference with her conduct. A smile turned up the corners of her mouth at the memory of Jason's expression of outrage when she'd dangled her little pistol in front of his nose. He'd been literally stupefied into silence, and since then there'd been no opportunity for him to lecture her. He'd been absent from London for almost a sennight. According to Henrietta, he was in New Market, overseeing the running of his horses in the First Spring Meeting.

As the carriage turned into New Bond Street and neared the entrance of Bruton Street, Araminta suddenly exclaimed, "It's such a lovely day, let's not waste a moment of it indoors. Shall we go to Gunther's pastry shop for an ice?"

Damaris said doubtfully, "You haven't forgotten about the ball tonight, Aunt Araminta?"

"No, indeed, but surely we can spare half an hour from our primping?"

"*Tiens,* Mademoiselle Damaris," Odile said with a laugh, "five minutes in your *cabinet de toilette* is all you will need to outshine every other female at the ball!"

Blushing prettily, Damaris made no further objection.

A little later, as they sat in their carriage under the tender spring green of the plane trees in Berkeley Square, spooning their ices with relish, Araminta said dreamily, "The white currant ice is just as delicious as I remembered it. I was only here once before, but I've never forgotten it. I was eleven or twelve, and my governess had brought me to London to have an impacted wisdom tooth drawn. After my agony in the dentist's chair, that white currant ice was a cool sweet miracle. We stayed overnight with your mother in Bruton Street, Gillian. You and Damaris were tiny girls, and your brother was a baby."

Odile put a wispy black handkerchief to the corner of her eye. "You are so fortunate, all of you, to be a family. Myself, I have nobody. Even Roger . . ." She shook her head, two large tears sliding gently down her cheeks.

"But Madame Lacoste, I thought your husband's

name was Armand," Gillian exclaimed.

A startled look crossed Odile's face, and then, her shoulders shaking, she buried her face in the black handkerchief. Seized with a familiar desire to strangle her friend, Araminta said sadly, "Roger was Armand's brother. The last surviving member of his family. He died fighting Napoleon."

"That's strange," said Damaris suddenly. Taking little part in the conversation, she had been idly watching the changing scene in the square, the elegant carriages coming and going, the waiters scurrying back and forth across the roadway with their trays between Gunther's shop and their waiting customers. "I could swear that Mrs. Everley recognized me, but when I smiled and nodded to her, she stared at me as though I were a perfect stranger and turned her head away."

"That *is* odd," said Araminta. "Is this Mrs. Everley an old friend of the family?"

"Well, no, I met her only last week, but I remember her very well."

"I shouldn't refine on it. Doubtless the lady is a little near-sighted. Depend on it, that's the case."

Damaris' flowerlike face turned pale. "I've known Susan Slade since she was five years old, and I know *she* isn't near-sighted," she choked, staring after the occupants of the open carriage that had just passed them. "That was Susan with her married sister Jane in that carriage, and they *cut* me!"

"Oh, you must be mistaken—"

"I don't think so, Aunt Araminta. I must have done something to offend Susan. . . . But then, what about Mrs. Everley? Could we go home now, please? I think I'd like to rest awhile before the ball."

"I'm so eager to hear your opinion of this latest chap-

94

ter. I think it's my best work yet, but I daresay every author thinks that!"

Araminta turned away from her mirror to smile at Gillian, who had come to watch her dress for the first big event of the fledgling London season, a ball at the home of the Duke and Duchess of Cathcart. "Another whole chapter finished? You must have been keeping your nose to the grindstone! I can't wait to read the new chapter. I'll leave it beside my bed so that I can read it the moment I return from the ball tonight," exclaimed Araminta enthusiastically, noticing with a little pang of sympathy that Gillian's reddish curls were in wild confusion, her simple muslin gown was grubby, and the fingers of her right hand were spotted with ink. "I wish you were coming with us tonight. You'll be by yourself in the house, with only the servants to keep you company."

Gillian's eyes crinkled in a smile. "You forget that I'm not out yet. And then I always feel uncomfortable on grand social occasions, and I'm really not a very good dancer. So I'm just as happy to stay home tonight. Actually, I like being alone. I plan to finish another chapter this evening. Do enjoy yourself at the ball, Araminta—there, for the very first time I wasn't even tempted to call you aunt!" As Gillian left the bedchamber, she nearly collided with Odile.

"Pauvre petite. How I should like the dressing of her," Odile remarked after Gillian had left the room. "The child always looks as though she had slept in her clothes." Odile turned slowly in front of Araminta. "What do you think? It's not my best color, *certainement,* but I do think the gown is becoming, don't you?"

Araminta examined Odile's ball gown of violet gauze and her long matching veil fastened with a pearl ornament confining a tiny bunch of violets and an aigrette. "You look charmingly, as always. I'm happy to see that

95

you're overcoming your disinclination for society. The British Museum and Gunther's sweet shop this afternoon, and a ball this evening. You're becoming quite giddy!"

Seemingly unaware of the ripple of amusement in Araminta's voice, Odile replied seriously, "Oh, I am trying very hard to take your advice to heart, *ma chère*. I quite see that I can't continue to immure myself in this house in fear if I'm to be a proper wife to my Roger." Her eyes lighted up. *"Actuellement,* I'm looking forward to this ball. It's been such a long time since I danced a waltz."

Glimpsing Damaris hovering rather shyly at the open door, Araminta called, "Do come in. Odile would like your opinion of her ball gown."

"You look simply lovely, Madame Lacoste," said Damaris as she advanced into the room.

Accepting the compliment with a pleased nod, Odile looked with admiration at Damaris's robe of white lace over a pale blue satin slip trimmed with artificial cornflowers. "My child, I have seldom seen so beautiful a gown complemented so perfectly by such a beautiful face," Odile exclaimed, her voice tinged by the faintest hint of envy.

Damaris blushed deeply, her porcelain skin suffused not with an unbecoming red, Araminta noted, but with a delicate rosy glow. "You're far too kind. Actually I came to ask Aunt Araminta—and you, too—about the arrangement of my hair. Do you like it? It's called 'a Madonna.' My abigail thinks it's a little old for me."

Araminta glanced at Damaris's golden hair, parted in the center and flowing in loose curls over the crown of her head. "I like the style very much," she said. "And I don't need to ask if you're feeling more the thing. I can see you've recovered your spirits."

Damaris nodded. "I was being silly this afternoon,

imagining things. Mrs. Everley simply didn't recognize me, and as for Susan—well, why on earth would one of my oldest friends cut me? I'll see her tonight, and we'll have a great laugh about it."

Odile had been studying Damaris's coiffure in absorbed silence. At last she said, "Yes, I think the arrangement is perfect, *ma petite*. If it does make you look a trifle older, that is all to the good, *n'est-ce pas? Monsieur le Duc* is, I understand, some years older than you are."

Damaris blushed even more deeply. "Please, Madame Lacoste, you mustn't couple my name with the Duke's. Not yet. Nothing has been announced." To hide her embarrassment, she went over to the cheval glass, holding her hand to her hot cheek as she examined her image in the mirror. "Jas—the Duke once told me that blue is his favorite color," she murmured with a pleased little smile. Araminta wondered if her niece realized how much of her feelings for her not yet officially announced husband-to-be she was giving away.

"Monsieur le Duc, he will be at the ball?" asked Odile.

"Yes, he told Mama last week that he'd return from New Market today."

"Araminta, I must talk to you." Hurrying into the bedchamber, Henrietta stopped short when she observed her daughter and Odile.

"I was just going, Mama," said Damaris hastily, and Odile, murmuring something about completing her toilet, left with her.

"If there are any other members of the household who would like to see me, I'm quite at their disposal," said Araminta jokingly. "I'm beginning to feel a little like Mr. Lawrence's latest portrait at the Royal Academy—I've had a constant parade of visitors since I started dressing this evening!" Her merriment faded as she looked more

97

closely at her sister, whose features seemed etched in doom. "What is it? Is something wrong? Are you ill? Have you received some bad news?"

"The worst, the very worst," said Henrietta tragically. She collapsed into a chair. "I just discovered that you will be denied a voucher for Almack's."

"For what? Oh, Almack's Assembly Rooms. They sponsor balls during the season, don't they? Well, why am I being denied admittance to this place, and why should I consider it of any great moment to be excluded?"

Henrietta put up her hands in horror. "I can't believe your ignorance. No great moment to be turned away from Almack's? Don't you realize that only a quarter of the girls from the noblest families in England succeed in obtaining vouchers of admittance?" She sat down, expelling a discouraged sigh. "The news came as such a shock. I've just returned from taking tea with my dear old friend Sophie Marsden. Mrs. Drummond Burrell was there—she's one of the patronesses of Almack's—so naturally I broached the subject of obtaining a voucher for you. You can imagine my distress and mortification when she said that she would be unable to recommend granting you a voucher because of the scandalous rumors about you that are sweeping London."

The amusement fading from her face, Araminta straightened in her chair. "Rumors? What kind of rumors?"

"Vicious ones," Henrietta snapped. "I blush to repeat them. One woman told Mrs. Burrell that you'd been the inmate of an Arab harem. Another said you'd joined a band of desert slave traders. Someone else swore you'd become the tenth wife of a camel driver!"

Araminta broke into a whoop of laughter. "Oh, this is ridiculous, Henrietta. These cork-brained gabsters have never met me, and yet their tales grow more preposterous with each telling. What will they do, I wonder, when they meet me in the flesh? I'll warrant that before they're done they'll have me usurping the throne of the Sultan of Turkey!"

Henrietta looked at her grimly. "You needn't tell me these rumors are untrue. I know they're pure drivel. I don't think Mrs. Burrell really believes them, either, but it makes no difference. Mrs. Burrell can't go against public opinion, and she's sure that the other patronesses of Almack's will concur with her judgment. I fear she's right. Oh, I might ask Lady Jersey to intercede for us; she's the kindest and most liberal minded of all the patronesses. But even then . . . suppose for a moment that our inability to obtain vouchers for Almack's is the least of our troubles! What if all the prominent hostesses of the Ton cross you off their invitation lists?"

She reached into her reticule for a handkerchief and dabbed at the corners of her eyes. "I'm not blaming you. It's all *my* fault," she declared. "I should have fought to prevent you from ruining your life by going off with Sir Wilfrid. But just at the time you were leaving England with him, the children came down with the mumps—Philip, especially, was so ill that I thought he might die—and I didn't like to leave them all alone in Lincolnshire, even though Nurse was so devoted to them, and, besides, how was I to know that Sir Wilfrid would take you to live among the savages, depriving you of the opportunity of learning the proper deportment for a gentlewoman?"

Araminta's lips tightened momentarily at this latest slight to Uncle Will by Henrietta. Realizing, however, that her sister was too distraught to think of guarding her tongue, Araminta said calmly, "Don't be a goose. You're not to blame for anything I've done. Perhaps the situation isn't as bad as you think it is. Or, even if it is, perhaps Lady Jersey will come to my rescue! Mean-

99

while, for the evening at least, let's put Almack's out of our minds. Do dry your eyes and go dress for dinner and the ball. You wouldn't want to put a damper on my very first venture into the London social scene now, would you?"

After Henrietta had left the room, Araminta sat for several minutes before her dressing table in thoughtful silence. Then, glancing down with a hint of regret at her ball gown of yellow crepe, purchased just two days ago at the most expensive dress shop in Mayfair, she rang for her abigail. When Jessie arrived, Araminta said, "Quick, help me out of this dress."

The Duke of Harwood looked out his window to observe with surprise that his town carriage had joined a long line of vehicles that was inching slowly into Mount Street to deposit passengers in front of Cathcart House. He couldn't remember a single detail of the journey from his town house in South Audley Street, he admitted grimly to himself, because all his thoughts had been concentrated on Lady Araminta Beresford. He had never before met a woman who could so easily ruffle his composure, who could put him on the defensive with a look or a smile. And now, unless he could think of a solution to turn the situation around, she was about to cause an upheaval that would alter the course of his well-ordered existence.

He'd arrived in town from New Market this morning glowing with satisfaction over the performance of his stud at the race meeting, and filled with the determination to treat Lady Araminta with a firm formality that would put her in her place and keep her there. However, scarcely had he sauntered into Brookes's Club in late afternoon when he became aware that, during his short absence from London, Araminta had become the talk of the town. Concerned friends, knowing his relationship to Lady Middleton as the guardian of her children, had informed him about the scandalous rumors circulating about Araminta's travels in eastern Europe, rumors that seemed to grow more licentious and more wildly exaggerated with each passing moment.

The carriage stopped in front of Cathcart House, blazing with lights from every window, and Jason stepped down from the vehicle to walk to the door beneath the ornate canopy erected to shelter the Duchess's guests from wind and rain, past the stiff double row of liveried footmen lining the steps. As he began slowly to mount the long steep staircase to the first floor, he wondered gloomily if Lady Middleton and her sister were aware as yet of the rumors besmirching Araminta's reputation, and if so, whether the alarming situation might cause them to cancel their appearance this evening at the Cathcart ball. He set his mouth. One way or the other, he'd have to find some way to scotch the scandal, not for Araminta's sake, to be sure, but to prevent any damage to the reputation of his future wife. The very best solution to the problem, obviously, would be to rid the metropolis of Araminta's infuriating presence. However, as the image of a lithe, Titian-haired girl astride a camel in the desert, or sailing in a *dhow* down the Nile, popped into the Duke's mind, he suddenly felt an acute sense of loss.

The ball had been in full swing for some time when Jason entered the ballroom, but the Duke and Duchess of Cathcart and their son and daughter were still in the receiving line. The Duchess greeted him graciously. He had always been a favorite of hers, and indeed several years previously she had nourished hopes that he would offer for her older daughter, now happily married. But behind her gracious smile Jason thought he could detect a note of questioning, of doubt, of concern.

His nerves tightening, he left the receiving line and glanced around the ballroom, already comfortably full. Soon, with relief, he spotted Damaris's golden head and slender figure. The music hadn't yet started up for the next dance, and she was sitting beside her mother at the side of the room. As he came up to them, he noted with a faint sense of foreboding that the chairs to their immediate left and right were unoccupied. Damaris was usually surrounded by admiring friends of both sexes. And Henrietta looked wan.

Bowing to Lady Middleton, he sank into a chair next to Damaris. "You always look beautiful, my dear, and tonight is no exception," he murmured.

Damaris accepted his compliment with the shy smile and faint blush that he had always found so enchanting. He'd been in no hurry to marry until his brother Rupert's death at Waterloo had forced him to consider the necessity of providing an heir to the dukedom, but now that he'd made the decision to do so, he reflected, he'd certainly chosen a perfect candidate for his bride. Damaris was beautiful, elegant, amiable, well bred. She would be, like her own mother, a graceful hostess and a devoted mother. He wasn't passionately in love with her, of course, nor, he rather thought, was she with him. He preferred it that way. He liked his privacy and his independence. He was sure he and Damaris would rub along together very comfortably, and if, at some future time, he should discreetly pursue other interests, Damaris would never betray by the flicker of an eyelash that she was aware of his activities.

However, when her faint and lovely blush faded, it became quite obvious that Damaris wasn't her usual self. There was a suggestion of strain in her beautiful face, and her fingers were energetically shredding a gossamer lace handkerchief.

"What is it?" Jason asked in a low voice.

She shook her head, trying to smile, and then, when a tall young man approached her, making his bow, she rose quickly, saying, "Pray excuse me, Duke. I've promised this dance to Mr. Weston."

Jason moved over one chair to sit beside Henrietta. Looking out over the dancers as he leaned back easily in his chair, his face calm, he murmured, "Trouble, Lady Middleton?"

Henrietta, too, managed to preserve an outward calm. Her voice was another matter. She sounded like Mrs. Siddons as Lady MacBeth. "Catastrophe, I fear," she muttered. "Perhaps you don't know about the dreadful rumors —"

"I've heard the rumors. The gabblemongers are inventing new ones by the minute."

"I daresay. I'm at my wit's end. It's like a plague. Where will it end? Damaris's bosom friend, Susan Slade, actually cut her today in Berkeley Square, and again tonight at the ball. No more than a handful of her young female acquaintances have exchanged a word with her. The young men" — Henrietta's tone became bitter — "the young men are pursuing her as usual. Naturally. *They* needn't fear to appear fast by associating with a young woman who's been tarred by scandal."

"Come now, Lady Middleton. No scandal attaches to Damaris."

"It's contagious," said Henrietta mournfully. "Araminta is my sister. The loss of her reputation is bound to affect Damaris and Gillian and *me.*"

Jason tightened his lips. Lady Middleton's comment was irrefutable. He scanned the dance floor. "I don't see Lady Araminta or Madame Lacoste. Didn't they accompany you this evening?"

"No. Araminta refused to come with us."

"Perhaps it's as well . . ."

"You mistake the matter. She plans to arrive later.

103

Yes," Henrietta nodded at Jason's quick look of alarm. "You may well fly up into the boughs. I fancy Araminta is up to some sort of farradiddle. I begged and implored her to tell me what she was about, but she just shook her head, with that expression she has sometimes when she's ripe for any spree. *You* know!"

Jason did know. Glancing in the direction of the door, he froze. "Oh, my God!"

The young footman who came to assist the occupants out of the hackney coach wore a supercilious expression at the sight of the hired vehicle. His expression changed to pure shock when Araminta emerged from the coach. A moment later the young man's shock was mirrored in the faces of the rigid servants lining the steps as Araminta and Odile walked past them and entered the Duchess of Cathcart's house.

"Je ne sais pas, ma mie," Odile murmured fretfully, following Araminta up the long staircase. "I ask you again, why are you doing this? You know Madame Middleton will not approve. Perhaps they will not even admit us into the ballroom! We shall be thrown out, like the cat!"

"Oh, I shouldn't think so, Odile. In any event, we'll know soon, *n'est-ce pas?*" Araminta sounded calm, but she felt an inward quake as she looked down at her clothing. The shock in the faces of the Duchess's servants was fully understandable. Probably she was wearing the most bizarre costume ever to be seen in a London ballroom. It consisted of a flowing caftan of thin, pale green damask, embroidered with gold flowers, over billowing pantaloons of the same green damask topped by a tight-fitting white and gold damask waistcoat with long fringed sleeves. The caftan was fastened with a four-inch-wide jeweled girdle, and on her head

Araminta wore a little green velvet cap with a gold tassel. Her bright hair, divided into plaits braided with pearls, hung over her shoulders.

Her feet dragged as she approached the top of the stairs. All too soon she crossed the threshold of the ballroom. The guests gathered in small groups near the door fell silent as she entered. Holding her head high, her face serene, Araminta stood in the doorway, looking around her with an air of polite interest. After some moments, a tall, imposing woman in purple brocade and a towering turban left the guests with whom she was talking and came over to Araminta, examining her from head to toe with a chilly eye. At last she said, "How do you do? I am the Duchess of Cathcart."

Outwardly self-possessed, though her heart was beating unpleasantly fast, Araminta curtsied gracefully. "How do you do, Duchess. I am Araminta Beresford, and this is my friend Madame Lacoste." She smiled, motioning to her caftan and pantaloons. "I do hope I haven't made a perfect idiot of myself by wearing my Turkish costume. It was given to me by my good friend, the wife of the Bey of Chahba." Araminta mentally crossed her fingers. There was no Bey of Chahba, as far as she was aware, and she'd had the costume made from the gorgeous fabrics she herself had selected in one of the great silk bazaars in Damascus. But the situation was desperate and seemed to warrant an innocent lie. She went on, "I thought my new London friends might enjoy seeing how the ladies of Syria dress."

The seconds ticked by. Her face impassive, the Duchess stared at Araminta without replying. The music had stopped as Araminta entered the ballroom, and the sound of conversation had died away. Now she was aware, without looking around, that she and the Duchess were the target of every curious eye in the room. Her self-possession began to slip away. Then, tentatively, the music struck up again, and a friendly voice said, "Lady Araminta, your servant. May I have the honor of this waltz? I'm Alverston."

A glimmer of recollection enabled Araminta to place the Marquis of Alverston. She smiled at the lanky, red-headed young man standing before her and said, "I'd be delighted, my lord." Her confidence was coming back. If she couldn't turn to her advantage this dance with her hostess's eldest son, the heir to the Dukedom of Cathcart, she didn't deserve to wriggle out of her predicament.

Across the room, Jason had his hands full dealing with Araminta's sister and niece. As the full horror of Araminta's appearance dawned on her, Henrietta fell into a fit of the vapors. "My vinaigrette," she whispered in failing accents. "Could you help me, Duke? It's in my reticule."

"My dear ma'am, you must get along without your vinaigrette," the Duke said urgently. "Try to compose yourself."

Henrietta blinked and swallowed hard. "Yes, of course. I mustn't allow myself to faint. I quite see that. It would only make matters worse. Only"—she looked up at Jason with haunted eyes—"only I can't imagine how matters could get any worse."

"Nor can I, Mama," said Damaris in a trembling voice as she came up to her mother. "Aunt Araminta has ruined us. We'll never be able to hold up our heads again. How could she do it—exhibit herself in such a ramshackle way in full view of all our friends?"

The rising hysteria in her voice caused Jason to snap, with a harshness he had never before used toward her, "Sit down, Damaris, and stop making a cake of yourself. Our only chance of carrying this off—a minuscule one, I admit—is to convince people that Lady Araminta had such an unconventional upbringing with her uncle that she's unaware of how much her conduct offends."

White-faced, shocked, Damaris sank into a chair. Jason rose, saying, "Pray excuse me. I think I should ask Lady Araminta to dance. When it's seen that I'm not scandalized by her outlandish garb, it might persuade others to take the same view."

But he was thwarted in his good intentions. Approaching Araminta as she was coming off the floor at the end of her waltz with Lord Alverston, Jason found her attention completely absorbed by a knot of eager young men begging for a place on her dance card. Before he could speak to her, a dark, intense-looking gallant had whisked her away to take part in a quadrille. With a sinking feeling, Jason retired to the side of the ballroom, watching the dancers with an air of deceptively negligent calm. He knew there was very little chance that an expression of support from himself and Araminta's family would enable her to pull her chestnut out of the fire. While he thought it likely that she wouldn't lack partners for a single dance this evening, her popularity with the masculine guests at the ball would do nothing to improve her standing with the outraged hostesses of the Ton.

He had been keeping an eye on Araminta as she moved through the intricate figures of the quadrille, and when it came to an end, he again tried to approach her, only to find her surrounded by an even larger group than before. His superior height enabled him to see over the shoulders of the people—mostly males, he observed with irritation—who were crowding around her. His blood ran cold when a young buck with a nipped-in waist and overly high collar points said laughingly, "Is it true, Lady Araminta, what Alverston has been telling me, that you actually lived with the Arabs in the desert?"

"Why yes, I lived with the Arabs for several weeks,"

Araminta replied matter-of-factly. "My guardian was extremely interested in how primitive peoples lived, and of course I discovered that the Arabs weren't primitive at all, just different from us. At times I felt as though I were living in another world. Imagine seeing sixteen hundred camels coming to water at the same time. Or hearing ancient poets reciting tales of heroes from before the time of Moses. Or becoming intimate with women so different from myself—helping them to draw water, or erect tents—women who had tattooed their faces and dyed their lips a bright blue." Araminta's lips curved in an amused smile. "It was quite humiliating to realize how unattractive I was in the minds of the Bedouin tribesmen with my fair hair and my lack of tattoos! Some of them thought I had the Evil Eye!"

A ripple of appreciative laughter greeted Araminta's sally, and Jason, glancing around him, could detect nothing but rapt interest in her circle of listeners. Certainly not a hint of condemnation.

Another man said, with a hint of incredulity, "Someone was telling me at White's today, Lady Araminta, that you once took part in a camel race!"

Araminta burst into laughter. "Oh, how amused my guardian would be to hear that. I never could learn to ride a camel. I always fell off!"

Beside Jason, a voice murmured drily, "That is a very clever young woman. She's dulled the knives of gossip. They will never be turned against her again. You must be feeling a certain amount of relief, Duke, since the lady is so closely related to your wards."

The bemused Jason turned in some confusion to greet one of the redoubtable patronesses of Almack's, Mrs. Drummond Burrell. He said, with a hastily assumed sangfroid, "Relief, Mrs. Burrell? Surely not. I can assure you that any so-called gossip about Lady Araminta never occasioned the slightest concern in my mind or in that of my wards' family."

Mrs. Burrell smiled thinly. "I'm relieved to hear it." She moved away, saying, "If you'll excuse me, I must see Lady Middleton. I believe she is interested in obtaining a voucher to Almack's for her sister. I will tell her that I see no reason why Lady Araminta should not receive one."

She's done it, by God, thought Jason, watching Araminta with a feeling of reluctant admiration as she began to spin yet another tale of her life among the Bedouins. She's spiked their guns, she's turned the tables on them, she's completely disarmed the gossips. First of all, wearing the outlandishly colorful dress of the East had been a master stroke, a proclamation without words that she had nothing to hide. Then her constant references to her Uncle Will had left the distinct impression that he'd accompanied her on her Syrian travels. And by speaking freely of her adventures she had rendered them innocuous; especially, by her wry, self-deprecating reference to her lack of charms in the eyes of the tribesmen, she had destroyed any credibility to the rumor that she'd entered an Arab harem.

A discordant series of sounds announced that the orchestra was tuning up and was about to begin playing. As the circle around Araminta showed signs of breaking up, Jason made his way to her side. "Congratulations on the performance you just gave," he said in a low voice.

Araminta did not pretend to misunderstand him. "Thank you," she said calmly. "Was I convincing? Henrietta was so distressed by all the silly rumors, I thought I should do something to scotch them."

"Convincing? Entirely so. The scandalous Lady Araminta Beresford is by way of becoming a refreshing original! Even so severe a critic as Mrs. Drummond Burrell has now gone off to inform Lady Middleton that you are to receive a voucher for Almack's."

"Bless Mrs. Burrell. Henrietta thinks I'll be an utter pariah if I'm excluded from Almack's."

"I'd like to talk to you, Araminta. Dare I hope that all your dances are not yet taken?"

She tossed him a quick, questioning glance. "Yes, I think we should talk," she said, nodding. She consulted her card. "You may have the next waltz but one." Then, breaking into a teasing smile, she added, "Lord Alverston's already claimed it, but I really can't dance three times with the same man, now can I? I *must* be careful to observe the amenities now that I've rescued my reputation, don't you agree?"

Before he could reply, Odile fluttered up to them on the arm of Viscount Manning. "*Chère* Araminta, observe who is here. I have been giving *Milord* Manning a tiny scold for neglecting us this past week."

"Press of business at the Foreign Office, I assure you, Lady Araminta. You know my inclinations, I trust," said Manning. He bowed stiffly to Jason, his face composed but his eyes revealing a telltale flash of angry dislike. "Evening, Harwood."

Jason inclined his head a fraction of an inch. "Sir." He moved away, saying to Araminta, "Until the next dance but one, then."

After he had gone, Odile said earnestly to Araminta, "*Ma mie,* how grateful I am that you forced me out of my shell. I see now I was only nourishing my grief. I must tell you that everyone here has been so kind." She flourished her dance card with a childlike pleasure. "Entirely filled, as you can see!"

Araminta couldn't resist asking, "All your partners speak French, do they?"

"*Mais non,*" replied Odile blithely. "But then, one dances with one's feet, not with one's tongue, *n'est-ce-pas?*" Beaming at a young man who came up to claim

110

her next dance, she went off with him to take her place in the line forming for a country dance.

Looking after her, Manning remarked with a smile of amusement, "I hardly think Madame Lacoste's inability to speak English will be a barrier to her conquest of impressionable males." Sobering, he added, "Will you allow me to tell you again how much I regret what happened at my house when you honored me with a visit?"

"Oh, I never like to dwell on past unpleasantness," said Araminta with a laugh. Nodding to her next partner, hovering hopefully in the background, she went on, "No doubt you've heard that I've become the talk of the town?"

Manning's expression became grave. "Indeed. The clubs have talked of nothing else for days. I've done my poor best, naturally, to squelch the rumors, but . . ." He spread his hands in a gesture of helplessness.

"At first, when I heard that I was supposed to have taken part in a *camel* race, I did just wonder if you'd mentioned that you once saw me riding in that horse race in Damascus . . ."

The Viscount cut in reproachfully, "But Lady Araminta, I gave you my word!"

"Well, of course you did! After that first moment of dismay I was positive you hadn't said a word about that dreadful race." To the relief of her partner in the country dance, she turned to him, taking his arm, smiling over her shoulder at Lord Manning as she walked off. But as she moved up and down the line of the dance, she found herself concentrating on the Viscount rather than on the dancing.

She was morally certain that Manning was responsible for the rumors about her that had flooded London. There could really be no other source for the salacious stories. Manning had been deeply humiliated at being milled down in his own house by a man he already held in acute dislike and in front of a woman he'd hoped to impress. Doubtless, too, he'd been irritated by her impatience and lack of sympathy for his predicament, and by the fact that in the end she'd left his house in Jason's company. Possibly he hadn't deliberately planned to spread scandal. More likely, he'd let slip in a fit of pique that he'd once seen her engage in a horse race against an Arab sheik in Damascus. After that, with no further assistance from him, the rumors would have multiplied from their own momentum. Even a tiny item like her groom Hassan's Arab dress would have fed the fire.

She hadn't felt it wise to confront Manning with her suspicions. If she were to cut their acquaintance, she would only make him her enemy, as he already seemed to be Jason's implacable enemy. Out of malice, Manning might start spreading the rumors anew. Much better to let sleeping dogs lie. She would continue to treat the Viscount with an off-hand friendliness that disguised her determination never to trust him again.

The country dance ended, with no serious missteps on her part, and soon the Duke strolled up to claim his waltz. Eyeing his evening costume of dark blue coat, cream-colored kerseymere breeches, and striped silk stockings that displayed his well-shaped legs to perfection, she thought Jason was easily the most elegant man in the room. The orchestra struck up, leading her on to the floor, he slipped his arm loosely around her waist, saying, "I prefer waltzing to the country dance. It makes conversation so much easier."

He was a splendid dancer, she thought, as he guided her expertly among the throng of waltzers. Somehow she'd known he would be. She closed her eyes, leaning back against the gentle but firm support of his arm, enjoying the feeling that she was floating effortlessly above the floor. For just an instant she allowed herself a vagrant wish that he would hold her more closely, that the dance would go on forever. Then, forced back to reality by the sound of his voice, she opened her eyes.

"I daresay you know that wearing that costume was a stroke of genius," he was saying.

Araminta glanced down at her green and white and gold damask. "You like my Turkish dress? I hoped it would catch the eye."

The Duke involuntarily tightened his arm around Araminta and pulled her closer to him. "You must know that you're as alluring in that costume as one of those—what do you call 'em—those nymphs who welcome Muslim warriors to Paradise," he muttered.

"Oh, what a lovely compliment, to be compared to the beautiful *houris!*" She cocked an inquiring eye at him. "You wanted to talk?"

Jason seemed to have recovered his composure. "It's more a matter of necessity than desire," he said coolly. "Look, Araminta, we're about to become relatives, and yet we've done nothing but quarrel since you came to London. Once, in Hyde Park, we agreed to a truce—"

"Which lasted all of five minutes," Araminta interrupted with a laugh.

"Exactly. I'm proposing a renewal of that truce. Not just a cessation of hostilities, but a real peace treaty."

"And the terms?"

Jason drew a deep breath. "I'll engage to do my best not to interfere in your life, if you'll agree to be more circumspect about your conduct. More specifically, I must insist that you drop all plans to set up your own household."

Araminta could feel the angry color rising in her cheeks. Jason stiffened. Then his jaw dropped as she said, "Agreed."

His eyes narrowed. "Araminta, are you trying to bamboozle me?"

"No, I meant what I said." She looked up at him steadily. "Listen carefully. I'm not accustomed to eating humble pie, and I may not ever be able to bring myself to say this again. Jason, you've been right and I've been wrong. Because of Odile's harem history and my own near-catastrophe with these poisonous rumors—and, mind, I don't admit to *any* fault on the part of either Odile or myself—I realize I can't be too careful in the future about creating scandal. I concede it would be tempting fate for me and Odile to rent a house and live in it alone. It would be particularly dangerous to rent Lord Manning's house."

Jason's brows drew together. "Explain that remark," he said curtly.

"I think Lord Manning started the rumors. The day I went to inspect his house he remembered having seen me race in Damascus."

The hand holding hers tightened convulsively and the Duke missed a step.

"But you're not to do anything about it," Araminta said quickly. "Remember your decision not to accept Lord Manning's challenge. It's the same principle. You knew that a duel would only cause more gossip. We'll just keep an eye on him."

Gradually Jason's hand relaxed. "Score a point for your side," he said with a wry smile. "You're quite right."

"I very often am, my lord Duke."

Jason laughed outright. "Damn your impudence. If you'd been a man, and Napoleon had been clever enough to enlist you as one of his generals, I'll warrant Wellington would have had a much nearer thing at Waterloo."

The strains of the waltz died away, and Araminta thought Jason removed his arm from her waist with a shade of reluctance. As they walked slowly toward the side of the ballroom, he looked down at her, saying, "It's agreed, then? We have a peace treaty?"

"Well, at least a cease-fire. It's really up to you. I warn you, I still intend to lead my own life."

The Duke lifted an eyebrow. "Of course you do. I've learned my lesson. Never again, Araminta, will I try to tell you what to do."

"*Never* is a dangerous word," said Araminta provocatively, but Jason refused to take the bait, merely shaking his head and grinning. However, as they walked on, he murmured, "How much more comfortable it will be to have you as a friend rather than an enemy. But I must confess that life won't be half as exciting!" He brought her over to the corner where Henrietta, looking as though the cares of the world had been removed from her shoulders, was sitting with her elder daughter and Odile, and claimed Damaris for the quadrille that was forming.

"They make such a handsome couple," murmured Henrietta, her eyes following the pair. "Don't you think so?"

"Mm, yes." Thinking back to her waltz with Jason, Araminta's eyes grew a little wistful. She and the Duke had resumed the teasing repartee that had marked their encounter in Dover, quite as if their recent quarrels had never been. Quite as if they were meeting for the first time, their identities still unknown to each other, groping to determine just what their relationship might be. . . .

Araminta straightened in her chair. She couldn't afford thoughts like these. Perhaps if she and Jason had met under different circumstances . . . But no. They were merely friendly enemies, soon to be aunt and nephew. She burst into a laugh, quickly smothered.

"What is it, Araminta?" asked Henrietta.

Araminta looked at her dance card and rose from her

chair. "I need a favor. I have the next dance with Mr. Weldon, that gangling youth over there in the bottle green coat. He stepped on my feet unmercifully during our first dance, and I simply will not risk being made a permanent cripple. Henrietta, I'm off to take refuge in the library."

"But what will I tell Mr. Weldon when he comes looking for you?"

"Tell him that I've come down with the pox!"

Chapter Seven

Odile watched critically as Araminta adjusted the tall-crowned hat with its curling plumes of ostrich feathers. "You look *très* dashing, *ma chère*," she pronounced. "Perhaps a trifle too dashing? That hat looks exactly like a cavalryman's shako!"

Araminta laughed, rising to obtain a full-length view of herself in the cheval glass. "The hat is supposed to look like a shako. My new riding habit is very *à la militaire,* didn't you observe? You can't have failed to notice the epaulets and the frogs and the braid halfway up my sleeves!"

"Mais non, nor have I failed to notice that bright green color," Odile retorted. "You will be visible a good half a mile away! You should have allowed me to accompany you when you chose your new habit."

Araminta laughed again. "I fear I must live with my mistake, if mistake it was. Well, I'm off," she said, picking up her riding crop. "I've persuaded Damaris to ride with me in the park this afternoon." She paused on her way to the door. "It's such a shame that you don't ride, Odile. Wouldn't you like to take lessons? I collect it would give you something to occupy your time."

Odile shuddered. *"Quelle horreur!* Me, climb on top of one of those huge beasts? Never! Araminta, before

117

you go I must talk to you. You recall that *Milord* Manning visited us this morning?"

"It's not difficult to remember," said Araminta drily. "He arrives as regularly as clockwork." In the week since the Duchess of Cathcart's ball, she hadn't changed her mind about the wisdom of avoiding an open break with the Viscount, but the price of preserving a surface friendship with him was beginning to seem rather high, since it meant that he was continually underfoot. He called every day at Middleton House, and he'd contrived to be present at several of the functions she'd attended elsewhere in these, the early days of the Season. Nothing seemed to disturb his friendly imperturbability. He didn't appear to notice the slight distance Araminta was maintaining between them, and he'd expressed only a mild regret when she informed him that she'd decided against renting his house.

"Yes, I look forward to *Milord's* visits," said Odile happily. "And you'll never believe the marvelous idea he has for our amusement. Araminta, he wants to take all of us—Madame Middleton and the little Damaris and you and me—to Vauxhall Gardens one evening soon. It sounds like such an exciting place—dancing and concerts and midnight suppers and thousands of fairy lanterns swaying in the breeze."

"Very poetic," said Araminta, even more drily. If she and her family were to accompany Manning to Vauxhall, she hadn't the slightest doubt that he'd find some graceful way of luring her into a tête-à-tête in one of the secluded paths, illuminated by those famous fairy lanterns, in which the Gardens abounded. "Lord Manning is very kind, Odile, but we'll have to decline his invitation."

"But Araminta!"

"No, our calendar is becoming entirely too crowded now that the Season is in full swing," said Araminta

118

firmly. "Look, Odile, I've been meaning to talk to you about his lordship. I think you're becoming a trifle too friendly with the man. You realize, don't you, that my sister disapproves of him? She regards him as a rake and a fortune hunter. No, wait, I'm not passing judgment on him myself. But you and I are guests in Henrietta's house, and we wouldn't want to distress her by becoming too intimate with a man she cannot like, now, would we?"

Odile sounded shaken. *"Naturellement,* I would not displease Madame Middleton, but not to see any more of *Milord* Manning. . . . He is so charming, he speaks such perfect French."

"I didn't say we should drop him. Just don't get too friendly, I beg you."

"You may depend on me to do what is proper, *chère* Araminta. I will leave you now. Do have a pleasant ride with the little Damaris," said Odile with dignity. But her shoulders drooped as she walked to the door and opened it, and she brushed past with only a wan smile when she found Gillian waiting in the hallway outside the bedchamber.

"Madame Lacoste isn't ill again?" asked Gillian, watching Odile's receding form.

"Oh, no." Araminta studied her niece's expressive face. "What's happened, puss? You look as if you'd swallowed the cream."

"Oh, Araminta, the Duke has spoken to Mama, agreeing that it will be unnecessary for me to have another governess."

"Agreeing? Gillian, have you been writing to His Grace again?"

"Well, yes. You see, Mama's in correspondence with a lady she says will be a *perfect* governess for me. This lady's been in charge of the education of the Marquis of Rotherham's daughters and Mama says they're the most refined creatures in all of England. So I *had* to write to the Duke."

"What did you say to him?" asked Araminta with a shade of apprehension.

Gillian dimpled. "I was *most* circumspect. I didn't say a word about female equality, or taking charge of my own destiny. I merely pointed out that in just over a year I'll be preparing for my come out, and I hardly thought I needed a governess for so short a time."

"And you brought the Duke around to your point of view. That should teach you, my love, that a soft answer turneth away wrath!"

Araminta was smiling reminiscently about her conversation with Gillian as she walked down the stairs to keep her riding appointment with Damaris. She was only mildly surprised that Jason had supported Gillian's pleas to remain without a governess. He knew Araminta's views on the subject, and she guessed that his softened attitude had a great deal to do with the declaration of peace they'd made at the Duchess of Cathcart's ball. To give him his due, she thought he was trying his best to avoid playing the tyrant. And while she had a suspicion they might well clash again one day, she was still feeling chastened by her near-brush with notoriety, and she was determined not to provoke Jason by any ill-advised burst of independence.

"Oh, Araminta, how I wish I could ride as well as you do." Damaris spoke with wistful admiration but without a trace of envy as she watched Araminta calm Selim, suddenly skittish after a curricle and four had driven past him rather more closely than he was accustomed to on his regular outings in Hyde Park. Araminta's unconscious mastery of her mount caused a gleam of appreciation to cross Hassan's normally impassive dark face. Riding behind the two girls on the mare, Balkis, the Arab groom looked far more unobtrusive now that he had abandoned his flowing native robes.

"I wish we'd decided to ride this morning, though, rather than this afternoon," Damaris went on. "The park is so crowded at this hour."

Though it was only the first week of May, it was such an idyllically lovely spring day that an unusually large number of riders and carriages thronged the paths of the park. At the sudden swift approach of a high-perch phaeton, Damaris pulled abruptly on her reins, causing her well-behaved little mare to shy slightly. "There, you see. The head groom at our estate in Lincolnshire once told Mama I didn't have good hands, and I daresay he was right."

"You ride very well, Damaris. All you need is a bit of practice," said Araminta with an encouraging smile. But privately she had to admit that Damaris, though she looked quite impossibly beautiful in a riding habit of fine pale blue broadcloth trimmed in darker blue, was a very indifferent horsewoman.

Gathering her reins rather nervously, Damaris craned her neck to peer around her, murmuring, "The Duke said he would join us at five, but I don't see—" She drew a sharp breath. "Martin Corby! What's he doing here?"

Araminta glanced at her niece in surprise. Usually so demurely self-possessed, Damaris looked quite flustered. Comprehension dawned a moment later when a young man pulled up his horse beside Damaris, whose damask cheeks were turning a delicate rose. She sounded distinctly ill at ease as she made the introductions. "Aunt Araminta, may I present Martin Corby? Martin, this is my aunt, Lady Araminta Beresford."

Martin Corby was a sturdy, dark-haired young man of about Araminta's own age, or perhaps a year or two

121

younger. His pleasant, rather plain features looked puzzled as he said, "You're Damaris's aunt, Lady Araminta? But how can that be? You two seem exactly of an age."

"Pray continue, Mr. Corby. You're making me feel younger with every graceful word," replied Araminta with a laugh.

"Aunt Araminta is Mama's younger sister," put in Damaris quickly. She added, to Araminta's secret amusement, "But of course, I'm really some years younger than my aunt. Martin, what are you doing in London? I thought—I heard that you were living on your farm in Surrey."

"Mama wrote that you and your mother were in London for the Season, so I decided to come up for a visit," said Martin with a hint of embarrassment. "When I called at your house this morning, Lady Middleton told me you were riding in the park, so here I am. I'm so glad I found you. May I ride with you for a little?"

"I—yes—I daresay that would be all right." Damaris still sounded flustered. To Araminta she said hurriedly, "Martin is a very old friend. Our families have adjoining estates in Lincolnshire, and I've known him practically from my cradle."

"Yes, when I wasn't at school I spent more time playing with Damaris and Gillian at Middleton Hall than I did at my own home," grinned Martin. "Poor Lady Middleton actually became concerned that the girls would never develop any interest in female concerns like painting on glass, or netting, or shell work. Or really important things like ball gowns!" He looked at Damaris's artfully arranged golden curls and modish riding habit with open admiration. "I'll wager that your mama has no worries on that score now."

To rescue Damaris from the evident embarrassment she felt at Martin's impulsive compliment, Araminta remarked, as the trio put their mounts to a brisk walk, "So you're from Lincolnshire also, Mr. Corby. I thought I heard Damaris say that you were farming in Surrey."

"Well, yes, an old uncle died and left me this little property," began Martin, breaking off when he observed Damaris's radiant smile at the sight of the tall man on the powerful bay stallion who had just ridden up beside them.

Jason touched his hat. "Miss Middleton, Lady Araminta." He glanced inquiringly at Martin, and Damaris hastened to make the two men known to each other.

"So, Mr. Corby, you're an old friend of the Middleton family," said the Duke affably. "I quite envy you the experience of knowing Miss Middleton for so many years." To Araminta he said, "Since you have Mr. Corby as your escort, I feel sure you won't object if I whisk your niece away for a quiet canter."

Martin's eyes lingered on Jason and Damaris as they rode off. "I hope you won't think I'm too forward, Lady Araminta, but could you tell me—that is to say, my mother writes that the *on dit* has it that Damaris—Miss Middleton—may soon be betrothed to the Duke of Harwood."

Araminta eyed Martin's tense young face with considerable sympathy, but said merely, "I'm sorry. I'm not at liberty to speculate on any marriage plans that may be in the offing for my niece. Shall we ride, Mr. Corby? There's a very pretty path over there beside the Serpentine." She motioned to her groom, Hassan, to fall in behind them.

It soon became clear that Martin's attention was not on his surroundings. He rode along beside Araminta in a moody silence that she interrupted after several minutes by saying, "Will you be staying very long in London?"

"What? Oh—no. One night only." He glanced at Araminta with a boyishly disarming smile. "I've been rude, haven't I? Lord knows, I'm no Pink of the Ton, but I certainly know better than to ignore one of the most beautiful ladies in London. Will you forgive me?"

"Indeed, yes. I'm not in the least offended. It was obvious that you were a trifle blue-deviled."

Martin sighed heavily. After a moment he blurted, "Lady Araminta, could I talk to you? If I don't talk to *somebody*, I may well end up in Bedlam!"

"Talk away. I must warn you, however, that I suspect I know what you're going to say. It's about Damaris, isn't it?"

"Is it that obvious?" Martin's shoulders slumped. "For so many years, Damaris and I were simply friends. My only brother is much older than I am—much like you and Lady Middleton, I daresay—and there were few children of our age in the neighborhood, so Damaris and I became very close. But two years ago we discovered that what we felt for each other was more than friendship. Suddenly we realized that we'd fallen in love. And then, almost as quickly, the bubble burst. Lady Middleton was kind, but firm. She could not allow Damaris even to consider marrying a younger son with pockets to let. I had to agree with her. What could I offer Damaris? With her beauty and breeding and fortune, she could marry anyone. I left Lincolnshire to live on the farm in Surrey that I had inherited from my uncle a short time previously."

Martin sighed. "Even though I'd given Damaris up, I suppose I nursed a secret hope that someone would wave a fairy wand and bring us back together. Perhaps she wouldn't fancy any of the eligibles who were certain to swarm around her. Or I might earn such a respectable income with my stud farm that Lady Middleton would judge me prosperous enough to be considered as an eligible suitor myself. Then Mama wrote me about the gossip connecting Damaris with the Duke, and I hared straight up to London to find out if the rumors were true."

Martin glanced hopefully at Araminta, who shook her head, smiling. "No, no, you'll not catch me out," she said. "I simply can't discuss Damaris's plans—or lack of them!—with you. If it will be of any comfort to you, however, I must tell you that I think you and Damaris would make a splendid couple. I'd hate to think that a vulgarity like lack of money would keep you apart!"

"Thank you, but I fancy the situation is a little more complicated than that. Or perhaps a great deal simpler. Perhaps Damaris just outgrew her childhood affection for me," said Martin quietly. Putting on a determinedly cheerful face, he changed the subject, saying, "That's a sweet-going bit of blood you're riding. The mare, too. Arabian, are they?"

"Yes. I bought Selim and Balkis in Syria. Did you say that you own a stud farm?"

"In a very small way. Last spring two of my mares dropped promising foals, but of course it will be another year before I can race them. I've also begun to train horses for several owners. I'm entering one of these horses in the Second Spring Meeting at Newmarket. If he wins, well and good. Otherwise . . ." Martin shrugged.

Knitting her brows thoughtfully, Araminta broke a short silence by saying, "You're quite a young man, Mr. Corby, and by your own admission you have very little experience in racing. Do you consider yourself a good trainer?" As Martin shot her a quick glance, half startled, half resentful, Araminta hastened to add, "Oh, my wretched tongue! Truly, I didn't mean to sound so lowering. It's just that I think I'm a good judge of character, and if you tell me that you're a skillful trainer,

125

I'll believe you."

Martin's expression of hauteur slowly faded into a grin. "I'm dashed if I can imagine why you want to know, but yes, I'm a *very* good trainer."

"Famous. How would you like to train Selim? I'd like very much to enter him in this year's Derby."

"You're bamming me, of course."

"Why do you say that?"

"Oh, come now. I may not be awake on every suit, but . . . You must know that ladies of quality don't race horses. Why, for one thing, females aren't eligible to join the Jockey Club."

"Is that essential?"

"Well, no. Not every man who races belongs to the Jockey Club. But really, for you to enter a horse in a race wouldn't be at all the thing."

"So I've been told," Araminta conceded. "I see no reason, however, why I should abstain. Is there a law against my entering Selim in the Derby?"

"N-no. Not that I know of. It's just—you wouldn't care to have people say you were fast, or—or—"

"Or even worse. I know," sighed Araminta. Perhaps she'd better rein herself in. She'd already flouted the rules of convention to the limit, and she'd escaped disaster by a hairsbreadth, thanks to quick thinking and her exotic Turkish caftan. One more lapse, and she might find herself ostracized once again by the guardian patronesses at Almack's.

Martin took another long look at Selim. "My eye and Betty Martin, that's an elegant tit. If I had the training of him, who's to say he couldn't win the Derby?" Martin paused, an expression of envy creasing his forehead. "I wonder. It's done often enough. If you were only a man . . ."

"Yes? Do go on."

"Oh, I had a silly notion. You see, I know a man—it

126

was young Lord Easterbrook—who entered his horse Paladin in a race last autumn at the Doncaster meet, giving the name of his groom as the owner."

Araminta looked puzzled. "I fear I don't see the point."

"It's quite simple. Lord Easterbrook's father had forbidden him to race, because he'd lost a fortune betting on horses at Tattersall's Subscription Room. So Easterbrook raced under an assumed name."

"Are you suggesting that I could do the same? Pretend that Selim is owned by someone else and enter him in the Derby?" asked Araminta, breaking into a laugh. "Let me see, now. Selim, property of Mr. John Jones. No, not a soul would believe in that name. How about Sheik Ahmed? Too exotic, I fear. I have it: Mr. Middleman. Perfect, don't you think? Our imaginary owner is the middle man between me and Selim."

"Lady Araminta, pray forgive me for suggesting an idiotic idea like that," said Martin, aghast. "It wouldn't fadge, I assure you. For one thing, your horse Selim would be recognized. He's no unknown horse fresh off some stud farm in the North. Doubtless you've been seen riding him by half of London. I suspect his name is almost as well known to the Ton as your own. Even if there weren't other objections, you couldn't sneak him into the Derby under a false name."

"We're a pair of dolts, not to have thought of that." Araminta's eyes narrowed. "Wait. What if I were to sign a bill of sale transferring Selim to Mr. A. Middleman?"

"I don't think—well, it might do, I suppose. Unless—wouldn't it look very strange if Mr. Middleman never appeared?"

"Gout," said Araminta triumphantly. "Poor Mr. Middleman has such a bad case of gout that he seldom ventures out of doors. That's settled, then. You'll train Selim for the Derby."

The bemused look faded from Martin's eyes. "No, Lady Araminta," he said regretfully. "I'll not lend myself to a scheme that might involve you in scandal."

"What's this about a scandal, Corby?" demanded the Duke, riding up with Damaris. His mouth had tightened into a hard line, and Damaris seemed to be turning faint at the possibility that her aunt had become entangled in still another imbroglio.

"No scandal at all, Duke," said Araminta. "Discovering that Mr. Corby owns a stud farm, I asked him to train Selim for the Derby and he refused, on the grounds that ladies of quality don't race their own horses. So, since I consider such an attitude both lowering and unfair, I've been trying to change Mr. Corby's mind."

"Don't," said Jason curtly. "You'll find yourself out of curl if you don't heed Corby's advice."

"Oh yes, Aunt Araminta, it would be most improper for a lady to patronize the turf," Damaris exclaimed.

Araminta paused, frowning. Only a few days ago, she reflected, she would stubbornly have persisted in her determination to do as she pleased in a matter that involved nothing more serious than a fancied breach of impropriety. But now . . . She looked at the three serious faces confronting her. At last she said slowly, "If you all truly believe that I might be risking scandal by racing Selim, I won't do it."

As she observed the Duke and Damaris breathe a collective sigh of relief, Araminta's eyes began to twinkle, and she flashed Jason an impish challenge. "It positively hurts to sing small, when I thought I'd found such a clever way to have my cake and eat it too. I proposed to Mr. Corby that I pretend to sell Selim to an imaginary gentleman named A. Middleman, who would then hire Mr. Corby to train Selim for the Derby. I still think it's a capital notion, but Mr. Corby warned me I'd catch cold at it."

To her surprise, an instant flicker of amusement crossed Jason's face. He raised an eyebrow, saying coolly, "If you expect me to remonstrate against your scheme, you're quite out, Lady Araminta. Now, of course, no one would be in the least taken in by your imaginary owner, Mr. 'A. Middleman.' However, I suspect that such a flimsy masquerade would enable you to enter your horse in the Derby without incurring the censure of society, since you'd at least be paying lip service to the conventions. I'd advise you to sell Selim to Mr. Middleman immediately."

"Duke, you can't mean that!" cried Damaris in horror.

Ignoring her niece, Araminta looked at Jason blankly. Having expected to lure Jason into one of their usual sparring matches, she felt distinctly let down when he hadn't risen to the bait. The corners of his mouth were quivering, and she knew that he was enjoying her discomfiture. *I'll give you that round, Jason,* she thought, *but just wait until the next one.* "I'm so pleased that you agree with me," she told him with a gracious smile. "It was my thought, exactly. As long as I don't admit to being A. Middleman, society will look the other way." She turned to Martin. "Well, Mr. Corby? Will you take Selim on?"

Looking hopelessly confused, Martin stammered, "I don't know . . . Naturally, if the Duke thinks it permissible . . ." He swallowed hard. "Yes, I will, Lady Araminta. I'll be honored!"

"Splendid. Now, then, what about jockeys? Can you lay your hand on a bang-up rider?"

"Er—I fancy that won't be a problem. We'd want a top jockey for the Derby, of course." Martin sounded a little unsure of himself. Clearly, matters were moving too fast for him.

Turning to Hassan, Araminta spoke in rapid Arabic.

"Would you like to ride Selim in the most famous of English races?"

"Allah be praised, lady. What a glorious deed, to defeat the infidels on their own soil."

"It would mean leaving my employ temporarily to live on a farm owned by this gentleman." Araminta motioned to Martin. "Mr. Corby will train Selim for the race, and I would expect you to obey his orders as you do mine."

Hassan's dark eyes flicked over Martin, who sat his horse listening to the incomprehensible guttural speech with a growing puzzlement reflected also in the faces of the Duke and Damaris.

"It shall be as you say, lady."

"Mind you remember that." To Martin, Araminta said, "No need to bother yourself with finding a jockey, Mr. Corby. Hassan will ride Selim. He knows the horse, and among the Bedouins he's the best rider I ever saw."

"I see." Martin eyed Hassan with a kind of horrified fascination. "Does the man speak English? If he doesn't, how am I to give him orders?"

Araminta dismissed the problem with a wave of her hand. "Around horses, Hassan doesn't need words. Besides, he's learning English fast. You'll have no difficulty working with him." She added, "It's just occurred to me that perhaps I should send you Balkis, also. It's more than time for her to be bred."

Martin's eyes glowed. He impulsively extended his hand to Araminta. "Shall we shake hands on our new venture?"

"Gladly. How does it feel to be the trainer of the next Derby winner?"

"Doing it rather too brown, Lady Araminta," Martin grinned.

"Martin, come ride with me for a little," said Damaris suddenly, an oddly shrill note in her voice. "I'd like you to catch me up on all your doings."

Looking puzzled but flattered, Martin rode off with her, while Jason, sitting his horse, gazed after the pair with a slight frown. "I take it Damaris and this Corby fellow are very old friends?"

"Oh yes, childhood playmates," replied Araminta easily. What was Damaris about? she wondered. The girl had been unusually abrupt, not to say almost rude, in ordering Martin to come away with her. "Shall we go see the powder magazine? I understand it's north of the Serpentine," Araminta said aloud.

"The *powder magazine?* In heaven's name, why?"

"Because it's there? We must go somewhere, after all. We can't just sit here letting our horses get restless while we wait for Damaris and Martin to come back."

Jason chuckled. "Very well. The powder magazine it shall be." As they began to walk their horses sedately along the path, he said, "I've been wanting a word alone with you. I thought you'd like to know that I went to the Admiralty to place an inquiry about Madame Lacoste's lieutenant. I should have news for you soon."

"Oh, thank you. Odile will be so pleased." Araminta smiled at him. *"I'm* pleased. You didn't say a word about the possibility of my being compromised by Odile's presence."

Jason grimaced. "My dear girl, haven't you noticed? I'm strictly observing the terms of our truce." He leaned over to pat Selim's glossy coat. "That horse is real blood-and-bones. I fancy you'll miss riding such a magnificent animal."

"I hadn't thought of that." Araminta looked stricken. "And here I've already promised to send Balkis to Mr. Corby's stud for breeding, so . . . Duke, would you do me a great favor? Will you select a suitable mount for me at Tattersall's?"

"I — with pleasure." Jason seemed taken aback.

Quickly regaining his composure, he said with a trace of malice, "I marvel that you aren't planning to go to Tattersall's in person to choose a horse."

"I shouldn't dream of doing such a thing," Araminta said primly. "It's my understanding that females of good breeding never set foot in Tattersall's!"

After a startled moment, Jason began laughing. "Hoist with my own petard, am I? You're never at a stand for long, are you, Araminta? I don't doubt you'll come through this latest cork-brained scheme of yours with flying colors." He smiled wickedly. "What a shame you won't win the Derby, however. I'm entering a horse, too, and Selim, marvelous creature that he is, hasn't a chance against my Caesar!"

"Oh? Do you care to back that remark with a small bet?"

"A hundred pounds, shall we say?"

"A trifling sum. Make it five hundred!"

They rode on in the direction of the powder magazine, exchanging lighthearted banter, laughing at each other's jokes. Their estrangement might never have been, Araminta thought. They were back to the easy companionship they'd enjoyed during their first meeting at the inn in Dover.

"Aunt Araminta, you were only funning about racing your horse in the Derby, weren't you?"

Damaris's remark broke into Araminta's delightful reverie of watching Selim thunder to victory in the Derby. Having said good-bye to the Duke and Martin Corby at the gates of Hyde Park, she and Damaris were riding back with Hassan to Middleton House.

"You were just trying to tip the Duke a rise, wasn't that it?" Damaris said with a coaxing smile. "I've noticed—that is to say, you sometimes speak quite teasingly to him."

"Why no, I'm perfectly serious. I've wanted to enter Selim in the Derby since I arrived in England. What a stroke of luck to meet Mr. Corby in the park today! Oh, by the by, now that Mr. Corby and I are to be so closely connected, don't you think I might start calling him Martin?"

"Call Martin anything you like," replied Damaris shortly, her cheeks suddenly bright with color.

Araminta stared at her niece in mild surprise. Was that jealousy in Damaris's voice? Even though she seemed to be fond of the Duke, could it be that Damaris retained a proprietary feeling for her childhood friend that made her resent Araminta's association with Martin?

But no, Damaris might be feeling jealous, but she was also very angry. "I'll tell you what, Aunt Araminta," she burst out, "you're making a very big mistake, planning to enter your horse in the Derby. You'll plunge all of us into disgrace again. I can't see why the Duke doesn't realize that. And Martin! He calls himself my oldest friend, and yet he absolutely refused to listen to reason when I begged him not to train your horse. He thinks he'll become rich and famous doing so!"

She lapsed into an aggrieved silence during the rest of their ride home, and her low spirits were still in evidence when the ladies of the household gathered for a cup of tea in the morning room before going to their bedchambers to prepare for the rout party hosted by Lord and Lady Massingham.

Looking askance at her usually sunny-tempered daughter, Henrietta inquired, "Did Martin Corby find you in the park this afternoon, Damaris? I own, I was so flabbergasted to see him that I didn't put him off as I perhaps should have done. Well, he *is* such an old friend, but there's no denying the situation is a bit deli-

133

cate, my love. I trust you weren't too embarrassed to see him."

"Oh yes, I saw Martin, Mama."

As usual, the conversation was being conducted in French to accommodate Odile, who now chimed in, "You met a young man in the park today, *chère* Araminta? An old friend of *la petite* Damaris? What is he like, this young man? Handsome? Of good family? Perhaps with a small competence at least?" She tossed Damaris an inquiring glance. "This Martin—that is his name?—would he be an eligible *parti* for our Araminta, do you think?"

Trust Odile to get to the heart of the matter, thought Araminta, smothering a grin. Damaris, whose lips had tightened at Odile's artless question, was spared the necessity of a reply by the arrival of a footman who gave Araminta a message in a low voice. She rose, saying, "Will you excuse me, Henrietta? Mr. Corby is here to see me."

"Martin wants to see you?"

Damaris said acidly, "Martin and Aunt Araminta are partners now, Mama. He's going to train the horse she's entering in the Derby."

Henrietta choked. When she recovered her breath she gasped, "Araminta, how could you? After you were so nearly refused a voucher from Almack's . . ." She put her hand to her head. "Damaris, my dear, could you bring me some hartshorn?"

"Henrietta, the Duke agrees with me that it would be a capital idea to run Selim in the Derby."

"He does?" Lady Middleton said doubtfully. She pursed her lips. "Well, in that case . . ."

"Why do you not invite the young man to come in, *ma mie?* You know I always like to meet new friends," said Odile, wide-eyed with interest.

When the footman ushered Martin into the morning

134

room, he appeared awkward and ill at ease at being confronted by a roomful of females, though Araminta noted that his eyes flew instantly to Damaris's face and lingered there, like a man searching for water in the desert.

"I'm sorry to intrude, ma'am," he apologized to Araminta after he'd been introduced to Odile. "The thing is, I must return to the stud first thing in the morning, and it occurred to me after I left you this afternoon that you might want me to take your horses back with me. So if I could have a word with your grooms to make the arrangements . . ."

"A capital notion. Selim can begin his training at the earliest possible moment."

"And if at any time you'd care to visit the stud to see how the horse is coming along, you'd be more than welcome, I assure you."

"Why, thank you. I'd love to visit the stud."

As if struck by a sudden idea, Martin added, "Perhaps you and Damaris would like to come too, Lady Middleton. Oh, and Madame also, of course."

"Oh, I scarcely think so," said Henrietta quickly. "I know nothing of horses, and Damaris—"

Her daughter cut in, shifting her straight, unsmiling gaze from Araminta to Martin, "On the contrary, Mama, I should very much like to go. You forget, the Duke also has a stud farm near Epsom. I daresay he'd be delighted to show us *his* horses."

Chapter Eight

As it happened, when the Duke was informed about Damaris's proposal to combine an expedition to see Martin Corby's stud farm with a visit to his own establishment, he was enthusiastic. Henrietta was less eager, at least so far as the scheme involved Damaris. Her motives were quite transparent to Araminta. Lady Middleton didn't want any unwelcome echoes from the past to jeopardize Damaris's opportunity to make the match of the year.

"My love, I hardly think it wise to visit Martin Corby's farm," Henrietta ventured at one point to her elder daughter. "It might—how shall I say it?—reopen old wounds."

Damaris blushed at her mother's remark. "Mama, forgive me, but you're talking fustian. Martin and I were never—" She broke off, biting her lip. "We were just children, childhood playmates who were fond of each other and imagined for a very little while that"—the lovely rose color deepened—"that we had fallen in love. I daresay Martin is as grateful as I am that you pricked our romantic bubble! So there's no reason why either of us should feel embarrassed if I were to visit him at his farm."

At this, Araminta lifted a mental eyebrow. Damaris had seemingly recovered from the snit into which she'd fallen when both the Duke and Martin had seconded Araminta's plans to run Selim in the Derby, and she was once more her demure, charming self. But did she really believe what she'd said in her little speech to her mother? At her meeting with Martin in Hyde Park, it must have been as apparent to her as it had been to Araminta that her childhood friend was still wearing his heart on his sleeve. Surely the gentle Damaris wouldn't wish to visit Martin solely out of curiosity, to see if her powers of attraction were as strong as ever?

On the morning fixed for the jaunt to the stud, a week following her meeting with Martin Corby in Hyde Park, Araminta came down the stairs a few minutes early to encounter Odile in the foyer, about to walk out the door on the arm of Lord Manning. As Araminta stared at her in considerable surprise, Odile turned a dull red and the violet ribbons on her widow's veiling began to shake agitatedly. Bowing with his usual aplomb, the Viscount said politely, "Madame tells me you're off to Epsom, Lady Araminta. I trust you'll enjoy your outing. You have a lovely day for it."

"I'm sure I shall."

Gazing with frank admiration at her pelisse of dove gray *gros de Naples,* trimmed with deep coral velvet and worn with a wide-brimmed bonnet edged with a fall of blond lace, Manning said, "Will you allow me to tell you how much your costume becomes you?"

"Thank you," replied Araminta composedly. "Lord Manning, could I ask you to wait outside for Odile, please? I must have a word with her."

After the door had closed behind the Viscount, Araminta asked pleasantly, "Where are you off to, Odile?"

Odile eyed her defensively. "Silvanus is—"

"Silvanus?"

"That is *Milord* Manning's name," said Odile, lifting her chin. "He has asked me to use it. Silvanus has invited me to ride with him in Richmond Park this morning. I am eager to see the Pen Ponds with all the fish, and the herds of deer, and the oak trees. Hundreds of years old the trees are, Silvanus says. And you need not glare at me like that, Araminta, it is most respectable to go to Richmond Park, and I am sure I will enjoy it a great deal more than driving down to see that young man's horses. I hate horses!"

Araminta sighed. "Yes, of course Richmond Park is respectable, but I wonder you didn't tell me beforehand about your plans to go there. And I thought we'd agreed that it would be better not to see so much of Lord Manning."

"I did not inform you, Araminta, because I knew you would look at me with that disapproving Friday face!" Her eyes brimming, Odile dove into her reticule for the ever-present lace-edged black handkerchief. "You keep forgetting how alone I am in this strange country, and how few friends I have," she sobbed. "You begrudge me this kind, good man's company!"

Flinging up her hands, Araminta exclaimed in exasperation, "I don't begrudge you anything. I only wish—Oh, be off with you, Odile. Have a lovely time."

Wiping her eyes, Odile went off with a forgiving smile, and Araminta indulged herself in some hard thoughts about Silvanus Manning. He and Odile were growing entirely too close. Araminta didn't suspect for a moment that Manning was falling in love with Odile. It was much more likely that he was using her as a stalking horse to maintain his ties with Araminta. But in her growing intimacy with Manning, there was a definite possibility that Odile might grow too attached to him. It had been so many months since she had seen her sailor lover, and she was so susceptible to male admiration and attention.

The arrival of the Duke forced Araminta to put Odile's problems out of her mind. Jason reined in his team in front of Middleton House just as Araminta's coachman, Ben, was driving her new town chariot around from the stables.

Stepping down from his curricle, Jason tossed the reins to his tiger and walked over to Araminta, waiting on the walkway with Damaris and Gillian. Smiling a greeting at the Middleton sisters, he took an appreciative look at the elegant vehicle with its pair of matched bays and the liveried footman standing in impassive solitude between the rear wheels. "What a spanking turn-out," he exclaimed with a grin.

"Isn't it?" Araminta agreed, her eyes twinkling. "It was so kind of you to accompany me to the carriage maker's and help me to select just the right town carriage. Oh, and for choosing the horses, too. I'm very much in your debt."

He bowed. "My pleasure." His lips curved mischievously. "Young Corby will be overwhelmed by such magnificence. He probably expects you to arrive on horseback, riding *ventre à terre!* Or, at the very least, driving your own high-perch phaeton!"

"Believe me, I would *adore* driving a high-perch phaeton, especially if I could do so behind a pair like your grays. You wouldn't consider letting me drive your curricle, would you?"

"Certainly not!" The Duke asked curiously, *"Have* you ever driven a phaeton?"

"Not a phaeton, but I've driven a gig many times, and once, in the Peloponnese when Ben took ill"—Araminta smiled at her coachman—"Uncle Will allowed me to drive our berline. I didn't overturn us, in any event."

The Duke shook his head. "You may be a pretty whip with a gig or a berline, Lady Araminta, but you've never tried to drive my grays in city traffic!"

"Oh, well," Araminta sighed. "Perhaps it's for the best. As you know, I'm making every effort these days to be more conventional than the Queen!"

Jason burst into a laugh. "Pray don't turn into an out-and-outer of a high-stickler, Lady Araminta, or you'll send all your friends into a state of shock," be teased. "Now, to avoid appearing like too much of a slow-top, you might attract a bit of attention by putting your footman into those flowing garments your Arab groom used to wear—"

"How fortunate that the day is so fine, Duke," Damaris declared. "If it had been raining, I shouldn't have had the pleasure of driving to Epsom with you in your curricle."

The laughter dying out of his face, the Duke looked at Damaris with the faintest suggestion of a frown. His thoughts must be echoing her own, Araminta reflected. Making all allowances for Damaris, her comment could only be considered a deliberate interruption. After a slight pause, Jason extended his hand to her, saying politely, "Perhaps we should be on our way, then. With our variable English weather, there's no telling when it might start to rain."

Araminta watched Jason drive off in the curricle with Damaris with a slight pang. She would have much preferred to travel to Epsom with him in an open carriage rather than to ride with Gillian in the new town chariot. However, as it turned out, the fifteen-mile journey from London to Epsom in her younger niece's engaging company was far from dull. Gillian was full of plot ideas for a new novel featuring a ghastly Egyptian mummy.

Across Westminster Bridge they went, the town carriage following Jason's curricle, through Clapham Common and Tooting, Merton and Kingston. Soon they were entering Epsom, a large and rambling town seated in a depression of the great chalk downs of northern Surrey. The High Street seemed strangely quiet and humdrum to

140

Araminta, recalling the tales she'd heard of the days in the past century when Epsom had been a brilliant and fashionable watering place. After the carriage left Epsom, however, her disappointment quickly faded when, after passing the magnificently wooded grounds of a large estate, the carriage emerged onto a vast open heath, thickly covered with furze and redolent of wild thyme and juniper. Horses and riders covered the heath like a vast herd of cattle, walking, trotting, galloping. The horses were being ridden without saddles by wiry, poorly dressed lads, one of whom was thrown by his mount almost under the wheels of the carriage. The rider picked himself up immediately and ran, half limping, to catch his horse.

Peering excitedly out the window, Araminta craned her neck, searching for a glimpse of Hassan's dark-browed face and Selim's sleekly powerful form, but if they were there, they were lost in the throng. Then Gillian exclaimed in disappointment, "Botheration, Araminta, all the horses are leaving." As they watched, the riders and their mounts began streaming away from the heath like a vast movement of the tide.

From the heath it was only a few miles down a narrow, winding country road to Martin Corby's stud. As the two vehicles rolled to a stop in the courtyard, Martin emerged from the house. First greeting the Duke and Damaris, he walked over to the town chariot. "Welcome to Longridge Farm, Lady Araminta," he said cordially, handing her down from the carriage. He smiled at Gillian. "Hallo there, puss. I vow, you've grown a foot since the last time I saw you."

Gillian wrinkled her nose at him. "Did you expect me to stay a child forever, Martin?"

Araminta gazed around her with approval at the trim farmhouse, surrounded by neat flower beds, vivid with early spring flowers, and at the well-kept stables and outbuildings lining the courtyard. "This seems like a very snug establishment, Mr. Corby." She cocked an inquiring eye at him. "I hate standing on ceremony. May I call you Martin? And I am Araminta, of course."

Looking a little bemused at this sudden turn into informality, Martin said hastily, "I'd hoped to see you on the heath this morning to watch Selim being exercised, La—Araminta."

"Alas. We were all slugabeds. On my next visit, be sure I'll arrive much earlier. May I see Selim?"

"Hassan just returned from riding him on the heath. It will be some time before he's properly cooled down. Meanwhile, won't you come into the house to have some refreshments? My housekeeper has been in a fine taking ever since she learned I'd be entertaining three ladies and a Duke! If you don't partake of the delicacies she's prepared, I fear she may fall into a fit of the dismals!"

A little later, seated at table in the painfully neat parlor of the farmhouse, Araminta bit into a scone, lavishly spread with country butter and preserves, and munched thoughtfully for a few moments. "Sheer ambrosia, Mrs. Felton," she exclaimed appreciatively to the hovering housekeeper, whose anxious middle-aged face relaxed into a smile of thankful relief.

During the light meal, Araminta began to note with amusement that Martin, though he may have believed he was taking an active part in the conversation, was silent much of the time, gazing surreptitiously at Damaris as though she were his vision of the Holy Grail. Catching Jason's eye at one point, Araminta realized from his lurking twinkle that he was quite aware of Martin's befuddlement and was having difficulty keeping his face straight. Henrietta's worries had been quite needless. Self-assured man of the world that he was, the Duke of Harwood wasn't disturbed by the devotion of his future wife's childhood swain.

Damaris was her usual serene, collected self, seemingly oblivious to the effect she was having on poor

Martin. She chatted pleasantly during the collation, effusively praising the housekeeper's baking, and then, with an arch smile, she requested a tour of the house. Araminta had never before observed any strong interest in domesticity on Damaris's part, but her niece appeared much taken with Martin's living arrangements. "This is such a comfortable house," she told him when they returned from their tour. "The rooms are so large and well appointed, and I can see that your housekeeper is taking excellent care of you."

At Martin's look of gratified delight, a sudden suspicion seized Araminta's mind. Could Damaris possibly be playing a double game? Was she encouraging Martin's attentions in an attempt to make the Duke just a shade jealous?

Feeling irritated—though what was it to her, after all, how Damaris chose to conduct her affairs?—Araminta said, "Well, Martin, now that we've seen the interior of your house, let's go visit Selim."

On the way to the stables, Martin mentioned that they had not yet decided on Araminta's racing colors. "What do you say to red and blue?"

"Certainly not," said Araminta firmly. "Those colors would clash with my hair. A pretty picture of fun I'd look."

Gillian giggled. "But what difference does it make? *You* won't be riding the horse."

"Come now, Gillian, it's the principle of the thing," suggested Jason, grinning.

"Precisely," said Araminta. "Make my colors pale green and white, Martin."

As the group paused at the open door of Selim's large and immaculately kept loose box, a stableboy was industriously rubbing down the magnificent Arabian under Hassan's watchful eye.

"Well, love, you're looking more beautiful than ever. I've missed you," crooned Araminta, reaching up to scratch Selim gently between his ears. The horse inclined his head to nuzzle Araminta affectionately.

Damaris took an involuntary step backward. "Aunt Araminta! He—he doesn't bite, does he?"

Araminta tossed her a look of blank incomprehension. "*Bite* me? Damaris, what a shatterbrained thing to say! Selim is as gentle as a kitten. Gentler!"

Martin said hastily, "I think Selim has missed you too, La—Araminta. He's looking well, don't you think?"

"Indeed, yes." Araminta turned to Hassan, who, though he was dressed like the other stable hands in breeches and gaiters and rough jacket, still looked exotically out of place. "How are you coming along, Hassan? Do you like working for Mr. Corby?"

"I'm quite satisfied, lady," replied Hassan in swift Arabic. "The infidels treat me very well—I have my own room, and the food, though atrocious, is at least plentiful. Also, making things easier, I am learning your language very rapidly. The stableboys tell me they have never seen a foreigner become so fluent in so short a time. And Corby *effendi* allows me to manage Selim's training without undue interference. We understand each other."

"I'm happy to hear it," said Araminta, stifling a quick grin of amusement. She had always been able to cope with Hassan's Bedouin male arrogance, and now it was apparent that Martin Corby also possessed the ability to manage Hassan without ruffling his feathers. "Do you think Selim will be ready to race in the Derby?"

"He is ready now, lady. And, Allah willing, he will win this English race by many lengths. The infidels have no horse to match him, nor any rider who can compete against a true son of the desert."

"Allah be praised for my good fortune in owning a horse like Selim and for having a servant like you," said Araminta drily. The sudden answering gleam in Hassan's dark eyes told her what she had often suspected, that he thoroughly enjoyed testing the boundaries of their mistress-servant relationship. "Continue your good work."

She turned back to the others. "The oracle has spoken," she informed them. "Hassan assures me that Selim can't lose the Derby." She smiled impishly at Jason. "I'd advise you to scratch your entry in the race, Duke. Why waste time and effort in a forlorn cause?"

"You'll be singing a different tune after you've seen my Caesar," the Duke retorted. "Shall we go along to my stud now? Corby, do you care to accompany us?"

Martin chuckled. "I wouldn't miss the chance to scout the opposition, sir."

After the carriages were brought around, Jason proposed a change in the seating arrangements. "Perhaps you'd like to ride with me, Lady Araminta? You might take the ribbons for a spell. We're not likely to encounter much traffic in these quiet country lanes."

Out of the corner of her eye Araminta saw Damaris's pretty mouth harden into a straight line. "Why, thank you, I'd like that," Araminta told the Duke without an instant's hesitation. Damaris had been indulging herself quite enough for one day, and, besides, Araminta fairly yearned to drive those grays.

Ten minutes later, watching Araminta feather-edge a blind corner, Jason relaxed beside her. "You're a first-rate fiddler, Araminta. I haven't a doubt you could drive a high-perch phaeton in Hyde Park. What's more, 're-freshing original' that you are, I fancy you wouldn't cause an eyebrow to lift when you appeared in it. Shall I help you select a dashing model?"

"Would you do that?" Araminta exclaimed, gratified. "What a swath I'd cut, to be sure! I wonder what the patronesses at Almack's would say?" Her eyes crinkling with amusement, she added, "I collect you realize you're oversetting all my good resolutions to be prim and proper and above all unnoticeable! Why this change of heart?"

"I'm faithfully observing our truce, of course," Jason grinned. Then, the merriment leaving his face, he said, "Actually, I should long since have admitted to you that I was a trifle high in the stirrups about your goings-on. Perhaps the Ton has become entirely too rigid and artificial in its standards for young women if it tends to destroy spontaneity like yours."

Araminta felt her throat constricting and searched her mind frantically for something to say. The Duke saved the moment by remarking casually, "You need to pay a shade more attention to pointing your leaders."

Jason's training stables were considerably more impressive than Martin's modest establishment. Directing Araminta to turn into a set of imposing entrance gates leading into an extensive, well-maintained parkland, the Duke explained that the property had once been his maternal grandfather's principal seat. "Grandfather lived for horse racing. My mother was an only child and her father's sole heir, and she left the estate to my younger brother Rupert. I inherited the place when he died. Rupert and I and my sister Felicity spent parts of every summer here with my grandfather before his death."

"You had just the one brother and sister?"

"Yes. I don't see very much of Felicity these days. She's been married for some years now, and Rupert . . . Rupert died at Waterloo."

Araminta glanced sideways at him, her heart full of sympathy at the desolate note in his voice. She remembered Henrietta telling her how close the brothers had been and how much Rupert's death had affected Jason.

"Was your brother on General Wellington's staff?"

"Lord, no." Jason gave a sudden reminiscent chuckle. "He was in the Blues. Rupert was the most joyous, dashing cavalryman who ever threw his leg over a saddle. I'll warrant he enjoyed every moment of that last charge with Uxbridge until the very second he was hit." Clearing his throat, he said, "Take that turning over

146

there for the stables."

Soon Araminta drove into an enormous paved court-yard surrounded on all four sides by storerooms and loose boxes, from the half-doors of which a number of equine heads peered out inquisitively. A pleasant-faced middle-aged man in gaiters and riding coat came hurrying out of an office near the entrance, his eyes widening in curiosity at the sight of a female driving the Duke of Harwood's famous grays. "Welcome, Your Grace. We don't see you down here often enough."

"Afternoon, Smithers. I should come more often, I daresay, but then I have every confidence in your train-ing methods. As I indicated in my letter, I've come with several guests. This is Lady Araminta Beresford, and—yes, here they are, my wards, the Misses Middleton, and Mr. Corby of Longridge Farm."

The town carriage rolled into the courtyard as he spoke and Martin jumped out to help Damaris and Gil-lian down. The introductions were interrupted by a sharp cracking noise from one of the loose boxes on the opposite side of the quadrangle.

"He's a bit restless today, Your Grace," Smithers apol-ogized. "Off his feed a trifle. It's been quite warm the past few days, and Caesar likes cooler weather."

The Duke nodded. "How about his training? Progress-ing as well as you'd like?"

"Oh, indeed, Your Grace. He ran an incredibly fast mile yesterday. He'll be at his peak for the race."

"Be sure to inform Mr. A. Middleman about his com-petition." Jason murmured teasingly to Araminta under his breath. To his trainer, he said, "Let's have a look at him."

Smithers raised his voice to the short, wiry figure lounging beside the loose box. "Blake. Bring Caesar out."

Moving cautiously, the groom opened the loose box door and led out a large coal-black stallion who snorted

147

nervously as he sidled skiddishly into the courtyard, jerking his head and shying away from imaginary dangers. Caesar wasn't a particularly beautiful animal, but Araminta, examining the horse with a critical eye, noted with approval the broad, muscular breast, the short, well-developed legs, the small rounded feet, wide and open, and the alert, well-pricked ears.

"A grand horse," she murmured to Jason, walking forward several steps for a better view.

"That's far enough, Araminta. Stand back," said the Duke sharply.

She turned her head in surprise. "What is it?"

"His Grace is right, my lady," intervened the trainer. "The horse is dangerous. You could be seriously injured."

Narrowing her eyes, Araminta took another long look at Caesar, edging a few inches closer. She didn't flinch when the horse, rolling his eyes, jerked violently on his reins, nearly tearing them from the hands of the groom. "I can see Caesar has a lot of spirit," she commented at last, "but surely you don't think *I'm* in any danger around him? You've seen me with horses. . . . Well, you'll recall Selim has a lot of spirit, too—"

"Araminta, stow your whid," exclaimed the Duke impatiently. She widened her eyes at the remark, and behind her she could distinctly hear a shocked gasp. From Damaris, probably. Beyond doubt, Jason had never offended his future betrothed's delicate ears with such a bit of rude slang.

He went on, as if unaware of what he'd said. "Let me explain the situation to you. That horse is practically unrideable. He literally will not allow human beings to approach him, with certain rare exceptions: Smithers here, the groom, Blake, who's looked after the horse since he was a foal, and myself. And oh, yes, we've found one veteran jockey who's somehow managed to ingratiate himself into Caesar's black soul. No one else can ride him. If he couldn't run like lightning, I'd have given up the notion of racing him long ago." Jason smiled grimly. "Incidentally, Caesar especially dislikes females. Something about the timbre of their voices, or possibly the distracting fluttering of their skirts."

Araminta burst out laughing. "Now I know you're trying to bubble me. Why should Caesar prefer males to females? Look, I'll show you, I'm perfectly safe with this so-called rogue horse . . ."

Before she could put one foot ahead of the other, Jason lunged forward, snatching her up in his arms and dragging her to the edge of the courtyard.

Momentarily paralyzed with astonishment, Araminta exclaimed angrily, "You've no right—let me go, Jason."

Ignoring both her glare of rage and her determined struggle to free herself, the Duke looked over her head, saying calmly to the groom, "Blake, get that horse back to his loose box." Only after Caesar was safely secured behind the closed half-door of his stall did Jason relax his hold, though he maintained a sinewy grasp on Araminta's wrist.

"Listen to me," he said in a low, tense tone. "We've come to points again, as we always seem to do, but neither of us wants to make a scene. Won't you take my word for it that Caesar might have injured you?"

Araminta felt a sudden electric jolt from the touch of the long slender fingers gripping her wrist, and she was acutely aware of Jason's scent, an indefinable blend of tangy shaving soap and immaculately laundered linen. At the same time, her anger beginning to fade away, she remembered the presence of Damaris and Gillian and Martin. She looked up at Jason with a rueful smile. "It's safe to release me now," she said softly. "I'm sorry. Such scaly behavior on my part. You have a perfect right to enforce any rules you see fit in your own stables."

Visibly relaxing, the Duke released her wrist. "Thank you. I knew I could rely on your good sense." His mouth twisted wryly. "Don't tell me, you dreadful female," he muttered. "Lombard Street to a China orange, you still believe you had nothing to fear from Caesar."

"Oh, my thoughts are something else again," Araminta said airily, and went off to join Martin and her nieces. Damaris edged close to her, speaking in a near-whisper.

"Aunt Araminta, I was so frightened for you when you went near that dreadful beast. I clutched poor Martin's arm so hard that his sleeve got all wrinkled. Why didn't you pay heed to the Duke's warning? I've never seen him so angry!"

Araminta gave Damaris a long look. The faint hint of smugness in her niece's expression belied her solicitous words. Araminta swallowed her irritation. Damaris was pleased that her aunt had incurred the Duke's public disapproval!

Mr. Smithers, the trainer, insisted that the Duke's guests come into the main house for a spot of refreshment that they were unable to refuse, and then it was time to drop Martin off at Longridge Farm and begin the journey back to London.

"I'll be back soon to check on Selim," Araminta promised her trainer as she stepped into the town chariot with Gillian. Damaris was once more seated beside Jason in the curricle.

As they neared Kingston, Gillian uttered an excited squeal. "Look! Gypsies! Oh, can't we stop?"

Following Gillian's pointing figure, Araminta looked out the window of the coach at what appeared to be a small encampment of gypsies in the courtyard of a modest inn set back from the road. A number of brightly dressed figures were gathered around a dilapidated wagon, while others stood idly near the door of the inn. Several women with babies in their arms sat under a nearby tree. Half-naked brown children played in the dust. Two men wearing kerchiefs tied around their heads and sashes around their waists stood dickering about the sale of a mule with a man who seemed to be a local farmer.

Lowering the glass, Araminta called up to her coachman, "We're stopping here for a moment, Ben. Miss Gillian wants to see the gypsies."

"Drat, my lady, that card will win you no tricks," the coachman called back in grumbling tones. "I don't like the look of the place, and that's a fact. No telling what bobbery these folk be up to." However, despite his disapproval, Ben obediently slowed the chariot and drove into the innyard. By the time Araminta and Gillian had stepped out of the vehicle, Jason, noticing the town chariot was no longer following his vehicle, had swung his curricle about and had reined in behind them.

Jumping down from the curricle, he strode over to them. Casting a quick look at the horses, he observed to Ben with relief, "I thought you might be having a problem with Lady Araminta's new team."

Before Ben could reply, a young woman sauntered up to Gillian, who stared in fascination at the gypsy's flowing, exotic clothing and her armful of clinking bracelets. "Tell your fortune, my pretty?" said the woman in wheedling tones.

"Oh, Araminta, could I?"

The gypsy girl didn't seem threatening. Araminta glanced at Jason, a question in her eyes.

He shrugged. "I see no harm in it."

But Damaris, who came hastening up a moment later, was horrified. "How can you, Gillian?" she hissed. "The woman's a heathen. And she's dirty. Look at her hair. It might have—things—in it."

"Now, Damaris, don't get on your high ropes," Gillian said as she prepared to follow the gypsy girl. "Nothing will happen to me. You'll see, I'll be back before the cat washes behind his ears."

The gypsy ushered Gillian into the dilapidated wagon,

after first chasing from the interior of the vehicle a rather large number of people of assorted ages. The minutes passed, and Araminta stirred uneasily. She murmured to Jason, "She's been in there for so long."

"She'll be right as a trivet," he assured her. Then he chuckled. "She probably wants to get full value for her shilling."

Soon after that Gillian emerged from the wagon. Her eyes were shining with excitement. "Araminta, I had no idea that gypsies could tell fortunes in so many ways—with a crystal ball, or Tarot cards, or just by reading one's palm."

"Which method did you choose?"

Gillian grinned. "All of them. I owe the lady another two shillings."

"And did you like your fortune?"

"Oh, yes."

"Well?"

But Gillian shook her head. "It's a secret," she said mysteriously.

Coming up to claim her extra two shillings, the gypsy woman beamed with delight when Jason handed her a pound note. "I knowed ye was a proper gentry-cove the instant I cast me winkers over ye," she told him. "Let me do somefing fer ye, ter show how much I 'preciate yer kindness. I'll read yer palm fer free. The other young ladies, too." She held out her hand invitingly.

"Why not?" said the Duke with a good-natured smile. "Lady Araminta, will you go first?"

"Oh, of course. You know I'm up to every rig and row in town," said Araminta, laughing. She extended her hand to the gypsy.

First putting her hand to her forehead as if to collect her powers, the woman looked intently into Araminta's palm. "I see love," she said sibilantly. "Ye'll have a fine husband, tall, handsome, wealthy."

"I like that," said Araminta. "When will I meet this

paragon?"

"Ye've knowed him fer some time, lady. But true love won't be easy fer ye. I see another woman. She be a beautiful mort, wi' hair like the sun." The gipsy sucked in her breath sharply. "Be on your guard, lady. Ye'll face danger—nay, 'tisn't clear. Mayhap 'tis a friend who is in danger?" The woman lifted her head. "That be all I see. If ye'd wish me ter deal the Tarot cards—"

"Thank you, but no. I fancy I've learned quite enough about my future!" said Araminta, withdrawing her hand. "Damaris, will you go next?"

But Damaris edged away in alarm to a position nearer the Duke. The gypsy murmured under her breath to Araminta, "It be jist as well. Sometimes I can't read the palms o' the young uns. Their futures be too far ahead fer me. The other young lady, now—*she'll* be having a grand future!"

"Well, then, Duke, it seems to be your turn," said Araminta saucily. "Or are you reluctant to find out what's in store for you?"

"No more than you, certainly!" Jason held out his hand. The gypsy took a quick, cursory look at his palm. And disaster struck. "Ye'll have riches and a great house and a beautiful wife and many young uns," she informed him. Unexpectedly she reached out to grasp Araminta's hand and joined it to Jason's. Bathing them both in the radiance of her smile, she added, "Nuffing but happiness awaits ye and yer fine lady 'ere, yer honor."

Araminta refused to look at Damaris. Nor, for one of the few times in her life, could she think of anything to say. The silence dragged leadenly. Then Jason smiled, saying to Damaris, "Are you quite certain you don't wish to take your turn, my dear? Considering the falderal your Aunt Araminta and I have been listening to, there's no telling what the gypsy will say about *your* fortune. Perhaps you'll discover you're destined to become

153

the next queen of England!"

There was a tiny pause, and then Damaris replied with a tinkling laugh, "La, sir, what would the Princess Charlotte have to say to that?"

Chapter Nine

"What a squeeze," Araminta murmured to Henrietta, as they waited with Damaris on the staircase of Lady Onscott's house in Manchester Square for the opportunity to greet their hostess in the receiving line. "Half of London must be here."

"Everyone who matters in the Ton," Henrietta murmured back complacently. "I understand some people literally fight to receive an invitation to one of Lady Onscott's rout parties. Well, of course, she *is* such a prominent Whig hostess. Almost as prominent as Lady Holland."

Later, edging her way with Henrietta and Damaris into the drawing room, Araminta found herself wondering why invitations to Onscott House were so coveted. The room was very crowded, crammed with at least twice the number of people who might have constituted a comfortable gathering, and the noise level from so many people talking at once made conversation difficult.

"What are we expected to do now?" Araminta said into Henrietta's ear. "Will there be dancing? Cards? Music?"

"Oh, dear, no. Not at a rout party. No, we'll just wander about the drawing room and the other public rooms, greeting friends and acquaintances, and then after a bit we'll go home again."

"That's *all*? What it amounts to is we've come here merely to see and be seen?" At Henrietta's reproachful look, Araminta subsided, resigning herself to the dullest evening she'd yet spent in London. A few moments later, however, she heard Damaris exclaim with pleasure, "Oh, there's the Duke, Mama. But who's the lady with him?"

Henrietta said in surprised tones, "Why, it's Lady Salford. I had no idea she was in London."

Looking up, Araminta spotted Jason walking toward them, a young woman on his arm. He was experiencing no difficulty making his way through the crowded room. His unconscious air of serene self-confidence in his own precedence seemed to cause his fellow guests to melt before him to right and left, rather, Araminta thought wickedly, like Moses parting the Red Sea. Coming up to them, he said with a smile, "Lady Middleton, I'm sure you remember my sister, Lady Salford. Felicity, Lady Araminta Beresford and Miss Damaris Middleton."

"Why, of course I remember you, Lady Salford," said Henrietta warmly. "We met often in the year you came out. Are you and your husband here for the Season?"

"Alas, no. I arrived this afternoon without my husband to spend a few days only with Jason. Well, perhaps I can stretch my stay to a sennight."

Araminta observed with interest that the former Lady Felicity Windham, now the Countess of Salford, was a softer, feminine version of her brother. Like him, she was tall and slender, with the same dark hair, bright blue eyes, and that provocative cleft in the chin.

"Augustus and I had every intention of opening Salford House for the Season," the countess went on ruefully, "but then the children came down with the measles! They're recovering now, but they still aren't very stout. Nor am I, in Augustus's opinion, after I helped nurse the children for several weeks. Solicitous husband that he is, he insisted I indulge myself for a spell among the fleshpots of London! But here I am, rattling on as usual, forgetting my manners! Lady Araminta, Miss Middleton, I'm so happy to meet you."

"How do you do, Lady Salford," said Araminta, smiling in response to the other's easy friendliness. "Speaking of fleshpots," she added with a laugh, "I fancy it's not likely you'll be tempted into dissipation in *this* place."

At this heresy, Henrietta bridled, and Damaris pursed her lips slightly in disapproval, but Araminta spotted a quick answering gleam of amusement in each of those two pairs of intensely blue eyes that were so much alike.

Casting a critical eye around the room, the Countess remarked to the Duke, "Lady Araminta is quite correct, Jason. Lady Onscott's parties always were a dead bore. Why did we come here tonight?"

"That's enough of your impudence, my girl," retorted Jason with a brotherly rudeness. "We came because I'd already accepted the invitation, and because Lady Middleton was to be a fellow guest, and I knew you'd wish to renew your acquaintance with her." He turned to Araminta. "Was the phaeton delivered on schedule today?"

"Indeed it was," Araminta replied, laughing. "My coachman recoiled at the sight of it! Ben says a bright red phaeton is immoral. He doesn't wish to be seen anywhere near me when I drive it in Hyde Park tomorrow."

Henrietta said anxiously, "I know you helped Araminta choose the carriage, Duke, but are you quite sure it's safe for her to drive a high-perch phaeton? It looked positively dangerous to me."

Jason laughed. "I have every confidence in Lady Araminta. She can drive to an inch."

Her eyes lighting up, the Countess exclaimed, "You're really going to drive a high-perch phaeton, Lady Araminta? Oh, how I envy you. I always longed to take the ribbons of a phaeton — any kind of phaeton — and Jason would never let me."

"And with good reason," declared her brother. "You can't drive. What a prime gudgeon I should be if I allowed you anywhere near a pair of sweet goers!"

Lady Salford made a face at him, and Araminta, enjoying the good-natured banter between the brother and sister, said to the Countess, "If the Duke won't permit you to tool *his* phaeton, perhaps you'd like to take the air in mine tomorrow? I promise not to overturn you."

"Oh, I'm not in the least worried. Like my brother, I have every confidence in you, Lady Araminta!"

"Jason was right. You *are* a pretty whip," Lady Salford said impulsively to Araminta.

"I don't make you nervous?"

"Oh, no. I must say, though, it's a very long way to the ground," said the Countess with a little shiver, looking down at the roadway from her seat beside Araminta. The rear wheels of the dashing "high flyer" were eight feet in diameter.

It was a perfect May afternoon, and Hyde Park was thronged with members of the Quality out to enjoy the brilliant sunshine. Heads had turned, and carriages had slowed, and horses had reined in from the moment Araminta had driven into the park with her passenger in the blindingly red high-perch phaeton. Secretly amused by the minor sensation she was causing, Araminta kept a straight face and pretended not to notice the stares, whether they were curious, admiring, or critical.

"I can't wait to tell Augustus about this when I get home," Lady Salford said, her eyes twinkling. "For a settled old matron, I feel all the crack!"

Araminta reined in the phaeton when Jason drew alongside in his curricle, Damaris seated at his side. "At home to a peg, I see," he observed to Araminta. "You'll be the talk of every drawing room in London tonight, and deservedly so."

"I collect I ought to explain to everyone that you deserve the credit," Araminta replied. "*You* chose the phaeton and the team."

"I prefer to blush unseen, thank you," he retorted. Raising a casual hand in farewell, he drove off.

"What a lovely girl, your niece," said the Countess, gazing after the curricle. "She's so young, though. So—so unformed. But what am I saying? Miss Middleton must be eighteen, nineteen, the same age as any other girl making her come out." She hesitated. "Tell me, are you in Lady Middleton's confidence?"

"Moderately, I daresay," replied Araminta cautiously. "Why do you ask?"

"Well . . . Oh, the devil, I won't be mealy-mouthed! Do you know about Jason and Miss Middleton?"

"In what respect?"

Lady Salford burst out laughing. "Oh, I like you, Araminta! May I call you that? And please, I'm Felicity. As I'm very sure you know, I'm talking about Jason's plans to marry your niece at the end of the Season. Will you think me a real busybody if I tell you I came to London primarily to see what kind of a girl Damaris is? I do want Jason to be happy." She hesitated again. "You see, I always thought he'd marry someone a little older, someone with more—more *spark*. Someone who'd put him in his place occasionally, which I can assure you he often richly deserves!"

The Countess's remark struck an answering chord in Araminta. She, too, had wondered once or twice lately if Damaris, with her gentle, yielding ways, was quite the right wife for Jason. Not, of course, that it was anyone's affair except the Duke's! But refusing to be drawn, Araminta kept her eyes forward, concentrating on her driving. She felt a modest swell of pride as she lifted her whip and jauntily took a fly off her leader's ear. After a moment she said noncommittally, "You seem very fond of your brother."

"I am, yes. It's odd in a way, because I really didn't know him well until I was almost grown. Jason is eleven years older than I am, and as a child I rarely saw him. I'm sure he thought of me as a perpetual infant until I turned fifteen. My father died then, and Jason became the head of the family. Suddenly he discovered that I was on my way to becoming an adult. We became very good friends after that. My brother Rupert and Jason were always very close, almost like twins. They were less than two years apart in age." Felicity sighed. "I was so worried about Jason when we received the terrible news that Rupert had died at Waterloo. Jason grieved so much that I actually feared for his health. Oh, there was no outward indication. To most people he was his usual suave self. But *I* knew. That's why I took it as a good sign when he told me he was thinking of getting married. It meant that he was healing."

Araminta listened sympathetically. She was seeing a softer side of Jason, a side he apparently revealed only to those with whom he was very close.

"Lady Araminta, what a spanking turn-out! If you didn't already have a passenger, I'd beg you to take up a weary pedestrian."

At the sound of the laughing voice, Felicity gave a sudden gasp, and Araminta, with a muttered "Oh, the deuce," reluctantly halted her team. Even as she gazed down into Silvanus Manning's smiling face, she saw his expression alter dramatically as he recognized her passenger.

"Felicity." It was almost a whisper. Manning's face had turned pale.

Felicity was also pale. Making what was obviously an enormous effort of will, she managed to say with a semblance of calm, "How do you do, Lord Manning. It's been — oh, I can't remember how many years — since we last met."

"I remember exactly. It was the second of March, 1808. We were having breakfast at a little inn near the cathedral in York," Manning said slowly. He stared at Felicity as if mesmerized.

A sudden color showed in Felicity's cheeks. In a quick burst of enlightenment, Araminta surmised that Manning was recalling his ill-fated elopement with Felicity. That inn in York was probably the place where Jason had caught up with the pair.

"Was it that long ago?" Taking a deep breath, Felicity raised her chin, fixing Manning with a level, unsmiling look. "I haven't thought about that time for so many years that I really don't recall much about it. I've been too busy with my home and family."

Bravo, thought Araminta. Or was it *brava?* No matter. She was proud of Felicity.

Manning gave a start, a quick flush replacing his pallor. Then, recovering his poise, he said, "Yes, I'd heard that you were the mother of a young family. How many children do you have, Lady Salford?"

"Four. Three boys and a girl."

"I'm happy for you. Are you and Lord Salford here for the Season?"

"Oh, no. I'll be returning to Gloucestershire in a few days."

"I see. Then allow me to wish you a safe journey home. It's been a great pleasure seeing you again." His urbane mask once more in place, he bowed formally to Felicity and walked around the phaeton to look up at Araminta. "I collect you're bored to tears by the subject, Lady Araminta," he said with a whimsical smile, "but Madame Lacoste still cherishes the ambition to go to Vauxhall Gardens. Could I possibly persuade you to reconsider my invitation?"

"You're kindness itself, my lord," replied Araminta, "but my answer must be the same. My calendar is filled for weeks ahead."

Lord Manning struck his forehead in mock despair. "I'm desolated. Or I would be, if I didn't know I'd be seeing you often, even if not as my guest. You're attending the Lymond ball on Wednesday? Good. I'll see you then." With another bow and a jaunty wave, he was off.

As Araminta put the phaeton in motion, Felicity said, her voice sounding constricted, "I feel one of my headaches coming on, Araminta. Would you mind very much if we cut short our drive?"

"No, not all."

During the short journey from Hyde Park to her brother's house, Felicity seemed lost in her thoughts, thoughts that shadowed her pretty face. Arriving at Harwood House, she roused herself to say, with a rather forced smile, "I haven't been very good company for the last few minutes, have I? Won't you come in and let me offer you a cup of tea, a glass of wine? Please. There's something I'd like to discuss with you."

In the drawing room of Harwood House, Felicity made small talk until after the footman had brought in the tea tray and left the room. Then she said, hesitating, "I fear you'll think me a hopeless gabblemonger for asking, but . . . are you and Lord Manning good friends?"

Stirring liberal amounts of sugar and milk into her tea, Araminta shook her head, saying, "No, we're the merest acquaintants, and I intend to keep our relationship on exactly that level."

"I fancy that isn't *his* intention, however," Felicity blurted. "Forgive me. I have no right to pry. No right to give you advice, either. But I must tell you, I know Silvanus Manning very well. I also know, from something Jason told me, that you're a considerable heiress, and I could see for myself in Hyde Park today that Silvanus is throwing out his lures to you. I don't say he's interested in you only for your fortune. He may well be very fond of you. But don't admit him into your circle of friendship, Araminta. He's—he's not a nice man." Felicity paused, biting her lip. "I wonder—it's possible you've heard some ancient rumors about me—"

"I don't pay any mind to rumors."

Felicity smiled crookedly. "I see you know all about my elopement with Silvanus. Henrietta Middleton, perhaps? It's such an ancient scandal. Most people stopped talking about it years ago. It's not important anymore, and I wouldn't have brought it up if we hadn't met him in the park today—"

"Felicity, there's no need for you to distress yourself like this," Araminta interrupted. "Thank you for your warning, but I'm in no danger at all of falling in love with Lord Manning. Almost from the first moment I met him, I realized he was a fortune hunter."

"I'm glad." Felicity still seemed troubled. "There's one more

162

thing. Be careful how you refuse his offer of marriage, if it should come to that. Let him off lightly. Try not to injure his self-esteem. I think he nurses grudges." Averting her eyes, she said in a low, strained voice, "When Jason caught up with us at that inn in York, and I agreed to go home with him, Silvanus took me aside and told me he'd find some way to get even with me and Jason if it took him the rest of his life."

Araminta felt a frisson of foreboding invading her heart, but she quickly shook it off. "Oh, I shouldn't worry about a toothless threat like that. How long has it been? Seven, eight years? He hasn't caused you any trouble in all that time, has he?"

"N-no." Felicity's face brightened. "Oh, Araminta, you're like a breath of fresh air. I'd like so much to know you better. I've been so busy rearing children that I don't have any friends my own age anymore. How I wish I could stay a little longer in London. But the children—"

"The children will be fully recovered from the measles very soon now, won't they? I'm giving a ball for Damaris in three weeks' time. Why don't you and your husband plan to attend it?"

"We'll be there. Augustus hates London, and he'll try to use the children's measles as an excuse to stay in the country, but I shan't let him," said Felicity. "And of course, if we're to open the town house and take part in all the activities of the Season, I shall need some new clothes. Will you go shopping with me tomorrow?"

"Take care," said the Duke, striding into the drawing room. "My dear sister, I'm happy you've decided to spend some time with us during the Season, but do think twice about going shopping with Lady Araminta. I fear she's a bad influence. According to her niece, Damaris, Lady Araminta bought out half the shops in London when she first arrived. Augustus may be full of juice, but you wouldn't want to drive him to Point-non-plus!"

Chapter Ten

As the Harwood landau swung around the corner into Bruton Street, Araminta looked at the bandbox on her knees and at the parcels on the seat opposite her, and remarked to Lady Salford with a laugh, "When I get out of the carriage, you'll have much more room for your purchases."

Felicity gazed, conscience-stricken, at the mound of parcels. "I must have been queer in my attic to buy all these things. I couldn't wear them all in *two* Seasons. What will Augustus say? For that matter, what will Jason say?"

Araminta said merrily, "He'll look at you in that toplofty way of his and inform you that he told you so! Your brother will lay all this extravagance at my door. He considers me a bad influence!"

"Oh, don't talk fustian, Araminta!" Felicity stole another look at the parcels. "Well, I daresay I should thank you for helping me to choose all these lovely things. I appreciate it. I think."

Araminta laughed again, shifting the bandbox she was holding to the top of the pile on the opposite seat as the landau came to a stop in front of Middleton House and the footman opened the door and let down the steps. Stepping out of the carriage, she looked up at Felicity, saying, "Goodbye. I enjoyed shopping with you. I'll see you before you return home, I'm sure. Perhaps at the Lymond ball?"

With a parting wave, she walked up the steps of the house, accompanied by one of Felicity's grooms. The footman who answered her ring seemed distracted, keeping his head half turned to listen to the sound of voices coming from the drawing room. "It's Miss Middleton, my lady," he said in answer to Araminta's questioning look. "A French lady came to see 'er, and before long I starts to 'ear screeching, like, and I begins to wonder if somefing might be amiss in there, do y'see, but I dunno — I didn't quite like to go in wifout I was sent for."

"Thank you, Beeson. I'll look into it."

As she approached the drawing room, Araminta could distinctly hear a sudden loud wail. She opened the door and entered the room, saying, "Pray forgive me for interrupting you, Damaris."

"Oh, Aunt Araminta, I'm so happy to see you," exclaimed Damaris in heartfelt relief. "This — this lady seems to be very distressed, and I'd like to help her if I could, but she's speaking so fast, and you know my French isn't fluent like yours, and of course dear Madame Lacoste always speaks to me more slowly. I can make out a word or two here and there — I hear my name and the Duke's, and something about a — a baby . . ." Damaris broke off in embarrassment.

Araminta turned an interested gaze on the strange young woman standing near Damaris. The newcomer was a strikingly pretty girl, dark of hair and eyes. She was also very large with child. She had fallen silent when Araminta entered the room, but now she burst into a torrent of French interspersed with wrenching sobs. She fell to the floor, clutching at a bewildered Damaris's knees. *"Chère Mademoiselle* Middleton, you have such a kind face, and I know that you must have a kind heart, also. I cannot believe that you will leave me in my misery, poor desolate creature that I am."

Araminta tapped the agitated young woman on the shoulder. She said in French, *"Tiens, Madame.* Mademoiselle Middleton's French is not fluent. She doesn't understand what you're saying. You may speak to me. I am Lady Araminta Beresford."

Slowly the stranger disengaged herself from Damaris,

who moved abruptly away, her delicate features rigid with distaste.

"*Grâce à Dieu!* To find someone in this great cold unfriendly city who can speak a Christian tongue!" The young woman rose with difficulty, leaning for support on a nearby chair. "It is permitted that I sit down? I am *enceinte,* as you see."

"*Oui, certainement.*" Araminta seated herself on a sofa opposite the Frenchwoman. "Now, then, Madame. You seem to be in some distress. How may I help you? What is your name?"

"I am Stéphanie Windham. Lady Rupert Windham, I believe you would say. I am the widow of the Duke of Harwood's younger brother."

Araminta's eyes widened. Glancing at Damaris, she said to her in English, "The duke had only the one brother, did he not? Lord Rupert? Who was unmarried, surely, when he fell at Waterloo?"

"Araminta! Is this creature claiming to be Rupert's widow?"

"It seems so." Turning back to "Lady Rupert," Araminta said, "There must be some mistake. If Lord Rupert Windham left a widow at his death, his family and friends are unaware of it."

"*Sacré,* I assure you there is one person who has been aware of my identity for many months, and that is *Monsieur le Duc,* himself!" exclaimed Stéphanie.

"What's she saying about the duke?"

Ignoring Damaris's anguished question, Araminta tossed Stéphanie a quelling stare, saying coldly, "I cannot allow you to defame the Duke of Harwood. Please explain yourself."

Stéphanie sat up straighter in her chair, clasping her hands together tightly over her enlarged abdomen. She fastened her eyes on Araminta with an almost frightening intensity. "I was born Stéphanie Despard, in a little village near Ninove, west of Brussels. *Milord* Rupert was stationed there for some weeks before the great battle. We fell violently in love at first sight of each other, *vous comprenez,* and we were married just two days before Rupert was ordered into action in the Waterloo campaign. This is his child I carry beneath my heart."

"You've waited until rather a late date to assert your claim, *n'est-ce pas?*"

"*Pas du tout, Miladi* Beresford. I wrote to *Monsieur le Duc* immediately after the battle, as soon as I received the news of my beloved husband's death. I wrote again a few weeks later, when I knew I was *enceinte.* The Duke of Harwood ignored me, worse, he denied me any recognition as a member of his family. Finally, after months of waiting, I decided to come to London to see him, hoping that if I could talk to him in person he might see the justice of my case. Madame Beresford, I am destitute. I have no money, no friends, no place to bring my child when he is born, and yet the Duke will not help me. He says that I am a liar, a swindler. He will not even see me, he no longer answers my letters. Today, in desperation, I came to see Mademoiselle Middleton."

Araminta flashed a sharp look at the Belgian woman. "Why did you do that? You say you're a stranger here. What do you know of the Middleton family?"

For a moment Stéphanie seemed embarrassed. "Why, one asks about town for information, one hears things . . . Is it not true that *Monsieur le Duc* is *le gardien, le curateur* of Mademoiselle Middleton? And also I have heard — forgive me if it is not true — that Mademoiselle may soon be betrothed to him. So I thought that as a woman she might have more sympathy, more *tendresse,* than *Monsieur le Duc.* I hoped that she would intercede with him for me."

The girl certainly sounded sincere, Araminta thought. Could her story possibly be true? Well, there was one way to find out. She said quickly, "I assume that you have no proof of your relationship to Lord Rupert. Otherwise, in the face of such proof, the Duke of Harwood would hardly have refused to receive you."

"Proof? You want proof?" Stéphanie tore open her reticule. "There's your proof!" she cried, handing Araminta several letters, a small miniature set in an ornate pendant, and an official-looking document.

In spite of herself, Araminta was shaken as she stared down at the miniature. The dark-haired young man in the picture, with his bright blue eyes and deeply clefted chin, bore a strong resemblance to the Duke and also to Lady Salford. The miniature itself, needless to say, was no proof of marriage. Stéphanie could have acquired it in a number of ways, all of them questionable. Riffling through the letters, Araminta noted that the writer had pledged passionate and eternal love to his Stéphanie and had signed his name "Rupert." But again, without having seen a sample of Rupert's handwriting, who could say if the letters were genuine? The document—Stéphanie's marriage lines—was something else altogether. Next to Stéphanie Despard's name was that of her bridegroom, Rupert Octavianus Windham. The date was June 14, 1815.

Looking up with a troubled frown, Araminta asked, "Has the Duke of Harwood actually seen your marriage lines?"

"He has. Or rather, his agent has seen them. After he received my first letter, last summer, the Duke sent one of his hirelings to Belgium to investigate my story. I showed this man the miniature, the letters, my marriage lines, everything. I also directed him to the parish register in my village, where my marriage was recorded."

Araminta's frown deepened. "Apparently the Duke wasn't convinced. Why was that, do you suppose?"

"C'est tout simple, Miladi Beresford," declared Stéphanie with an angry toss of her head. "His noble Grace is a snob. If my child is a boy, he will be the duke's heir, at least until the duke himself fathers a son. My father is a butcher, vous savez, and Monsieur le Duc cannot bear the thought of a nobody's child being his heir. Probably also, in spite of his great wealth, he is a miser. If he acknowledges me and my child, he will be forced to part with enough money to enable us to live according to our station in life." Stéphanie's eyes flashed. "Do you know what he did, this man of honor, to

168

avoid giving me my due? He had his agent tear out the page in the parish register, hoping to cast doubt on my marriage. Fortunately, I have my marriage lines. I have never allowed this precious piece of paper out of my possession. Regardless of his cruelty, his—his duplicity, *Monsieur le Duc* cannot disprove the fact that I married my beloved Rupert on the day before the great battle began."

Damaris had been listening to the exchange of rapid French with growing frustration. Now she burst out, "Aunt Araminta, in the name of heaven, tell me what's going on!" She peered over Araminta's shoulder to look at the miniature. "Why, that looks like—it *is* Lord Rupert! How did this woman lay her hands on his likeness?"

As Stéphanie waited expectantly, her eager eyes glued to Araminta, the latter said carefully, "Damaris, I want you to stay calm. As I told you, this young woman claims to be Rupert Windham's widow and the future mother of his child. She has this miniature, some letters reporting to be from Rupert, and a marriage certificate which certainly seems to be genuine. She also says that the Duke refuses to recognize her claim out of pure snobbery."

Reaching out her hand for the letters and the marriage lines, Damaris studied them carefully. "These must be forgeries," she said scornfully. "Rupert Windham would never have lowered himself to marry a strumpet. As for the miniature, the woman could have stolen it." Contemptuously, she tossed the documents and the miniature to the floor in front of Stéphanie's chair. "There, that's where this refuse belongs. Tell the woman to go, Aunt Araminta, before I ask the servants to throw her out."

The English words might have been incomprehensible, but Damaris's gesture was not. Throwing herself to the floor to pick up her treasured belongings, Stéphanie began to rock back and forth on her knees, wailing loudly and despairingly. The sounds reminded Araminta of the professional women mourners whose keening cries she had heard at several harem funerals in Syria.

"Aunt Araminta, can't you stop the woman? She'll soon

arouse the whole house."

But Damaris was already too late. The door opened just enough to allow the footman, Beeson, to peer cautiously into the drawing room. A moment later, Henrietta pushed past him, followed by Odile and Gillian. "Merciful heavens, who is making that dreadful noise?" Henrietta exclaimed. "We could hear it all the way back to the morning room—" She paused, staring in stupefaction at Stéphanie, who, seemingly unaware of the presence of the newcomers, continued to rock herself back and forth. Her movements, however, were less vigorous, and her wailing had become little more than plaintive cries.

"Who is this woman? And what is she doing in my drawing room?" Henrietta inquired, holding herself stiffly. After hearing a short account of her visitor's story, she said coldly, "The woman's lying, of course. Her bastard child the heir to one of the greatest dukedoms in England? The Duke of Harwood a defrauder of widows and orphans? I can't imagine how she had the effrontery to invent such calumnies . . . and then to inflict herself on my daughter! The Duke will be furious."

Araminta said quietly, "But what if she isn't lying? What if her story is true?"

Henrietta gasped. "I cannot credit my ears! Are you telling me that you believe there is any substance to these outrageous charges made by a person who's probably no better than a common street tart against so eminent a personage as the Duke of Harwood?"

"I'm not sure what I believe," replied Araminta honestly. "If the girl's story is true, it seems incredible that an honorable man like the Duke would have refused to recognize his brother's widow. But then, what about the young woman's marriage lines? They looked genuine to me, and I understand that the Duke himself has never seen the marriage certificate, or these letters either. Perhaps his agent made a mistake when he investigated Mademoiselle Despard's claims. If we were to help her to a personal meeting with the Duke, she might be able to convince him of the justice of her claim."

"Help her—" Henrietta recoiled, and Damaris chimed in indignantly, "Really, Aunt Araminta, this is too bad of you! Help this—this person to prove her wicked tale? No, it's as I told you. We should have her put out on the street where she belongs."

Araminta had been speaking to her half sister and her niece in English. Odile, whose command of the language—or at least her understanding of it—had been improving rapidly since her arrival in London, now favored Henrietta and Damaris with a withering stare. *"Mon Dieu,"* she cried. "Never in all my life have I seen such a lack of charity toward a poor unfortunate wronged woman!" She rushed to Stéphanie, placing a tender arm around the girl to help her into a chair. *"Pauvre petite,* we must see what we can do to help you." Her French, as she continued to speak in low-voiced, soothing concern to Stéphanie, poured out faster and faster. Araminta, listening with only half an ear, caught scattered impassioned words and phrases—*scèlerat, mauvais sujet, faire honneur à ces affaires*—from which she gathered that Odile was making mincemeat of the Duke of Harwood's reputation.

"Well! I had thought better of Madame Lacoste," an outraged Henrietta was saying, when Odile called out urgently, "Araminta, *vite, vite!* The child, it arrives!"

Hurrying over to Stéphanie, who was doubled over in what appeared to be severe pain, Araminta asked anxiously, "Do you really think the baby's coming, Odile? Perhaps Stéphanie—Mademoiselle Despard—Lady Rupert—oh, hang it, whatever she calls herself—is just having an attack of the cramp? A—a false alarm?"

"Not a false alarm, *Miladi* Beresford," murmured Stéphanie, lifting a wan face. "I am overdue, *vous savez,* and my—how do you say it—my waters, they have broken." She gasped, clutching her abdomen in a fresh contraction.

"Good God, that's torn it." Straightening, Araminta returned to Henrietta, saying, "Please have a chamber prepared immediately for Mademoiselle Despard's lying-in.

And send a servant for your doctor. The child could arrive at any time."

"You must be dicked in the nob! Allow a strumpet to use a bedchamber in my home for her lying-in? Never! She must leave immediately."

"But where would she go? She told me that she has no friends and no money, so I assume she's been living in a single room somewhere. We can't just turn her out, throw her on the mercies of some down-at-the-heel lodging keeper. Do have a little compassion."

"Where the creature goes is no concern of mine." Turning to summon a servant, Henrietta caught sight of her younger daughter, who had been standing quietly in the background, drinking in the situation with spellbound attention. "Gillian, you shouldn't be here. These goings-on are unsuitable for the ears of a young female. Pray go to your bedchamber. I'll speak to you later." After Gillian's reluctant departure, Henrietta pulled vigorously on the bell rope. When the footman appeared, she snapped, motioning to Stéphanie, "Procure a hackney cab for this person."

"No hackney cab," Araminta intervened. The glance she turned on Henrietta was cold and unsmiling. She said to the footman, "Tell my groom to have my carriage brought around. I will be escorting Mademoiselle Despard to her home."

During the few minutes that elapsed before the carriage drew up in front of the door, it seemed to Araminta's nervous gaze that Stéphanie's accouchement became speedily more imminent. As she and Odile came out the door of Middleton House, supporting Stéphanie on either side, the Belgian woman doubled over in pain. Araminta motioned to her coachman. "Quick, Ben. Have the groom give you a hand and carry Mademoiselle to the carriage."

At that moment Lord Manning drove his curricle into Bruton Street. Making a hasty stop, he jumped down from the vehicle and flipped his reins to his tiger. "Good God, what's this, Lady Araminta, Madame Lacoste?" he exclaimed as he came up to them, staring at the coachman and the groom, who between them were lifting a groaning Stéphanie into the carriage. "That young woman is about to give birth, if I'm not mistaken. Can I be of any help?"

Odile clutched at his arm, her eyes swimming with tears. "Oh, *Milord* Manning, how glad I am to see you. You will be able to tell us, Araminta and me, what we should do. We are at our wits' ends. This *pauvre petite,* the widow of *Monsieur le Duc's* brother, has no money, no home, no *nothing,* and Monsieur will take no responsibility for her."

Manning's eyes narrowed. "The lady's a Windham? Poor girl. Naturally, I should be only too happy to —"

Araminta suppressed an unladylike impulse to curse the unlucky chance that had brought Manning into the situation. There would be little she could do to curb his spiteful tongue if he got wind of embarrassing gossip and decided to turn it against the Windham family.

However, she kept the annoyance out of her voice as she said, "Thank you, Lord Manning, but there's no cause for you to concern yourself. We have the situation well in hand. We'll take the lady to her lodgings and then find a doctor for her." She went to the open door of the carriage, peering in. "Mademoiselle — Madame — Despard, what's your direction?"

A quavering voice answered weakly. "My rooms are in St. Giles, off the High Street. A side street called Sylvester's Alley. *Miladi* Beresford, could we hurry a little?"

"Drive to St. Giles," Araminta ordered her coachman. "Odile, are you coming with us?"

"One moment, Lady Araminta," said Lord Manning, giving Odile's hand a quieting pat. "I cannot allow you to go into St. Giles parish without an escort. You and Madame Lacoste are newcomers to London. You doubtless are unaware that the area is one of the worst stews in the city. If you insist on going there, I'll follow along behind you in my curricle."

Odile gazed up at him, her eyes wide with gratitude. "Oh, thank you, *Milord* Manning. I shall feel so safe with you beside us while *chère* Araminta and I perform our act of mercy."

"Odile. Please get into the carriage and wait for me. Try to make Mademoiselle Despard more comfortable," Araminta said sharply. Making an effort, she smiled at Manning. "I thank you for your good intentions, but as you can see, I already have an escort in my coachman and two sturdy grooms." With a friendly nod of dismissal, she turned to climb into the carriage.

"Your pardon, Lady Araminta." Manning spoke firmly to her back. "I couldn't forgive myself if any harm came to you. I shall follow along behind in my curricle."

"*Chère* Araminta, this is a dreadful place, *hein?* How could the little Stéphanie bear to live here?" With a moue of disgust, Odile pulled the skirts of her pelisse closer around her to avoid contact with the grimy walls of the litter-strewn hallway.

"I presume she had little choice of lodgings. She told us that she was out of funds." Araminta spoke calmly, but she had been as appalled as Odile to enter the run-down house in a garbage-choked alley off St. Giles High Street. If she had not arrived here in a carriage, accompanied by her elderly coachman, Ben, and several sturdy young grooms, she knew it would not have been safe for her to venture into the area. Short though her stay in London had been, she had become aware of the rookeries of lawlessness and criminality that existed in the parishes lying immediately outside the boundaries of the City. She glanced at Manning's tall form, standing beside her and Odile. Vexed as she was with him for insisting on coming with her, she had to admit that his presence gave her an added feeling of security.

"This birth, it is taking so long. Could something have gone wrong?" said Hippolyte Augé suddenly, staring at the closed door opposite. He winced as a muffled cry of pain came from inside the room.

Araminta looked sympathetically at the thin, dark young Frenchman, who, he informed her, had been living in the

174

room next to Stéphanie's in the lodging house. Araminta and Odile had encountered him when they brought Stéphanie into the house, carried in the arms of one of the grooms, and Hippolyte had volunteered to fetch a doctor.

"You seem quite fond of Mademoiselle Despard, monsieur," said Araminta. "I understood her to say that she had no friends in London."

"No friends who could help her," said the young man bitterly. "Myself, I liked the poor lady. I felt sorry for her, coming all alone to this strange, cold land. I tried to do what I could, but that was precious little. It comforted her, I think, that I spoke her language, that I could tell her how to find her way around in this vast city, but I couldn't direct her to any persons of influence who might advise her, I couldn't give her money when she exhausted her funds." He spread his hands. "I work as a waiter in a French restaurant in Soho. *Vous comprenez,* I earn barely enough to keep body and soul together." He smiled at the two women. "It's like a little miracle that you kind ladies—oh, and this kind gentleman, also—have come to her aid." He broke off as the doctor emerged from Stéphanie's room.

"Your friend has a fine boy. It wasn't a difficult delivery, and she should recover her strength very soon," said the beaming doctor, rolling down his sleeves and shrugging himself into his coat. His attitude had changed dramatically since his arrival at the house several hours before. His practice lay outside the squalid confines of St. Giles, and he had reluctantly agreed to come here to attend Stéphanie only after the most desperate of entreaties by Hippolyte. One look, however, at the elegant toilets of Stéphanie's friends had apparently convinced him that he was not dealing with penniless foreigners.

"Oh, I must see the precious *bébé*," cried Odile. She rushed past the doctor into Stéphanie's room.

"Thank you, Doctor, for coming so promptly," said Araminta, reaching into her reticule. "I'm sure Mademoiselle Despard had excellent care. Please accept this with my thanks."

175

The doctor's eyes widened as he glanced at the two golden guineas that Araminta had deposited in his palm. "A pleasure to be of service, ma'am." He cleared his throat. "With respect, may I suggest that the young mother and her child might recover more quickly in — er — more healthful surroundings?"

"I'm sure you're right, Doctor." Araminta looked around the dingy hallway with distaste. Shifting to French, she said to Hippolyte Augé, "The doctor thinks, and I agree, that your friend Stéphanie should move to more comfortable rooms. Will you help her find something appropriate? Money won't be a problem."

Hippolyte's face lighted up. "You are an angel, madame. May I suggest Marylebone? It is a very nice area, where there are still a great many French residents. They came here as *émigrés* at the time of the Revolution, you understand, and never went back to France. Some of them are willing to let rooms."

"Excellent. Will you make the arrangements? And let me know Stéphanie's new direction? She knows where I live. Mind, there's no need for you to quibble about terms with these landlords. I want Stéphanie and the child to be comfortable. And now I think it's time for us to make the acquaintance of the newest resident of London."

Hippolyte Augé said eagerly, "I may come with you, madame, to see the *bébé?*"

"Yes, come along. Lord Manning?"

He shook his head, grimacing. "No, thank you. A lying-in chamber is the last place I would wish to be."

The tiny airless room, though furnished with only a few pieces of shabby furniture — a bed, a small chest of drawers, a rickety table and chair — seemed impossibly crowded when Araminta and Hippolyte joined Odile at Stéphanie's bedside. The new young mother, though she seemed tired from the birth, smiled with happiness as she lifted the blanket from her son's face.

"See, I told you my child would be a boy," she told Araminta. "He looks exactly like my adorable Rupert, I think. A true Windham! And as of the moment, the next Duke of Harwood!"

Privately, Araminta considered that the tiny wizened red face bore no resemblance at all either to Lord Rupert Windham's picture, or to Jason and Felicity, but she said merely, "Congratulations on your son's birth. Monsieur Augé and I have a little scheme to make life easier for you, but we can talk about that later."

Stéphanie reached out to take Araminta's hand. "You've already done so much for me, *Miladi* Beresford. But for you and Madame Lacoste, I might have given birth to my child on the street."

"Not at all. We were glad to help. And it's not Lady Beresford. I'm Lady Araminta." Motioning to Odile, Araminta added, "We'll leave you now to get some rest."

Outside the room, Araminta handed Odile a handful of coins, saying, "Would you be afraid to stay here without me if I left you for a spell? I could leave one or both of the grooms with you."

Odile looked puzzled. "No, I should be quite all right. But where are you going?"

"I'll tell you about it later," Araminta replied evasively. "While I'm gone, see if you can arrange to have another woman, perhaps someone living in the house, stay with Stéphanie. Perhaps the landlord could suggest someone. I don't think Stéphanie should be alone just now. In the meantime, of course, Hippolyte will be looking for new lodgings for her. Have some food sent in for her, and ask the landlady to bring fresh sheets and more candles. I'll send the carriage back for you in about two hours' time."

"Mais oui, certainement. I will go see the landlord immediately." Looking excited and self-important, Odile bustled away.

"I'd be happy to remain here with Madame Lacoste if you wish," said the Viscount. "In fact, why don't you allow me to drive her home when she finishes her arrangements?"

Araminta disliked the idea intensely. Staying here with Odile would give the Viscount an opportunity to pump her and Hippolyte about Stéphanie, in the event that he was curious. On the other hand, Araminta could hardly force Manning to leave the house, and in any case, he visited Middleton House so regularly that he could always ferret out from Odile any information that he wanted later. All Araminta could do was to try and contain the damage.

"Lord Manning," she said abruptly, "will you do me a great favor?"

"You've but to ask, you know that."

"I'll be frank with you. Mademoiselle Despard tells a very strange story. It might prove harmful to certain of my friends. Would you please put out of your mind any—any preconceptions about her until I've had the opportunity to look into her case?"

"I told you that all you had to do was ask. My mind is a blank, and I'll make every effort to keep it that way," said Manning cheerfully. "No preconceptions, not a one."

"Oh. Well, thank you. And yes, it would be a kindness if you waited with Odile and drove her home. I'd be easier in my mind."

The Viscount reached out to take Araminta's hands, holding them gently, but releasing them immediately when she pulled against his fingers. "Lady Araminta, I wish you'd ask me for favors more often. Don't you know I'd do anything to please you? Unfortunately, you give me so little opportunity to see you or talk to you!" For a moment he waited expectantly, and then, when she didn't reply immediately, he gave a smiling shrug. "Come, you'll at least let me escort you out to your carriage?"

Ushered into the drawing room of Harwood House by a silent-footed butler, Araminta was too tense to sit down while she waited for the Duke to appear. She paced up and down on the thick-piled Persian carpet, fighting a cowardly impulse to leave the room and the house.

She didn't want to be here. The visit was very likely to result in a quarrel with Jason, and yet she would have transgressed her own standards of justice and fair play if she had stayed away. Almost despite herself, she'd become convinced of the truth of Stéphanie Despard's story, and had decided that she must intercede for the girl with Jason. At the very least, she felt obligated to inform him of the birth of Stéphanie's child. But she wasn't hopeful about the possibility of influencing him. It wasn't that she doubted his code of honor, his innate sense of decency. However, she knew how much pride he took in his family lineage, and she knew also, from past experience, that he wasn't given to easy change in his opinions or his ideas. If he believed he had good and sufficient reason to doubt Stéphanie's story, it was going to be very difficult to persuade him to think otherwise.

"Lady Araminta."

At the sound of the Duke's voice, she looked up to see him standing in the doorway with Felicity, both of them dressed for the street.

"I can see this isn't a good time to call," said Araminta hastily. "You're about to go out."

"Felicity and I were merely planning to pay a duty visit to our great-aunt Maria," said Jason, advancing into the room. "You've saved us from a very boring half an hour—" He broke off, looking intently at Araminta. "Is something wrong?"

"I—yes. I'm not sure," Araminta floundered. She glanced from the Duke to his sister. "Actually, it—it concerns family. If I could speak to both of you . . ."

"Of course. Won't you sit down?" Jason settled himself into an armchair. "Now, then, what's this about a family matter?" he demanded, his expression puzzled. "And what family, by the by? Yours or mine?" Suddenly he chuckled. "Is it Gillian? Has that saucy piece found another school she wishes to attend?"

"No, this has nothing to do with Gillian." Araminta took a deep breath. "I've come to talk to you about Stéphanie Despard."

Jason's brows drew together and his blue eyes turned

179

chilly. "Stéphanie Despard?" he asked curtly. "What have you to do with that woman?"

"She came to visit Damaris today, since you'd refused to see her."

"She came to visit Damaris?" Jason echoed incredulously. His mouth hardened. "If you know I've refused to see her, then you know I'm not interested in discussing her," he said even more curtly.

Araminta's temper began to flare. "Well, if you're not interested in Stéphanie, you ought to be," she snapped. "While she was at Henrietta's house this afternoon, she went into labor, and shortly afterwards she delivered a son."

"Araminta!" Felicity's face flushed a deep crimson. "As an unmarried woman, you really shouldn't speak of such things to a gentleman! And who, pray, is this Stéphanie?"

"Oh, we all know that Lady Araminta doesn't hesitate to speak her mind about anything," said Jason coldly. "Stéphanie Despard is a Belgian woman who claims to be Rupert's widow. Now that she's had a son, I presume she'll also claim that the child is my heir."

"Rupert married?" Felicity exclaimed. "Surely not. While he was in Belgium, before the battle, he wrote to me often, and in almost every letter he'd go into raptures about some new charmer who'd captured his heart. He seemed to fall in love with a different girl every week, but I'd swear he never came close to proposing marriage. Who is this Stéphanie Despard?"

"She's the daughter of a man who kept a butcher shop in a little town near where Rupert was stationed," Jason replied, his lip curling. "Ravishingly pretty, I'm told, but common as dirt."

Felicity's jaw dropped. "I don't believe it. Oh, I know Rupert was active in the petticoat line, but he'd never have considered *marrying* a girl like that!"

"I agree with you. The girl's a fraud. You've been taken in by a clever liar, Lady Araminta. Last summer, when I received the first of many letters from Mademoiselle Despard, I, of course, took steps to investigate her story, sending my secretary to Belgium as my agent. I did this as a matter of simple justice, even though I considered it virtually impossible that my brother, even though he'd always had a tendency to become enamored of barques of frailty, would have lowered himself to marry the daughter of a common butcher. My secretary learned almost immediately that there had been no civil marriage as required by the Code Civil. Mademoiselle Despard herself freely admitted this; she said that Rupert's decision to marry her was a hasty one, that he wanted to make her his wife before he went off to battle, promising to enter into a legal ceremony later. Therefore, whether or not a religious ceremony was actually performed, this woman was never legally married to my brother. As to the child, he may or may not be Rupert's son. I will point out to you, however, that the battle of Waterloo took place on the eighteenth of June, 1815. It is now the month of May, 1816."

"But that's . . ." Felicity paused, her brow creased in thought, her lips moving silently. "Rupert died almost eleven months ago," she exclaimed triumphantly. "Even if this girl conceived as late as the day before the battle, she should have given birth weeks ago."

"I can count as well as you can," declared Araminta with a hint of asperity. "There are such things, you know, as ten- or even eleven-month babies." She looked at Jason. "What about Stéphanie's marriage lines? The certificate appeared genuine to me."

"Mademoiselle Despard allowed my secretary to glance at her marriage lines, and several letters purporting to have been written to her by Rupert, for a few minutes only. She wouldn't permit my secretary to take away the documents for closer study, but he's convinced, even after such a cursory examination, that both the signature on the marriage certificate and the letters are well-done forgeries."

"But that's so flimsy a reason—only a brief glimpse at such important papers—to declare Stéphanie a fraud," protested Araminta. "Don't you think you're being unfair? Let's concede that her marriage may not be strictly legal, at least not in Belgium. She sincerely believes that she was married in her church and that her child is legitimate. Surely that entitles her to some consideration on your part. Oh, I don't mean that you should recognize her child as your heir, necessarily. But couldn't you provide her with an income? Welcome her as a member of the family?"

"So I might, if I were convinced of her 'sincerity.' I am not. I daresay she failed to tell you of another circumstance that casts doubt on her story. My secretary discovered that a page, recording the marriages that were performed in her village church during the period in which she claimed to have married Rupert, had been torn from the parish registry."

"As it happens, Stéphanie did tell me about that. She thinks that you had your agent destroy the page in an effort to discredit her."

Jason's eyes glinted with anger. "You think me capable of such behavior? You'd take this woman s word over mine?"

Felicity chimed in, her face troubled, "Yes, Araminta, surely you don't believe that Jason could be so unjust?"

"No, of course, Duke, I wouldn't take a stranger's word over yours without a good reason," flashed Araminta, "but I do think you're guilty of not giving enough consideration to a defenseless girl who means well. I shouldn't have come here, I see it now. I should have known that it would be impossible to make any impression on a mind as rigid as yours. Perhaps, after you think about it, you may decide to do what's right. In the meantime, be assured that I will provide for Stéphanie and her child. A child, may I remind you, who may possibly be the only real remembrance you have of your brother Rupert." She rose, picking up her reticule. "Will you ring for my carriage, please?"

"With pleasure," Jason retorted, white to the lips with barely controlled rage. He stalked to the bell rope. Following him, Araminta walked with dragging feet to the door, where she paused, saying, "Please believe me, I didn't do this maliciously. I've no desire to interfere—"

"You'll forgive me if I find that hard to believe," gritted

the Duke. "Your entire association with Mademoiselle Despard has been one of unwarranted meddling in my affairs. An aspect of your personality with which I may say I'm entirely too familiar. I should have remembered that the female of the species never changes her spots!"

Araminta tossed her hat on the bed, shrugged off her pelisse, kicked off her shoes, rang for her maid, and sat down in a chair by the window, gloomily reviewing the events of the day. It was not that she regretted coming to the rescue of Stéphanie Despard. No, she firmly believed that the girl had been treated unfairly, but couldn't she have been more adroit, more diplomatic, in presenting Stéphanie's case to the Duke? Now, apparently, Araminta had not only further prejudiced Stéphanie's case in Jason's eyes, but she'd also forfeited every shred of liking and trust that he'd ever felt for her. Not to mention her newly formed friendship with his sister Felicity, who would probably never speak to her again.

Araminta sighed, feeling a distinct sense of loss. She also felt ravenously hungry, and suddenly remembered that not a morsel of food had passed her lips since an early breakfast. When her abigail, Jessie, answered her ring, Araminta sent her down to the kitchens for tea and sustenance.

When it arrived, Araminta was pleased to see that the lavishly appointed tea tray contained not only toast and biscuits but a generous assortment of cold meats. A short time later, pouring herself a second cup of tea and reaching for another piece of toast, Araminta found that her normally ebullient spirits were reviving. Surely, with a little care and thought, it shouldn't be too difficult to straighten out Stéphanie's affairs and to mend the breach with Jason.

A soft knock sounded at the door. "Come," called Araminta, absently examining the tea tray and wondering if she could possibly have consumed six biscuits.

"Thank heaven you're back," said Henrietta, hurrying into the bedchamber with Damaris in her wake. "I was beside myself, worrying about you. *Anything* might have happened to you, accompanying that woman to her lodgings. Gentlewomen simply don't venture into the side streets of the East End. Of course, if you had taken my advice – but there, let us think no more about it. That dreadful creature is out of my house and out of our lives. There's no need for any of us to see or hear of her again."

Araminta stared at her sister. "Don't you want to know what happened to Stéphanie? She gave birth to a son this afternoon, and she and the baby are doing well."

"The woman is nothing to me, or to you, either."

"Oh, but you're wrong. I intend to see that Stéphanie has a secure future, even if her child isn't recognized as the Duke's heir, and so I informed Jason not an hour ago."

"Jas – " Damaris bit back the name in a strangled whisper.

Henrietta, ignoring Araminta's unconscious use of the Duke's given name, exclaimed in horror, "You went to see the Duke about that woman? You championed that – that sluttish creature against the very man that she's attempting to injure?"

Sweeping into the bedchamber, Odile announced cheerfully, seemingly unaware of the air of tension that pervaded the room, *"Ma chère* Araminta, I have returned, as you see. The *bébé,* and the sweet little mother, too, are doing very well, and that *gentil* young man, Hippolyte, he will see to it that Stéphanie and her child move to better lodgings when they are stronger. How fortunate, *ma mie,* that our Stéphanie has *one* man friend who will help her. My blood, it boils when I think of how *Monsieur le Duc* has treated her."

"Madame Lacoste, hold your tongue," screamed Damaris to an astonished Odile. Swinging on Araminta, Damaris continued, her voice trembling on the edge of hysteria, "I regret the day you stepped foot in this house. You've done nothing but stir up trouble for Mama and me and – and the Duke since you came here!" She ran out of the room sobbing bitterly.

Henrietta stared at her sister, her expression a mixture of consternation and resentment. "Damaris shouldn't have

184

spoken to you like that, Araminta, and so I shall tell her. But you provoked her, you know you did. It was bad enough that you defended that dreadful woman. Why, why, did you feel you must confront the Duke?"

Araminta shrugged. "Would you have wanted me to go behind his back?"

Henrietta winced. Stalking to the door, she paused to say with a glacial dignity, "Never, Araminta, did I conceive that you would place the welfare of a common slut before that of your own family!"

After the door closed behind her, Odile exclaimed, *"Mon Dieu,* what a *brouhaha.* One would have thought the little Damaris — yes, and her mother, also — would be more — how do you say it? — more *sympathetique."*

Chapter Eleven

"Well, which will it be, my lady?"

"What?"

"I said, will you wear your pearl earrings today or your amethysts?" repeated Jessie.

Seated at her dressing table, Araminta glanced down at her gown of primrose sprigged muslin. She'd been so lost in thought that she hadn't even noticed the gown's color when the abigail had helped her into it a few minutes before. "Oh—I think the pearls would look better with the dress."

As she slipped on the earrings, Araminta reprimanded herself. She'd been doing entirely too much woolgathering during the past week, since the rupture of her short-lived truce with Jason over the claims of Stéphanie Despard. Araminta smiled wryly. She'd grown so used to being on good terms with the Duke that now it felt positively uncomfortable to be on the fringes of his regard again. Not that she had any intention of knuckling under to him. His treatment of Stéphanie was inexcusable.

Araminta shifted uneasily. Her efforts on behalf of the Belgian woman were, predictably, also causing strains with her sister and her niece. Actually, after her initial reproaches, Henrietta had been avoiding the subject of Stéphanie, but she appeared nervous and peevish in the midst of her social rounds, and she seemed perpetually on the verge of an attack of the vapors. Damaris's gentle charm had turned brittle. Ladylike to the core, she'd apologized, albeit rather limply, for her outburst on the day of Stéphanie's arrival, but she'd tended to avoid Araminta's company as much as possible. The atmosphere at Middleton House felt both uncomfortable and foreboding, as if the other shoe could drop at any time, with disastrous consequences.

As the abigail adjusted the last curl in Araminta's shining topknot, she said, sniffing, "Miss Odile, she went out bright and early this morning. She left a message for you, reminding you of your promise to visit that foreign woman in her new rooms this afternoon."

"Thank you, Jessie. I'm afraid I *had* forgotten."

"For once, Miss Odile has a sensible idea," said Jessie, her tone reflecting her long-standing disapproval of the Frenchwoman. "You're paying for those rooms. You might as well see that you're getting good value for your money."

"Oh, don't be so high in the instep, Jessie. Poor Mademoiselle Despard and her son do need a respectable place to live. You wouldn't credit your ears if I described the mean hovel where she gave birth to that baby. I think Odile has performed wonders in finding new rooms so quickly. Of course she had the help of that young man in the lodging house—what was his name? Oh, yes, Hippolyte Augé—but Odile was in charge of all the arrangements. She told me with tears in her eyes that her conscience wouldn't allow her to leave poor Stéphanie in that dreadful place an hour longer than necessary."

It had, in fact, been a stroke of genius, Araminta thought complacently, to give Odile the task of helping Stéphanie to become established. In her role as Araminta's factotum during the past several days, Odile had been far too busy with Stéphanie's concerns to sit in Lord Manning's pocket, or to lapse into melancholy about her continued separation from her naval lieutenant.

A tap at the door was followed by the sight of Gillian's tousled head poking around the doorpost. "Do you have a moment, Araminta?"

Araminta smiled a welcome. With Gillian, at least, she was still on affectionate terms. Her younger niece had quietly let her know that she sympathized with Stéphanie's plight, and with Araminta's efforts to help. "Come in, Gillian. I have lots of time. Jessie, I won't need you anymore."

On her way to the door, the abigail cast a sharp look at Gillian. "My lord, miss, what have you been up to?"

"Oh. I've spilled some ink," said Gillian guiltily, looking down at her hands. "I hadn't noticed."

"It seems to me, Gillian, that you have more ink on your hands than you can have used on your manuscript," said Araminta with mock severity after Jessie had left the room.

"Well, I couldn't help it. I spent most of last night and the early hours of this morning making a fair copy of the last chapters of my book. Araminta, you'll never guess what I'm about to tell you. A publisher is interested in *Castle of Horrors!*"

"Good heavens, sit down with me on the settee and tell me all about it. I didn't realize you'd even finished your book."

"Actually, I wrote to the publisher, Mr. Loman, two weeks ago, before I *had* finished it. I told him what kind of a book it was, and asked him if he'd like to see it when I'd completed it. He wrote right back, Araminta, urging me to send it to him!"

Araminta's brows knitted in a puzzled frown. "I don't quite see . . . I know the butler delivers all the letters that come to the house directly into your mother's hands. How . . . ?"

Gillian grinned impishly. "You must think I have no more sense than a zero! I knew I couldn't allow Mama to have any suspicion that I was writing a novel, let alone corresponding with a publisher. When I wrote to Mr. Loman, I told him my name was Margery Tavistock. Margery is my old nurse. When she left us, she married a man who keeps a sweet shop in Holborn. I enclosed my letter to Mr. Loman in a note to Margery, asking her to send it on to him."

"What a clever puss you are. With this arrangement, Mr. Loman can't possibly discover your real name, and Henrietta won't know anything about Mr. Loman." Araminta's conscience gave a decided thump. Sympathizing with Gillian's writing ambitions was one thing; now that publication of *Castle of Horrors* seemed possible, the situation suddenly appeared full of pitfalls. Clearing her throat, she said, "Gillian, I feel bound to say this: I really shouldn't be encouraging you to deceive your mother."

A shadow of remorse crossed Gillian's face, which was marred by a streak of ink reaching from her left eyebrow to her chin. "I know I shouldn't be going behind Mama's back, but I can't think of any alternative, can you? I haven't done anything wrong, or—or immoral by writing a book, but if Mama should learn about *Castle of Horrors,* she wouldn't allow me to publish it. And the book is so much better now, because I've added bits to make Count Ugolino an even nastier villain. I think it would be really immoral *not* to publish it!"

"But Count Ugolino was already such a monster," said Araminta, momentarily distracted. "I find it hard to believe he could get any worse! How did you make him more villainous?"

"I won't tell you," Gillian said with a teasing look. "It'll be a surprise for you when you read the published version of the book." Getting back to essentials, she went on, "So would you do me a great favor, Araminta? If you're planning to go out in your carriage today, could you deliver my manuscript to Margery? Her husband's sweet shop is only a few streets away from Mr. Loman's offices in Chancery Lane."

Still feeling a twinge of guilt, Araminta said ruefully, "In for a penny, in for a pound? I daresay I'm already your partner in crime! Yes, I'll deliver your manuscript. Give it to Jessie before we leave."

Scarcely had Gillian, bright-eyed with excitement, left the room when a footman knocked at the door. "Will you see Lady Salford, my lady?"

"Why, yes. Tell her I'll be with her in a few moments—" Araminta stopped short as Felicity swept into the bedchamber.

"Forgive me for intruding on your privacy," said Felicity

when the door had closed behind the footman. "I wanted to see you alone, and I feared I might encounter Lady Middleton if I waited for you downstairs."

Araminta indicated a chair. "I'm happy to see you. Please sit down. Will you have some tea? Lemonade?"

"No, nothing, thank you."

Felicity seemed ill at ease. The fingers of one hand pulled nervously at the fingers of the other, and her eyes avoided contact. "I can only stay for a moment," she said after a moment. "I'm on my way home to Gloucestershire. As a matter of fact, my traveling chaise piled high with luggage is standing at your door."

"You spoke of returning to town for the ball I'm giving for Damaris."

"Oh. I'm not sure . . ." At last Felicity lifted her head and looked directly at Araminta. "I'd like to come. I'd like to continue being your friend, but under the circumstances . . ." She shook her head.

"I understand." And Araminta did. She and Felicity had taken an instant liking to each other, but it was asking too much of human nature to expect Jason's sister to side with her new acquaintance against her brother—misguided and stubbornly wrong-headed though he was!—in a matter affecting the Windham family. "The Duke is still very angry with me, I collect."

Felicity's eyes kindled. "That, yes. Jason has such a stiff-necked sense of honor. He can't fathom how you could accuse him of attempting to cheat his legitimate flesh and blood out of a farthing. However, if that were all—but it isn't. Are you aware that all of London knows about this wretched girl and her spurious claims? The rumors have been sweeping the clubs. Jason can't step into White's, or Brookes's, without being stared at. No matter how much you disagreed with him, he naturally thought you'd be discreet. As did I, I confess."

Araminta stared at Felicity, aghast. Her premonitions had been correct. The other shoe had dropped. A private quarrel between her and Jason, and the reason for it, was now apparently public knowledge. But how, in the space of such a few days, had the gossip about Stéphanie spread to Jason's own turf, the elegant men's clubs in St. James's Street? Not through Stéphanie herself, surely, though she'd certainly been vociferous enough about her grievances. She simply didn't move in such rarified social circles. And Araminta had specifically asked Odile not to discuss Stéphanie's situation with anyone. Her eyes narrowing, Araminta thought of one solution to the puzzle. It was undoubtedly far too late to contain the source of the gossip, if what she suspected was true.

"As if the situation wasn't bad enough already," Felicity went on, her voice trembling, "last night Jason brought home the worst rumor of all. They're saying that you, Araminta, have bought that creature a house. From that the gossips are concluding that the woman's story about being Rupert's widow must be true, or why would Lady Araminta Beresford be supporting her? I simply couldn't credit that you'd do such a thing, and so I told Jason, but I had to come here today to hear your denial from your own lips. *Have* you bought a house for Stéphanie Despard?"

Araminta's heart felt as if it were plummeting into her stomach. "No, I haven't bought Mademoiselle Despard a house," she said with dry lips. "However, the rumor does have a basis in fact. My friend, Odile Lacoste, has rented rooms for the young woman at my expense."

Looking stricken, Felicity rose from her chair. "There's nothing more to say, then, is there? Except for one thing, perhaps. Jason said last night he intended to write to your sister, telling her that he proposed staying away from Middleton House for the time being to avoid the embarrassment, both on your part and his, of any meeting with you. I told him it was an overly harsh set-down, but now I'm inclined to think he was right. I see little basis for any further connection between you and our family. Good-bye, Lady Araminta."

Araminta made no effort to detain Felicity. What would be the point? The situation was beyond mending. If there had ever been a possibility that she and Jason could iron out

191

their differences about Stéphanie, it was gone now. Felicity had spoken of his stiff-necked sense of honor. Call it pride, and the result was the same. All London was discussing Jason's family affairs; worse, the Ton was condemning his actions. Goaded by his anger and his wounded self-esteem, Jason would have little reason to change his mind either about Stéphanie or about Araminta's interjection into his affairs.

She put her hand to her forehead, conscious of the beginning twinges of a headache, willing herself not to think of the reactions of Henrietta and Damaris when they read Jason's letter informing them he would no longer be visiting Middleton House. One calamity seemed to be leading into another, and what could she do about it? For the first time in her life, she found herself lacking in both resourcefulness and optimism. For a fleeting moment she wished she'd never become embroiled in the Belgian woman's troubles. But that was a lowering thought, soon dismissed. It might be cold comfort, indeed, but it was right and proper to help Stéphanie in her legitimate claims. Jason was *wrong*. Somehow her conviction of her own righteousness didn't help to raise Araminta's spirits. *I feel like a pariah, or a flea carrying the plague,* she thought in a burst of self-pity. *Ever since I came to London, I've been putting my foot wrong.*

By early afternoon, however, as she rode with her abigail in the town chariot, heading north out of Bruton Street toward Holborn, Araminta was no longer wallowing in a fit of the dismals. She was no closer to a solution of the Jason-Stéphanie problem, but her ingrained buoyant cheerfulness had bubbled to the surface. All was not lost. Something would turn up. Meanwhile, her errands this afternoon would help to take her mind off her troubles.

"What can be in this package Miss Gillian gave me?" asked Jessie, poking a curious finger at the bulky parcel, wrapped in several sheets of the *Times,* that she was holding on her lap. "She said as how it was something for her old nurse, but it can't be food, nor yet clothing. It's too heavy. It don't rattle, neither."

192

"If she'd wanted us to know, she'd have told us, no doubt," said Araminta. She glanced out the window. "We must be almost there. Gillian said her nurse lived in a side street near Gray's Inn. Yes, here's the sweet shop. Jessie, take the parcel to the proprietress, Mrs. Tavistock."

But the abigail was gone only a minute or two before she was back at the open door of the carriage. "Mrs. Tavistock says please, my lady, would you come in for a glass of her homemade wine?"

In the tiny, neat-as-a-pin parlor behind the sweet shop premises, Araminta confronted a round little lady with anxious eyes and iron gray curls escaping from her prim white cap.

"Lady Araminta Beresford? Ye'd be Lady Middleton's sister? I'm that glad to see ye. I'm nearly at my wits' end with worrying."

Accepting a glass of the homemade wine, Araminta inquired, "Is there a problem, Mrs. Tavistock?"

"Yes, my lady, it's Miss Gillian! I know that girl, and it's my belief she's under the hatches, or will be, as soon as makes no difference! She sends me letters I'm to pass on without telling a soul, and now here's this package I'm to take to that man Loman, and she says I'm not to tell a soul about *that,* neither. Now, I'm no green'un, and I know it's Carlton House to a Charley's shelter that Miss Gillian's mama don't know about this bobbery, and so I ask you, my lady, as that child's aunt, is it my bounden duty to inform Lady Middleton about this scrape afore Miss Gillian makes a cake of herself?"

Suppressing her own faint stirrings of guilt, Araminta said soothingly, "Please don't fly up into the boughs, Mrs. Tavistock. I'm familiar with what Gillian's doing, and I assure you she's in no danger of being under the hatches. Actually, it's all quite innocent. Cutting up a lark, if you will. If it will relieve your mind, I'll take full responsibility for any consequences. Lady Middleton will have no reason to reproach you."

It took several more minutes to calm Mrs. Tavistock, and

to do so Araminta had to accept a second glass of what proved to be a ghastly wine and a sampling of the more superior wares of the sweet shop, but at last she and Jessie made their escape.

Traveling east from Holborn on Oxford Street, they turned right into Orchard Street, a continuance of Baker Street. The carriage stopped at the northern end of Baker Street, immediately before its junction with Marylebone Road, in front of a narrow three-storied house that was almost a duplicate of its neighbors. It was, thought Araminta approvingly, as she descended from the carriage, a modest, respectable middle-class neighborhood. Stéphanie should be very comfortable here.

Leaving Jessie to wait for her in the carriage, Araminta walked up the steps of the house. Scarcely had she lifted the knocker when the door was opened by a trimly dressed maidservant.

"Good afternoon. I believe that Mademoiselle—or perhaps it's Madame?—Despard has rooms in this house. Will you show me up, please?"

The maidservant gaped at Araminta. "I'm that sorry, ma'am, but ye've come to the wrong 'ouse. There's no'un by the name o' Despard 'ere."

Odile appeared on the stairway behind the maidservant, calling, "That's all right, Sophie. Lady Araminta has come to visit Mrs. Windham."

Walking into the small entrance hall, Araminta observed to Odile, "Is it really necessary for me to see the mistress of the house? Mrs. Windham, is that her name? What a coincidence, she has the same name as the Duke's family. You know, Odile, she really ought to keep her servant informed about the names of her tenants. This girl seemed unaware that Stéphanie lives here."

Odile's smile was a little strained. "No, no, Araminta, it's *Stéphanie* who is Mrs. Windham. She didn't like to be known as *Mademoiselle* Despard, when she is really a widow and the mother of a child, so she decided to adopt her dead husband's family name. *Pourquoi pas?* Why not?"

"It sounds a little awkward, but—" Araminta shrugged. "There's no real harm, I daresay."

Odile beamed. "I knew you would approve. Every little comforting detail helps, when one is, like *pauvre* Stéphanie, in such awkward circumstances! But come, let me show you around the house."

Bisected by a central hallway, the narrow house had only two principal rooms on the ground floor, commodious parlors facing each other across the corridor. The rooms were furnished tastefully in what appeared to be the latest fashion. Araminta noted particularly a Grecian settee with roll-curved ends, a gilded rosewood chair with lion's paw feet, an ornate convex wall mirror with a gilded frame surmounted by an eagle with spread wings, and a sparkling cut glass fire lustre, or chandelier. Descending to the cellar, to be shown around the kitchen quarters by the plump, immaculately dressed cook, Araminta observed that both kitchen and pantry seemed to have been recently refurbished.

"And now for the bedchambers and the nursery," said Odile, her eyes glowing with satisfaction as she prepared to lead the way up the stairs.

Araminta detained her with a hand on her sleeve. "My dear Odile, I'm beginning to feel slightly embarrassed. Where *is* the landlady, the mistress of the house? Should we be poking around her establishment in her absence? Isn't this really an invasion of her privacy?"

Odile froze, refusing to meet Araminta's eyes. Staring down at her hands, she said in a small voice, *"Chère* Araminta, I have a small confession to make. Stéphanie— Mrs. Windham, as I told you she now calls herself— is the mistress of this house."

Araminta gasped. "You've rented this entire three-story house for Stéphanie? Or perhaps you've actually bought it?"

"Not bought it, no," Odile assured her hastily. "I've merely taken a year's lease."

Araminta's heart sank. So the scandalmongers had been very close to the mark. She hadn't bought a house for

Stéphanie, but renting one, especially a house this large, was almost the same thing. Felicity, and by extension, Jason, would never believe she hadn't intended to deceive them when she'd insisted she had only rented a few rooms for Stéphanie.

"How could you think I would be so prodigal with your money?" Odile went on reproachfully. "When I lived with my uncle in Athens, I assure you I was a most careful housekeeper. I pinched every sou! But you did say that I should find the little Stéphanie and her *bébé* suitable quarters, *n'est-ce pas?* We could not allow her and her infant to remain in that dreadful place where we found her, so filthy, so unsafe." Odile shuddered. "I saw a *rat* running across the floor of Stéphanie's room!"

"Good God, I'm not disputing the necessity for Stéphanie to move," Araminta retorted. "Are you forgetting I gave you *carte blanche* to find her suitable lodgings? But you told me that her friend from the rooming house—that nice young man, Hippolyte Augé—was looking for *rooms* in a respectable house in the Marylebone district. You didn't tell me he was looking for a *house!*"

"Hippolyte did find some rooms, Araminta, but they looked so small, so cramped, so—so unhomelike for a new mother and her child. It didn't seem right that Stéphanie, after all her hardships, after all the injustice inflicted on her by *Monsieur le Duc,* should be obliged to live like a laborer's wife. So I rented this house." Odile looked at Araminta pleadingly. "It's not such a very large house, after all, and the rent, it's really quite modest." She paused, looking away. "There's one more thing you may not like," she said at last. "The house was let furnished, but everything was so old and worn, in such bad taste, that I had no choice. I had to buy a few sticks of furniture, some rugs, some new draperies."

Araminta sighed, recalling the Grecian settee, the rosewood chair with the lion's paw feet, the mirror surmounted by an eagle. She said resignedly, "So how much will the rent and the new furnishings cost me?"

Odile named a sum that raised Araminta's eyebrows.

After a moment she shrugged, saying, "Oh well, what's done is done. The amount won't send me to the poorhouse. I know you had the best of intentions." She stood patiently as Odile smothered her in a hug.

"Vous êtes un ange," exclaimed Odile. "Now come see our Stéphanie."

The new mother was reclining on a chaise longue in a snug sitting room on the second floor. A new-looking Aubusson carpet covered the floor and the flowing satin damask draperies looked recently installed. A nursemaid was just taking her infant from Stéphanie's arms when Araminta and Odile arrived at the door. It seems that I'm paying for a staff of three, at least, thought Araminta: a maidservant, a cook, and a nursemaid.

Spying Araminta in the doorway, Stéphanie exclaimed in delight, *"Miladi* Beresford, you've come at last."

As Araminta entered the room with Odile, a tall graceful figure rose from his chair beside the chaise longue. "Good afternoon, Lady Araminta," said Lord Manning with a bow.

Shooting a long look at Odile, who colored faintly, Araminta inclined her head slightly to Manning, saying coolly, "And so, are you a frequent visitor, my lord?"

"I've dropped by occasionally since Mademoiselle — I beg your pardon — since Mrs. Windham moved here," acknowledged the Viscount. "I feel a certain proprietary interest in the newest Windham heir. After all, I was present — or nearly so! — at his birth."

"Oh, *Milord* Manning is *très sympathetique,"* Stéphanie said, smiling. "He was saying, just before you arrived, *Miladi,* that he would be happy to be my son's *parrain,* his godfather, because he is such an old friend of my husband's family."

Manning's eyes met Araminta's with a look of limpid innocence. "I also told Mrs. Windham that her brother-in-law would doubtless insist that the honor of being godfather should belong to him, and I certainly would never compete with a ducal claim!" To Stéphanie, he said, "I'll take my leave, Mrs. Windham. You'll want to have a comfortable

197

cose with Lady Araminta. With your permission, I'll call again tomorrow."

As he turned to go, Araminta said, "I'd like a word with you, Lord Manning. Could you wait for me downstairs?"

"Certainly. I look forward to it."

After the Viscount left, Stéphanie said happily, "And now, *Miladi* Beresford, you must have a look at my son."

The nursemaid took the infant from his lacy, beribboned cradle and folded back the blanket from his face, holding him up for Araminta's inspection.

"Is he not beautiful?" sighed Stéphanie.

"Indeed, yes," said Araminta, gazing at the baby with suitable admiration. "His mother is looking blooming, also."

It was not an idle compliment. Dressed in a pale pink silk dressing gown, with a soft fleecy shawl covering her legs, Stéphanie Despard looked glowingly beautiful. She was also well mannered and well spoken, despite her seeming inability to remember Araminta's title correctly. It was not at all difficult to believe that she might have touched the heart of the Duke of Harwood's younger brother.

As Araminta pulled up a chair and sat down beside the chaise longue, Stéphanie took her hand, saying softly, "I am so glad to be able to thank you in person for all you have done for me."

"You must rather thank Odile. She did all the work!"

"Chère Odile," breathed Stéphanie, misty-eyed. Out of the corner of her eye, Araminta watched Odile's futile attempt to disguise her gratification.

"Tell me, Stéphanie, about your long-range plans, in the event that the Duke of Harwood doesn't recognize your claims," said Araminta after a moment.

"Eh bien, I realize I cannot presume on your kindness forever . . ."

"Don't worry about that."

"No, really, I do not wish to be a permanent object of your charity. That man *must* recognize me as the mother of his heir. If he will not do so voluntarily, I think I should pursue my son's case in the courts," declared Stéphanie. "What do you think?"

Araminta groaned inwardly. A sensational court proceeding would not only crucify Jason's pride, it would ensure that *l'affaire Windham* would remain in the public eye for many months. She said cautiously, "I think you might gain more through negotiation, compromise. I'm sure your lawyer, when you obtain one, will say the same. You mustn't forget that the Duke of Harwood has tremendous power and influence."

Before Stéphanie could reply, a man burst into the room, brandishing a small painting. "Look what I have found, *chérie*," he exclaimed excitedly. "The artist might have had you in mind when he painted these beautiful roses. It will look so charming on the wall of your boudoir—" He broke off as he realized that Stéphanie had visitors. *"Miladi* Beresford, I am honored to meet you again," he said, with an enthusiasm that seemed rather forced. "You remember me, Hippolyte Augé?"

It had taken Araminta several seconds to recognize the face of the thin, dark young man. "Oh, yes, you're the man who befriended Stéphanie at her old lodgings," she said after a long look. "I understand you also found this house for her."

A muscle twitched in Augé's face. *"Vraiment,* I know I suggested rooms, which would have cost much less," he said apologetically. "But Madame Lacoste, she agreed with me, none of the available rooms seemed suitable for a lady who is the widow of an English *Milord* and the mother of a future Duke!"

"It doesn't signify. You did what you thought best." Araminta glanced at the painting, a small still life depicting a vase of flowers. She knew a great deal about classical art, thanks to her travels in eastern Europe, but she had a scanty knowledge of painting. Nevertheless, to her unschooled eyes, the still life appeared to be a brilliant piece of work. "You've brought Mademoiselle—Mrs. Windham—a gift. That was kind of you."

"Pas du tout, pas du tout," murmured Augé. "I merely thought to do something to brighten Stéph—Mrs. *Windham's* day." He kept his eyes down, turning the painting round and round between his hands and looking so uncomfortable at being the object of Araminta's direct but not unfriendly gaze that she was not at all surprised when he mumbled his excuses and left.

"Poor Hippolyte. He's so shy," said Stéphanie with an indulgent smile. "But he's been such a good friend, my only friend, until my great fortune in meeting you and *chère* Odile."

"My uncle Will always said that if a man had even one good friend, his prospects could not be entirely bleak," remarked Araminta. She rose, saying, "I must go. I've enjoyed seeing your baby and your new home. I hope you'll be happy here. If you need anything, tell Odile. And one more thing—please think about what I said concerning a court case. Neither you nor the Duke will like being pilloried in public."

Downstairs, in one of the large, newly furnished parlors, the Viscount was standing by the fireplace, leaning against the mantel as he looked down into the small fire that was taking the spring chill off the room. He straightened as Araminta entered, indicating a small table drawn up in front of a sofa. "I asked the maidservant to bring us some wine and lemonade. Won't you sit down?"

"I'd rather stand. Lord Manning, a scant week ago you promised me you would keep silent about Mademoiselle Despard's situation. During those few days apparently all London has become aware of her supposed connection with the Duke of Harwood. *I* haven't spoken about this in public, nor have my sister and my nieces. Certainly the Duke hasn't done so. I can only conclude that you are the source of these rumors. Do you care to deny it?"

Manning reddened. "I deny doing anything to injure or embarrass you, or Mademoiselle Despard."

"I don't consider that an answer. You've certainly injured the Duke. And obviously you've broken your word to me."

Manning's eyes sparked angrily. "Look, I've no obligation to defend the Duke of Harwood. I promised you—yes, I admit it, I did it because I wanted to please you—I promised you I would keep my mind open about the Despard woman, nothing more. Well, after coming to know the lady, I've decided she's in the right. Why should I keep silent about such injustice? The more the world knows about Harwood's venality, the better Stéphanie Despard's chances of obtaining her just dues."

"It won't fadge, sir," said Araminta, her lip curling. "You don't care a fig about Mademoiselle Despard's welfare. You hate the Duke of Harwood and you're out to destroy him if you can. I've withheld judgment on you for a long time, partly because I think you'd make a very bad enemy. Now I know you for what you are. In future, I want nothing more to do with you. If you come calling on me or Odile Lacoste at Middleton House, you'll be turned away."

His flush fading to a pasty white, Manning's voice was cold and level as he replied, "You'll be sorry for this, you know. You and Jason Windham. I don't take kindly to being kicked in the teeth."

"Thank you for the warning. I'll be sure to watch my back. I suggest you leave now. You're no longer welcome in this house, either. Not as long as I'm paying the rent."

The interview with Manning left a bad taste in Araminta's mouth. Despite her bold words, she was apprehensive that he could cause even more damage to Jason's reputation, and probably to hers, with his venomous tongue. Later, on the drive back to Bruton Street, with Jessie nodding inattentively in her corner of the carriage, Araminta had to force herself out of her black thoughts to listen to Odile, who seemed bent on describing in minute detail every purchase she had made for Stéphanie's house in Baker Street.

"Don't you think so, Araminta?"

"What?"

"I said, don't you think the draperies in Stéphanie's boudoir are a perfect match for the new carpet?"

"Oh. Yes, indeed." Yawning against the indifference she

felt for Stéphanie's furnishings, Araminta asked idly, "Does that young man — Hippolyte — come around very often?"

"Well, yes. Quite often."

There was an evasive quality in Odile's voice that caused Araminta to look at her more closely. "Do you mean *very* often?"

"Yes. No." Odile nervously twisted and untwisted the clasp of her reticule. "Actually, Hippolyte . . . *Eh bien,* the fact of the matter is that Hippolyte is living at the house in Baker Street. I haven't told you because I thought you might not approve."

Araminta sat bolt upright. "Do you mean to say — ?"

"No, no, of course not. How could you think such a thing?" Odile exclaimed indignantly. "The widow of a nobleman romantically involved with a cook-waiter? *Inimaginable!* You see, Stéphanie was afraid to live alone in that house, without a manservant to protect her against thieves, or — or worse. And Hippolyte was happy to vacate his room in that dreadful lodging house. Now Stéphanie feels safe in her bed at night, and Hippolyte pays for his lodging by taking care of all those little problems that crop up in a household. Today, for example, he was out searching for a team and a carriage that might meet Stéphanie's needs."

And my pocketbook, thought Araminta. Her stomach felt hollow. She remembered that expensive-looking oil painting Hippolyte had given Stéphanie. She remembered his use of the endearment, *chérie,* before he realized that a visitor was in the room. If he wasn't already Stéphanie's lover, he was probably well on the way to becoming so. Araminta couldn't condemn the pair out of hand. Stéphanie had badly needed a friend when she first came to London. Perhaps it was only human nature that she should respond to Hippolyte's kindness by falling in love with him. Unfortunately, their romantic relationship, if such it was, could only tighten the coils in which Araminta was entangled. Now she could be accused, not only of supporting Stéphanie in her claims against Jason, but of supporting Stéphanie's lover as well!

Aloud she said to Odile, "Be as tactful as you can, spend as much money as necessary, but get Hippolyte out of that house. He can rent a room nearby, if Stéphanie leans on him so much. If she objects, give her a friendly warning. Tell her that if she really intends to go to court about her son's inheritance, she should avoid even the appearance of a scandal in her establishment."

A rather subdued Odile was still digesting Araminta's curt order when their carriage stopped in front of Middleton House, where Araminta discovered that her disastrous day wasn't over yet. As she trailed into the house with Odile and Jessie, the butler gave her a message. Lady Middleton would like to see her in the library.

Henrietta was sitting at the desk and Damaris was sitting opposite her in an armchair when Araminta entered the room. Mother and daughter were wearing identical expression of frozen shock. Henrietta stood up, extending a rather crumpled letter to Araminta. "I think you should see this."

Accepting the letter, but giving it only a cursory glance, Araminta said quietly, "I don't think I need to read it. Lady Salford visited me earlier today. I believe the note says that the Duke has decided not to visit Middleton House as long as I'm residing here." She placed the letter on the desk. "What do you want me to do, Henrietta? I quite see we can't go on like this. Would you like me to move out? You needn't have any qualms about casting me out into the cold cruel world. You know I've always wanted to set up my own establishment, and I'm perfectly capable of taking care of myself."

There was a long silence. From Henrietta's expression, she was obviously battling between her lifelong devotion to propriety, her affection for her sister, and her very human desire to advance her elder daughter's marriage plans. At last she said, "It might be best if you started looking for a suitable house, Araminta."

Chapter Twelve

Araminta threw down her pen and pushed her chair away from her desk. She'd been sitting here for half an hour and hadn't made a dent in her correspondence. Her mind had obstinately refused to cooperate, veering away from tradesmen's bills and the invitations to balls and dinners and routs that had continued to pour in despite the titillating rumors sweeping London about her connection with Stéphanie Despard's claims against the Duke of Harwood.

It was three days since her visit to the Belgian woman's house in Baker Street. During that time she'd made no progress in extricating herself from her difficulties. After looking at so many houses in the West End that their facades and interior appointments all tended to blur together in her mind, she still hadn't discovered a suitable place to rent. Henrietta and Damaris were being studiously polite to her, no more, and it would probably take only a spark to ignite a full-fledged quarrel. To avoid such a catastrophe, she'd begged off accompanying her sister and her niece to engagements for several days running, on the theory that she could best head off a quarrel by being in their company as little as possible. The one infallible solution to all her problems, of course, would be to find some way to prove the truth of Stéphanie's story to Jason's satisfaction. So far, no inspiration had been forthcoming.

One small thing she *had* accomplished. Hippolyte Augé

had moved out of Stéphanie's house, so one tiny source of scandal had been eliminated. She'd asked Odile curiously, "Was Stéphanie offended when you told her Hippolyte must leave?"

"*Mais non.* She saw at once that she must avoid even the appearance of impropriety. Like Cleopatra, you know, in that old play. She has to be above suspicion."

Araminta blinked. "Do you mean Calpurnia, Caesar's wife?"

Shrugging, Odile said impatiently, "What does it matter, a name?" She added, *"La petite* Stéphanie, she was so distressed to hear that you could even *think* she has a *tendresse* for Hippolyte. Araminta, she so values your good opinion."

And well she might, thought Araminta now, recalling the conversation. Without me, she'd soon be fast aground. Araminta sighed. She intended to continue helping Stéphanie, because she was convinced that her claims were legitimate, but there was something about the girl that made it difficult to like her personally.

A soft knock sounded at the door. "Come," Araminta called, rather glad than otherwise to be distracted from her depressing thoughts.

A footman opened the door. "The Duke of Harwood has called to see you, my lady."

"The Duke wishes to see me, Beeson? Not Lady Middleton, or Miss Damaris?" Araminta asked in surprise.

"No, my lady. His Grace specifically asked for you."

After a hasty look into the cheval glass, Araminta walked down the stairs, sternly suppressing a tingling feeling of pleasurable anticipation. Entering the drawing room, she inclined her head to Jason in a cool, formal little nod. "How kind of you to call."

His rangy powerful form impeccably dressed as always in a form-fitting blue coat, creaseless fawn-colored breeches, and an intricately tied cravat that would undoubtedly cause the most exquisite of Corinthians to gnash his teeth in helpless envy, Jason rose from his chair with a punctiliously formal bow. "Lady Araminta."

"I hope the butler offered you some refreshment. A glass of claret, perhaps?"

"No, I thank you. This is not a social call."

That was obvious, thought Araminta. She gazed at Jason's lips, set in a straight, unsmiling line above that sensual cleft in his chin. His resentment and animosity were clearly as strong as ever beneath his facade of polished courtesy.

"I see. Or rather, I don't see. Perhaps you'll enlighten me."

"Certainly. I'm about to visit Stéphanie Despard, and I would like you to accompany me. Inasmuch as you've seen fit to become the lady's ardent champion, I consider it only proper that you should be present at her unveiling."

"Unveiling?"

"Yes." The Duke shot her a level, unfriendly glance. "I've always maintained that Stéphanie Despard is a liar and a fraud. Now I can prove it."

Araminta's mouth suddenly felt dry. Could she have made a ghastly error of judgment about Stéphanie? With an effort, she said calmly, "I'm quite willing to accompany you, but I warn you, it will take a great deal of proof to convince me that I've misplaced my trust in Stéphanie."

Seated beside Jason in his curricle a few minutes later, Araminta refused to allow her mind to dwell on the possibility that she would soon be proved wrong about her Belgian protégée. She concentrated her attention on Jason's driving, watching him handle the ribbons with the easy, expert grace that had always elicited her admiration. Soon, however, she began to feel more and more uncomfortable at the chill and awkward silence that enveloped them. She stole a quick sideways glance at him, but she could detect no softening in his grimly uncommunicative profile. Involuntarily her mind leapt back to their first meeting at the inn in Dover, remembering the laughing, flirtatious, quicksilver charm that had tempted her to indulge in a very unladylike dalliance. He was making no attempt to charm her today.

Determined not to allow Jason to keep her off-balance with his taciturn silence, Araminta remarked, "I've been wanting to tell you how much I regret that your personal affairs have become a matter of public knowledge. I hope you believe that I had no part in spreading the gossip."

"Your apologies are quite unnecessary. Whether you helped fan the rumors is a matter of complete indifference to me."

The harshness of the reply startled Araminta. It also made her angry. "It's not a matter of indifference to me," she snapped. "I'm no scandalmonger, and it was never my intention to injure you. As it happens, I've recently discovered who did spread the rumors. It was Lord Manning."

He flicked her a disdainful glance. "That, too, is a matter of indifference to me."

Grinding her teeth so hard that her jaw began to ache, Araminta averted her head from Jason, ignoring his presence entirely for the remainder of the journey. When they arrived in front of Stéphanie's house in Baker Street, she stared stonily for several seconds at his outstretched hand before she accepted his help in descending from the curricle.

The maid who answered the door, wide-eyed at the mention of the Duke's title, showed Jason and Araminta into the parlor to the left of the door. Jason sat down on the Grecian settee and studied the room's furnishings. "Charming. Do I detect your taste in the decor, Lady Araminta? Or did you merely open your purse strings?"

She flicked a contemptuous glance at him, not deigning to give him the satisfaction of a reply, and settled into a chair at the far side of the room.

After a short wait, Stéphanie entered the parlor, obviously nervous and ill at ease, her lips set in a rather forced smile. *"Miladi* Beresford, what joy to see you again," she exclaimed, speaking in French. "And you, *Monsieur le Duc.* At last we meet. No, no, please sit down," she added as Jason rose from the settee, bowing slightly. "We have so much to discuss, so many things to settle. Later, *bien entendu,* you will want to see your new little nephew."

Jason remained standing. "We do, indeed, have much to discuss," he said coldly, also speaking in French. "The first order of business is this: how soon can I expect you to pack up your belongings and leave England?"

Stéphanie's face paled. "Monsieur, what are you saying? I am your brother Rupert's widow, the mother of his child. You owe me—"

"I owe you nothing," Jason cut in. "Your claims are completely fraudulent. Oh, I don't doubt you were Rupert's doxy, but I'm positive you aren't his widow, and the odds are enormous that he wasn't the father of your child. Infants of eleven months' gestation are extremely rare. Some would say an impossibility."

Stéphanie turned to Araminta, tears streaking her carefully painted face. *"Miladi* Beresford, you've always believed in me. Won't you help me now?"

Crossing the room, Araminta put a protective arm around Stéphanie and glared at Jason. "I'm not going to permit you to browbeat this woman. Any doctor could tell you that the birth of an eleven-month child is not impossible. If that's all the evidence you can bring against her—"

"I told you earlier I had proof."

"Really? Please show it to us."

"How about this?"

Taking the document Jason handed to her, Araminta read it carefully. She looked at Stéphanie, her brows knit. "This seems to be a copy of a civil marriage record," she said slowly. "According to this, a woman named Stéphanie Despard married one Hippolyte Augé on September fourteenth, 1815, in the city of Brussels, Belgium. Is this an authentic document, Stéphanie? Are you married to Hippolyte?"

"Yes, she's married to me," came a voice from the doorway. Hippolyte Augé strode into the parlor to stand by Stéphanie's side. "What difference does our marriage make to my Stéphanie's case? She was a widow, *n'est-ce pas?* She had every right to remarry. We decided to pretend to be strangers when we came to England because we thought the marriage might prejudice Lord Rupert's family against her."

A note of distaste in her voice, Araminta said to Jason, "I wish Stéphanie hadn't deceived me about this man, but he's quite right, you know. She was perfectly free to marry anyone she chose after your brother died. It doesn't affect her claim at all."

"Not if she had a valid claim, no. It does indicate a good deal about her character, though, don't you think?" Jason turned his attention back to Stéphanie. "As you well know, after I received your first letter, requesting recognition as Rupert's widow, I sent my secretary over to Belgium to look into the matter. He didn't make a prolonged investigation, because almost at once he found several clues that completely disproved your claim: a page had been torn from the registry of the church where you and Rupert were supposedly married—a page covering the period of the ostensible ceremony—and a search of the town records turned up no indication of a civil marriage, as required under the terms of the *Code Civil.*"

"Your agent, that secretary of yours, removed the page from the parish register, and well you know it, *Monsieur le Duc,*" flared Stéphanie. "As for a civil ceremony, I never claimed that it had taken place. There was no time for Rupert to legalize our situation before he went off to be killed at Waterloo."

Jason listened to Stéphanie, unmoved by the passion of her outburst. "Are you finished? Very well. I'll proceed. When you came to England to pursue your claim, and after I learned that you had enlisted Lady Araminta and her purse in your cause, I decided to search for definitive proof that you were lying. Back went my secretary to Belgium. This time he had a long conversation with Father Gilbert, the pastor of the Church of Sainte-Anne in the village of Vardon—ah, I see you recognize the name. Yes, Father Gilbert is the priest who you say officiated at your marriage to Rupert, and Vardon, of course, is the little village on the Dender River where my brother was billeted during the Waterloo campaign."

"So?" Stéphanie lifted her chin defiantly.

"So Father Gilbert wasn't familiar with your name or Rupert's, which wasn't at all strange, because you had only recently arrived in Vardon, and Rupert wasn't a Catholic. However, the good father did notice something significant about the date of your 'marriage.' June fourteenth, 1815. The day before the start of the battle of Waterloo. The day the good priest's mother died in Brussels, surrounded by all her children, including Father Gilbert. The priest had been summoned to his mother's deathbed two days previously, and remained in Brussels for another week."

Araminta drew a sharp breath. "So Father Gilbert couldn't have married Stéphanie and Lord Rupert in Vardon on June fourteenth. He was in Brussels that day. Stéphanie's marriage certificate must be a forgery."

"Quite right. Mademoiselle Despard apparently didn't wear the willow for Rupert for very long. She immediately took up with Hippolyte Augé—or it may be that she had been carrying on with Rupert and Monsieur Augé at the same time, who knows?—and became pregnant. She and Augé, recalling that my brother came from a wealthy family, then hatched a scheme to make their love child my heir. Unfortunately for them, they were a pair of amateurish bunglers. Their little plot never had a chance of succeeding."

Hippolyte Augé had been listening to Jason's exposé in a grim silence, his dark face betraying a growing agony of disappointment. Now, stung by Jason's note of careless contempt, Augé launched himself at the Duke, slashing wildly with the knife that he had snatched from an inside pocket of his coat. "Amateurish bunglers, are we," he screamed. "We made just one mistake, your high and mightiness. We didn't check into the whereabouts of that damned priest."

Wary-eyed and cool, Jason managed to grab Augé's knife hand, twisting it with a steely strength. The knife fell to the floor, and Jason, jerking Augé upright with his left hand, clipped the Belgian neatly and surgically on the chin with his right fist. Stepping over Augé's prostrate form, the Duke walked to the door of the parlor. On the threshold, he turned, fixing Stéphanie with a chilly stare. "I want you out of England within the week. I'll pay for your passage home, and I'm also prepared to settle a modest yearly pension on you, on the off-chance that you've actually given birth to my brother's child. The pension will cease the moment you again set foot in this country. Lady Araminta, are you coming with me?"

Araminta opened her mouth to speak to Stéphanie, but immediately closed it again. Any conversation with the ashen-faced woman would be so embarrassing that it would be demeaning to both of them. Averting her gaze, she marched past Stéphanie and out the door.

In the curricle, Araminta sat looking down at her hands, nervously pleating the material of her gown. For the first time in her life she felt completely in the wrong. How could she have been so blind to all the signs that should have indicated to her that Stéphanie Despard didn't ring quite true? The missing page from the church register. The curious failure to persuade Rupert to marry her in a civil and legal ceremony. The refusal to allow her marriage certificate and Rupert's alleged letters out of her possession so they could be verified. The quick friendship with Augé and the subsequent permission for him to reside in her home. Above all, Araminta thought wretchedly, why hadn't she put more trust in Jason's fundamental honesty and sense of justice? Stiff-necked and arrogant he might be, but she had never found him dishonorable.

"Jason, will you accept my humble apologies?" she said in a small voice. "I should never have taken Stéphanie Despard's side against yours without acquainting myself with more of the facts."

"No apologies are necessary," came the curt reply. "You're entitled to hold any opinion you like, and to befriend anyone you like."

Araminta felt the beginnings of a slow rage building up inside her as she realized that Jason was not yet prepared to bury his grievances. "In that case, why did you go to so much trouble today to inform me of Stéphanie's misdeeds?" she demanded.

"I felt it to be my duty to prevent an adventuress from taking advantage of you."

Resisting the impulse to hit him over the head with her parasol, Araminta forced herself to count to ten. "Thank you so much for your solicitude, but I'm quite able to fend for myself."

Back in Bruton Street, after a most uncomfortable drive in which she and the Duke had not addressed another word to each other, Araminta jumped down from the curricle, narrowly avoiding a nasty fall to the pavement as she did so, and marched up the steps of Middleton House without a backward glance. She went straight to her bedchamber, where she vented her angry feelings by tossing her bonnet on the floor and stamping on it. Amid a shower of feathers from the ostrich plumes, floating around the room like the aftermath of a pillow fight, she threw a book against the wall, and then, for good measure, followed it with her favorite gilded mirror.

Jessie walked into the midst of this carnage, turning pale with shock. "Merciful heavens, my lady, what's wrong?"

"Nothing's wrong," replied Araminta crossly. "I'm in a towering rage, that's all, and I mean to enjoy it!" By this time, however, the destruction of her property had had a calming effect on her temper. She sat down at her desk, reaching for a pen. "Send Ben up to me, please, Jessie."

A little later, entering the bedchamber, the coachman, Ben, paused to look down at his feet when his stout boots crunched against a broken shard of glass. At the same time he lifted a hand to brush from his face an errant wisp of ostrich feather from Araminta's bonnet. "Yes, my lady?" he inquired impassively.

"Ben, you packed away Uncle Will's effects after his death. Can you lay your hand on that gold scimitar presented to him by the Vali of Aleppo?"

"That I can, my lady. Sir Wilfrid, he set great store by that there sword wi' all them diamonds and rubies. I have it packed away all right and tight in Sir Wilfrid's trunk."

"Good. Send it to the Duke of Harwood, along with this note. See that His Grace receives it today."

As the door closed behind Ben, Araminta grinned wickedly. Jason had ungallantly refused to accept her apology today. How would he cope with an even handsomer gesture, the gift of a magnificent bejeweled scimitar, once the property of a powerful Turkish official?

Almost immediately her face sobered. Jason was now vindicated, but the echoes of scandal might linger on, causing him embarrassment for years to come. Something would have to be done. Taking a sudden decision, she raced to the door, calling after the coachman, "Ben, wait. I want my carriage immediately. One of the grooms can take the scimitar to the Duke."

Waiting in the opulent drawing room of Lady Jersey's town house in Berkeley Square, Araminta rose as her hostess entered the room, saying, "Thank you for seeing me."

A pretty, graceful woman in her early thirties, Lady Jersey had been dubbed by some the "Queen of Fashion." Certainly she was one of the most influential political hostesses of the day, and she was a member of the all-powerful committee of women who ruled the assemblies at Almack's with an iron hand. If anyone could be said to rule over London society, the Countess of Jersey was a strong candidate. She was reputed to be exceptionally kind and good-humored, but today, as she inclined her head to Araminta and begged her to be seated, there was an air of reserve, almost of aloofness, about her.

"Lady Jersey, I find myself at a standstill, entirely through my own fault," began Araminta with an air of candor. "I need advice, and I've been told that you give the wisest advice in London!"

Lady Jersey shook her head. "I think you've been listening to too many Banbury stories, Lady Araminta. However, I should be glad to help you if I can." No doubt about it, the slight chill in her ladyship's manner was beginning to thaw.

"Well, you see, I've been taken in by a—I'm sorry to speak so frankly, but I can't think of another word for that adventuress!—by a scheming lightskirt! Perhaps you've heard something about the Belgian woman who claimed to be the widow of the Duke of Harwood's brother?"

"I did hear some rumors," said Lady Jersey cautiously.

"Everyone has, I fear," Araminta exclaimed, sighing. "I took her part because I thought she'd been tragically wronged. Now, too late, I've discovered that her story was a tissue of lies. In the meantime, however, the Duke has suffered damage to his reputation. It's all my fault, and I'd do anything to set things right, but I don't know how to go about it. I can hardly contact every one of his acquaintances and tell them the Duke wasn't at fault!" Araminta leaned forward in her chair, her hands clasped tightly together. "Lady Jersey, you have a much greater experience of the Ton than I do. What would you advise me to do?"

The Countess's face was a study in mixed emotions. She was interested, she was flattered, she was irresolute. She said tentatively, "You're to be commended for having such a sense of responsibility. So many young people these days are unthinking . . ." Pausing, her brow knit in thought, she seemed to come to a decision. "Lady Araminta, I do have some advice for you. Don't do anything. Let me drop a word here and there. It's quite true, I have a good many friends in London, and many of them are kind enough to value my opinion. I fancy it won't be long until everyone who matters knows the truth of the situation."

Araminta rose, extending her hand. "Thank you. I was informed correctly. You *do* give the wisest advice in London!"

"Oh, as to that, I'm not so sure," Lady Jersey said modestly. Then she added, her eyes twinkling, "Are you a devotee of horse racing? If so, you may be interested in some information I received the other day from a friend. He tells me that a horse owned by a mysterious gentleman named A. Middleman has an excellent chance to win the Derby. I myself have placed a substantial wager on the horse—what was his name?—oh, yes, on Selim."

Well! thought Araminta as she left the house. At least I won't be causing any fresh scandal by racing Selim in the Derby. If Lady Jersey is amused by "A. Middleman," no one else will lift an eyebrow over it.

When Araminta returned to Bruton Street from her visit to Lady Jersey, she found Odile getting out of a hackney in front of Middleton House.

"I could not resist paying another little visit to Stéphanie," Odile bubbled, walking up the steps of the house with Araminta. "The adorable *bébé*, he seems to grow an inch every day!" She frowned. "One thing troubles Stéphanie, however. *Milord* Manning hasn't visited her in several days. She wonders if she could have offended him. But then, he has not called here recently, either. It's not like him, he has been so kind, so devoted."

Araminta opened her mouth and then thought better of it. When the footman opened the door, she said, "Beeson, please ask Lady Middleton and Miss Damaris to join Madame Lacoste and me in the morning room for tea."

As soon as the footman left, Odile said in a stage whisper, "But what is this, *chère* Araminta? Madame Middleton and the little Damaris, they have not been *en rapport* with us lately, since we rescued poor Stéphanie from the gutter, *non?* In fact they have spoken to us hardly a word. Indeed, Madame Middleton seems happy to see us leave her house. So perhaps she and Damaris, they will not wish to take tea with us. And in any case I should prefer chocolate, as you know."

Henrietta and Damaris arrived in the morning room as the footman appeared with the tea tray. Neither of them seemed especially eager to be there. "Well, Araminta, I daresay you're about to tell us that you've found a house to rent," Henrietta said heavily.

"Why, no. Actually I've decided not to rent a house. You see, I learned something today that I hope makes it unnecessary for to set up my own establishment. Something you and Damaris should know, and you, too, Odile." Briefly Araminta described her visit with Jason to Stéphanie's house in Baker Street.

"So that dreadful woman's story was a tissue of lies. I knew it!" exclaimed Henrietta in triumph.

"We *told* you, Aunt Araminta," said Damaris reproachfully.

Odile's reaction was even stronger. Far from displaying any reluctance to accept the charges against her friend, she flew into a towering rage. I *believed* in that woman, *chère* Araminta! I worked my fingers to the bone—to a nubbin!—putting that house in order, and shopping for all that lovely furniture. I poured out my heart's sympathy to her, I admitted her into the bosom of my confidence, and now you tell me she was *scélerate*. I could throttle her with my bare hands!"

"It won't be necessary to do anything that drastic. We can make her suffer enough by other means! The Duke has ordered her to leave England by the end of the week, and tomorrow morning you, Odile, will go to Baker Street to inform Stéphanie that she will get no more money from me. You will also give her a stack of tradesmen's bills for her new clothes and furnishings, with a request for immediate repayment. *That* request, I fancy, will drive the woman out of the country faster than anything else!"

As a diabolically pleased expression began to spread over Odile's face, Araminta said to Henrietta, "When I realized how wrong I had been about Mademoiselle Despard, I, of course, apologized immediately to the Duke. Now I'd like to apologize to you and Damaris for causing you so much anxiety. I should never have taken up that woman's case unless, or until, I'd had the opportunity to investigate her thoroughly."

Henrietta exclaimed, "Oh, Araminta, I've felt so wretched these past few days, knowing we were out of charity with each other. We're *sisters,* the last living members of our family. I'm delighted that you're not leaving my house. Everything will be comfortable now that the Belgian woman has been revealed for the snake she is!"

Araminta looked past her sister to her niece. "How about you, Damaris? Are you going to forgive your erring aunt?"

"Well, to be sure, Aunt Araminta, I don't *like* feeling at odds with you. As Mama was saying, you're our only relative on the Beresford side of the family," replied Damaris, her tone as stiff as the set of her slender shoulders. "But when I saw you helping that wicked woman in her false claims against the Duke—"

"It was very bad of me. The Duke is the soul of honor, and I should have recognized that," said Araminta solemnly. Perhaps a shade too solemnly, for Damaris stared at her aunt with a trace of suspicion, doubtless recalling those occasions when Araminta had displayed a less than serious outlook on life.

Henrietta glanced up as the butler entered the morning room. "Yes, Simpson?"

"A Lieutenant Craddock is at the door, my lady. I told him, naturally, that you do not receive callers at this hour, but he was insistent. He said he must see you on a matter of great urgency—"

"Craddock? Did you say Craddock?" Odile interrupted. Without waiting for a reply, she jumped up from her chair and ran out of the room, followed by the astonished butler. Seconds later, the sound of loud shrieking sent the startled occupants of the drawing room rushing out into the hallway, where they found Odile locked in the arms of a gentleman in the uniform of the Royal Navy.

The butler coughed loudly. "Sir. Madame Lacoste. You are not alone."

Slowly, reluctantly, Odile unwound her arms from around the neck of the naval officer, whose handsome face turned a bright red as he realized that several pairs of interested eyes were observing him.

"*Chère* Araminta, this is my Roger, home from the sea at last," exclaimed Odile, clinging tightly to the lieutenant's arm.

"I'm very happy indeed to meet you, Lieutenant Craddock," said Araminta, extending a cordial hand.

"Not as happy as I am to meet you, Lady Araminta," said the lieutenant, wringing her hand. "I've been in such agony for so many months, not knowing Odile's fate or her whereabouts, and now I learn that she's safe and has kind new friends." He looked inquiringly at Henrietta and Damaris.

"Allow me to introduce you to my sister, Lady Middleton, and my niece, Miss Damaris Middleton. But look, Lieutenant, we can't welcome you properly out here in the hallway. Pray come into the drawing room." She smiled at Henrietta. "This is such a happy occasion for Odile. Don't you think it warrants a celebration? May I ask Simpson to bring us a bottle—no, several bottles—of champagne?"

"Certainly. Ask Simpson for anything you wish," replied Henrietta, looking utterly bewildered. In the drawing room, she and Damaris seemed unable to tear their fascinated eyes away from Odile, who had plastered herself so close to her Roger on the settee that a piece of paper could hardly have been wedged between them. Odile nestled her head against Roger's shoulder and cuddled against him without a hint of self-consciousness, but the lieutenant, a tall, attractive young man with a hint of shyness in his manner, looked distinctly uncomfortable at this public display of affection. Henrietta murmured, "Who *is* this young man, Araminta? Did I misunderstand Madame Lacoste's situation? I thought she was widowed within the past year."

Oh, my God, thought Araminta, experiencing a sudden hollow sensation in the pit of her stomach. What a dolt she had been, not to anticipate the need for explanations when Roger reappeared in Odile's life. It had seemed so clever at the time to make her a widow. The primary purpose of the story, of course, had been to conceal the fact of Odile's residence in a Syrian seraglio, but this new identity had also enabled her to avoid embarrassing questions about her background. It would have been awkward for Araminta to introduce into London society a young unmarried Frenchwoman of doubtful origins, but a pathetically grieving widow—especially one so beautiful—was quite something else again! However, grieving widows do not customarily pine for new lovers, so Lieutenant Craddock's name had never been mentioned to Odile's new London friends. Now, Roger must be explained, and fast.

Araminta said quickly, "Henrietta, could I speak to you for a moment privately? Odile, Damaris, Lieutenant Craddock, will you excuse us?"

In the hallway, Araminta said in a low voice to her mystified sister, "I have something to tell you, but it concerns such a—a delicate subject that I don't think you would wish a young unmarried female like Damaris to hear it."

"Good heavens, Araminta, what is it?"

"Well, poor Odile, she would die rather than admit it, but . . . Araminta turned her head away, as if the subject

219

was too painful to discuss. After a moment she leaned toward Henrietta, whispering urgently in her ear.

Henrietta gasped. Araminta could almost see the lurid images she'd invoked racing through her sister's horrified mind. Odile forced into a loveless marriage with a man of good family whose handsome face and exquisite manners concealed his dissolute character. Odile beaten senseless by a brutish husband. Unnatural practices, nameless vices. And the one shining spot in Odile's ordeal, the friendship and help of Lieutenant Craddock.

Henrietta looked at Araminta with tears in her eyes. "Poor, poor woman. I understand why you didn't tell me this before. It would have been so humiliating for Madame Lacoste to reveal her sufferings at the hands of her husband. Under the circumstances, I don't begrudge her the affections of Lieutenant Craddock, although normally, as you know, I would frown on the spectacle of a young woman falling into the arms of another man when her husband hadn't been dead in his grave for a year. Indeed, I wish her very happy!"

"Oh dear, perhaps I shouldn't have—" Araminta tried to look conscience-stricken. "You won't tell anyone, Henrietta? I shudder to think what would happen if the gossips should get hold of Odile's story. They might even accuse her of misconduct with Lieutenant Craddock."

Henrietta looked grave. "Couldn't we just say that the lieutenant is an old friend of the family? Then, after he's been here for a few days or weeks, he might begin to 'fall in love' with Madame Lacoste. That would be unexceptionable. But I think you should hint to Madame Lacoste that she and the lieutenant might be more—er—circumspect in public."

"The very thing!" Araminta beamed, feeling limp with relief. Perhaps there was something to thought transference, after all. Henrietta had certainly said exactly what her sister had been hoping she would say.

Returning to the drawing room with Henrietta,

Araminta reached for a glass of champagne from the tray the butler was extending to her and turned her attention to the lovers, who, she decided, had been wrapped up in each other for long enough. "When did you arrive in London, Lieutenant?"

Recovering slightly from her first paroxysms of joy, Odile lifted her head from the lieutenant's shoulder to say solicitously, "Roger, *mon chou,* you look so weary. Have you been traveling a long time?"

"Ten hours and a bit. We docked at Portsmouth at dawn, and I was on my way to London by seven o'clock in a hired post chaise and four."

"And how long can you stay? They won't be sending you back to sea right away, will they?"

"I have indefinite leave, owing, I'm told, to the good offices of the Duke of Harwood."

Seated next to Damaris, Araminta could hear her audible gasp of surprise.

The lieutenant continued, with a loving smile for Odile, "I feel as if I've been living in a dream for some weeks now, ever since the *Bellerophon* landed in Gibraltar and I found my new orders waiting for me there and the letter from the Duke."

"You say the Duke of Harwood wrote to you?" said Henrietta. "You were perhaps previously acquainted with him?"

"Oh, that was my doing," said Araminta. "I asked the Duke to use his good offices at the Admiralty to locate Lieutenant Craddock."

"I see," said Henrietta, as if she didn't see at all.

"Naturally, I'm very anxious to make His Grace's acquaintance," said the lieutenant, "so that I can thank him in person for his kindness. When I read his letter telling me about Odile's experiences—"

Araminta deliberately spilled her wine over the skirt of her gown. She could see another disaster looming. Henrietta had accepted the fiction of Odile's ill treatment by a

221

brutish husband, but never, never would her ladyship's forbearance extend to Odile's deflowering by a lascivious Turk. She exclaimed, "Lieutenant, could you help me, please?" When the lieutenant rushed over to daub solicitously at her gown with his handkerchief, she whispered fiercely, "Roger, if you say one word about Algerian pirates or Syrian harems, I'll see you hanged on the nearest yardarm in His Majesty's Navy!"

Chapter Thirteen

As she was about to mount the steps to the front door of Middleton House after her morning ride, Araminta paused on the pavement to greet Lieutenant Craddock, who had just driven up in a curricle.

"Good morning, Lady Araminta," he said. "Odile tells me that you're quite the horsewoman. Do you ride every day?"

"As often as I may. Later today I hope to ride my Arabian, Selim, when I go down to Epsom with my nieces to visit the stud where Selim is being trained." She smiled at the lieutenant. "Your powers of persuasion must be enormous," she said. "You're the first person I've met who's been able to break Odile of a lifelong habit of late rising."

During the past several days Roger Craddock had become a familiar figure in Bruton Street, arriving every morning to take Odile sightseeing in London or in one of the surrounding communities. Yesterday they'd gone to Richmond Park, taking with them an elaborate picnic hamper from Gunther's pastry shop in Berkeley Square. Nothing had yet been said publicly about an engagement, but, thought Araminta, even the most unromantic onlooker could hardly have failed to observe that Roger and Odile were lovers. At first Roger had been somewhat in awe of Araminta, but her genuine friendliness had soon melted his reserve and they were now on excellent terms. "I'm preparing Odile for her new life, Lady Araminta," he said now with a chuckle. "As a sailor's wife, she'll be expected to rise at the crack of dawn to have breakfast with me, at least when I'm in port."

"And what are your plans for today?"

"I thought we might go to the museum at the Egyptian Hall, where I'm told there is an exhibition called the Pantherion, a collection of all the world's known quadrupeds."

Araminta burst out laughing. "Hardly Odile's cup of tea."

"Possibly not," grinned the lieutenant, "but the museum also has Napoleon's bulletproof traveling carriage on display, and I'm sure Odile will love seeing that."

Each time she saw Odile and Roger Craddock together, Araminta marveled at the attraction between such an unlikely pair: Roger, so sedate and serious-minded, a man who seemed to have little interest in the social scene but whose tastes, it had developed, ran to a study of history and the sciences; and Odile, whose beauty, vivacity, and beguiling sweetness of manner could not mask entirely her strong sense of self-absorption and her frequent lapses into shallowness. But the lieutenant apparently was oblivious to his love's faults, or at worst, passed over them with an uncritical acceptance.

"Before we go into the house, I'd like to ask you a question about Odile," Araminta said abruptly.

Looking faintly puzzled, Roger replied, "I'd be happy to tell you anything I know, but surely you're closer in many ways to Odile than I am, especially during these past months."

"Actually, my question concerns you more than Odile. You see, I'm very fond of her, and I feel at least partially responsible for her happiness." Araminta paused, wondering how to phrase herself most diplomatically.

"You've been most kind to Odile. I'll be grateful to you as long as I live," said Roger, still sounding puzzled.

Throwing up her hands, Araminta exclaimed, "Oh, the

devil, there's only one way to put it, even if I embarrass you to tears! Has it been difficult for you to accept Odile's stay in the Syrian harem? Do you think it might—well—might cause problems for you in the future?"

"You don't embarrass me," replied the lieutenant with a simple directness. "I think you're asking me if in the future I might resent the fact that Odile had belonged to another man. The answer is no. Odile was sold into the harem against her will. Why should I blame her for something that wasn't her fault?"

Oh, Odile, you lucky, lucky woman, Araminta thought with a twinge of envy. The door of the house opened just then, and the object of her envy swept down the steps to join her and Roger. Dressed for the street, Odile was a vision in a gown of pale pink muslin and a pelisse of zephyrine silk in a deeper shade of pink, worn with a straw gypsy bonnet laden with roses.

"Here I am, Roger," she exclaimed. "The footman, he informed me you were standing on the street in front of the house with Araminta." Odile planted a kiss on Roger's nose, causing him to look around him apprehensively for possible spectators. "Only for you, *mon bien-aimé,* would I leave my bed so early. It's not yet ten o'clock!" Tugging gently at his heavy silk cravat, she added with a coaxing smile, *"Chéri,* could we go to this place—this Egyptian Hall—another time? I would like to go shopping today. I've decided to come out of mourning. Why should I go on pretending grief for somebody who never existed? I want to wear colors again, and my wardrobe"—she glanced down disparagingly at her gown and pelisse—"my wardrobe is at least two years out of date."

"We'll do anything you like, my love," replied Roger promptly.

"Just don't let Odile anywhere near Madame Lyon's millinery shop," Araminta said, laughing. "Madame prides herself on selling the most expensive hats in London."

* * *

After Odile and Roger had gone off in the curricle, Araminta went up to her bedchamber to change out of her riding habit into clothes more suitable for her trip to Epsom. As she was adjusting the tilt of her hat in the mirror, Gillian wandered into the room, looking far more presentable than usual in a neat pelisse and modest bonnet. She wrinkled her nose in distaste at the tiny cup of syrupy Turkish coffee that Jessie had just deposited on the dressing table. "How can you swallow that vile drink?" she inquired.

"I got so used to drinking this coffee in the Levant that now I can't start the day without it," said Araminta cheerfully. "You should try it sometime. It will put iron in your backbone. By the way, you look charmingly, my dear. Different, of course, without all those ink stains on your hands and your clothing!"

"It's been so nerve-racking, waiting to hear from the publisher about *Castle of Horrors,* that I haven't been able to begin my new book," sighed Gillian. "I keep thinking, what if Mr. Loman hates my work? That's why I'm so happy to be going off with you for today, Araminta. It will take my mind off my troubles!"

"I'm glad. I'll enjoy having you with me. Is Damaris ready to go?"

"Oh, she asked me to give you her apologies. She had to change her mind about going with us to Epsom. Lady Slade sent around a note this morning with the news that Susan has taken a chill and won't be able to attend Mrs. Carleton's ball tonight. So Damaris felt she ought to spend some time with Susan today."

"That was kind of Damaris. She and Miss Slade are such good friends."

Driving over Westminster Bridge a little later with Gillian, Araminta reflected that the day would probably be more enjoyable without Damaris's presence. She'd never tried to disguise from herself that she felt more affection for Henrietta and Gillian than she did for Damaris. And even though the Stéphanie Despard disaster had been resolved—the Belgian woman, according to Odile, was making plans to leave England immediately—Araminta could detect in Damaris a slight edge of coolness that said without words that her elder niece hadn't entirely forgiven her.

Nor had Jason. Not a word had come from him, not even an acknowledgment of the Turkish scimitar. Araminta had been telling herself for several days that she shouldn't allow her estrangement from the Duke to weigh heavily on her mind. His position in her life, after all, was merely peripheral, as Damaris's future—if yet unannounced—husband. He was also unjust, narrow-minded, prejudiced against the female sex, and thoroughly infuriating. She shouldn't care a whit about his good opinion of her, but unfortunately she did. She missed his company. She'd enjoyed their constant battle of wits, and it had been curiously comforting to know that there was at least one person in London to whom she could safely make any outrageous remark that came into her head.

The fifteen-mile journey from London into the lovely rolling countryside of Surrey's North Downs seemed to take a shorter time than usual, probably, thought Araminta, because both passengers in the carriage were lost in thought. Gillian was obviously a prey to anxiety about the fate of her book, and Araminta continued to brood on Jason's iniquities. Before it seemed possible, they had passed through Epsom into the lonely stretches of the open heath and then down the narrow winding lane leading to the courtyard of Martin Corby's neat farmstead.

As Martin helped Araminta and Gillian down the steps of the town chariot, his expectant smile faded. He cast an involuntary look into the recesses of the carriage. "Oh. I thought perhaps Damaris might come."

"Damaris is visiting a sick friend, Martin," said Gillian.

Martin's face lighted up. "That's like her. She always thinks of others first. Lady Araminta, will you come into the house before we visit your horses? Mrs. Felton has been baking scones all the morning!"

"Selim and Balkis first, please."

As she and Gillian walked with Martin to the stables, Araminta reflected on the change in Martin's attitude toward her since their first meeting. This was her third visit to the stud, and by now he'd largely lost his awe of her and treated her as he would any male client for whom he was training horses.

Selim's head was peering out of his loose box as Araminta entered the stable area, and he immediately whinnied a welcome to her. "Oh, Selim, you're more beautiful than ever, and I've missed you so much," Araminta crooned, brushing her hand gently across the horse's head and mane. She nodded a greeting to Hassan, who had been standing apart with folded arms, keeping a watchful eye on the stable boy who was rubbing Selim down. "Well, Hassan? Do you still think Selim can beat any horse in England?"

The Arab lifted his hooded gaze to say disdainfully in his rapidly improving English, "Lady, provided your servant was in the saddle, Selim could outrun any horse in the world!"

Araminta laughed. "There speaks the voice of authority, Martin." To Hassan she said, "Please have Selim saddled up in about an hour. I haven't had a really satisfying gallop since I arrived in England. A ride in Hyde Park can't compare with a ride in open country."

Hassan shook his head. "No, Lady."

"What?" Araminta stared at Hassan in disbelief. "Are you refusing to obey my orders?"

"I am. Selim has finished his training for the day. I wish him to rest now."

Martin cleared his throat. "Actually, Lady Araminta, I

228

agree with Hassan. Selim worked out strenuously this morning on the heath. May I offer you my own horse as a mount? Wizard isn't as fast as Selim, but I think you'd enjoy riding him."

The combative look died out of Araminta's eyes. "What a caper-witted creature you must think me, Martin. Of course I don't wish to interfere in Selim's training. I'd be happy to ride Wizard."

A gleam of mischief crossed her face. She spoke in her swift, fluent Arabic to Hassan, who listened in glum disapproval. He bowed stiffly. "As you wish, lady."

Turning to Martin, Araminta said, "Now can I see Balkis?"

"Indeed. She's in the south pasture. Gillian, are you coming with us?"

But Gillian had found another interest. She came up to them holding a tiny coal-black kitten with white paws and a white spot on its nose. "Look, Martin, it has the same markings as that cat I had years ago on our estate in Lincolnshire. Remember Lucifer?"

Martin chuckled. "Do I not? It landed on my head once. There's a whole litter of identical ones in the stables, if you care to have a look at them."

Leaving Gillian to visit the kittens, Araminta strolled with Martin to the south pasture to visit Balkis. They stood side by side watching the dainty Arabian mare placidly feeding on the lush spring grass.

"I'm reasonably certain she's in foal," remarked Martin. "We'll see, won't we, eleven months from now."

"Oh, how I'd love to have her back in London," Araminta sighed. "The Duke of Harwood has found me a very suitable mount, but I do miss my Arabians."

"The way you ride, so I hear, Balkis is much better off with me in her delicate condition," grinned Martin. "We'll give her plenty of exercise, never fear." After a moment he said in a carefully careless tone, "I daresay this a very exciting time for Damaris."

"Yes, a girl's come out season is always exciting."

"Is—oh, I know you can't comment on any plans she may have for marriage—but is Damaris happy?"

"Very happy, I think." Araminta looked at Martin with sympathetic eyes. Surely only very young men wore their hearts on their sleeves so openly. In Martin's eyes, Damaris was obviously a figure of perfection, a saint on a pedestal. It was not a position that Araminta had any desire to share; she much preferred being a flesh and blood woman with a normal share of faults and virtues. In contrast to Martin, the Duke of Harwood . . . Hastily she pushed the image of Jason, very improbably mooning over his heart's desire in public, out of her mind. "Do you know Lady Torrington?" she asked suddenly.

"Lady Torrington?" Martin looked momentarily blank at the abrupt change of subject. "Why, yes. She's a good friend of my Aunt Maybelle. Matter of fact, I received an invitation from Lady Torrington just last week. Seems she's having some kind of *fête.*"

"Exactly. Do you plan to attend?"

"Well, no. I'm no great hand for that sort of thing, to tell the truth. And also, I'm very busy with the stud."

"I really think you ought to attend the *fête,*" Araminta said earnestly. "Damaris will be there, and others of your friends, I collect. I think it so important for old friends not to lose sight of one another, don't you? Why, I remember Damaris saying, that first day I met you in Hyde Park, that it had been much too long since she'd seen you."

"Well . . . perhaps I *have* been rusticating for too long at Longridge Farm. A change of scene might be just the thing for me. Thank you for the suggestion."

Now, why did I do that, Araminta asked herself as she and Martin walked back to the house. Why did I encourage poor Martin to seek out Damaris's company, when I know full well she fancies herself head over heels in love with Jason and, moreover, wants very much to be a duchess?

Fancies herself! Araminta's cheeks burned as she repeated the phrase to herself. What a strange expression to use in describing Damaris's feelings for the Duke. Could it be wishful thinking? In some deeply buried part of her mind did she harbor a secret desire to see Martin and Damaris paired off so that Jason . . .

Rubbish, thought Araminta. Jason and her niece were not yet formally affianced, so it would not be at all out of line for Martin to renew his friendship with Damaris. In any case, Martin had a perfect right to take his part in the London social scene. She, Araminta, would very much enjoy his company.

A little later, sitting in the farm parlor with Martin and Gillian, Araminta accepted a second cup of tea from the solicitous housekeeper, settled back in her chair, and said, "Well, now, do bring me up to date, Martin. What do you think of Selim's chances in the Derby? As he just informed me, Hassan is firmly of the opinion that it will be no contest, but then we have to remember that his opinion is very biased!"

"True, but Hassan may very well be as clever in the saddle as he thinks he is," Martin replied, smiling. "And Selim—"

"Permit me to say that I admire your finesse in handling Hassan," Araminta interrupted. "He seems to think that he alone is responsible for Selim's progress in training."

"Thank you. I've grown to like Hassan, but he can be a bit of a handful." Martin's face sobered. "In reference to your question about Selim and the Derby, I'm almost afraid to say this, for fear the gods of racing will punish me for my presumption, but I'm so certain that Selim will win the Derby that I'd be willing to wager everything I possess on the outcome. Never in all my experience have I seen a horse with such intelligence, such speed, such endurance, and above all such a desire to win. Barring some kind of disaster, you're the next owner of a Derby winner."

"Not I," retorted Araminta. "You're forgetting Mr. A. Middleman. Lady Araminta Beresford would never do anything so unladylike as to enter a horse in the Derby! By the by, has the public swallowed the fiction of A. Middleman's ownership of Selim?"

"Yes and no. I'm constantly being questioned about Selim—by onlookers at his exercise sessions on the heath, by gentlemen I meet in Epsom, by actual visitors to the stud—and they all inquire respectfully about Mr. A. Middleman. But then invariably their eyes twinkle, and they make remarks like, 'I understand Mr. Middleman has been resident in the Levant,' or 'I hear that Selim is a very good mount for a lady.' "

"Famous. I don't care what the turf world believes, as long as"—Araminta smiled at Gillian—"as long as there are no scandalous rumors to upset your long-suffering mama!" She set down her cup and rose. "And now, if you'll excuse me, I'm going to change into my riding habit. I'm really looking forward to my ride on your horse Wizard, Martin."

However, when she reentered the parlor some ten minutes later, Araminta was greeted by a stunned silence. She hadn't changed into the riding habit she'd brought with her from London. Instead, she was now wearing a long tunic belted with a scarlet sash under a flowing *abba*, or camel's hair cloak, striped gaily in red and white. A *kaffiyeh*, a large square of brightly striped cloth, was doubled over her head, held in place by an *agal*, a twisted band of camel's hair, with the two long ends of the headdress trailing over her shoulders.

"Araminta! What on earth—" gasped Gillian.

"I've borrowed some of Hassan's clothes," said Araminta, pirouetting to show off her costume. "How do you like me as a Bedouin tribesman?"

"You certainly look exotic," Gillian replied, still looking faintly shocked. "Is there a special reason why you're masquerading as a Bedouin?"

"Certainly. I want to ride astride. I can't do that in my regular habit, at least not without causing eyebrows to raise. What if one of Martin's neighbors should see me? It would never do to cause scandal, as I'm sure your mother would agree. So I decided to dress like an Arab."

"Araminta . . ." Gillian paused, biting her lip. "I know I don't have the right to tell you what to do, but I think you're making a mistake by wearing those garments in public. You keep saying you want to avoid scandal. But what if one of Martin's neighbors saw you dressed like that, and guessed you weren't really a man?"

"That won't happen. My disguise is perfect. If I meet anyone on the road, I'll simply drape a corner of my *kaffiyeh* across my face, the way I've seen the Bedouins do it, time and time again, to protect themselves from a desert wind storm."

Despite Gillian's continued protests, Araminta left the house and walked out to the courtyard in front of the stables, where Martin's horse, Wizard, was waiting for her. She circled the big rawboned stallion slowly, examining him with the keen eye of a natural horsewoman. Then she smiled at Martin, who had accompanied her from the house. "You're a fine judge of horseflesh. Wizard and I will get along extremely together."

Martin nodded at the groom who had just emerged from the stables, leading a saddled horse. "Josiah will ride with you."

"Oh, I don't need an escort."

"I insist. You're my guest. I feel responsible for your safety." The stiffness of Martin's tone revealed more clearly than his wooden-faced expression what he thought of Araminta's latest prank.

She shrugged, refusing to allow Martin's masked disapproval to mar her enjoyment. Mounting from his cupped hands, she rearranged the folds of her tunic and cloak and cantered out of the courtyard, followed by the groom. As she went down the driveway, she urged Wizard to a gallop, and by the time she neared the main road, she was crouched low over the horse's mane, exhilarating in a burst of speed that sent her headdress and cloak billowing out behind her. At the entrance to the main road she reined in abruptly to avoid colliding with a passing curricle. Behind her, the groom sawed on his reins, preventing himself from crashing into her by a hairsbreadth.

Fully occupied by Wizard, who was rearing sharply, Araminta paid no attention to the curricle until she heard the sound of a familiar voice.

"Damnation, fellow, what are you doing on a horse if you don't know how to ride him properly? You might have killed both of us," roared Jason, his angry voice contrasting with the steady hands that were keeping his skittish team from bolting. When he had his horses under control, he looked up, saying, "Now then, my man, if you speak any English perhaps you'll see fit to apologize—" Breaking off, he stared incredulously. "Araminta? What in God's name are you doing in those infernal clothes? They look like the shapeless things your Bedouin groom used to wear."

"As a matter of fact, these *are* Hassan's clothes, and he wouldn't thank you for the unflattering description. I've borrowed them because I wanted to ride astride at long last," Araminta retorted. She pointed at the driveway. "Have you come down to visit Martin's stud? It's down that way, in the event you've forgotten how to get there." Nodding a cool good-bye, she tucked a corner of her *kaffiyeh* around her face, gathered her reins, touching Wizard lightly with her boot, and moved off.

"Araminta, wait."

"Yes?" She edged Wizard back beside the curricle, surveying the Duke with calm green eyes, all that was visible in her veiled face.

"Dash it, must you hide behind that thing? I want to

234

talk to you."

"Oh, very well." Araminta released the concealing folds of the *kaffiyeh*. "But if someone comes along the road, I'll have to put on my disguise again. Mustn't scandalize the local gentry, you know. Now, then, I'm entirely at your disposal." Then she added, with a tinge of gentle curiosity, "What a coincidence that you and I should be visiting Martin's stud on the same day."

Jason looked up at the beautiful face—so polite, so bland, so impersonal, with an imp of provocation lurking beneath the surface—and squelched an urge to shake her out of the saddle and put her over his knee. She must know what he had in mind to say, but she was going to make it as difficult as possible for him to say it.

"Actually, my presence here isn't a coincidence at all," Jason began, mustering the shreds of his aplomb. "I wanted to thank you for your gift of that magnificent scimitar, but when I called in Bruton Street this morning Lady Middleton informed me that you had gone down to Surrey. So, since I already had plans to visit my training stables in the vicinity, I decided to go first to Mr. Corby's farm to have a word with you." He swallowed hard, battling against the stiff-necked pride that made it difficult for him to acknowledge an error. "Much as I admire the scimitar, I appreciated even more the note you sent along with it. It said, 'Jason, I know you must feel tempted to use this weapon on me, but I assure you that I meant you no harm at all when I befriended Stéphanie Despard, and I'm sincerely sorry for any discomfort I may have caused you.' "

The Duke shook his head. "It shouldn't have been necessary for you to send me either the scimitar or the note. I should have accepted your original apology. Better, I should have told you that you had nothing to apologize for. I refused to admit it to myself, but I always knew that you took up Stéphanie Despard, not to spite me, but because that generous heart of yours impels you to reach out to help people. Will you forgive me for being such a boor?"

A quick, radiant smile lighted up Araminta's face. "Oh, of course I will." Impulsively she reached down to extend her hand, feeling a curious warm tingling sensation when his strong slender fingers closed around her own. "Friends again?"

Jason squeezed her hand before releasing it. "Friendly enemies at the very least!"

"Thank you for such a generous apology," said Araminta. "Not that I deserve it," she added, smitten by a twinge of her normally untroubled conscience. "I was angry with you for rebuffing me when I tried to tell you how sorry I was about Stéphanie, so I sent you the scimitar just to make you feel small."

"Oh, I knew that." The Duke's intensely blue eyes danced with amusement. "You're the most outrageous female I've ever met, but you rarely surprise me anymore."

For a brief moment, Araminta stared at Jason, mouth agape. Then she collapsed over Wizard's mane in a storm of helpless laughter, inadvertently jerking her reins and causing the horse to shy nervously. Jason reached up in alarm to seize Wizard's bridle, but Araminta, with the lightest pressure of her knees and a gentle tightening of her reins, already had the horse under control, while at the same time she unconcernedly mopped her eyes, watery from her bout of laughter, with a corner of her *kaffiyeh*.

"By God, you're a horsewoman!" exclaimed Jason. "As good a rider as I know."

Feeling her spirits lift to absurdly giddy peaks now that she seemed to be back on her old irreverent terms with Jason, Araminta tossed him an impudent look. "Good enough to ride in the Derby?"

Jason shook his head, grinning. "I daresay I'm risking our newly recovered friendship, but no." He cocked an inquiring eye. "Araminta, be serious. If, by some aberration of the rules of society, females were allowed to compete in

236

the Derby, you don't really believe that you could win on Selim?"

"Oh, but I do. Not just on Selim. On any horse you care to name."

"Not a rogue horse like my Caesar."

"How can you be so sure of that?"

Smiling, Jason refused to be baited. "You've seen Caesar. That's all the answer you need. Is your heart set on a solitary ride? Would you care to accompany me on a visit to my stables?"

"Oh." Araminta glanced down at her Arab garments. "I'm hardly dressed—"

"No one will see you except Caesar's groom and possibly my trainer. I'll introduce you as a visiting Arab breeder. You can pull the front part of that cloth thing down over your eyes and it will be difficult to see your face."

"You're not afraid I might be recognized and cause another scandal?" Araminta asked demurely.

"I'll let you worry about that," he retorted. "Remember our peace treaty? I promised to allow you to be your own woman."

Touché, Araminta thought with a quiver of mirth. Life was certainly going to be more interesting now that Jason was back in his role of perpetual antagonist. She released her feet from the stirrups, swung her right leg around, and slid down from the saddle. Beckoning to Martin's groom, who had been waiting patiently during her conversation with the Duke, she ordered him to take Wizard back to the stables. "Tell Mr. Corby that I met the Duke of Harwood on the road and accepted his invitation to visit his stud." Jason's tiger came up to give her a hand into the curricle and then jumped into his place behind the driver's seat.

At one point during the drive, Araminta remarked, "I daresay you haven't heard the latest news. Lieutenant Craddock arrived in London several days ago. Odile is in ecstatics, of course, and Roger's heart is full of gratitude toward you. As is mine. Thank you for your efforts with the Admiralty."

"It was my pleasure. It's not every day that one can unite a pair of lovers! I hope the lieutenant's return means that . . ." Jason broke off.

"You hope that Roger's arrival means that Odile will be leaving me," said Araminta with a touch of asperity. "You're still convinced that her presence at Middleton House is a potential source of scandal."

"You have many excellent qualities, Araminta, but mind reading isn't among them," retorted Jason. "Pray allow me to keep my thoughts to myself in the interest of our newly established state of peace and mutual tolerance!"

Flashing him an appreciative grin, Araminta subsided, leaning back to enjoy the short trip to his stud through the lovely Surrey countryside. As they drove into the vast quadrangle of the stable courtyard at Jason's stud, Araminta pulled the folds of her *kaffiyeh* down to shadow her eyes before hopping down from the curricle. Smithers, Jason's trainer, came hurrying out of his office to greet them, his gaze lingering on Araminta's strange garb with a polite curiosity.

"Afternoon, Smithers," said Jason. "I've brought a friend, Sheik"—he paused for a split second, obviously searching his mind for a suitable Arab name—"Sheik Mohammed, to see Caesar. The Sheik is a breeder of Arabian horses." As Araminta bowed her head gravely, Jason added, "He doesn't speak English, unfortunately, only a smattering of French."

The trainer accepted the fictive sheik and the reason for his muteness with no apparent difficulty. "I'm pleased to make your acquaintance, sir. Now, Your Grace, Caesar's groom isn't here at the moment, so I'll bring the horse out myself. Oh, and have you warned the Sheik how dangerous Caesar can be? Only minutes ago, he kicked out the

238

entire rear wall of his loose box."

Led out by the trainer, the coal-black stallion seemed even more nervous and ill-tempered than he'd appeared when Araminta had last seen him several weeks before. When an errant gust of wind sent her headdress flying wildly around her shoulders, Caesar caught the movement of the cloth out of the corner of his eye and started to rear so violently that he wrenched his halter from the grasp of the trainer, who fell to the ground, rolling away from the horse's hooves. Before Jason realized what she was doing, Araminta darted forward. She grabbed the halter, calling out to the horse soothingly and hanging on with all her strength while Caesar shook his head from side to side, trying to dislodge her. In moments, before the trainer could stumble to his feet or Jason could hurtle himself to her assistance, Caesar had ceased rearing and was standing quietly, trembling and rolling his eyes but showing no signs of an imminent outbreak. Araminta continued to talk to him in a low voice while she blew gently into his ear and then, pulling his head down, rested her chin on his muzzle. "Please put a saddle and bridle on him, Mr. Smithers," she said.

"Araminta, are you mad?" Jason snatched Caesar's halter away from her. He was white to the lips, the immense relief he felt at seeing her safe apparently evolving irrationally into an explosion of rage. "Get away from that horse. He could turn on you at any moment. A few weeks ago he kicked a careless stableboy so violently that the lad may be crippled for life."

Araminta stood her ground. "Caesar is your horse, and if you say I'm not to ride him, I'll abide by your decision," she said calmly. "But Jason, be truthful: if I were a man, and I had just proved to you that I could control Caesar, would you refuse to let me ride him?"

Jason stared at her, his mouth set in a stubborn line. Gradually the uncompromising grimness of his expression faded. She could sense a note of uncertainty in his voice as he said, "Don't ask me to do this. If anything should happen to you while you were riding Caesar, I'd never forgive myself."

"Could you forgive yourself more readily if I were a man?"

Turning abruptly to the trainer, Jason said in a strangled voice, "Saddle Caesar."

The trainer looked helplessly from the Duke to Araminta and back again. "Your Grace, is this wise? Caesar seems quiet now, but what if . . ." He flicked another uneasy glance at Araminta. "You *know* how Caesar feels about"—he gulped—"about females."

"The only stranger you've seen here today is an Arab sheik. Remember that, Smithers," the Duke said shortly. "Now do as I say. Saddle that horse."

Slowly and unwillingly the trainer brought out a saddle and placed it over Caesar's back. He tightened the cinch and moved to the horse's head. Unfastening the halter, he put it around Caesar's neck. "As you'll recall, Your Grace, he hates being bridled. If you'll just keep a tight hold on the lead rope, just in case—there we are." He raised the bridle in his right hand until the crownpiece was just in front of the horse's ears, slipped in the bit by placing the fingers of his left hand between Caesar's lips on the far side, and brought the bridle up over the ears.

"Nicely done," said Araminta approvingly. "A head-shy horse really fights the bridle. Do you think the bit's a trifle low?"

The trainer eyed Araminta with increasing respect. "You're quite right, ma'am." He raised the cheek piece so that the bit ceased to strike against Caesar's teeth. Turning back to the Duke, he said uneasily, "I wouldn't be doing my duty, Your Grace, if I didn't warn you again—"

"Thank you, Smithers, I take full responsibility." Jason drew a deep breath, cupping his hand for Araminta to mount. Caesar reared sharply as he felt her weight, but subsided almost immediately into a state of quivering tension when she patted his neck and leaned over to whisper in his ear. She smiled down into Jason's anxious face. "Don't worry," she said softly. Moving slightly in the saddle to settle her weight, she relaxed infinitesimally her pressure on the reins, booted Caesar lightly with her heel, and put him to a walk.

Standing beside the Duke, the trainer observed Araminta's seat—head erect, back straight, seat and legs close to her mount, knees down and closed against the saddle—and muttered in relief, "She's with the horse, no doubt of that." He watched closely as Araminta, on the far side of the courtyard, put Caesar to the trot, rocking gently from the saddle and easing back into it with the two beats of the trot. "And she's posting beautifully. The young lady's a superb rider."

"She's a superb woman," murmured the Duke absently, his eyes intent on Araminta as she cantered briskly a full turn around the courtyard and reined in before him. Stroking Caesar's neck affectionately, she remarked with a grin, "I almost wish you hadn't given in to me, Jason. If I hadn't ridden this wonderful animal, I wouldn't have the slightest worry about Selim's chances in the Derby. Of course, without putting Caesar to the gallop, I don't have any real idea of how fast he is."

"Very fast, ma'am. Like the wind," put in the trainer.

Araminta rolled her eyes at Jason in mock alarm. "Good heavens. Perhaps I should reconsider the size of the bet I was going to place on Selim."

Later, as they were driving away from the stables, Jason observed, "You needn't worry that my tiger or Smithers will do any gossiping about your visit. Each of them is the soul of discretion, and Smithers admires you too much to say an unkind word. He's inclined to think that you must have some kind of miraculous power over animals."

"How flattering, if untrue," Araminta laughed. Growing quickly more serious, she put her hand on his arm, saying softly, "Thank you for letting me ride Caesar. I know it was against your better judgment, against your every instinct. No one has ever paid me a greater compliment."

She could feel the muscles in Jason's arm tighten at her touch. He flashed her a sideways glance. "I have a rather thick head, but you've finally convinced me that you have a right to make your own decisions, good, bad, or indifferent, wise or unwise." His voice roughened. "On the other hand, if you'd sustained a serious fall while riding Caesar, I think I would have had him destroyed immediately."

Araminta felt a curious little lump in her throat. Since their first meeting, she and Jason had fallen into an easy, bantering give-and-take as "friendly enemies," but during the relationship, almost by unspoken agreement, neither had probed below the surface of their emotions. Jason's remark edged dangerously close to breaching that unspoken agreement.

She snatched at the first remark that would shatter the emotional tension that had unaccountably developed between them. "Then I'm very happy indeed that I *did* ride Caesar successfully," she said gaily. "Without him in the Derby, there'd be no race of the century!"

As she was speaking, Jason turned out of the long driveway of his estate into the road leading back toward Martin's farm. Coming toward them was a heavily laden farm cart, the driver of which touched his forelock to Jason while staring as if mesmerized at Araminta's colorful Eastern garb. For some unaccountable reason, the man's curious gaze brought to Araminta's mind a sudden vision of Henrietta's disapproving face.

"Jason," she began in a small voice, "it might be better not to mention to my sister that I visited your stud dressed like an Arab shiek. She'd be bound to think I'd committed another terrible impropriety. Poor Henrietta, I've tried her sensibilities so often since I came to live with her, why risk scandalizing her again?"

After a short pause, Jason observed, "I think you're right. Lady Middleton would no doubt be distressed, also, to learn that you'd risked injury by riding my horse. But . . . didn't you say that Gillian came down from London with you?"

"Gillian was so shocked to see me in these clothes, I'm sure she'll be more than happy not to tell her mama about it."

Jason met her eyes in a glance of perfect understanding. Neither of them had mentioned Damaris's name.

Chapter Fourteen

Araminta read Felicity's letter again with a glow of pleasure. Now she was in charity with both Jason and his sister. She'd written a frank letter of apology to Felicity after discovering the falsity of Stéphanie Despard's claims, and now Lady Salford had replied promptly, expressing her joy and relief. "I'm in transports of happiness at the thought that we can be friends again," Felicity had written, "and Augustus and I—well, *I*, at any rate!—are looking forward immensely to attending your ball for Damaris."

Araminta looked up from her letter in surprise as Gillian burst into the bedchamber without knocking. As usual, she looked as though she'd thrown herself into her clothes, and her hair hung in wild ringlets on her forehead. "Oh, Araminta, I'm in *such* trouble! You *must* help me!"

"Of course, love, anything I can do," Araminta said soothingly. "But first you must try to get hold of yourself. Sit down and tell me about it."

"It's my book. Mr. Loman wants to publish it!"

"Gillian! How splendid! Why aren't you hopping with joy?"

"Well, you know I wanted to publish the book anonymously so that Mama wouldn't find out about it . . ."

"Yes, you said the title page would read, '*Castle of*

244

Horrors, by A Lady of Quality.' Does the publisher object to that?"

"No. That's not the problem. Mr. Loman's just written that he likes my book very much and would be happy to publish it under any pseudonym I chose."

"Well, then . . ."

"Don't you recall that I told Mr. Loman my name was Margery Tavistock—my old nurse, you know—and that I gave Margery's sweet shop as my address? Now Mr. Loman says he can't do business with an accommodation address. He wants to meet me. I fancy he's become a little suspicious because Margery's shop is so close to his office that one could easily walk from one to the other in minutes, so why the need for an accommodation address? Perhaps he suspects that I've stolen someone else's work. At any rate, he insists on knowing my real name, or failing that, he wants to be sure that a responsible person is acting as my agent. He says that either I or my agent must come in and discuss the terms of the contract personally."

"Well, I suppose Mr. Loman isn't being totally unreasonable."

"Of course he isn't. He's willing to give me one hundred pounds for the book in advance of publication, and I quite understand why he doesn't wish to hand over a huge sum like that to someone who won't even give him her real name. For a while I considered going to see Mr. Loman under a false name; I thought I could satisfy him that I had indeed written the book, and I could still use Margery's shop as an accommodation address, and all without Mama's being any the wiser. But I soon realized what a hen-witted notion that was."

"Oh—why?"

"It's plain as plain could be. I'm sixteen years old, and I look even younger. Mr. Loman would *never* believe that I wrote *Castle of Horrors*. Or if he did believe me, he would refuse to publish a novel written by a mere child.

And I can't send Margery to Mr. Loman as my agent. The poor thing can't read, she can barely sign her name." Gillian's voice trailed off, but she looked at Araminta with pleading eyes. Her nail-bitten hands were clutched convulsively together.

"Would you like me to go see Mr. Loman as your agent?" Araminta asked resignedly.

"Oh, Araminta, would you?"

"I think I'm obligated to do so, to ensure that *Castle of Horrors* finds its way to a waiting public." Araminta's eyes began to twinkle. "When I think, though, of the conventional, ladylike life your mother wanted me to live in England when I first came here! Well, no matter." She rose, walking to the door to ring the bell. "I'll have the carriage brought around immediately. However, I must tell you, Gillian, that I hope our errand to the publisher won't take long, because otherwise my abigail is going to be very displeased with me for going out. Tonight I'm attending Lady Torrington's *fête champêtre,* and Jessie has been planning to spend hours on my toilet!"

Half an hour later Araminta's town chariot rumbled along Oxford Street, continued into Holborn Street, passed the Lincoln's Inn Gateway to the Inns of Court, and came to a stop before a building in Chancery Lane. Leaving a nervous Gillian in the carriage, Araminta climbed the stairs to an office two floors up. The outer door carried in florid lettering the words "Loman and Son, Publishers." Inside, in a tiny anteroom barely large enough for a desk and a chair, sat a middle-aged, rather scruffy-looking clerk, industriously scribbling in a ledger. He stared curiously at the tall elegant woman in the gown of pale green jaconet muslin, worn with a spencer of canary-colored silk and a French bonnet trimmed with a large bunch of spring flowers and an enormous plume of ostrich feathers.

"Mr. Loman, please. Either the father or the son will do."

"Isn't but one Loman, ma'am. The old man, he died last year. What name shall I say, ma'am?"

Araminta frowned slightly, wishing she had given some thought to a pseudonym, since she had no intention of meeting the publisher under her real name. "I am Miss Cholmondely. Miss Saphira Cholmondely," she announced after a moment. "Tell Mr. Loman that I wish to see him about a book I've written."

Appearing both surprised and impressed, the clerk went into the inner office, returning almost immediately to say, "Go right on in, ma'am."

Mr. Loman was a stout, shrewd-looking man in his forties. He left the chair behind his desk to greet Araminta, pressing her to take a chair while his alert eyes were assessing every detail of her appearance. Resuming his seat, he said politely, "My clerk tells me you've written a book, Miss Cholmondely. I gather it's something you think I might be interested in publishing. Will you tell me a little about your book?"

"You've already read my book, Mr. Loman. I'm the authoress of *Castle of Horrors*. Since you've insisted on meeting me personally, I'll admit that my name is not Margery Tavistock, and I don't keep a sweet shop in Holborn. A lady must have a little privacy, as I'm sure you'll agree. Now, then, I've come to discuss my contract."

Mr. Loman appeared too surprised to speak for several moments. Then he blurted, "I hope you'll forgive me for saying so, but you really are not at all the person I expected to see. I was convinced that *Castle of Horrors* had been written by an older lady, someone not so fashionable, someone who was more of a—a . . ."

"More of a bluestocking? I'm very sorry if I disappoint you."

"Oh no, not at all. I'm delighted to meet so charming a lady," the publisher said hastily. "Well, now, shall we get down to business? I'm considering publication in the au-

247

tumn. Three volumes. Tooled leather. I believe I've already mentioned the sum of one hundred pounds in my letter to you. Do these arrangements suit you?"

"Not entirely. I consider one hundred pounds a paltry sum for a work of such merit. Shall we say two hundred?"

Mr. Loman was speechless. When he recovered his voice, he spluttered, "Two hundred pounds for a first book from an unknown writer? Impossible. I'm not in this business to go bankrupt."

Araminta rose, shaking out her skirts. "That closes our discussion, then. Pray return my manuscript to the sweet shop at your earliest convenience."

Jumping up from his chair, Mr. Loman exclaimed, "Let's not be overhasty, ma'am. I like your book, and I'm prepared to offer, say, one hundred and twenty-five pounds. There, that's fair enough, isn't it?"

Araminta looked at the publisher thoughtfully. The sums in question represented the merest pocket money to her, but she knew that a substantially larger offer on Mr. Loman's part would bolster Gillian's self-esteem enormously. On the other hand, the publisher could probably be pushed only so far before he gave up on *Castle of Horrors*. "One hundred and seventy-five pounds seems much fairer to me," she said coolly.

"You're not being reasonable, ma'am. Oh well, I daresay I could come up a bit. One hundred and fifty?"

"Done. You may pay me now, or a draft sent to Margery Tavistock's shop would be acceptable."

Mr. Loman seemed taken back by Araminta's sangfroid. Apparently he was accustomed to dealing with fledgling authors whose gratitude for being published made them quite humble in their dealings with him. "Ah—splendid. If you will just sign here, then . . ." While Araminta was reading over the dry-as-bones clauses of the contract, Mr. Loman observed, "I would much prefer to send your money to your actual address, ma'am. I dislike this hole-in-the-corner way of doing business."

"And *I* prefer the present arrangement. My friends and family don't know that I've written a book, and I propose to keep them in ignorance of it."

"Ah." Mr. Loman's round face lighted up. "You've put some of your friends into the book, and you don't want them to find out about it. I thought that might be the case. A *roman à clef* like *Glenarvon*. That book came out only last week, and I hear it's already going into a second edition. High jinks among the *ton*. That's what sells books."

Araminta bit her lip to keep from laughing. The latest *on dit* had it that *Glenarvon* was the work of Lady Caroline Lamb; in a rage at being jilted by Lord Byron, she had supposedly written an anonymous novel skewering Byron and a host of her society friends and relatives under fictitious names. There was no need to disillusion Mr. Loman, thought Araminta. Rather, his belief that she had written a scandalous *roman à clef* would go far to explain her desire to preserve the anonymity of her identity and her address. "I don't admit to anything," she said, smiling. "You must allow a lady to have some secrets."

After Araminta had gone, Mr. Loman sat at his desk for a few moments, chewing thoughtfully on the end of his pen. Miss Cholmondely was undoubtedly a prominent member of the Ton, not, as he had previously surmised, a mere hanger-on of society, a former companion or governess, say, or a disgruntled family member, now out of favor with her aristocratic relatives, who had decided to tell all. Miss Cholmondely's presumably exalted position put a different character on the proceedings entirely. Her book might be even more of a *cause célèbre* than he had originally thought. Perhaps he should publish it immediately in order to take advantage of the notoriety of Caroline Lamb's novel. Meanwhile, though, he'd much prefer to know Miss Cholmondely's real name.

Rising, Mr. Loman walked hastily into the anteroom of

his office. "Fisher, I want you to follow that lady," he ordered his clerk. "I daresay she came here in a private carriage, so you might try to get into conversation with her coachman. See if you can find out who she really is."

As she left the publisher's office and descended the stairs, Araminta's lips were still curved in amusement at Mr. Loman's transparent attempts to discover her real identity. Emerging from the building, she narrowly missed colliding with a tall gentleman who was passing by on the pavement.

"Lady Araminta."

"Lord Manning," Araminta exclaimed in surprise. She hadn't seen him since their unpleasant encounter at Stéphanie Despard's house, when she'd forbidden him to call on either her or Odile, and the memory of their association, and the unpleasantness connected with it, had largely faded from her mind.

"I hadn't expected to meet you in this part of town, Lady Araminta," Manning observed. His handsome face was calm and smiling, betraying no indication that they had parted on bad terms.

"You, too, are far from your usual haunts."

"Well, not entirely. Sometimes one is obliged to mend one's fortunes in unexpected places."

He's been visiting the moneylenders, thought Araminta. It was almost the one good quality she knew of him, that he never hesitated to admit openly his lack of funds.

"Are you still angry with me?" he asked, in a light, conversational tone. He might have been inquiring about the weather.

"I really haven't examined my feelings about you, Lord Manning, nor do I intend to do so in the future. Good day, sir." As Araminta walked to her carriage, she noticed the unkempt figure of Mr. Loman's clerk loitering outside the entrance to the building, and wondered vaguely what he was doing there.

As they drove out of Chancery Lane, Araminta told a

tense Gillian about her meeting with Mr. Loman.

"Three volumes, leather-bound? Publication in the autumn? A hundred and fifty pounds? Oh, Araminta! Thank you, thank you, thank you from the bottom of my heart! Oh, how I wish I could dedicate my book to you. But that would give us both away, wouldn't it? Well, I'll dedicate my *next* book to you!"

"*Chère* Araminta, I just popped in to say *au revoir*. Roger and I are leaving now." Odile, who had been standing at the door, walked into Araminta's bedchamber, looking at her with unfeigned admiration. "You are beginning to have such style, *ma mie*. I've often suspected that you must have a strain of French blood!"

"Not unless some ancestor of whom I'm not aware brought back a French bride from the Hundred Years War, or some such thing," laughed Araminta, turning her back to the cheval glass and craning her neck to check the hang of her skirt in the mirror. She was wearing a white net frock over a deep green satin slip, cut very low all around the bust and with extremely full short sleeves. The skirt was edged with a deep flounce of blond lace embroidered with green leaves and tiny white roses. On her hair she wore a Kent toque in Parisian green gauze, trimmed with white roses. A necklace and earrings of emeralds and diamonds completed her toilet.

"It will be a very grand affair, then, this *fête champêtre?*" Odile asked, a note of envy in her voice.

"Yes, probably. Lady Torrington is floating us up the Thames in barges to her estate at Kew, to start the evening. I hear that we're to dine al fresco, with music and dancing and fireworks to follow. I'm sorry you won't be going with us. I think you might have enjoyed it."

"Yes, *probablement*. Duty first, however. Roger's parents have come up to London especially to meet me. We're to have dinner with them at their hotel." Odile

251

sighed, her expression turning unwontedly serious. "Do you think Roger's family will like me, Araminta?" she asked wistfully.

"How can they not like Roger's choice of a bride?"

"Yes, but—I *am* a Frenchwoman, and I have no fortune."

"It won't make the slightest difference," said Araminta firmly, and prayed that she was right. It was not like Odile to display such a lack of self-confidence, but in this instance she might well be justified. It would be only natural for Mr. and Mrs. Craddock to prefer an English bride with a substantial dowry for their only son, although Araminta found it hard to believe that anything short of death and destruction could dissuade Roger from marrying his French love. Araminta continued, "I'm sure that Roger's parents and *all* his family will be delighted that Roger is acquiring such a beautiful wife, with style and charm to boot!"

"*Eh bien,* I hope so," replied Odile. "We will soon know. Roger is taking me to visit his parents' home in St. Albans next week. There I will meet all the rest of his family. His married brother—he will inherit the property, you know. His younger brother, who is still at school. Eton, I think Roger said. Assorted cousins."

"Next week?" Araminta frowned slightly. "How long will you be staying? You haven't forgotten the ball I'm giving for Damaris at the end of the month?"

"I wouldn't dream of missing the little Damaris's ball. Wait until you see my gown! Roger says there will be no problem about returning in time. He tells me that St. Albans is not so very far from London." Looking more cheerful at the prospect of future festivities, Odile peered past Araminta into the cheval glass and adjusted her bonnet. She pulled on her gloves and walked to the door, saying, "I mustn't keep Roger waiting any longer. Do enjoy yourself at the *fête champêtre* . . ." She broke off, turning to look at Araminta with twinkling eyes. "Why didn't you tell me that Mr. Corby was escorting you tonight? I was in the drawing room when Roger arrived here this evening, with Mr. Corby practically on his heels. *Chérie,* he's as handsome as I remembered him! A trifle young, *peut-être,* but . . ."

A romantic to her fingertips, Odile had never been able to understand why her friend's heart had remained impervious to the horde of male admirers who had besieged her since her first London ball. Araminta lifted a warning finger, saying, "No you don't, Odile. I won't have you matchmaking me with poor Martin. I didn't tell you he was escorting me tonight because I only learned about it a few hours ago. Martin sent me a note saying that he had decided at the last minute to attend Lady Torrington's *fête* and could he please accompany my party. Unfortunately, the Duke's carriage will hold only four bodies comfortably, so Martin and I will be obliged to drive separately in my town chariot."

"So much the better, you and Mr. Corby will have more time for a *tête-à-tête!*" Odile waved good-bye, throwing a parting mischievous remark over her shoulder, "I did not mean to offend, chère Araminta. It's just that you are not getting any younger, and I should hate to see you on the shelf!"

Laughing at Odile's impudence, Araminta made a final check of her appearance in the cheval glass, picked up her reticule and shawl, and left the room. As she walked down the stairs, she reflected that she would miss Odile when she married Roger. Fluffy-headed and self-centered though she might be, Odile was always amusing company.

When Araminta entered the drawing room, she found Martin chatting with Jason. She noted approvingly that her trainer, in his black coat and breeches, silk stockings, and buckled shoes, looked as much at home in Henrietta's elegant drawing room as did the Duke in his superbly tailored evening clothes.

"Good evening, Lady Araminta," said Jason, whom she

hadn't seen since their visit to his stud several days previously. "I realize I should never underestimate your powers of persuasion, but I must confess I was a little surprised to discover you'd inveigled Mr. Corby away from his duties. The Derby, after all, is only two weeks away." He was using her title, as he always did when others were present, but his tone, light and teasing, had no trace of formality.

"Oh, I don't begrudge Martin a night away from the stables," she smiled. "I think Selim will be quite safe in Hassan's hands."

"I fancy you'll soon be offered all the horses to train that you can accommodate," Jason observed to Martin. "Your name is becoming very well known. All they talk about in the clubs these days is Mr. Middleman's horse. Only yesterday I heard of a colonel in the Blues who'd borrowed five thousand pounds from one of the cents-per-cent for a wager on Selim. Colonel Milroy assures all his friends that Selim can't lose. Next thing you know, I'll be doubting my Caesar's chances of winning the Derby!"

Martin looked disturbed. "I'm sorry to hear that. I don't like to see Selim a big favorite. The legs will be out in force."

"Legs?" asked Araminta.

"Blacklegs. Fielders. Gamblers who lay bets at varying prices on every horse in a race. What they call 'betting around.' Often when a leg lays heavily against a fancied horse, he tries to make very sure that the horse can't win."

"You mean they harm the horse?" asked Araminta in horror.

Martin shrugged. "Sometimes. Four horses were poisoned to death at Newmarket Heath in 1811. But it isn't really necessary for the legs to kill a favorite. There are other means they can use to keep a horse out of a race—doping, bribing an official at the track, buying off a jockey. False starts are particularly effective. You do that by putting several bad horses into the race, who cause so many false starts that the favorite loses the will to run.

However, I don't want you to be concerned, Lady Araminta. From now until the Derby, I'll take extra precautions with Selim. Luckily, you needn't worry about your jockey. As well I know, Hassan's only loyalty is to you and Selim."

"Well, Martin, I'm sorry you must go to this extra trouble. Fortunately it won't be for long." Araminta looked at Jason. "Even if your horse also becomes a favorite in the betting, you needn't take extra precautions to guard him, I imagine. Didn't you tell me once that only four people can approach Caesar without taking their lives in their hands? His trainer, his groom, his jockey — and you yourself, of course."

Martin burst out laughing. "Oh, come now, Lady Araminta. You'll catch cold if you try to gammon me. Only four people who can approach Caesar without fear of injury? That's a real bouncer if I ever heard one. Not ten minutes ago the Duke was telling me how you actually rode Caesar at his stud the other day when you and Gillian came down to see Selim." He laughed again. "Lord, I'd have given a monkey to see your trainer's face, Duke, when this man dressed in those outlandish Arab clothes not only turned out to be a woman but actually rode that evil-tempered brute of yours!"

Even as she flashed Jason a look of displeasure for his loose tongue, Araminta glimpsed out of the corner of her eye the unwelcome sight of Damaris's figure entering the drawing room. Her heart sank. Surely Damaris must have heard at least the last part of Martin's remarks.

She had. Advancing into the room, her lips stiff in a frozen smile, Damaris said, "Good evening, Duke, Martin. Araminta, how was it you never mentioned such an interesting visit to the Duke's stud? Did you really wear Arab clothes and ride that dangerous horse?"

Trying for a tone of disarming candor, Araminta replied, "I'm afraid I did. And then, you know, I was so ashamed of myself for doing something so childish, I de-

255

cided not to tell you and your mother!" She turned with relief to the footman who entered the room, announcing that her carriage was at the door. Consulting the tiny jeweled watch pinned to her bodice, she said to Martin, "Lady Torrington expects us at Westminster Stairs at six o'clock. Shall we go?"

Jason stepped down from his town carriage, which was stopped near the head of the landing stairs at Westminster Bridge, and reached up his hand to assist Lady Middleton and then Damaris from the carriage.

Henrietta glanced around her, noting the large numbers of carriages that were discharging passengers, and said in dismay, "Do you suppose that all these people are Lady Torrington's guests? Oh, I do hope this affair won't be too much of a squeeze. If the boats should be overcrowded . . ."

The Duke hastened to assure her that she would be perfectly safe in the barges rented by Lady Torrington, and Henrietta, somewhat comforted, moved off to greet an acquaintance.

"Aunt Araminta and Martin are already here," observed Damaris, looking across the intervening carriages to the opposite side of the landing.

"Shall we join them?"

His eyes wary, Jason glanced down at Damaris, observing the bright spot of color on either cheek. During the ride from Middleton House to Westminster Stairs, she'd hardly spoken a word. "You're offended with me, aren't you?" he said slowly.

"Offended? Why would you ask me a question like that?" replied Damaris with a flustered laugh.

"Don't be missish. I think you're angry because I took Lady Araminta on a private tour of my stables," he said bluntly.

Damaris's delicate features smoothed into a polite

mask. "La, sir, why would I object to that? Aunt Araminta is her own mistress. She can go wherever she likes. Just as you may invite whomever you choose to visit your properties." Abruptly turning her back to Jason, she waved at Araminta and Martin and began walking across the pavement to join them.

Instinctively, the Duke took several hasty steps after her, saying, "Damaris, wait a moment." When she ignored him, he paused, staring after her with narrowed eyes. Her action, which could hardly be interpreted as anything but deliberate rudeness, disconcerted him, accustomed as he was to her usual demure complaisance. With an impatient shrug, he followed after her, only to find when he caught up with her a few moments later that she had already plunged into an animated conversation with Martin.

"I'm so pleased you decided to join us, Martin," she said archly. "We've seen much too little of you since you began training race horses. Aunt Araminta insists her horse will win the Derby, and when that happens, I fancy you'll be busier than ever and we'll scarcely see you at all. Perhaps you'll even find new customers for your services at Lady Torrington's *fête!*"

Martin's open face registered a momentary amazement — clearly he hadn't expected such a warm reception from his old playfellow — but he recovered almost instantly. "Oh, I wouldn't dream of looking for customers tonight, Damaris, not while there's an opportunity to dance with *you*," he replied. For him, it was a daring remark.

On arriving at the landing, Araminta had spotted Jason's tall, rangy form immediately, and she'd observed from a distance the byplay between him and Damaris. She looked at him closely as he came up to them. His bland face didn't reflect any annoyance he may have felt at Damaris's behavior or Martin's impulsive attempt at gallantry.

"Lady Torrington is treating us like nabobs," Jason observed to Araminta with a smile, motioning to several long barges moored at the foot of the landing stairs. The boats were luxuriously carpeted and shaded by bright red awnings. Forward on the deck of each barge, chairs had been set out for the guests, and on the aft decks were seats for the rowers. Amidships of each barge, a trio of musicians was playing softly, and footmen stood at attendance to provide refreshments.

Minutes later, as the barges glided away from the landing and pulled upstream under the high, balustraded arches of Westminster Bridge, Araminta found herself, quite to her surprise, sitting beside Jason. It had been sheer happenstance. When she boarded, she'd sat down next to an empty chair, she'd met Jason's eyes as he stepped onto the barge, and without an instant's hesitation he'd dropped into the seat beside her.

Soon the tree-lined terraces in front of Westminster Hall had fallen behind them and they were approaching the gloomy hulk of the new Milbank Penitentiary. "Been trying out your riding skills on any other Derby contenders?" Jason said in a low voice, handing Araminta a glass of arrack punch from the tray extended by a hovering footman.

Her eyes crinkled with amusement. "Hush, before you give the gossips a juicy morsel. Since I 'sold' Selim, my position has been that I haven't the slightest interest in the Derby!"

Henrietta wandered up to them, looking harried. "Araminta, have you seen Damaris? I don't think she's on this barge."

"There's no cause for concern, Lady Middleton. I saw Damaris boarding the barge behind us with Martin Corby," said Jason coolly.

"But why didn't you . . ." Henrietta broke off, drawing herself up with an air of dignified calm. "Thank you. I'm sure Damaris is being well looked after. Martin is one of her oldest friends. They've known each other from the cradle."

After Henrietta had returned to a seat next to one of her cronies, Araminta flashed Jason a sideways glance, murmuring, "Trouble in paradise?"

"A small shadow, perhaps, confound your impudence. Your niece is—ah—a trifle displeased with me for the moment. I trust she'll soon recover her good nature. Fortunately, it's not every woman who has your supreme gift for driving a man to exasperation," the Duke retorted.

"I'm sorry. Would it help, do you think, if I had a word with Damaris?"

"No, I thank you, it wouldn't help at all, since you're . . ." Jason paused, looking uncomfortable.

"Since I'm what? The worm in the apple?" Araminta sighed. "I seem to have a gift for ruffling my nearest and dearest. I shouldn't have borrowed Hassan's clothes, I shouldn't have ridden Caesar . . ."

"Oh, the devil, Araminta, humility doesn't become you. Don't worry about Damaris. It's just nonsense, melting butter in a wig," replied Jason, dismissing the subject. He took a sip of punch, gazing at her appraisingly. "You're looking very handsome tonight. I don't recall seeing that gown before. And your emeralds are magnificent. The gift of a Turkish Pasha or an Arab sheik?"

Araminta laughed. "No, the necklace and earrings belonged to my mother. The gown is new, however. Odile insisted that I buy a new ensemble for the occasion. She says I mustn't lower my standards by appearing too often in public in the same gown. Possibly you've noticed that I've been dressing in the first style of elegance since Odile has been managing my wardrobe! She paid me the supreme compliment this evening. She said that I have such good taste that I must have French blood in my veins!"

Jason failed to look amused. He hesitated, saying, "I know I promised faithfully not to interfere in your affairs any longer, but I still think that young woman could cause you infinite embarrassment. She's like a piece of

259

flint awaiting the first touch of steel to create a spark that will ignite a blazing scandal. Don't bother to say it," he added as Araminta opened her mouth to protest. "What happened to her wasn't her fault, but society simply will not accept a Turkish Pasha's leman into its ranks." His mood softening, he flashed her a crooked grin. "I thought you were about to wash your hands of Madame Lacoste by marrying her off to her sailor."

"Oh, indeed, you can almost smell the orange blossom at Middleton House! Roger is introducing Odile to his parents this evening—they came up to London especially to meet her—and he'll be taking her to St. Albans next week to meet the rest of the family. Soon, I fancy, we can begin planning for the wedding. Odile is talking in terms of St. George's, Hanover Square, but I daresay we should choose a less conspicuous church. What's your opinion?"

"As inconspicuous a location as possible would be my suggestion. Why don't they elope to Gretna Green?"

Araminta made a face at Jason. "This talk of Odile's wedding reminds me of something. How would you like to give the bride away?"

"Me?" he spluttered. "You sound as queer as Dick's hatband. I scarcely know the girl, I'm not related to her, and what's more, I don't even like her!"

"Well, but Jason, Odile doesn't have any family here, and you've known her longer than any other gentleman in London. After all, she's been living in Henrietta's house for a number of weeks now. If she's not your intimate friend, she's at least a close acquaintance of Damaris. I think it might be considered quite natural for you to give Odile away."

The Duke fixed a grim eye on Araminta. "Have you ever been suspected of witchcraft? There must be *some* explanation for your ability to charm your friends and acquaintances down the path to insanity!"

"You'll do it, then?"

"Yes! Anything to get rid of that Frenchwoman!" Jason

suddenly leaned across Araminta, bracing his hand against the railing, to peer out at the wooden arches of the Battersea Bridge looming dead ahead of them. When the barge emerged on the other side of the bridge, he settled back in his chair, saying with a cheerful grin, "I just wanted to be sure that our rowers were on their toes. Many's the boat that has been wrecked on the piers of Battersea Bridge while attempting to shoot the arches."

During those brief moments of closeness, Araminta had been shocked to realize how acutely aware she was of Jason physically—the pressure of his powerfully muscled shoulder against her arm, the faint clean scent of his crisp linen, the accidental brushing of his fingers across her thigh when he withdrew his hand from the railing. Gazing now at those intensely blue eyes, alight with laughter, and at the sensual curves of his smiling mouth above that deep cleft in his chin, she thought that his striking good looks and the severe perfection of his black evening clothes made Lady Torrington's other male guests seem like clumsy imitators of the fast-fading Beau Brummell.

To her horror, she heard herself saying, "It seems so long ago since we sat together over a quiet glass in the inn parlor at Dover. Have you ever wondered what would have happened if . . ." She broke off, biting her lip.

Thoroughly taken aback, Jason blurted, "I *know* what would have happened that evening if you'd given me the slightest encouragement!"

She said hastily, "I should never have brought up that evening. We both had too much champagne for our own good."

"Was that what it was? Just champagne? Araminta . . ."

"Just champagne," she repeated firmly.

"The best champagne I ever drank, and the most unforgettable evening I ever spent," Jason shot back, but when Araminta shook her head at him, he subsided with a rueful grin and lifted his finger to an attentive waiter for an-

261

other glass of arrack punch.

Araminta leaned back in her chair, exchanging an occasional companionable comment with Jason while she sipped her glass of punch and dreamily enjoyed the gentle beauty of the May evening as it slipped into early twilight. Violins played softly amidships, hardly disturbing the balmy clear air, almost still save for a vagrant breeze so ethereal that Araminta did not bother to cover her shoulders with her fringed silk shawl, and the faint, beguiling scent of growing things wafted from the gardens of the Middlesex villas scattered along the banks between Hammersmith and Chiswick.

Near the top of the next great lazy curve of the river, the barge passed under Kew Bridge and edged into the Surrey shore. A myriad of colored lanterns suspended from the trees and from the supports of a large open pavilion illuminated the landing place. More lanterns edged the terraced walk leading up to a gleaming white mansion and lighted the winding paths of the surrounding wooded park. The awning-shaded pavilion near the water's edge was filled with small round dining tables, and off to one side of the pavilion an orchestra was playing on a large temporary stage.

After landing on the wharf, Araminta stood with Jason, Henrietta, Damaris, and Martin in the long receiving line to greet their hostess. The guests were then urged by smiling servants to enter the dining pavilion. "May I?" asked Jason, extending his arm to Araminta. She hesitated, glancing around the milling crowd of guests. "Shouldn't you be sitting with Damaris?" she asked in a low voice.

"Miss Middleton is otherwise occupied," he said coolly, motioning ahead of them to Damaris and Martin Corby, who were already entering the pavilion. They were flanked by Henrietta, whose very back looked reluctant.

Be it on your own head, Damaris, thought Araminta blithely. "I'd be delighted to share your table, Jason," she smiled, taking his arm. They were joined at their table for four by the Honorable Mr. and Mrs. Winston, a rather dull young married couple with whom Araminta was barely acquainted. Their presence didn't detract from her enjoyment of the occasion. She was rarely bored in any gathering, and she had certainly expected Lady Torrington's *fête champêtre* to be an pleasurable affair, but she was soon asking herself why this evening seemed to be composed of pure magic.

It wasn't the food, lavish though it was, two courses consisting each of more than twenty dishes, served by an army of liveried footmen—carp and tench and venison, turkeys, chickens, partridges and pigeons, a vast haunch of beef, every imaginable kind of cake and pastry and a luscious cornucopia of hothouse fruits. Nor was it the entertainment on the outdoor stage next to the pavilion, though the acts presented—acrobats, mimes, rope walkers, jugglers, singers, and dancers—rivaled the performances she had seen at Sadler's Wells. No, the difference between this evening and any other she could remember had to be the interplay between Jason and herself. Like a pair of skilled fencers, they attacked and partied, feinted and riposted, in a scintillating verbal swordplay that reduced Mr. and Mrs. Winston to helpless mirth and attracted the interested attention of diners at adjoining tables.

"I can't top that story," conceded Araminta at last. "Are you really asking me to believe, Jason, that this Colonel Kelly burned to death while attempting to save his *boots?*"

"On my honor. What's more, his valet had developed a secret formula for blacking that had made the Colonel's boots the envy of the military. So after poor Kelly died, his friends and enemies all vied with one another to hire the valet and get their hands on that special formula."

Dusk had fallen when the guests emerged from the pavilion after dinner. The multicolored lanterns, swaying and flickering in the breeze, created an effect of fairylike enchantment against the deepening darkness as the guests began strolling up the gently inclined path to the mansion for the start of dancing on the terrace.

Footmen with trays of glasses circulated among the crowd on the terrace while the orchestra regrouped itself and tuned up. Glass of Madeira in hand, Jason strolled over to speak to Damaris, standing with her mother and Martin Corby. Henrietta murmured a rather incoherent excuse and drifted away. Martin, looking uncomfortable, soon followed suit. The orchestra struck up the first notes of a waltz.

"May I have this dance, Damaris?"

She fixed her gaze at a point over his left shoulder. "I'm sorry, but I promised this dance to Martin."

"Damaris, please look at me. Isn't it time to end this unpleasantness? I'll gladly explain how I happened to meet Lady Araminta the other day and invite her to visit my stud—it was all quite innocent, I assure you—and then, if you still think I've done something amiss, I'm prepared to apologize."

Damaris lifted her eyebrow. "I wasn't aware of any 'unpleasantness,' so there's no need for you to explain anything, and certainly no need to apologize." A ripple of familiar laughter attracted her attention, and she turned her head to look at Araminta, surrounded by half a dozen eager would-be partners.

"The only solution is to dance with you alphabetically. Mr. Brown, shall we waltz?" Araminta was saying gaily.

Watching her aunt swing by her, Damaris snapped, "Aunt Araminta has the manners of a hoyden. Mama's been very concerned about her behavior tonight."

"Lady Middleton distresses herself unnecessarily," said the Duke curtly. He bowed to Damaris and headed straight across the terrace to the daughter of Lady Combermere, who watched with considerable pleasure as her eldest girl glided away in the Duke's arms. Lady Combermere was well aware of the rumors placing Harwood and Damaris at the altar at the end of the Season, but she was an optimistic woman as well as a worldly one. She knew that the Duke would not be hopelessly lost to the matrimonial market until the definite announcement of his betrothal had been sent to the *Times* and the *Morning Post*.

Araminta was attempting to arbitrate the claims of Mr. Stanwyck and Mr. Stoner by pointing out that the letter *a* precedes the letter *o* when Jason, carrying several glasses, pushed his way into the center of the circle surrounding her.

"I thought we might enjoy a glass of punch together before our dance," he announced.

"For shame, Duke, we've already passed the h's," protested Mr. Stanwyck.

"Ah, but mine is a prior claim, sir," Jason replied suavely. "Lady Araminta, shall we sit down on one of those benches over there at the side of the terrace?"

"You're a rogue, Jason," said Araminta, adjusting her skirts to allow him enough room to sit on the bench. "It really was poor Mr. Stanwyck's turn." She took a swallow of the punch that Jason had just handed to her, and made a face. "You know, I don't really like arrack punch. What does it taste mostly of, would you say? Coconut or dates or molasses or—ugh—rice? Besides, I've had rather too many glasses tonight. I feel a little giddy."

"I'm a trifle foxed myself. Lady Torrington has provided an excellent port." Jason raised his head to watch the first rocket of the evening's fireworks shoot up into the sky behind the house. "Shall we go for a stroll in the park? We can see the fireworks much better from there."

Very much against her better judgment, Araminta allowed Jason to slip her hand under his arm and lead her down the steps of the terrace into one of the paths winding through the gardens. While she'd been dancing with her alphabet of partners, she'd caught numerous glimpses of Jason out of the corner of her eyes and she knew that he'd spent the greater part of the evening—aside from the one dance with Lady Combermere's hopeful daughter—watching her from the sidelines and liberally sampling Lady Torrington's port. He was clearly in an erratic mood, and it was challenging common sense to be alone with him.

"Is this wise?" Araminta murmured as she and Jason walked past a bank of pale pink rhododendrons coming into bloom.

"Lady Torrington is very proud of her gardens. She urged us all to see them before the end of the evening, remember? And we certainly aren't the only guests to take advantage of the invitation."

Jason was right. From a secluded bench off to her right, Araminta caught the sounds of giggling and a sudden scuffle, and around the next bend of the winding path she could see a young couple walking hand in hand up the steps of a miniature temple.

"I saw you talking to Damaris," said Araminta. "Have you cleared up your misunderstanding?"

"No," said Jason shortly. His tone was so forbidding that Araminta did not pursue the subject. Lapsing into silence, they wandered into a secondary path, lined with deodars and lime trees, which led down to a tiny artificial lake, spanned by a Chinese bridge.

The bridge proved to be an excellent vantage point from which to view the fireworks, and Araminta leaned on the railing, entranced, watching a rotating tourbillion forming its beautiful spiral lines of fire. Next a giant rocket soared into the sky, scattering its garniture of stars, crackers, serpents, and gold and silver rain. Some minutes later the climax of the display was a magnificent girandole, in which several hundred rockets were discharged simultaneously to pierce the sky like the glittering fan of a gigantic peacock's tail.

"I'm so glad you brought me here," Araminta exclaimed, turning to Jason with a radiant smile. "Wasn't that last display the loveliest you've ever seen?"

"I wasn't watching it. I was watching you. *You're* the loveliest thing I've ever seen," said Jason huskily. He put his arms loosely around her waist and bent his head to brush his lips against her bare shoulders, trailing a line of gentle, clinging kisses along her throat, across her cheeks, sending the blood leaping through Araminta's veins in a fiery torrent, and making her aware of Jason's insistent masculinity in every fiber of her being.

"Jason, please don't," she whispered weakly, even as she longed to feel his body closer to hers.

"Hush," he murmured, covering her mouth in a kiss that began tenderly but deepened into a bruising pressure that left Araminta gasping for breath. He lifted his head at last, looking down at her with eyes ignited with passion. "I've wanted to kiss you like that all evening. What am I saying—I've been wanting to kiss you since the moment I first laid eyes on you in Dover. Oh Araminta, you're completely irresistible."

Araminta felt curiously light-headed, knowing she was being drawn into a seething maelstrom of emotion but powerless to prevent herself from spinning out of control. "And I've been wanting to do this," she breathed, raising her hand to touch a finger to the cleft in his chin.

With a stifled groan, Jason swept her into his embrace, crushing her body brutally against his hard thighs and grinding his mouth against hers, gradually forcing open her lips until he could explore the sweetness of her tongue with his own. Carried along on a tide of overwhelming desire, Araminta came to her senses only when Jason abruptly swooped her off her feet and began carrying her to the concealing darkness of a grove of trees. She struggled frantically, kicking out and beating Jason's shoulder with her fist until he released her. Still breathing harshly, he stood staring at her with a dazed expression in his eyes.

267

"Araminta, what is it? You feel what I'm feeling . . ."

She drew a long hard breath, willing her clamoring heart to cease pounding. "Jason, whatever it is that we felt tonight, it isn't real. It's arrack punch and moonlight madness and shooting stars, but it isn't real. The reality is that you will soon announce your betrothal to my niece, and you and I, I hope, will continue to be friends."

His eyes clear again, Jason looked at her for a long, silent moment. He reached for her hand, raising it to his lips. "Real or not, Araminta, don't ask me to forget what I felt tonight," he said with a twisted little smile.

Chapter Fifteen

. . . Jason abruptly swept her off her feet and carried her into the concealing darkness of a grove of trees. He sank down with her on a velvety cushion of grass, holding her in such a close embrace that his male hardness seemed to meld into her soft curves. While his mouth sought hers with a hungry urgency, his long slender fingers lingeringly caressed her bare shoulders and then slipped lower into the brief bodice of her gown . . .

"No!" Araminta looked apprehensively around the dining room, realizing with horror that she'd spoken aloud. There was no harm done, she thought, relaxing. She was the only occupant of the room, having come down to a very late breakfast. Suddenly she felt a hot flood of color suffusing her face. She'd been allowing her unruly thoughts to take control of her mind again—those same treacherous thoughts that had kept her sleepless through an interminable night—as she imagined what might have happened if she hadn't stopped Jason from carrying her into the enticing darkness beneath the trees of Lady Torrington's garden.

She wasn't going to think such thoughts again, she resolved firmly. It had been a temporary madness that had taken hold of her and Jason, just as she'd told him last night. She'd always known there was a strong physical attraction between them, but that was all it was, a mere pull of the senses, transient and unimportant. Nothing that would keep him from marrying Damaris, or prevent Araminta from . . . Well, she didn't have any definite plans for matrimony. Doubtless someday she'd meet someone so mesmerizingly handsome, so sensually appealing and wickedly attuned to her every thought and emotion, that she couldn't resist him, but she wasn't actively looking for such a paragon.

"*Chère* Araminta, are you ill? You're so flushed. Do you have a fever?"

Startled, Araminta shook herself out of her thoughts to stare at Odile, who had just swept into the dining room and was looking at her closely.

"Ill? Of course not. I'm never ill."

"*Bien.* I am happy to hear it." Odile peered at Araminta's tiny cup of Turkish coffee. "Is there any more of that? I believe I will have a cup."

As Odile sat down at the table with her coffee, Araminta asked, "And so, did your meeting with Roger's parents go smoothly?"

"Oh, yes. Monsieur and Madame Craddock, they were so kind, so gracious. I told you, did I not, that Roger has only the two brothers, no sisters? *Eh bien,* Roger's mother actually said to me, 'My dear, at long last I will have a daughter!' "

"See, I told you, you had no reason to worry."

Odile nodded complacently. "Yes, I should have trusted your judgment. By the way, Roger is bringing his parents here later this morning. They wish to call on you and Madame Middleton. They are so grateful to both of you for befriending me. And Madame Craddock, she would like to speak with you about the wedding."

"Well, of course. I want to become acquainted with Mr. and Mrs. Craddock. In fact, Odile, I collect I've been remiss. I should have asked them to call when I learned they were coming to London. After all, I'll be taking the place of your mother in arranging your wedding, in effect, and soon the Craddocks and I will practically be members of the same family! Oh, I have news for you. The Duke of Harwood has offered to give you away."

"Oh, Araminta!" Odile put her cup down so hard that its contents splashed into the saucer. *"Monsieur le Duc* will do this great thing for me? But then, we positively *must* have the wedding at St. George's, Hanover Square, *n'est-ce-pas?* Anything less grand, and it would be an affront to *Monsieur le Duc's* rank."

Araminta thought feelingly of Jason's suggestion that Odile and Roger elope to Gretna Green, and counted to ten. "I have a much better idea. Why not get married in Roger's home parish? Didn't you tell me his uncle was the local vicar? I can see it now. So *intime* and yet so impressive. You'll walk down the aisle of the village church on the Duke's arm, with all of Roger's family present, even those too old and ailing to attend a London wedding. Roger probably has friends from the neighborhood who also might not be able to travel to London, and they'll be in the church too, and all of his childhood playmates. No one in that corner of Hertfordshire will talk of anything else except your wedding for weeks to come."

Watching an expression of misty delight spread over Odile's transparent face, Araminta rose from the table, saying, "If I'm to welcome the Craddocks properly, perhaps I should change into a more festive gown."

Walking down the hallway toward the staircase, Araminta paused as she was passing the drawing room. Someone was crying bitterly. Peering into the room, she saw with surprise that Martin Corby was sitting rigidly on a sofa, his arm draped across Damaris's heaving shoulders. Glimpsing Araminta in the doorway, Martin gently removed his arm, speaking to Damaris in a low, comforting murmur, and came over to speak to Araminta. "Thank God you're here," he said in a subdued tone. "You'll know what to do."

"But what *is* it, Martin?"

"Damaris was so upset and unhappy last night at Lady

Torrington's *fête*, I felt obliged to call this morning to see how she was feeling, before I left London to return to Surrey. I was appalled to find her in an even worse state. I didn't know what to say, I didn't know what to do. I kept thinking, what if Lady Middleton were to come into the drawing room just now and see her like this? And in *my* company?"

Araminta gave a mental shudder. "I understand, Martin. I'll take care of it. But first . . . is Damaris distressed about the Duke?"

"That's it. She seems to think she's offended him. Thank you, Lady Araminta. I know you'll be able to calm her," said Martin fervently, wringing Araminta's hand. "I'll go now, then. You'll tell me if—if there's any way I can help Damaris?"

Minutes later, having successfully spirited Damaris up to the girl's bedchamber without encountering Henrietta or any of the servants, Araminta settled her niece into a comfortable chair, bathed her eyes and face in lavender water, and sat down beside her, saying, "Now, then, why are you all to pieces?"

A flash of resentment appeared in Damaris's lovely face and then died away in a fresh flood of tears. "I've been a perfect goosecap, Aunt Araminta," she said at last, mopping her lovely gentian eyes. "I behaved atrociously to the Duke last night. I was—I was angry because he'd taken you to visit his stud, and I wouldn't let him explain, though he assured me it was all perfectly innocent. I refused to dance with him. I—I *flirted* with Martin. And now I don't know how to set matters right."

Araminta felt a nagging twinge of guilt, and promptly banished it to the back of her mind. "Were you a little jealous of me?" she forced herself to say. "You've no cause to be, you know. Will you let me give you a bit of advice?"

After a moment's hesitation, Damaris nodded. "Yes."

"When you next see the Duke, just be your usual self.

Dignified, charming, friendly. Forget what took place at Lady Torrington's *fête*. My Uncle Will never liked to dwell on the reasons for our quarrels when we had one of our infrequent fallings-out. He preferred to wipe the slate clean and pretend the quarrel had never happened. It was less embarrassing for him. I think most men are like that."

"Oh." Damaris looked thoughtful. "I shouldn't apologize?"

Araminta's eyes gleamed with mischief. "Oh, I wouldn't say that. But do so with a pretty smile and an air of gentle deprecation. *You* know! Don't enact a Cheltenham tragedy over it!"

Damaris put out her hand. "You've been very understanding, Aunt Araminta. Thank you."

Rising, Araminta patted Damaris's shoulder. "A shocking coil it would be if an aunt who's seen a bit of the world can't give some useful advice to her niece!"

Shortly afterward, when Araminta, suitably dressed to receive formal callers, entered the drawing room, she found that the elder Craddocks and Roger had already arrived and were chatting with Henrietta. Odile rushed over to her, murmuring, "I told Roger's *papa* and *maman* about *Monsieur le Duc,* and they were *so* pleased! And now come and let me introduce my dearest friend to my soon-to-be *beaux-parents.*"

Mr. and Mrs. Craddock were sedate, conservatively dressed people whose looks were so ordinary that no one would have given them a second glance while passing them on the street. Araminta soon discovered that their personalities matched their looks. They were, in a word, rather dull, although she had to admit the possibility that they were simply overawed at being entertained by one of the Ton's titled hostesses. As members of the minor gentry in their small corner of the world, they probably mingled with the county aristocracy only on Public Days, and rarely visited London.

Although Henrietta had apparently been doing her best to put her guests at ease, Mrs. Craddock seemed to relax her stiffness only when Araminta slipped into a seat beside her and began discussing the wedding.

"Lady Araminta, I must tell you how relieved I felt when Madame Lacoste—I mean Odile—told us of your suggestion to have the wedding in our village church. It will make things so much easier for so many of our friends and family members, and it isn't as if dear Odile herself had large numbers of friends and family in London. In fact, Mr. Craddock said to me only yesterday, 'How lonely it will be for Odile to be married without *any* of her family present.' "

Araminta shook her head, saying sadly, "I fear Odile is paying the penalty for belonging to a family that was loyal to king and country to the death. As I'm sure you know, all the members of her family, and her dead husband's, too, have either perished or are in exile."

Mrs. Craddock seemed much struck by this mendacious statement. Her reaction caused Araminta to feel a small spasm of guilt. By nature, she would much have preferred to tell the truth at all times, but the fact was that it would be impossible to establish Odile with her Roger in a snug English family setting if her real background became known. And surely these tales of Odile's past were very innocent lies that couldn't hurt anyone! Having dismissed without too much difficulty any guilt she was feeling, Araminta was soon deep in a happy discussion with Mrs. Craddock about the choice of fabric for Odile's wedding gown, arguing the competing claims of *crêpe lisse, gros de Naples,* and *soie de Londres,* from which they were distracted only by the unexpected entrance of the Duke of Harwood.

Standing on the threshold after being ushered into the drawing room by the butler, Jason appeared momentarily oblivious to everyone except Araminta. His eyes locked onto hers in a look that told her without words that he was thinking about shooting stars and moonlight madness and doubtless other things beyond the ken of gently reared females. Recovering himself instantly, he bowed to Henrietta and Araminta and Odile and gazed in polite inquiry at Roger and his parents. Then he advanced toward Roger with a beaming smile, extending his hand. "Lieutenant Craddock? It's time, and past time, that we met. Permit me to tell you how pleased I am that you've returned to England to be reunited with your betrothed."

Looking a little flustered, Roger thanked Jason for his kind offices at the Admiralty, and hastened to introduce his parents.

"What a coincidence," Jason remarked. "Last evening at Lady Torrington's *fête,* Lady Araminta asked me to give Madame Lacoste away, and I, of course, immediately accepted with great pleasure. Then this morning it occurred to me, Mr. and Mrs. Craddock, that we really ought to know each other better, so I came here this morning to ask Lady Araminta for your direction so that I could visit you at your hotel." Smiling at Roger's parents, he said, "Will you do me the honor of dining with me this evening at my house with Lieutenant Craddock and Madame Lacoste? Lady Middleton, I hope you and Damaris and Lady Araminta will be able to come also."

The Craddocks were plainly much impressed, not only by the invitation to dine, but by Jason himself. Flawlessly turned out in his blue coat, striped toilinette waistcoat, pale buff pantaloons, and glossy Hessians, he looked every inch a Duke and a leader of the Ton, and his manner, easy and unaffected though it was, without a hint of condescension, conveyed the unmistakable aura of ancient lineage and power.

Staying only long enough to have his invitation accepted, Jason made his graceful departure, followed shortly afterward by the elder Craddocks. Roger and Odile were soon gone, too, on a rather bourgeois shopping expedition to Grafton House, where, Odile assured

Araminta, one could find bargains quite *formidables*. Araminta watched them depart with the glimmer of amusement she usually felt when Odile artlessly proposed to spend money from her patroness's inexhaustible purse. It wouldn't be fair or accurate to accuse Odile of being greedy, or of taking advantage of her benefactor. She was just Odile.

"Well, I must say the Duke is being unusually gracious, Araminta," said Henrietta when they were alone. "Inviting the Craddocks to dine at his house. Agreeing to take part in Madame Lacoste's wedding, when she has no claim on him at all. She's really only the merest acquaintance. But I daresay he's paying her and the Craddocks these attentions because of their connection with *our* family."

Having satisfied herself about the reason for Jason's generosity toward the Craddocks, Henrietta dropped the subject in favor of a matter of more pressing importance. "I've been meaning to ask you something, Araminta. Do you know why Damaris is so out of curl? She's in her bedchamber now, sleeping. Sleeping in the middle of the day! She says she's tired."

"Well, a come out season *is* fatiguing. Damaris has had several engagements a day for weeks now. Why shouldn't she be tired?"

"She didn't complain of fatigue yesterday, or the day before that," replied Henrietta sharply. "Araminta—do you know if Damaris has had a quarrel with the Duke? She spent scarcely any time with him last night at Lady Torrington's *fête*. She didn't have supper with him. She didn't dance with him. She was in Martin Corby's pocket the whole evening. Martin Corby! What the Duke must have thought of that!"

"Nothing at all, you goose. He knows Martin is an old childhood friend," said Araminta, placing a soothing hand on her sister's arm. "As for Damaris being in bad skin, well, perhaps she did cut up a bit stiff with the

Duke. It was probably over a trifle. Lovers's quarrels are like summer showers. They never last long. You'll see. By tomorrow or the next day, Damaris will be herself again."

When Jason sets out to do something, he certainly does it in the first style of elegance, Araminta thought appreciatively as she watched the footmen bringing the dessert course into the dining room of the Duke's house in South Audley Street. The dessert course had been preceded by two main courses containing at least twenty entrées and an equal number of entremets. The table setting, all in exquisite silver gilt, was even more impressive than the food, and included a dessert stand with a foliated central column and a basket supported by three gryphons. Ranged on the sideboard was a rather overpowering display of the famous Windham plate.

Jason had also exerted himself to make Mr. and Mrs. Craddock feel at ease amid the ducal splendors of Harwood House, and had succeeded admirably. He commiserated with Mrs. Craddock about the inconveniences of her post journey from St. Albans, and the rarity of the great Mrs. Siddons's appearances on the stage since her official retirement several years previously. He drew out Mr. Craddock on the practicability of growing turnips and clover and on the pleasures of trout fishing. Deeply flattered by his attentions, the elder Craddocks were obviously enjoying their evening. To Roger he behaved like a solicitous older friend, offering at one point to put in another word at the Admiralty if Roger wanted a spot of shore duty before going back to sea. At this, Odile squealed with joy. "Oh, *Monsieur le Duc,* you have a heart as big as the ocean. *Mon cher* Roger and I, we cannot thank you enough!"

In Araminta's opinion, if Jason could be faulted as a host, it was in his treatment of Damaris. After she had joined the ladies in the drawing room, leaving the gentlemen to their port, Araminta studied her niece closely but unobtrusively. Damaris was trying very hard not to show her feelings, but to her aunt, who knew her so well, it was obvious that she was in very low spirits.

"I did what you said," Damaris murmured when Araminta took a seat beside her on the carved and gilt settee with its scrolled arms and bulbous gadrooned legs. "It didn't mend matters. The Duke simply looks *through* me, as if I wasn't there at all."

Araminta knew exactly what Damaris meant. She'd seen Jason in many moods—angry, teasing, amused, beguiling, icily aloof—but she'd never seen him as he was tonight with Damaris. He was meticulously polite, but it was the impersonal politeness of an uninterested stranger.

"Aren't you imagining things, Damaris? Perhaps the Duke isn't paying you as much attention as he usually does because he's making a special effort to become acquainted with Odile's future in-laws."

Damaris shook her head, looking unconvinced, and Araminta, unconvinced by her own arguments, changed the subject to one she hoped might brighten her niece's frame of mind—the ball she was giving for Damaris on the eve of the Derby. Soon Damaris had recovered sufficiently to take an interest in the orchestra Araminta proposed to hire, one recommended enthusiastically by Lady Jersey herself. With the entrance of the gentlemen into the drawing room, Damaris found still another distraction from her problems when Roger and Mr. Craddock proposed a game of whist.

It had long been a private source of merriment to Araminta that her sister and her niece shared a passion for whist. The staid and conventional Henrietta and the demure and charming Damaris seemed to undergo personality changes at the prospect of a game, when both of them turned into sharks, as Gillian had once laughingly suggested. The two ladies jumped at the opportunity to play whist with Roger and his father.

Odile had no card sense, and was in any case too indolent to learn to play, and Mrs. Craddock, too, was uninterested in whist. They settled instead into an absorbing exchange of ideas about bridal veils and wedding breakfasts. Soon tiring of the subject, Araminta wandered over to the pianoforte, where she sat playing softly until the inevitable—and the expected—happened. Jason, the odd man out in the drawing room, appeared by her side.

Continuing to play, she murmured, "I'd like to thank you for entertaining the Craddocks so magnificently. As I'm sure you've noticed, Odile is in raptures."

"Oh, the devil with the Craddocks. I'm doing this for you." There was a faint slur in his voice, and when he leaned over the instrument to help Araminta turn her page, she was immediately aware of the strong smell of port. Roger and Mr. Craddock had appeared perfectly steady when they entered the drawing room; apparently Jason had imbibed several glasses of wine to each one enjoyed by his guests.

Darting a quick upward glance at him, Araminta recognized the hot little leaping flame in his eyes and dropped her hands from the keyboard. "Your sister Felicity once told me you have a very handsome conservatory at Harwood House. Would you care to show it to me?"

"With the greatest of pleasure." Glancing around the room, Jason said with a straight face, "My other guests seem fully occupied. We won't trouble them to come."

As they walked toward the door, Araminta paused beside Odile and Mrs. Craddock to say, "The Duke wants to show me his prize camellias. We'll be back in a moment." Without giving either of the ladies the opportunity to express a desire to accompany them, she and Jason left the room.

The conservatory was quite small by country house standards, but it had been skillfully designed to give the impression of much greater size. The air inside was warm and moist and from one of the corners came the trickling sound of running water. Dimly lighted by a number of hanging Chinese lanterns, the beautifully arranged plantings looked more like a tropical garden than a conservatory attached to a fashionable London house.

"It would break my gardener's heart if I didn't show you his pineapple plant," Jason remarked. "He dotes on it like a besotted grandparent. And over here are the camellias. By the by, how did you know I prided myself on my camellias? Or rather, that my gardener prided himself on my camellias?"

"I didn't know. We had to have some excuse to come here," said Araminta coolly. Slowly she walked over to join Jason as he stood beside several large pots containing bushes with glossy green leaves and masses of white or red blossoms. In the soft light of the gently swaying lanterns, inhaling the intoxicating scent of growing things, she was suddenly intensely conscious of Jason's maleness in every nerve of her body, and she knew she was as much in danger as she'd been last night in Lady Torrington's gardens. And still she didn't move away when he severed a giant double white blossom and tucked it into the curls on the crown of her head.

"We came here to see the camellias," he murmured, his eyes gleaming with amusement. "We'd best return with proof of our good intentions." His hands strayed slowly to the exquisitely sensitive skin of her throat and shoulders, and as he bent his head, Araminta was aware of his heavy, unsteady breathing and the telltale whiff of too much port. Making a quick, abrupt movement, she broke the spell.

She backed away. "I didn't come out here to see your camellias," she said breathlessly. "I came to tell you that you're making Damaris very unhappy. She's very sorry that she behaved badly last evening, and you must stop sulking about it and forgive her."

He stared at her, his mouth hardening. "Nothing in my life is engraved on stone yet," he blurted. "Not

280

after last night—"

"Last night didn't mean anything," she interrupted.

"Araminta!"

"It's true. We kissed each other and we both enjoyed it immensely, and if I'd been a lightskirt . . . But I'm not. You're going to marry Damaris, and I'm going to attend your wedding. You'll live happily ever afterward and I'll be off on my travels again. Who knows, this time I might win a camel race!"

"Is that what you really want?"

"Yes."

He gave her a long look, almost as though he were memorizing her features and saying good-bye. Then he turned back to the camellia bush, carefully breaking off a richly red flower. "I think Damaris might fancy one of my prize camellias. As a peace offering, perhaps, or a symbol of love. Aren't flowers supposed to be the language of love?"

ing for the ball. She would be dressing in Thomas's bedroom, the room that would be hers until they were married after their trip.

"It's true, we all do care about each other if we acted it improperly, and if I'd been a lady of the *ton* . . ."

Thomas wanted to marry Araminta who never . . .

Chapter Sixteen

"I'm sure you have everything under control, Simpson." Araminta smiled at Henrietta's butler. "However, I'd like to check a few of the last-minute details. The canopy over the entrance, for example. It wasn't up when I glanced out at noontime."

"It was installed at one o'clock, my lady. And the extra kitchen helpers and servers from the Labor Exchange arrived several hours ago."

"Good. How about the broken lusters in the ballroom chandelier?"

"Replaced, my lady. And I can assure you that the footman who broke them will be more careful the next time he's set to cleaning the chandeliers."

Araminta laughed at the wrathful expression on the butler's face. "Don't be too hard on the lad." She glanced about the morning room, where several card tables had been set up. "I'm glad you agreed with me that we needed additional seating for the card players."

"Indeed, my lady. Oh, the florist is just finishing in the ballroom now. He asked me to give you his apologies for arriving so late."

"Oh, I'm sure the poor man couldn't help it if his horse dropped dead! Thank you, Simpson. I believe that takes care of everything."

After the butler left, Araminta glanced at the clock over the mantelpiece. In an hour she must starting dressing for the ball she was giving in Damaris's honor. A ball the success of which would have seemed quite dubious only two weeks ago, when Damaris and Jason had been on the verge of an open quarrel over her visit to the Duke's racing stables. She had just time to check on the florist's work before going upstairs. This ball was entirely her responsibility, and she didn't propose to leave any detail to chance.

Shortly afterward, as Araminta was patiently accepting yet another round of apologies from the tardy florist, Henrietta and Damaris joined her in the ballroom.

"Oh, Aunt Araminta, it's lovely," Damaris exclaimed, gazing in delight at the profusion of spring flowers massed in front of the orchestra platform and at the garlands of greenery interspersed with blossoms that festooned the wall sconces. "It's as if you'd transplanted an entire garden indoors."

"I'm glad you like it," smiled Araminta. "And now, isn't it time for you to think of dressing for your triumph?"

"She's so happy," said Henrietta, watching Damaris leave the ballroom. "It *will* be a triumph, I think. Your arrangements are superb, Araminta. I'm tempted to ask you to take over the planning for *my* ball at the end of July, when I'll announce Damaris's engagement. You do everything so effortlessly."

"Oh well, I've always enjoyed being a dictator!"

"And the best part of it all, you know," Henrietta went on, patting Araminta's shoulder fondly, "is that the Duke and Damaris have mended that little rift they had several weeks ago. The Duke's attentions to Damaris are so marked when they appear together in public, I daresay my announcement ball will be an anticlimax!"

As she sat in her bedchamber a little later, having a cup of her beloved Turkish coffee before it was time to dress, Araminta recalled her sister's remarks. Jason and Damaris *had* resolved their differences, and she told herself firmly that she was happy for them. Certainly she hadn't allowed herself to dwell on the alluring memories of that passionate interlude at the Chinese bridge in Lady Torrington's gardens. That had been purely the result of Jason's injured ego, too much wine, and supremely romantic surroundings. Jason had apparently recognized the truth of this as well as she had, and she was glad they'd been able to remain friends.

"Could I talk to you for a moment, *chérie?*"

Araminta looked up from her coffee at Odile, standing in the doorway of the bedchamber. "As many moments as you like. You're back from St. Albans in good time. Did you enjoy your visit to Roger's home?"

Odile drew up a chair beside Araminta. She sat with downcast eyes, nervously pulling at the strings of her reticule. "Not really. I don't think Roger's family liked me very much."

"Nonsense. I *saw* you with Mr. and Mrs. Craddock on several occasions. They're very fond of you."

"Oh, Roger's mother and father. I was talking about the rest of his family. They came flocking to the house and sat there like *toads,* pretending not to understand a word I said, and you *know,* Araminta, that everyone here in London tells me how remarkably well I've learned to speak English!" Odile brooded for a moment. Then she burst out, "I was so surprised at the Craddocks' estate. Estate! It's a tiny property, not above a few hundred acres, more like a—a farm. And Mr. Craddock doesn't have a title, he's a plain mister, and Roger says that his papa has only two thousand pounds a year. And since Roger is only a younger son, he won't inherit even that much. Araminta, the Craddocks are so—so *bourgeois!*"

"Well, to be fair, I'm sure Roger never told you his father had a title and an enormous fortune. I believe he said that Mr. Craddock was a country gentleman living on a small estate."

"So he did, but—you see, I've observed that here in England many untitled people occupy the most prominent

284

positions in society. Not as it was in France before the Revolution, where a man could not be presented at Court, *vous comprenez,* unless he could prove a title of nobility going back to the fourteenth century. Here it is so different. Mr. Carstairs, whom you meet as the guest of the most aristocratic hostesses in London, has no title, but they tell me he is very rich. So, of course, when I learned that Mr. Craddock's estate has been in his family since the time of William the Conqueror, I naturally assumed that he was wealthy and socially prominent, though I did wonder why he had no title . . ."

"Odile, let me explain to you a few facts about the British aristocracy, which is nothing like the old *noblesse* in France. In England, only the eldest son inherits the title; other members of the family may style themselves 'Lord' and 'Lady'—the younger sons of Dukes and Marquesses, for instance, and all the daughters of Dukes, Marquesses, and Earls—but these are simply courtesy titles. Which means, in effect, that you will meet men of the most impeccable lineage and social standing who are plain 'misters,' like Roger's father, and who may or may not be wealthy."

"It sounds very illogical," said Odile with a touch of peevishness.

Araminta threw up her hands. "It may be illogical, but that's the way it is in this country. Odile, answer me one question: Do you love Roger?"

"Araminta!"

"And do you believe that he would never deceive you?"

"Yes, of course! Why are you asking me these questions?"

"Because if you love Roger and believe in him, the size of his father's fortune is beside the point. You can be sure he'll always be able to support you in modest comfort, at least, and I predict that you'll always be a reigning hostess, no matter where you live, or how much money you have."

The disgruntled lines faded from Odile's pert face, and she reached out to hug Araminta. "Thank you, for being so wise and so sensible. Of course you're right. I would rather have my Roger than the wealthiest Duke in England!" A comical look crossed her face. "What am I saying? Damaris's Duke *is* the wealthiest Duke in England!"

Araminta burst out laughing. "Yes, and he's already spoken for, unofficially at least. Go along with you now and dress for the ball. When Jessie was doing my hair this morning, she mentioned that she had taken a peek at your gown for this evening and she assured me you would be the sensation of the ball!"

Odile, her lips wreathed in a gratified smile, went away. A moment later a footman tapped discreetly on the open door. "A letter for you, my lady. Just delivered by hand."

Glancing casually at the sealed note, addressed to her in a tiny, crabbed handwriting, Araminta was about to place it on her desk for later reading when she noticed the underlined word "Urgent" in the lower left corner. "Thank you. You needn't wait for a reply," she told the footman.

She broke the seal on the letter and scanned the brief message with uncomprehending eyes before reading a newspaper clipping enclosed with it. The clipping was from the "Fashionable Intelligence" column of the *Morning Post*. One paragraph was circled: "We hear that Lady A., a well-traveled young lady recently arrived in London, has written a novel which will be published this week. The novel concerns an evil count who ruthlessly murders his nephew-heir, the son of his heroic younger brother, who has died fighting for his country. Lady A. is said to be a close acquaintance of the D. of H—."

Dazed, Araminta turned back to the letter: "My dear Lady Araminta: I think you will be interested in the enclosed. As you may recall, I once told you that you would regret throwing my friendship back in my face. Manning."

Shaking with rage, Araminta tore the letter and the

286

newspaper clipping into tiny bits, knowing as she did so that it was a futile gesture. By this time the half of London society who mattered would have seen the offending column, and the other half would swiftly be apprised of it.

She'd underestimated Lord Manning. Thinking back, she remembered encountering him outside the offices of Mr. Loman, Gillian's publisher. She also remembered seeing Mr. Loman's clerk loitering at the entrance of the building at the same time. It seemed that she'd underestimated Mr. Loman, too. Curious to discover the identity of "Miss Cholmondely," he'd ordered his clerk to follow her to her carriage. The clerk had seen her talking to Manning, and had in turn accosted the Viscount for information. . . .

In her mind's eye, Araminta could see Lord Manning introducing himself to the publisher. "Could you tell me something about the young lady who just called on you, Mr. Loman?"

The publisher would have been cautious, suspicious. "And what might that be to you, sir?"

"That I'm not prepared to say," Manning would have replied calmly. "However, if you answer my questions fully and truthfully, it might be worth a handsome sum to you."

From her brief experience with Mr. Loman, Araminta knew that he was not the man to turn aside from a profit, especially when the transaction involved nothing more than the admission that "the young lady," whose name he did not know, had written a novel. Well, as of this morning's *Post,* Mr. Loman did know her name, and so did all of London.

Araminta stood at the window, gazing at the traffic in

the street below without really seeing it, as she tried to understand how she had gotten entangled in the worst coil of her life. Gillian must have added passages to her book that she had never shown to Araminta; certainly in those parts of the manuscript that Araminta had read, there was no reference to a murder by Count Ugolino, no mention of a nephew or a younger brother. It wasn't difficult to pinpoint the inspiration for Gillian's additions: Stéphanie Despard's claims against Jason had triggered Gillian's fertile writer's imagination to invent yet one more villainy for Count Ugolino.

It made no difference that Gillian had almost certainly never meant to suggest any wrongdoing on Jason's part. It made no difference, either, that Araminta was not the author of *Castle of Horrors*. Readers of that paragraph in the "Fashionable Intelligence" column of the *Morning Post* would be convinced that Araminta had indeed written the book and that she had modeled Count Ugolino on Jason. Even though Stéphanie had left England, abandoning her claim to be recognized as Rupert's widow, there would always be a few people who would believe Jason was capable of injuring his own nephew. And the Duke, remembering how fiercely Araminta had championed Stéphanie, would have no choice but to conclude that Araminta had deliberately set out to expose him to public ridicule by making him the villain of her *roman à clef*.

"It's past time to start dressing, my lady," said Jessie's voice behind her, and she turned slowly away from the window, her hand curled tightly around the torn remains of envelope, letter, and newspaper clipping, which she handed to her abigail, saying tersely, "Burn them." Silently, and with no discernible facial expression, the maid dropped the scraps of paper into the fireplace and went to the wardrobe for her mistress's new ball gown of pale yellow *crêpe lisse* trimmed with *ailes de papillon,* tiny butterflies in silver net.

288

While Jessie arranged her hair, Araminta was so deep in thought that she was caught completely unawares by Gillian's stormy entrance into the bedchamber. Without knocking, Gillian pushed open the door and ran into the room. Sobbing wildly, she threw herself down in front of Araminta's chair and buried her face in her aunt's lap.

"Here, now, Miss Gillian, stop that," exclaimed an outraged Jessie. "You'll ruin my lady's gown with those crocodile tears."

"It's all right, Jessie. Leave us alone for a while."

After the maid had left the room, Gillian raised a tear-stained face, saying, "Something's happened, something so terrible I don't know if I can tell you about it."

Araminta reached for a handkerchief and gently wiped Gillian's face. "Hush, love. I already know all about it. What I don't understand, my dear, is why you had Count Ugolino murder his nephew. Didn't you realize that your readers might suspect you had modeled the Count on the Duke of Harwood?"

"It just didn't occur to me. Frankly, I'm convinced that no one *would* have noticed any resemblance if that dreadful item hadn't appeared in the *Morning Post*."

"I suppose that's true," said Araminta slowly. "Your book was to have been published anonymously, and besides, Mr. Loman told us he was planning to bring it out in the autumn, when all the furor about the Duke and Stéphanie Despard would have died down. It's only the revelation of my identity as the author of the book, and its imminent publication, that makes the resemblance between Count Ugolino and the Duke in any way credible. Well, my dear, we must think what's to be done."

Gillian's tears began to flow again. "It was so dreadful. I was in my bedchamber a few minutes ago when I heard a commotion from Mama's sitting room. I rushed in to see if I could help and found her in a fit of the vapors. Someone had sent her a copy of that paragraph in the *Morning Post*. Araminta, I know I must be the worst sort

289

of coward, but I couldn't admit to Mama that I had disgraced the whole family and defamed the Duke of Harwood by writing that horrible book."

Araminta put her arms around Gillian in a comforting hug. "It isn't a horrible book. It's a great book! And nobody is going to discover that you wrote *Castle of Horrors,* because we won't tell anyone."

Gillian took the handkerchief from Araminta and blew her nose. "You're a darling, but I can't let you take responsibility for what I did. I'll go straight to Mama and tell her the truth."

"You'll do nothing of the sort. *I'll* talk to your mother and Damaris." Araminta smiled at Gillian, whose face wore the faintest glimmering of hope. "Trust me. No one can touch me for sheer gall, you know. We'll brazen this out yet."

Despite her reassurances to Gillian, Araminta wasn't at all certain she could rescue the situation, and after her talk with Henrietta and Damaris, she was only marginally more hopeful.

Damaris was with her mother when Araminta came to Henrietta's sitting room. Both of them appeared to be in deep shock. "I didn't write that dreadful book," she told them, "and I haven't the faintest idea why the newspaper printed that item."

"Oh, Araminta, I *know* you wouldn't do such a thing," Henrietta replied, close to tears, "but it makes no difference how it came about. The damage has been done."

"How can we possibly appear tonight at the ball? Everyone will be staring at us. Everyone, that is, who bothers to come," said Damaris in a tight voice that betrayed how close she, too, was to tears.

"If that's to be your attitude, I daresay we'll all most certainly end under a cloud," said Araminta sharply. "Listen to me. It's fortunate that we're giving this ball tonight, because all our friends and acquaintances, and yes, our enemies, will be there. We can show them what we think of this scurrilous gossip by remaining calm and dignified, denying to anyone who brings up the subject that there's a word of truth in that paragraph from the *Morning Post*. If we maintain a front of outraged dignity, the public will soon conclude that the "Fashionable Intelligence" column is pure libel. Which it is. No one can bring a shred of evidence to prove otherwise. We're simply the victims of someone's malice."

"Well . . ." Henrietta sounded miserably uncertain.

"Oh, I don't know if—"

Araminta interrupted Damaris. "Can you think of another solution? No? Then let's try it my way."

Glancing down at the guests advancing up the staircase to the ballroom and noting with relief that the number of arrivals was thinning out, Araminta spotted the welcome faces of Jason's sister and her husband near the end of the line. She said in a low voice to Henrietta, standing beside her in the receiving line, "Look. Lord and Lady Salford are here."

"Thank God," Henrietta muttered between lips set in a fixed smile.

Araminta had met Lord Salford, a pleasant-faced, rather prosaic-looking man, several days previously, when he and his wife had called at Middleton House on their arrival from Gloucestershire. Neither he nor his wife betrayed by their manner that there was anything amiss when they passed through the receiving line, but as she turned away, Felicity murmured, "I must talk to you later."

Araminta smiled her assent, and then remarked to Henrietta, "I think we might call an end to the receiving line. Any latecomers can seek us out in the ballroom. Damaris, I know you're eager to dance, so go along with you and give that crowd of waiting swains the opportunity to fill up your dance card."

"Do you think they really want to dance with me, Aunt Araminta? Or are they simply curious, waiting like jackals to ask me about the family scandal?"

Araminta shot her niece a look of green flame, and Damaris dropped her head, mumbling, "I'm sorry. It's so *awful,* you see, not knowing what's going to happen."

"I know. Waiting for the other shoe to drop," Araminta nodded. "We all feel that way, but we must go on exactly as we've been doing. Go right into that ballroom, Damaris, pretend that you haven't a care in the world, dance the night away, and if anyone has the audacity to mention the *Morning Post,* flash him your most beautiful smile and tell him you haven't the faintest notion of what he is talking about."

Damaris swallowed hard and rose on her tiptoes to brush her aunt's cheek in a kiss. "Thank you so much for this wonderful ball, Aunt Araminta," she exclaimed in a clear, carrying voice, and walked with a smile toward her coterie of waiting partners.

"You handle Damaris so well," murmured Henrietta. "She's a bundle of nerves tonight, and small wonder. Tell me, do you think we have any chance at all to muddle through this evening? Nobody said a word to us about that infamous newspaper item while we stood in the receiving line, but I could almost *hear* the questions behind those polite smiles."

"Remember what I told you: the item in the newspaper is a pure lie, and if we stay calm, we can't be drawn into a nonexistent scandal."

"I'd like to believe that, but . . ." Henrietta tossed a worried glance at the now empty staircase. "It's growing so late. I was encouraged to see the Duke's sister and her husband arrive, but why isn't he himself here? If he doesn't come to a ball given in Damaris's honor . . ."

Araminta took her sister's arm. "Of course the Duke will come. He's been delayed a trifle, that's all. Now let's go mingle with our guests."

Dancing had been in progress for some time, and when Araminta and Henrietta entered the ballroom, a waltz was just ending. Odile came off the floor on Roger's arm. She was wearing a gown of near-transparent *aërophone* crepe in a brilliant shade of red over a white satin slip, with a white crepe bodice cut so perilously low that Araminta had wondered if it would hold up for the entire evening.

"*Chère* Araminta, Madame Middleton, I have just heard the most distressing news—"

Roger interrupted her. "Odile, I *told* you that was simply an ugly rumor. You shouldn't disturb Lady Middleton and Lady Araminta with it." He cast a quick, worried glance around him to see if anyone had overheard Odile's remark.

"Roger's quite right, Odile. You can enjoy the ball with a light heart. There's absolutely nothing to worry about." Giving Odile's arm a comforting pat, and excusing herself to Henrietta, Araminta walked over to speak to the Salfords. "You've heard the rumor?" she asked.

Felicity's eyes flashed. "Yes, and Augustus and I want you to know we don't believe a word of it. You a two-faced person who could stab my brother in the back with one hand and extend the hand of friendship to his sister with the other? Infamous!"

"You must have an enemy, Lady Araminta," said Lord Salford quietly.

"Yes. I can't do anything about it, I fear," Araminta replied without thinking. She quickly changed the subject. "Felicity, has your brother seen the paragraph in the *Morning Post?*"

A shade of worry clouded Felicity's face. "I don't know. We haven't seen Jason since this morning. Augustus and I had been planning to attend your ball with Jason, of course, but we waited and waited this evening for him to return to Harwood House and he never came."

"I'm sure he's just been delayed," said Lord Salford. "Lady Araminta, permit me to say that you and Lady

Middleton are behaving just as you ought. Scandal can't exist without proof."

"Thank you."

"Let's not talk about it," said Felicity firmly. "Araminta, Augustus and I are looking forward so much to joining your party for the Derby. We've agreed to split our loyalties. I'll cheer for Caesar, since Jason is my brother, and Augustus will place his money on Mr. Middleman's horse!"

Leaving the Salfords, Araminta moved through the crowd, flashing a sunny smile to the dancers swirling by her, stopping to chat with an imposing dowager seated at the side of the room, laughingly allowing her dance card to be rapidly filled out by her usual phalanx of admirers. She felt a little more confident in her ability to weather the storm after talking with the Salfords. Felicity's open support would go a long way toward silencing the gossips.

However, a nagging worry remained. She'd told Henrietta that the newspaper paragraph was a gross and groundless fabrication, and if that had only been the case, she didn't doubt that she and her family could have waited out the rumor until it died a natural death. But as it happened, the story was basically true, verifiable by anyone who was prepared to dig for the facts, and it would remain a potential source of scandal even if Araminta were willing to clear her name by throwing poor Gillian to the wolves. And what about Jason? It was too early in the evening to conclude that he was not going to make an appearance at the ball, but what if he never arrived? His failure to do so would set the gossips' tongues wagging more furiously than ever.

Martin Corby proved to be a greater source of comfort than Araminta would have imagined. As he led her out on the floor for a waltz, he murmured, "Damaris has been telling me about that item in the *Post,* and I've assured her that *nobody* could possibly believe that you would set out to slander the Duke."

Araminta gave silent thanks that she'd invited Martin to the ball. She knew she could rely on her trainer to exert a steadying influence on Damaris during the course of the evening. It occurred to her to wonder if Damaris realized how much she was coming to depend on Martin's calming strength. She said to him, "Thank you. People who really know me will feel the same as you do, I'm sure. How is Selim?"

Martin's eyes lit up. "At his peak. If I were a betting man, which I'm not, and if I were full of juice, which I'm not, either, I could look forward to being a much wealthier man after the Derby."

"Mercifully, the race is only two days away," laughed Araminta. "I don't think I could manage the suspense for any longer than that."

"You haven't been listening," said Martin reproachfully. "There's no reason for you to feel any suspense about the outcome of the Derby. Hassan told me this morning that he expects to win the race by at least ten lengths."

Araminta laughed again. "Oh, in that case I'll cease worrying immediately. Hassan is never wrong! Have you experienced any difficulty with those 'legs' you were telling me about?"

"One of the grooms found a stranger lurking around the stables the other day. The groom threw the man off the property and we redoubled the guard on Selim. The stranger may have been a simple vagrant, but I took no chances."

"You've done a splendid job for me, Martin. I appreciate it. I plan to go down to Epsom tomorrow afternoon. I'll see you then."

Her dance with Martin lifted Araminta's spirits only temporarily. The evening wore on to the interval, and her face felt tired with the strain of maintaining a carefree smile on her lips, but still Jason had not arrived. She was standing at the end of the ballroom, talking to Henrietta and Damaris, when out of the corner of her eye, she glimpsed a flutter of movement near the door. "The Duke has come," breathed Damaris.

Araminta turned to face the door. Jason remained near the entrance, head high in that arrogant pose she knew so well, his arms folded across his chest as he glanced slowly around the room. Spotting Araminta, he began walking toward her, looking neither to right or left, responding to greetings from acquaintances with a curt nod, keeping his gaze fixed on her in a deliberate stare as he approached. Gradually the sound of conversation died away, and the orchestra leader, poised to lift his baton for the next number, lowered his hand. In the odd stillness, Araminta could feel every eye in the ballroom fastened on her and Jason.

The Duke stopped a scant two feet away. She noted the faint twitch of a muscle in his cheek and the hard glitter of his eyes, and her heart sank. He was in a very dangerous mood. Then, incredibly, he smiled, bowing deeply.

"Lady Araminta, forgive me for being so late to your ball. I was detained on—er—pressing business. Lady Middleton, good evening. Damaris, dare I hope that you've saved a dance for someone so tardy? And you, too, Lady Araminta. Will you waltz with me a little later?"

After Jason had whisked Damaris out on the dance floor, Henrietta heaved a sigh of relief, muttering, "Thank God for the Duke's common sense. He wasn't taken in by that lying newspaper item."

Araminta knew better. One glance from Jason's furious eyes had revealed what he was really thinking. She spent the rest of the evening in a kind of blur, dancing every dance, taking supper with young Mr. Ness, who had been sighing for the privilege, and waiting for retribution. Jason bided his time until the last dance of the ball. He came up to her then, picked up her dance card, flicked his finger at the last space, occupied by a neat signature, and said coolly, "A mistake, surely? I was positive this was my waltz." He tucked the card inside his coat and extended his arm.

Araminta had been dreading the close contact of the waltz, but when Jason smiled down at her, told her an amusing story, and paid her a charming compliment, he was so much like his old self that she began to wonder if she had misjudged his frame of mind. Or was it possible that he hadn't yet heard of the offending newspaper item? She tried cautiously to bring up the subject. "Jason, there's a very disturbing piece of gossip going the rounds—" He interrupted her to say gaily, "Then I don't want to hear it. Disturbing gossip shouldn't raise its ugly head at a ball." But again his eyes gave him away.

At the end of the dance, as she and Jason were walking across the floor, several young men fell into step with them. One of them said laughingly, "I say, Duke, did you know that your horse and that fellow Middleman's horse had drawn even in the betting as of this afternoon?"

Jason grinned. "I'd heard that, but I hadn't mentioned it to Lady Araminta. She's convinced, you know, that Mr. Middleman's horse will win the Derby, and I never like to be in the position of contradicting a lady." He cocked an inquiring eye at her. "However, now that the subject is out in the open, dare I suggest that we increase the size of the wager we made several weeks ago? From five hundred to, say, a thousand, that Mr. Middleman's horse can't beat my Caesar?"

"You're on," said Araminta promptly, and amid a gale of laughter, she and Jason went off to join Henrietta and Damaris.

Gradually the guests made their farewells. Soon Araminta was alone in the ballroom except for the members of the household and Jason, who stood off to one side chatting quietly with Damaris.

"It was a lovely evening, but I'm glad it's over," yawned Odile. "I don't believe I can keep my eyes open for a moment longer. You won't mind if I go off to my bed?"

Watching Odile walk to the door, Henrietta said in a low voice, "I know she's French and very stylish, but really, Araminta, that dress!"

"Don't you like the color?" Araminta asked innocently. "A trifle bold, perhaps? Odile informs me that it's a brand-new shade. *Coquilicot,* I think she called it."

"I don't object to the color so much as the lack of material above the waist," Henrietta retorted, and then blushed. Araminta read her mind as Jason walked up to them. Henrietta had not only spoken indelicately, but had done so almost within hearing of a gentleman.

"I'll take my leave now, Lady Middleton," said Jason. "It's been a most enjoyable evening." He was his normal affable, debonair self, and if there was a gritty undertone to his voice, Henrietta didn't appear to notice it. As though he were stating an afterthought, he added, "Oh, before I go, might I have a word with you, Lady Araminta?"

When they were alone, Jason stared at her, raising an eyebrow. "You don't seem surprised that I wanted to talk to you."

"No. I knew you had something to say to me."

"I do, indeed," said the Duke savagely. "Well? Did it amuse you to charm me and lead me on and pretend to be my friend, all the while knowing that you were about to make me the laughingstock of London?"

The bitter anger in his voice caused Araminta to wince inwardly, but she tried to sound both calm and persuasive. "I know you're angry about that paragraph in the "Fashionable Intelligence" column, and rightly so, but you must believe me when I tell you it's nothing but a pack of lies."

Jason's lip curled. "You're denying you wrote *Castle of Horrors?* I thought you had at least a few shreds of honesty."

"Of course I'm denying it. Me, an authoress? I wouldn't have the faintest idea how to go about it." She tried to smile. "I've been criticized a great deal, but never for being a bluestocking. And why on earth would I play a trick like that on you?"

"It won't fadge, Araminta. Do you take me for a Johnny Raw? Before I confronted you with this, I went to see your publisher. Mr. Loman was somewhat reluctant to talk at first, but after I laid out a bit of blunt, he permitted me to examine the manuscript of *Castle of Horrors,* and later he described his anonymous new author in exact detail. A tall, elegant, beautiful young lady with red-gold hair and laughing green eyes. You to the life. How amusing of you to hold out for more money! Poor Mr. Loman. He hadn't the slightest suspicion that he was dealing with one of the wealthiest women in England."

Araminta said through stiff lips, "Jason, I did not write that book, but I *can* give you an explanation for my visit to Mr. Loman's office."

"I doubt that I'd find the explanation convincing. You see, after I visited your Mr. Loman, I called on the person in charge of the "Fashionable Intelligence" column at the *Morning Post*. He told me that he'd received a letter by hand, setting out the information he later printed in the column and enclosing the sum of fifty pounds with the request that the item be published as soon as possible. You do things very thoroughly, don't you, my dear? Not content to wait for my humiliation when the book was published next week, you decided to let me sway a little longer on the gibbet by planting that prepublication tidbit in the newspaper."

Araminta's mouth went dry. It was Lord Manning who'd had been thorough, devilishly so. The Viscount had anticipated that the Duke would investigate the newspaper item and had weighted the evidence heavily against her. She couldn't fault Jason for being taken in by Manning's intricately plotted chicanery. "Jason, please listen. I didn't write that book. I didn't plant that item in the newspaper column either, but I know who did. It was

Lord Manning. He's been biding his time, trying to injure both of us—"

Jason cut in. "Don't try to hoax me with your farradiddles, my dear. I'd believe anything of that hell-kite Manning. He'd ruin me if he could. But if he's behind this take-in, he had help. Yours, Araminta. Don't forget, *you* went to see Loman. Why would you do that if you had no connection with the book?"

Her heart leaden with despair, Araminta made one last effort. "Think about it, Jason. Why in heaven's name would I want to harm you? We're friends, we'll soon be connected by marriage—"

"How would I know what your reasons are? Perhaps it started out simply as a practical joke. You delight in being an emancipated female, and you probably wanted to cut up a lark by standing society on its ears with a *roman à clef.* You put me in the book, no doubt, because you resented being proved wrong in the case of Stéphanie Despard."

"Jason . . ." Araminta shook her head. It was useless. After a moment she said, "Thank you anyway for playing out that charade at the ball tonight. I think you stopped the gossips in their tracks."

"I didn't do it for you. I did it to preserve a little dignity for myself and to prevent Lady Middleton and her daughter from being harmed by a family scandal." Araminta looked away to avoid the sneer of contempt on the Duke's face, and then felt herself turning to stone as he continued: "However, I want you to know that, while I'm prepared to ignore this whole incident in public, I'm not prepared to play your little game in private. I intend to tell Lady Middleton and Damaris the truth about you. I'll also tell them that in future I will not willingly attend any function at which you're to be a guest. And that, Lady Araminta Beresford, should put an end to our brief and unpleasant acquaintance."

* * *

The Duke stalked past the footman and out the door of Middleton House to his waiting carriage. "White's," he barked to his coachman. He threw himself into a corner of the carriage, trying to extract some pleasure from the parting shot he'd delivered to Araminta, but succeeded only in feeling more miserable.

This afternoon when he'd heard the first titter of amusement over the newspaper column, at Manton's Shooting Gallery in Davies Street, he'd been furiously angry at this invasion of his privacy and determined to track down whoever was responsible, but he'd taken it for granted that Araminta was as much a victim of slander as he was. After talking to the publisher and the newspaper columnist, he had been plunged into such a hell of humiliation that his first impulse was to seek out Araminta and horsewhip her down the street. Reason prevailed, fortunately. He refused to give her the satisfaction of watching him make a fool of himself in public.

Every word she had ever spoken to him had been a lie, every glance, every smile. Every kiss. He writhed as he remembered how she had melted in his arms, pretending a passion as fiery as his own, while at that very moment she was probably mentally composing the letter she was about to send to the *Morning Post*. Difficult as it was to believe, there had to be something devilish, something perverse about Araminta, despite that incomparably beautiful face and her witching sweetness of manner.

The carriage stopped in St. James's Street in front of White's Club. The Duke walked up the steps and through the door to the left of the famous bow window, where Beau Brummell and his cronies had reigned for so many years. Handing his *chapeau bras* to a hovering minion, he went to the supper room, his glance sliding away from several acquaintances to avoid the necessity of recognizing them. Tonight he didn't care to talk to anyone. He ordered a light meal that he didn't touch and a bottle of port. He had consumed most of the bottle when the Marquess of Haslemere stopped by his table.

"Ah, Harwood. Just the man I wanted to see. Will you make a fourth at whist?"

About to refuse the invitation, Jason changed his mind. A game of whist might keep his thoughts at bay. Certainly the port hadn't helped. And Haslemere, an amiable lightweight, was a pleasant enough fellow.

In the card room, Jason stiffened as Haslemere introduced the other two whist players. One of them, a Major Cobb, was a stranger. The other was Silvanus Manning.

Jason stared at the Viscount, noting the smirk of amusement on his handsome mouth. Was Manning thinking of the titillating column in the *Morning Post?* Was he congratulating himself on being the author of it, with Araminta's willing compliance? Jason took an instant decision. He was damned if he was going to give Manning the satisfaction of knowing how badly he'd been stung. Nodding curtly to the Viscount, he sat down at the table and lifted a finger to the porter to bring another bottle of port.

"Well, Duke," smiled Manning, "I don't believe I've had the pleasure of playing with you before tonight. Shall we make it interesting? What do you say to five hundred pounds a point?"

Jason shrugged. "I'm entirely at your disposal."

In the draw, Lord Manning became the dealer and Jason, with the next highest card, was his partner. Lord Haslemere and the nondescript major, who rarely opened his mouth to utter more than a monosyllable, quickly won the first game in one hand, scoring nine tricks with three honors. In the next game, down by only two points, Manning and Jason had a fine opportunity to score in the second hand when the combination of too much wine and the lack of any real interest in the play caused Jason to revoke.

"Game and rubber!" crowed Haslemere. "Let me see,

302

now: we agreed to raise the rub to four points, and Cobb and I had two trebles. I make it ten points for our partnership, Major."

The taciturn Major Cobb became loquacious. "Ten points," he repeated with obvious pleasure. "Five thousand pounds. Not a paltry sum at all for a mere half hour's work."

"I don't think you were concentrating on the play, Duke," observed Manning with a cold scorn. "We might have had that second game if you hadn't revoked. Could it be that you were distracted by weightier matters? The *Morning Post,* for example. I understand there was a very interesting item in today's edition."

"I discuss my affairs only with my friends, Manning," snapped Jason. "Of course, I normally associate only with gentlemen. And I never play cards with Greeks if I can possibly help it."

Manning turned a dull purple at this reference to his reputation for cheating. No one had ever actually caught him fuzzing the cards, so he was still a member in good standing in the exclusive men's clubs, but the rumor that he was a Captain Sharp still clung to him.

With a supreme effort, Manning managed to control his temper. "I daresay a low stakes game like this one simply fails to hold your interest," he said smoothly. "How about a somewhat larger bet? Say fifty thousand pounds that your horse Caesar doesn't win the Derby. But perhaps you feel that would be too risky. I hear that the favorite in the betting is a horse owned by—now, what was that fellow's name?—oh, yes, by a Mr. A. Middleman."

"Too risky? Not at all. Make it a hundred thousand."

"By Jove, if you're that confident, why don't we double the bet?"

"Done," said the goaded Duke.

Rising from the table, Manning called to the proprietor of the club. "Raggett, the betting book, please."

Carrying the famous betting book, George Raggett, the

303

owner of White's, strolled over from his seat in a corner of the room, where he had been conducting his usual nightly vigil: at the end of each evening he made it a practice to send his servants to bed so that he could personally sweep the carpet in the card room and retrieve the gold sovereigns and gaming counters dropped by careless or drunken customers.

"The betting book, my lord," said Raggett. "What shall I write?"

In a loud, clear voice that reached even the deeply absorbed hazard players at the next table, the Viscount said: "Lord Manning bets the Duke of Harwood two hundred thousand pounds that the Duke's horse Caesar will not win the Derby in two days' time."

Chapter Seventeen

Araminta put down her teacup, nibbled halfheartedly at a piece of toast, and pushed her tray away. She threw back her coverlets and got out of bed, shrugging herself into the silk dressing gown that Jessie had left draped over the foot of the bed. Walking over to the window, she stood looking down without much interest at the nursemaids and their charges in the street below, on their way to take the air in Berkeley Square.

It was considerably past midmorning on the day after the ball she had given for Damaris. Normally she was an early riser, even after a late engagement the evening before. But last night Araminta had been unable to fall asleep. Twisting and squirming in her bed, she hadn't drifted into a restless slumber until well past dawn, and even now she didn't feel rested.

A light knock sounded and a moment later Odile poked her head around the door. "It is permitted I come in, *chère* Araminta? I was just passing your door when a footman arrived with a message, so I decided to bring it to you myself." She handed Araminta a note superscribed in Henrietta's familiar handwriting. Araminta read it quickly and set it down without comment.

"It isn't often, *ma mie,* that you are a greater slugabed than I," said Odile merrily. "I thought the ball went very well, didn't you? The beautiful Damaris was in dazzling looks and her *maman* seemed very pleased with the evening." A slight frown furrowed her brow. "Except—what was all that *brouhaha* about the newspaper? Oh, you and Roger both assured me it was of no consequence, but there must have been *something*. Roger said that someone had accused you of writing a dreadful book about the Duke, which is to laugh. You write a book? You don't even like to write letters!" A sudden thought struck Odile, and she paused abruptly, her mouth half open. *"La petite* Gillian!" she exclaimed. "Often I've surprised the little one scribbling away in her bedchamber. *She* wrote the book, *n'est-ce pas?* But why would that child wish to harm the Duke, her sister's future husband?"

"Odile! Don't say another word. Don't even think another thought."

For a moment, Odile looked perplexed. Then she said wisely, "I see what it is. You are protecting the little Gillian. That is like you, my dear, good friend." She put her arms around Araminta in an impulsive hug. "Well, now, tomorrow is the day of your big race, *hein?* You are still planning to go with Madame Middleton and Damaris to—what is that place?—to Epsom this afternoon?"

"Yes, I'm leaving today to avoid the crowded roads tomorrow morning, but I've just learned that Henrietta and Damaris won't be going with me." Araminta indicated the note Odile had brought her. "I think they're both feeling overly fatigued after the ball last night. However, Lord and Lady Salford will be accompanying me. We'll be staying at the King's Head Hotel. I'm sorry you're not coming with us."

"So am I. But you know Roger has a meeting at the Admiralty this afternoon. I'm on the pills and needles about that. Perhaps, in spite of *Monsieur le Duc*'s kind intervention, the Admiralty will send Roger back to sea soon? Oh, well. We will come down to Epsom tomorrow, then. I wish you and your horse *bonne chance.*"

When Odile had left the bedchamber, Araminta read Henrietta's note again. After the unpleasantness of last night, Henrietta wrote, she and Damaris simply didn't feel that they would enjoy attending the Derby. She hoped Araminta would understand.

The note was mournful rather than angry or reproachful. Evidently Jason hadn't yet written to Henrietta to denounce Araminta. It was only postponing the inevitable. Interest in the titillating little item in the "Fashionable Intelligence" column would soon fade away, as the Ton discovered more promising bits of scandal to engage its attention, but Araminta knew that her stay in England was over. Once Jason informed Henrietta and Damaris that she'd written *Castle of Horrors,* they would never forgive her, nor would they allow her to associate with Gillian. Without these family ties there was little reason for her to remain in London.

After Selim had made his run in the Derby, after Odile was safely married and snugly established either at the Craddock estate in St. Albans or in a comfortable little house in Portsmouth to wait out Roger's next tour of sea duty, Araminta would take to the road again. Another visit to Greece, Egypt, and Syria, perhaps. Or Istanbul. Italy. There were many fascinating corners of the world that she hadn't yet seen, or would like to see again.

The King's Head Hotel in Epsom was one of the largest and most fashionable hostelries in the town, and had maintained its reputation for more than a century; Samuel Pepys and the infamous Nell Gwyn had been among its guests during the reign of Charles II. On the eve of the Derby, Araminta sat in the dining room of the hotel, dining with Felicity and her husband, who had arrived in Epsom late that afternoon. Araminta was both pleased and surprised to see them. As her thoughts had grown steadily gloomier during the day, she'd become convinced that the Salfords wouldn't come to Epsom; by this time, surely, Jason would have informed them of her presumed connection with the scandalous book, and they

307

too would have turned against her.

"Have you talked to your brother?" she asked Lady Salford after the first course had been served.

Felicity looked troubled. "No. According to his valet, he didn't come home until the small hours of the morning. He hadn't yet made his appearance when Augustus and I left for Epsom. Steen—the valet—is very discreet, but I got the distinct impression that Jason had been dipping very deep last night."

"I see." If Jason had been drinking heavily the previous evening, it would explain why he hadn't yet written to Henrietta, or spoken to his sister. Araminta took a sudden decision. "Felicity, Lord Salford, I think I should tell you something. I didn't write that book, but I fear the Duke is convinced that I did. Before very long, I may be in very deep disgrace."

"Then it will all be a misunderstanding," said Felicity calmly. "I'll *never* believe you intended to harm Jason."

Araminta squeezed Felicity's hand. "Thank you." She looked up as a waiter stopped by the table with a note on a tray. "Ask Mr. Corby to join us."

When Martin strolled into the dining room, he announced that he'd eaten his evening meal much earlier, but accepted the offer of a glass of wine and sat down at the table. "Well, Lady Araminta?" he said smilingly. "Have you prepared a modest little victory speech, giving me and Hassan all the credit for your win?"

Araminta laughed. "I hadn't thought about it, but if and when I do give a speech, it won't be in the least modest! I shall positively gloat about Selim's win! Since you're here, I assume that Selim is in town also."

"Safely bedded down, with half a dozen of my sharpest stable lads to watch over him through the night. You're fortunate that Selim's first big race takes place so close to his training stable. When a horse is obliged to walk for days to arrive at a race course for his next meet, some of his speed and endurance, in my opinion, inevitably gets left on the highway. Of course, if you planned to race Selim at Doncaster or Ascot or Goodwood, traveling would be required."

"I'm not planning on any other races for Selim. Not in England, at any rate. I may start off on my travels again soon." She smiled, shaking her head at a chorus of disapproval, and changed the subject. "Are there still fourteen horses in the race? You thought there might be scratches."

"Still fourteen, yes. But several of the fourteen are inferior horses, entered, I suspect, purely to make a series of false starts that will throw off the front runners. I don't want you to be surprised by that. As to scratches . . ." Martin shot a glance of sympathy at Felicity. "There are none as yet, but Joe Smithers, the Duke of Harwood's trainer, told me an hour ago that he had sent a message to the Duke, recommending that Caesar be scratched."

"Scratch Caesar? But why?" Felicity inquired incredulously.

"Because Smithers has no jockey. I'm sure you know, Lady Salford, that your brother's horse is so vicious that he will allow only a handful of people to come near him, let alone ride him. Late this afternoon, Smithers learned that Jack Tobin, Caesar's jockey, had gotten involved in a tavern brawl and was so seriously injured that he won't be able to ride tomorrow. And since Tobin is the only jockey who's ever been able to ride Caesar . . ." Martin shrugged. "The worst of it is, Smithers suspects that the legs are responsible. Or worse."

"What do you mean?" asked Araminta.

"The jockey told Smithers that he was enticed into a tavern and then was deliberately set upon by a gang of thugs. Of course, Tobin shouldn't have gone near a tavern the day before a big race, but Smithers is inclined to believe the man's story because"—Martin shot another compassionate glance at Felicity—"because last night the Duke bet Viscount Manning two hundred thousand pounds that Caesar would win the Derby."

There was a shocked silence and then Lord Salford said

incredulously, "Good God, man, you must be mistaken. Two hundred thousand pounds! No sane man would bet so large a sum, not even Charles James Fox in his heyday."

Felicity turned pale, and there was a pinched look around her mouth. Araminta suspected she was distressed, not only because of Jason's predicament but because Silvanus Manning was once again casting his baleful shadow across her life. Araminta said suddenly, "It's well known that Viscount Manning is quite run off his legs. How was he proposing to pay the Duke such a large sum if Caesar were to win the Derby?"

"Well, I can't swear to the amount because I wasn't present when the bet was made," Martin said doubtfully. "But it must have been an outrageously large sum, because the story became the talk of London overnight and had reached Epsom by early afternoon."

"Do you know any other details?" asked Araminta.

"Again, this is hearsay, but as I understand it, the Duke left your house last night, Lady Araminta, and went straight to White's, where he . . ." His face turning a bright scarlet, Martin turned his horrified eyes away from Felicity. "Pray forgive me," he muttered. "I really don't make it my practice to discuss a man's affairs with the female members of his family. If you'll excuse me, I should be getting back to Selim."

"Sit down," Araminta snapped. "And spare us your gentlemanly compunctions about injuring our female sensibilities." She paused, biting her lip. "I'm sorry, Martin. I can't think how I came to bark at you like that. Do go on. If the Duke is in difficulties, I think Lady Felicity has the right to know about it."

"Oh yes, please, tell us what you've learned, Mr. Corby," said Felicity quickly. "I'd prefer to know the worst. However, I don't see how the situation could possibly be as bad as you say."

"There isn't a great deal more to tell you," said Martin, looking even more uncomfortable. "The Duke was apparently already foxed when he got into the whist game with Lord Manning, and I gather he continued drinking during play. If he hadn't been castaway, I'm convinced he never in the world would have made so large a bet with Manning, of all people."

"Yes," said Lord Salford quietly. "The man's been suspected for years of being a Captain Sharp. No one knew that better than Harwood."

"Exactly. That's why Smithers believes the jockey's story. Manning must have had a scheme in mind to injure the Duke's jockey at the time he made his bet. You were right, Lady Araminta. Manning couldn't possibly have paid off his debt if he lost the race, but he *knew* he couldn't lose. Smithers thinks that Manning hired those thugs to disable Tobin and prevent him from riding Caesar in the Derby."

Lord Salford said slowly, "If we only had some proof . . ."

Martin shook his head. "It would do no good, at least where the Derby is concerned." He looked Felicity squarely in the eye. "I fear the situation *is* as bad as I said it was. Lord Manning has already won his bet, because there's absolutely no hope of finding a replacement jockey. Caesar's reputation is so bad that Smithers won't even attempt to find a jockey willing to risk his neck to ride the horse."

Araminta sat silently digesting the implications of Martin's remarks. It seemed incredible to her that Jason could have made a bet approaching the magnitude of two hundred thousand pounds. Granted, he was a very wealthy man. His yearly income undoubtedly hovered around the hundred thousand mark. Probably he wouldn't be faced with total ruin if he lost this bet to Viscount Manning. Yet, faced with the necessity of producing this immense sum immediately, and in cash, Jason undoubtedly would be forced to liquidate a large portion of his holdings at terms that wouldn't be advantageous to him. He might come out of this crisis solvent, but the chances were good that he would no longer be considered one of the wealthiest men in England.

Some of this is my fault, thought Araminta miserably. *Jason must take the ultimate responsibility for his own actions, but if he hadn't been so angry at me because of that wretched newspaper column, he wouldn't have gone straight to White's from my ball last night to drown his problems in a bottle of wine.*

She heard herself saying, "Tell Smithers you've found him another jockey, Martin."

"I beg your pardon, but this is no time for practical jokes."

"I'm not joking. Just inform Smithers you can provide him with a jockey who's already proved that he can ride Caesar."

Obviously trying to control his temper, Martin retorted, "Will you also tell me where I can find this miracle horseman?"

Araminta took a deep breath. "Right in front of you."

Felicity exclaimed incredulously, "You can't mean what you're saying, Araminta. You, ride in the Derby?"

"Why not? Though Hassan wouldn't admit it, I'm a better rider than he is. What's more, a few days ago I rode Caesar and controlled him without any difficulty. Smithers saw me do it."

Lord Salford put in, "My dear lady, every feeling must be offended at the very thought of such a thing. Ladies of quality do not become jockeys."

"I don't propose to become a jockey," retorted Araminta. "I just want to prevent your brother-in-law from beggaring himself. If I don't ride Caesar, he doesn't run in the Derby. It's as simple as that. Well, Martin?"

"I'm beginning to believe that you can do anything you set your mind to," Martin said, "but I'll have no part of this madness. Yes, you've ridden Caesar. That could have been a fluke. The next time you approach him he might tear your head off. In any event, you could easily be killed or injured during the race itself. At the very least, if

312

your identity became known, you could lose your reputation."

"Or more probably, I might stay on Caesar's back until the end of the race and come in last?"

"That, too. Your Selim is the fastest horse in the field."

"But he doesn't have the best rider. Very well, Martin, if you won't help me, I must help myself." Araminta beckoned to the waiter. "Please tell my coachman to bring around my carriage."

"Where are you going?" asked Felicity in alarm.

"I'm off to talk to Smithers, of course. Martin, you'll give my coachman Ben directions to the stables?"

"This is madness, Mr. Corby," interrupted Lord Salford. "We can't allow Lady Araminta to do anything so dangerous and so ill-considered."

Martin braced his shoulders. "What else can I do? Lady Araminta has me in a position where I'm piqued, repiqued, slammed, and capotted!" Turning to Araminta, he said, "You must know I couldn't let you go to the stables alone, at this time of night. Very well, I'll go with you. Perhaps it's all for the best. You'll not be able to bamboozle Smithers into going along with your shatter-brained scheme."

"No," said Joe Smithers. "Absolutely not, ma'am."

He was standing with Araminta and Martin in the dimly lit stable area outside Caesar's stall. Around them, they could hear the faint sounds of horses and stable hands settling in for the night.

"I couldn't take the risk, ma'am. His Grace would dismiss me from his employ if anything should happen to you, and rightly so. Nor could I ever forgive myself."

"If Caesar doesn't win the Derby, you may not have a position in any event," observed Araminta. "The Duke will doubtless be hard pressed to maintain his racing stables."

Smithers shot her a startled glance. "Even so."

313

"Have you heard from the Duke, Joe?" asked Martin.

"No, I haven't," said Smithers with a worried frown. "I expected him in Epsom today. When he hadn't arrived by early afternoon, I sent a message up to London, but I've received no reply. I don't like to scratch Caesar without His Grace's express permission, even though it's only a formality. Without a jockey, Caesar can't run."

"He can run and he can win, if you allow me to ride him," said Araminta. "What do you have to lose, Mr. Smithers? I'll arrive at the stables just before the race, dressed in the silks you're about to give me, my hair tucked neatly inside my cap, my face blackened to a desert bronze. You'll tell everyone that I'm an Arab rider, a countryman of Hassan. At the end of the race, whether or not I win, I'll disappear into the crowd. No one will ever know that Araminta Beresford rode in the Derby."

"The Duke would know," said Smithers uneasily, showing the first signs of wavering.

"If the Duke arrives before the race, and if he recognizes me and refuses to allow me to ride Caesar, then the matter is out of your hands."

"Well . . ."

"Smithers!" Martin exploded. "Are you queer in your attic, man? You can't allow Lady Araminta to ride that rogue horse."

"Martin doesn't believe that Caesar likes me," said Araminta. She walked toward the stall, calling softly, "Caesar, here, boy." A head appeared in the door, whinnying in recognition. As Martin exclaimed in horror, Araminta reached up to pull Caesar's head down, blowing gently in his ear. Caesar affectionately nuzzled Araminta's neck.

"Look at that," said Smithers in an awed voice, as he and Martin watched Araminta engage for several minutes in a low-voiced soliloquy with Caesar. "She talks to that horse as if he were human."

"Perhaps that's why he responds as if he were human,"

said Martin thoughtfully. "Smithers, can she really ride Caesar?"

"She rode him at a canter around the stable yard, that's all I can say. If I didn't think that she could at least keep to the saddle without injuring either herself or the horse, I wouldn't allow her to ride."

Later, gazing out the carriage window while she and Martin were driving away from the stable area, Araminta exclaimed, "Ben is taking the wrong direction. This isn't the road to Epsom."

"I told him to drive to the Downs. Mind"—Martin's voice grew truculent—"I'd as lief not be involved in this damned hum, but if you insist on riding Caesar tomorrow, you at least ought to see the course. You'll find that it's nothing like those flat, straight stretches of desert sand where you've raced in the past. Epsom is all ups and downs and sharp corners."

The moon was rising as Araminta and Martin left the carriage at the Stewards's Stand and walked slowly and in silence along the grass to Tattenham Corner and then up the sweeping curve in the direction of the starting post. The gently undulating Downs slept peacefully in the moonlight. There were no travelers on the several roads that crossed the race course, no hint of the roaring thousands who would be watching the running of the Derby tomorrow. "As you can see, it's not an easy course," Martin commented on the return walk. "The horses run right in the middle of the crowd, who leave a cleared space just sufficient for the riders to pass through. Some years back, a jockey was thrown when a mounted spectator charged onto the course and rammed into him."

Nearing the waiting carriage, he stopped, placing a hand on Araminta's arm. "You're playing a dangerous, foolhardy game, you know. Please change your mind while you still have the time."

Araminta shook her head. "I'll not change my mind. The stakes are too high."

* * *

"I can't believe my own eyes," gasped Felicity.

Carefully adjusting the broad-billed cap over her pinned-up hair, Araminta turned slowly around in front of the cheval glass. "I think I look rather convincing," she said jauntily. Her face and hands, tinted a deep charcoal from a generous application of bootblacking, contrasted sharply with her high white stock and brightly colored cropped jacket. The white breeches were too large, and had been hastily tailored to her slim waist by her openly critical abigail, Jessie. Fortunately, the shiny black boots with their wide white tops were an almost perfect fit.

"If I didn't know who you were, I could swear you really were a jockey," said Felicity. "You look like a very short, very slender young man, and that's strange, you know, because you're a rather tall woman. As a matter of fact, with your face blackened, you look very much like Hassan."

"Thank you. It's good to know that my appearance passes muster. Soon we'll find out if my riding does the same."

Felicity's face changed expression. "What am I saying?" she exclaimed in dismay. "Anyone would think I approved of this mad prank of yours. Heaven knows, Augustus and I talked to you last night until our voices gave out, and we made no impression on you, but please, please listen to me while I tell you this one last time: if the gossips find out what you're doing, you can never hold up your head in society again. And I *know* that my brother would far rather lose that dreadful bet than allow you to put yourself in danger."

Araminta patted Felicity's shoulder. "Your conscience is clear. If I disgrace myself, it won't be your fault." She looked at the clock on the mantelpiece. "Time to go." She wrapped herself in a large, old-fashioned cloak with an enveloping hood that concealed every inch of her jockey's garb down to the heels on her boots. Such an unfashionable garment, of course, had no place in Araminta's wardrobe, but she could hardly have stepped out of her hotel bedchamber dressed in her racing silks without arousing comment. Jessie had slipped out early this morning to purchase the cloak in a market patronized by the hotel servants.

Lord Salford stood waiting beside Araminta's carriage in front of the hotel, his features rigid with disapproval. Silently he handed first Araminta and then Felicity into the carriage and climbed in after them.

The streets of Epsom were clogged with vehicles and with boisterously celebrating pedestrians, and the traffic grew progressively worse as Araminta's party approached the Downs.

"You can let me out here," said Araminta, wriggling out of her cloak and throwing it over her arm. "The stables are just over there." She walked quickly to the stable area, where a harried-looking Smithers was standing in front of Caesar's stall. She disregarded the curious stares directed her way by stable hands and trainers and loitering racing followers.

"Good afternoon, Mr. Smithers," she murmured. "I don't want my voice to give me away, so I'll pretend to very limited English. Have you heard from the Duke?"

"Not a word. It's not like His Grace. I've begun to wonder—could he have met with foul play?"

The same uneasy thought had crossed Araminta's mind, but she promptly dismissed it. "Nonsense. He's well able to take care of himself."

"Let us hope so." The trainer gave her a long appraising look. "I wasn't sure you could carry off those racing silks, but you'll do." His eyes dropped to her boots. "You've forgotten your spurs. Here, you can have mine."

"I don't use spurs. Any horse I can't ride without spurs, I won't ride at all."

"But that's . . ." The trainer looked suddenly conscience-stricken. "Lady Araminta . . ."

"The name is Mohammed."

"Er—Mohammed. You're still determined to go on? I

can scratch Caesar right up to post time."

"I'm in this to the finish." She sounded confident, but by the time Caesar was led from his stall, wild-eyed and wary, Araminta was already feeling the first qualms of nervousness. A crowd immediately gathered to watch her, careful not to approach too close to the renegade horse and his murderous hooves. The news that Smithers had found a replacement jockey for Caesar had, it seemed, spread like wildfire. A low murmur of admiration went through the crowd when Araminta walked up to Caesar without a sign of hesitation and placed her hand on his neck. Ignoring the onlookers as she was ignoring the onset of her own fears, Araminta muttered a few soothing words to the skittish and trembling Caesar and then vaulted lightly into the saddle.

With Smithers leading the horse, and Caesar's aged groom trotting alongside, Araminta began the walk to the starting post at one end of the roughly horseshoe-shaped course. She kept Caesar on a very tight rein; being in the midst of so many thousands of people, noisy, excited, intoxicated, was putting a tremendous nervous strain on the horse. It was ironic, she thought, that, of this enormous gathering of individuals, only a few people would actually be able to view the race: the favored guests in the Prince's Stand and those fortunate souls who had managed to find a spot next to the temporary rope barriers marking the course.

Araminta and Caesar were the first to arrive at the starting post, followed almost immediately by the other entries. Araminta kept her eyes fixed directly ahead, avoiding any eye contact with the onlookers while she tried to overlook the increasingly uncomfortable churning sensation in her stomach. She could not block her ears, however, and she soon became aware that she and Hassan were the objects of the spectators's avid attention. Phrases and snatches of comment filtered through her consciousness. ". . . the fellow called Mohammed, he appeared out of the blue . . . heard they were both camel riders . . . or

Bedouin sheiks . . . favorite jockeys of the Turkish Sultan . . . a race to the death . . ."

"Lady! Did you think to deceive the eyes of your servant? Have you fallen under the spell of an evil jinn?" hissed a familiar voice beside her. "It must be so, else why are you riding the horse of the infidel?"

Araminta slanted a glance at Hassan's glowering face. "No, I'm not bewitched," she muttered impatiently. "The Duke is my friend and he has no jockey, so why should I not ride his horse? And I'll thank you to forget that I'm your mistress. Today I'm your friend, Mohammed."

Hassan bridled with mortified pride. "And do you really think that misbegotten excuse for a horse has the slightest chance to win this race?" He struck a hand to his forehead. "Allah forbid, can it be that you expect me to hold back my beautiful Selim, allow you to come in ahead of us on that ugly spawn of Satan?"

Araminta swallowed hard. For a fraction of a second the impulse to lower the odds against herself was very strong. "Don't be an idiot," she snapped. "I would never ask you to throw a race. Ride as hard as you can. Beat me if you can."

The starter appeared, waiting until the jockeys had aligned their horses with the starting post. "Go!" the starter shouted, but one of the horses had already bolted out of position. Again the procedure was repeated, and again. Four times. Half a dozen times. Only one horse was responsible for the false starts, and Araminta, remembering Martin's warning that starts often consumed an hour or more, longed for the power to consign the offending jockey to perdition. She forced herself to remain calm, however, with Caesar growing more restive by the second. She kept him on a very tight rein, preventing him from carrying out his undisguised intention to savage the jockeys on either side of him.

At the next attempt to start, a shout of "They're off!" thundered from the vast crowd. Araminta found her nervousness disappearing with each of Caesar's great leaping strides. Within moments she was completely swept up in the rhythm of the race, feeling herself and Caesar dissolving into one smooth running machine. She held him back on the first steeply rising half-mile of the left-handed course, and was still in the middle of the pack at the head of the long sweeping descent to Tattenham Corner, three and a half furlongs from the winning post.

Making the abrupt turn at the Corner, Caesar lost stride as the horse to his left jostled against him, but Araminta quickly picked him up. She shortened her reins slightly, shifted her weight more heavily into the stirrups and leaned forward, digging her heels into his sides. Caesar responded as if galvanized, passing one horse after another on the straight, gradually descending stretch run. At the beginning of the last uphill fifty yards, another horse drew level with him, and Araminta knew with a sickening inevitability the identity of horse and jockey even before she turned her head to see Hassan making the run past her. He was raking Selim ruthlessly with his spurs, contrary to every instruction she had ever given him, and the sight so sickened and enraged her that she hunched over Caesar's neck, calling, "Now, boy, now!" as she desperately willed him into one last giant effort.

After making his staggering bet with Viscount Manning at White's Club on the evening of Araminta's ball, the Duke of Harwood had gone home to his house in South Audley Street, but not to sleep, although it was already close to dawn. He went to his library, calling for a bottle of port, and began drinking himself into oblivion. His valet ventured into the library at noon, finding the Duke sprawled comatose in his chair. With the help of one of the footmen, the valet poured his master into bed.

The Duke slept through the day, awakening near midnight with a headache of terrifying proportions and a stomach so queasy that he threw a boot at his solicitous valet and crawled back into bed again. By the following morning, the headache had moderated sufficiently to allow Jason to open his eyes without wincing, and his treacherous stomach actually welcomed a strong cup of coffee and a rasher of ham and eggs.

As he was tying his cravat, not giving it his usual punctilious attention, he ordered the valet, "Have my curricle brought around. I'm going to Epsom."

"Ah yes, the Derby." If the Duke had been attentive, he would have noticed a slight change in his valet's expression. There was not a soul in London, high or low, with any connection to the ton, who had not by this time heard of the Duke's ruinous bet with Lord Manning. "Would you care to look at your mail before you leave, Your Grace?"

"Later. The roads will be congested all the way from Westminster, and I want to be in Epsom by the start of the race."

Not only were the roads as crowded as Jason had predicted, but he encountered more serious obstacles on his way to view the Derby. Near Streatham, the inebriated driver of a gig forced him off the road, leaving his curricle with a splintered wheel. There was not a hired vehicle to be had in Streatham on Derby Day, so there was nothing for it but to wait out the labors of the wheelwright. Finally, arriving on the Downs well after the scheduled start of the race, the Duke left the curricle with his tiger and forced his way through the mob to a position near the Prince's Stand, just as a tumultuous roar rose from the spectators on the upper course to announce that the race had begun.

Jason had spotted Smithers standing not far away from him, but made no move to approach the trainer. Mired in his black thoughts, Jason had no wish to speak to anyone. The drive to Epsom, and the attendant delays, had given him more than enough time to review the course of events leading to his disastrous bet with Manning. There was no need to drive the nails any deeper into his lacerated ego by discussing Caesar's prospects with Smithers.

In three minutes—a bit less than that, now—he would learn for himself whether he had thrown away the largest fortune in England on a drunken bet.

The minutes, the seconds, ticked away. Off to Jason's right, the crowd noises swelled to a crescendo, and soon he could see the tightly bunched horses heading into the straight from the sharp curve at Tattenham Corner. At the start of the last uphill stretch, two horses were far in the lead, running neck and neck. Jason froze as his eyes fastened incredulously on the slender, dark-faced jockey riding Caesar. Moments later, Caesar passed Selim at the winning post by a scant half a nose.

Even before the Stewards' official decision, Araminta and Caesar were surrounded by a boisterous crowd, shouting congratulations, patting the horse, clapping her on the shoulder. Caesar's reaction was predictable. He reared and kicked out, fortunately scattering the happy race goers before he could inflict any real damage. Unsure that she could keep Caesar under control, Araminta breathed a sigh of relief when Smithers ran to the horse's head and took a firm hold on Caesar's bridle. He screamed in a frenzy of joy, "You did it, ma'am—I mean Mohammed! You did it!"

Martin pushed his way through the crowd. He reached up to seize Araminta's hand, smiling ruefully. "Congratulations, and I'm trying to mean that sincerely. This is the first time I've ever been glad to lose a race. It was beautiful, beautiful, the finest ride I've ever seen!" He turned, startled, as Hassan rushed up to Araminta, his face distorted with fury.

"Lady, you betrayed Selim, you betrayed me," Hassan shouted in spluttering Arabic, lifting his hands as if to drag her from the saddle. Twisting the Arab's arms behind his back, Martin said under his breath, "I'll take care of him, Lady Araminta. I'm sure he'll calm down soon."

As Martin marched the struggling Hassan away, Jason

appeared beside Smithers. "Your Grace," gasped the trainer. "I didn't know you'd arrived. Did you see the race?"

"Yes, I saw the race." Jason paused, staring at Araminta. Slowly the light of recognition dawned in his face. He rounded on his trainer. "You're no longer in my employ, Smithers."

Araminta slid down from the saddle to face the Duke, whose eyes were flinty in his haggard face. He edged close to her, muttering savagely, "How dare you ride my horse without my permission?"

"But Jason, I—I won the race," Araminta faltered. "I heard about your bet, you see, and I couldn't let you lose two hundred thousand pounds. I *had* to ride Caesar. I hoped it would make up for that dreadful book . . ."

"Smithers was a driveling idiot to let you substitute yourself for my jockey," Jason blazed. "You could have maimed the horse, you could have been killed or injured yourself. In any case, I would rather lose ten times two hundred thousand pounds than accept a favor from you!"

Lowering her head to conceal the tears that were blinding her eyes, Araminta ducked under Jason's arm and ran off into the crowd. She brushed off the congratulating hands and the curious questions, and plowed unseeingly ahead until she caromed head-on into one of the spectators.

"Lady Araminta, I'm happy I couldn't prevent you from riding in that race," said a familiar voice. "I'll be grateful all my life that I saw you do it."

She grasped at Lord Salford's steadying arm. "My lord, where's Felicity?"

"Why, right over there in your carriage, next to the Prince's Stand."

"Take me there. I want to leave Epsom."

Jason took a quick, involuntary step after Araminta, then stopped abruptly. Squaring his shoulders, he turned back to meet the mob of friends, acquaintances, and perfect strangers who were bent on congratulating him on his win. All of them kept a wary distance from Caesar, who, though still firmly controlled by Smithers and the aged groom, was growing increasingly nervous.

As soon as he could make his excuses, the Duke walked over to his trainer. His voice throbbed with barely suppressed fury as he said, "Now, Smithers, you'll tell me why you allowed Lady Araminta to ride Caesar in this race. Didn't you realize how dangerous it was, to the horse and especially to Lady Araminta's safety and reputation?"

The trainer faced his employer squarely. "I make no excuses. When Jack Tobin was injured in a tavern brawl yesterday and couldn't ride, and I received no instructions from you, I should have scratched Caesar. Granted, I was disturbed to hear that you had so much money riding on the race, but I should never have allowed myself to be persuaded by her ladyship."

"Tobin injured? Why wasn't I notified?" Jason paused, thinking of the neglected messages and letters that had accumulated during his descent into the bottle, thinking also with a sudden grim certainty that Manning had made his incredible bet with the express intention of disabling Caesar's jockey.

"It's all right, Smithers," said Jason slowly. "I'm as much at fault as you are. If I'd come to Epsom yesterday as I'd planned, I could have prevented Lady Araminta from riding." He reached up to stroke his horse's flank. "Forget what I said about discharging you. Take Caesar back to his stall now for a rubdown and some rest. He deserves it."

Besieged by his friends to take a glass of wine or share a celebration supper at the Spread Eagle, a favorite haunt of the sporting fraternity at Derby time, Jason managed to decline all the invitations without giving offense, and walked slowly in the direction of his curricle. Near the Prince's Stand he encountered Lord Manning, who appeared in some indefinable way to have shrunk physically since their last meeting.

"Ah—Harwood. May I offer you my congratulations on your win?"

Acknowledging Manning's greeting with the barest of nods, Jason continued walking toward his curricle.

"Harwood, wait, please."

Jason swung around to confront Manning. "Yes?" he inquired coldly.

"About our wager. I'm by no means in Dun territory at the moment, but two hundred thousand pounds is not a small sum. I must confess that I would find it awkward at this time to raise the wind for that amount. If you could wait a little . . ."

Jason stared into Manning's haunted eyes. If the Viscount reneged on this debt of honor, he'd be a ruined man, both socially and in his diplomatic career. Jason didn't feel a shred of pity. The man deserved everything that was coming to him.

"I'm afraid I can't wait, Manning. I'll expect you at Tattersall's on settling day. Until next Monday, then."

Chapter Eighteen

Araminta's carriage turned into Bruton Street, and she breathed a sigh of relief. She was very tired, physically and emotionally, from the exertion of riding in the Derby itself and from her stressful interview with Jason. And it had been a long, wearying drive from Epsom, even though she'd avoided much of the congestion on the roads by starting her return trip to London well ahead of the general exodus of race goers from the town.

Lord and Lady Salford had offered to drive back with her from Epsom, but she'd refused, even though Felicity's presence would have been comforting on the return trip. Araminta needed to be alone, to sort out her thoughts and her emotions, and to make some kind of tentative plans for the future.

Descending from the carriage in front of Middleton House, and leaving Jessie to manage the luggage, she trudged wearily up the steps. As she walked into the foyer, Henrietta was coming down the staircase. She stared at her sister. "Araminta. I didn't expect you today. Didn't you tell me you were staying two nights in Epsom? Well, I'm glad you're here. I must talk to you."

Araminta's heart sank. Henrietta's face was pinched with anxiety. She must have received Jason's letter, and she was now about to barrage Araminta with reproaches and recrimination about her supposed authorship of the infamous *Castle of Horrors*. It was more than Araminta

326

wanted to face at the end of this disastrous day, but there seemed little point in putting off the evil. "Could we talk over a cup of tea?" she asked with a sigh of resignation. "Or better yet, could I have some of my Turkish coffee?"

After Henrietta had ordered the tea and coffee, she and Araminta walked to the morning room, where Damaris was already sitting, working desultorily on a piece of embroidery. She, too, looked pale and upset. "Aunt Araminta!" she exclaimed. "Back so soon? Did your horse win the Derby?"

A flicker of surprise passed through Araminta's mind. Damaris had never displayed much real interest in the Derby. It was odd she would do so now, when her attention must be entirely concentrated on the enormity of her aunt's conduct in writing that scandalous book. Perhaps it was her natural politeness speaking. Or perhaps her mother hadn't yet told Damaris about Jason's letter.

"No, alas, Selim lost the race," Araminta replied. "The Duke's horse, Caesar, was the winner."

"Oh, too bad! Poor Martin! I daresay he was devastated," said Damaris with what seemed like genuine regret. "He was counting on a Derby win with Selim to make his name as a trainer." She added perfunctorily, "I'm sure the Duke will be pleased that his horse won."

"Well, to be sure, I'm sorry your horse lost, Araminta, but we have more important things to talk about," said Henrietta, waving her hand impatiently. Then, as she peered closely at Araminta, the harried expression disappeared momentarily from her face. She said with disapproval, "There's a black spot on your right cheek, below your ear."

Trust Henrietta to concentrate on the essentials of life, thought Araminta, fighting an impulse to laugh. In the rush to pack up and leave the hotel room in Epsom, she must have been careless in removing all traces of the bootblacking that had disguised her face during the race. Glancing down at her hands, she could see traces of stain

327

around her fingernails. She shrugged. "It's a grimy business, traveling. What did you want to discuss with me, Henrietta? Has the Duke written to you?"

"The Duke? No. Why? I want to talk to you about Gillian."

"What about Gillian?"

"Oh, it's that ghastly book again," cried Henrietta. "It was bad enough when everyone suspected *you* of writing it, but now . . . Oh, Araminta," she wailed. "What am I to do about Gillian? Where *is* Gillian?"

Araminta sat up straight. "What do you mean? Is she gone?"

"My dear, I thought I would have palpitations this afternoon when my abigail brought me this letter—but there, read it for yourself."

Araminta gazed blankly for several seconds at Henrietta before reading the crumpled note that her sister had handed her. "Dearest Mama and Damaris, I know you'll be so disappointed and angry with me," it began, "but I must tell you that I wrote *Castle of Horrors*. I simply can't allow Aunt Araminta to take the blame any longer for what I've done. No matter how much she denies writing the book, no matter how much support our family shows toward her, some people are always going to think she did it, and I can't have that on my conscience. Please believe I never meant to hurt the Duke. I'm going away so that I won't embarrass you anymore. Don't worry about me, I shall be quite safe."

"Gillian's disappeared," cried Henrietta, reaching for her handkerchief. "She must have left the house about midday, taking with her only a small portmanteau with a few changes of clothes. Where can she have gone? What does she intend to do?"

"She took her writing materials, Mama," said Damaris, "so I'm sure she had no plans to—to injure herself . . ."

As Henrietta stared at Damaris in open-mouthed shock, Araminta said quickly, "Of course Gillian's not

328

planning to put an end to herself or anything so ridiculous! She's gone off to write another novel! I'm sorry, Henrietta, but the child *is* a writer, and you must resign yourself to it." She broke off as the butler appeared in the doorway.

"Yes, Simpson?" said Henrietta. "We're not seeing callers today."

The Duke of Harwood pushed past the butler. "I don't wish to intrude, Lady Middleton, but I must talk to Lady Araminta—" He interrupted himself, seeing Henrietta's expression of distress. "Is something wrong?"

Misery and embarrassment were mingled on Henrietta's face. "I don't know how to tell you this," she faltered. "It's Gillian. She's disappeared, leaving behind a letter in which she confessed to writing that dreadful, lying book."

"She wrote to me, too. I found her letter when I returned from Epsom a short time ago." Jason tossed a faintly irritated glance at Henrietta and Damaris. It was clear that he would have preferred to speak to Araminta alone, but he continued doggedly. "That's why I'm here, Araminta. I owe you an apology."

"Thank you, but I don't think my feelings matter now," said Araminta quietly. She noted that Jason's many-caped driving coat and elegant boots were thick with dust, and reflected with a flicker of satisfaction that he had probably left Epsom very shortly after her own departure, going straight to his house in South Audley Street. There, after examining his mail, he must have driven immediately to Bruton Street to make his apologies, without stopping to change his clothes.

"Gillian should be our only concern," she went on. "She never meant to do you any harm, you know. And now the poor child feels so guilty about what she did that she's run away, we have no idea where."

"Wherever she went," said Henrietta, "she must have gone on foot. She had no money."

"We-l-l." Time to confess, thought Araminta. "Actually

Gillian did have money. The publisher of her book paid her one hundred and fifty pounds."

"How did you—" Henrietta closed her mouth, thinking better of asking the question.

"Money being no problem, perhaps Gillian traveled by stagecoach to your estate in Lincolnshire," suggested Araminta.

"I don't think so. It's too obvious. She'd know it would be the first place we would think of," said Damaris, breaking her silence for the first time. She carefully avoided looking at Jason, and Araminta suspected that the revelation that Gillian had written *Castle of Horrors* was more deeply mortifying to Damaris than her original conviction that her aunt had written it. "If my sister really doesn't want to be found—" Damaris interrupted herself. "Mama! What about Great-aunt Tabitha? Gillian's godmother," she added in an aside for the benefit of Araminta and the Duke. "Only a few days ago, Gillian was saying that Aunt Tabitha was growing too old to live by herself in the wilds of Northumberland."

"Of course, that must be it," exclaimed Henrietta, jumping to her feet. "I'll send an express immediately to Aunt Tabitha, and another to the estate in Lincolnshire. Come, Damaris." She rushed toward the door, uttering a stifled scream as she caught sight of her butler in the doorway. Simpson inched past her into the room, supporting a battered-looking Lieutenant Craddock. The lieutenant's cheek sported several ugly welts, one eye was blackened, he wore his left arm in a sling, and he was limping badly.

"Good God, Craddock," Jason ejaculated, lifting his quizzing glass to his eye. "You look as though you should be reporting to sick bay after taking part in an engagement with the Channel fleet."

"Here, Roger, sit down," said Araminta, guiding the lieutenant into a chair. "Now, what's happened to you? And where's Odile? I understood you were

330

taking her to Epsom today."

"We never got there. Odile is gone. Kidnapped," said Roger tragically. "We started out for Epsom in good time this morning, but we were held up when we reached Mitcham. There was such a crush of vehicles there that we were barely able to crawl along. I noticed without much interest that two horsemen were galloping in our direction from across the Common. These men trotted along the line of slowly moving carriages, peering at the occupants, and then, before I realized fully what was happening, they stopped beside my curricle. One of them snatched Odile out of her seat, the other lashed out at me with his riding whip, causing me to crash to the ground against a boulder. I was knocked unconscious by the fall. When I recovered my wits, I found that my left arm was broken and I had severely twisted my leg. Odile, of course, was long gone with her captors, over the Common."

"That was this morning?" Jason demanded.

"Yes, shortly before noon." Roger seemed dazed by the question.

Jason reached under his waistcoat for his watch. "It's seven o'clock, man. Where have you been since noon?"

The lieutenant flushed. "I resent your implication. My tiger took the reins, naturally, since I couldn't drive, but he had to pull off the road and wait for the long line of carriages to pass us before we could even begin our journey back to London. Then we had to stop in Streatham, where we found a doctor to splint my arm, and when we finally arrived in the City, I decided to go around to the Bow Street Magistrates' Court to report Odile's abduction. That's why it took me so long to get here."

"Roger, why on earth would anyone set out to kidnap Odile?" demanded Araminta. "She has no fortune. She has no enemies that I know of. Did the kidnappers say anything at all to indicate why they . . ." Araminta paused, apprehension growing in her face. "Roger! Did the kidnappers look foreign?"

331

The lieutenant's eyes widened. "Yes. They were very dark-complexioned, and one of them spoke a few words to the other in a harsh, guttural language I'd never heard before."

"Arabic," said Araminta. "Why didn't I listen to Odile? She was always so afraid that the Pasha's men would come after her, and now they've done it."

"Pasha?" repeated Henrietta blankly. "I don't understand any of this. Who is this Pasha, and why should he be pursuing Madame Lacoste?"

Araminta could see the word "seraglio" forming on Roger's hapless lips, and she rushed in to say, "While we were in the Levant, Odile incurred the enmity of a powerful Turkish official, who vowed to seek revenge. Odile was frightened by the threat, but I never believed for one moment that the Pasha would reach clear across Europe to harm a defenseless girl. How wrong I was. Well, Roger, now that we know who abducted Odile, we can do something about it." Ignoring the quick, amused grin that appeared on Jason's lips, she crossed the room to pull the bell rope; when a footman appeared, she told him to have her carriage brought around.

"Where are you going?" exclaimed her sister.

"She's off to one of the Channel ports, of course," said Jason impatiently. "Araminta, I'm coming with you. We'll try to catch up with the Pasha's men before they take ship. I'll bring around my chaise. We'll make faster time that way."

Roger Craddock struggled to his feet. "I can't allow you to do that. Odile is my betrothed. It's my place to go with Lady Araminta."

"Stop acting like a paper-skull," Jason retorted. "You can scarcely hobble, and you have one good arm. How much help would you be to Araminta in your condition?"

"None," said Roger, biting his lip. "I accept your help gladly, Duke. Thank you."

"I, too, Jason," said Araminta. "Jessie will have my

portmanteau packed, and I'll be all ready to go when you return in your chaise. Say half an hour's time?"

"What are you thinking of?" gasped Henrietta. "Go off with the Duke unchaperoned on a night-long journey to heaven knows where? Supposing you arrive at Dover or New Haven or Folkestone, only to find that this—this Pasha has already sailed with your friend Odile. What then? Would you go on to France? To Syria, even? At the very least, you might find it necessary to spend several nights away from London in the Duke's company."

Araminta lifted her chin. "Are you implying that society might pin the label of demirep on me and throw me out of its ranks?"

Henrietta looked shocked. "Of course I'm not suggesting anything so vulgar. But Araminta, do think. You can't deny there's a good chance your reputation might be tarnished by such an escapade. Let the authorities take care of the problem."

"I'll have to risk the gossips' tongues. I'd do anything rather than see Odile back in the—in the clutches of that Turk."

"You don't know what you're saying, Araminta. I positively forbid you to go off like this."

Jason intervened. "Remember, Lady Middleton, that no one will know anything about our journey except you and Damaris and Lieutenant Craddock."

"But—"

"The Duke is right, Mama," said Damaris quietly. Her voice sounded a little brittle, and the color was high on her pretty face, but she seemed quite composed. "If we're all discreet, the gossips will never get hold of the story. And I think you must allow Aunt Araminta to do what she thinks best for her friend. Think how you'd feel if somebody had carried me off to a harem!"

Jason gave Damaris a long look, in which surprise was mingled with respect. "You have a very level head on your shoulders, Damaris. Thank you," he said. Then, laughter dancing in his eyes, he added to Araminta, "Lady Middleton may have a point, however. I daresay we can't be too careful about the proprieties. Do you think you can lay hands on those widow's weeds that Madame Lacoste used to wear?"

Araminta whooped with delight. "The perfect touch! What a co-conspirator you are, Jason!"

As the chaise rattled across the great camel-back curve of London Bridge, Araminta could hear a noise like the sound of artillery fire. Turning her head, she glanced inquiringly at Jason through the concealing folds of her widow's veil.

"The London Bridge Waterworks," he explained. "The water surging through the arches of the bridge turns giant wooden water wheels which in turn direct the flow into great iron cylinders. There's talk of replacing the wooden wheels next year with iron ones."

The sun was sinking as Jason drove the chaise along the old Kent Road, although the long early-summer twilight had not yet begun to draw in.

"I hope we've guessed right," Jason observed with a touch of unease. "For lack of any information about the kidnappers's route, we're obliged to go by the law of probabilities. More likely than not the Pasha's men are heading for a French port, intending to travel south through the country and take ship at a Mediterranean port for Syria. In that case, Dover and Folkestone are the ports closest to France, and of the two, Dover is by far the more widely used port."

Araminta realized that Jason was speaking more to reassure himself that he had made the right choices than to impart any information. She said quickly, "I trust your instincts. I *know* we'll reach Odile in time." He responded with a quick little smile of appreciation, reaching over to touch her hand. They did not speak of Odile again immediately. It was as if, by not mentioning her name, they were also dismissing any possibility of failure in their attempt to rescue her.

Passing through New Cross and Blackheath, the chaise began the steep climb up the wooded slopes of Shooters Hill to the Bull Hotel at the top of the hill, where they were to change horses for the first time. The hostlers literally flung themselves to attention in their eagerness to serve an obvious swell like the Duke, and Jason and Araminta were on their way after the briefest of stops. As they drove out of the inn yard, they could hear the long blast of a horn, and Araminta craned her neck to catch a glimpse of a Royal Mail coach, smartly painted in maroon and black and with the royal arms emblazoned on its panels, pulling into the Bull behind them. Throughout the rest of the long night, Jason and Araminta paced the Dover Mail, always ahead of it, sometimes by a substantial margin, often in sight of it.

"We should reach Rochester about midnight," Jason observed. "Be sure to tell me if you feel tired. We can stop at any time to allow you to rest."

"Thank you, but I'd like to push on as fast as we can."

"That's what I would have expected you to say," Jason grinned. He slanted a quizzical glance at her. "You look very authentic in those widow's weeds. But then, as we know, you have a gift for disguises."

Araminta chuckled. "So you didn't recognize me in my racing silks?"

"Not immediately, no. As you rode past me, I could see that you weren't Jack Tobin. It was only when I approached the winning post, bent on learning why Smithers had made a substitution for Tobin—and how he had managed to find another jockey, and an Arab at that— that I realized who you were." Jason's voice changed. "I thank God I didn't know you were riding Caesar until the race was over. Araminta, why did you take such chances? You could have been killed, or maimed for life."

335

"You're my friend, even if we had quarreled over that silly book. I couldn't let you lose a fortune for lack of any help I might give you." Never one to be serious for long, Araminta added provocatively, "Actually, I didn't do it for you at all. I wanted to prove that I could ride and win in the Derby, and of course I couldn't expect Hassan to give up his chance to ride Selim!"

"You relieve my mind no end," said Jason drily. "I can't tell you how comforting it is to know that I needn't feel beholden to you."

"Exactly," beamed Araminta. "I was just trying to show you what an independent woman I am."

"That was unnecessary. You've done nothing but flaunt your independence since I met you!"

It was growing dark now, and they stopped to light the carriage lamps. They reached Rochester a little before midnight. The night wore on, growing chilly. Jason wrapped a robe around Araminta's legs, and she drowsed intermittently, scarcely aware of the towns through which they were passing. Sittingbourne. Faversham. Canterbury. Barham. At six in the morning, Araminta jerked awake to find the chaise entering the outskirts of Dover. It was windy and overcast, with a fine, cold rain beginning to fall.

"We'll find you a room at the Ship while I go down to the pier to have a word with the harbormaster," said the Duke.

"You should rest for a bit, too," Araminta replied with a remorseful glance at Jason, whose shoulders were drooping with weariness. "I was able to snatch a few minutes of sleep during the night, but you look tired to death."

"You need rest more than I do. I didn't ride Caesar in the Derby yesterday." Jason drove into the courtyard of the hotel, which, despite the early hour, was bustling with activity as a stagecoach and several private vehicles were preparing to depart. Escorting Araminta into the hotel,

336

Jason faced down the obsequious landlord who informed him apologetically that all his rooms had been taken the night before and there would be a wait before a vacated chamber could be prepared for the lady.

"I trust that the wait will be short," said Jason coldly. "Not only has my sister suffered a great loss recently, but at the moment she is very fatigued. I certainly hope that your establishment will not add to her discomfort by forcing her to wait unduly for a bedchamber."

"Not a minute, not a second longer than necessary, Your Grace," the landlord assured him.

Jason's quelling eye and peremptory orders produced a bedchamber for Araminta in under ten minutes. Removing her bonnet and enveloping widow's veil with a sigh of relief, she threw herself down on the bed, feeling herself drift into a blissful euphoria as her cramped limbs began to relax. She fell into a deep sleep, rousing most unwillingly when a servant girl entered the room to tug gently on her shoulder.

"What time is it?" Araminta yawned, struggling to sit up.

"Close on eleven, ma'am. The gentleman—your brother, I reckon—is waiting for you in a private parlor downstairs."

Jason rose as Araminta entered the parlor. After she had closed the door, she threw back the veil that she had donned before leaving the bedchamber.

"Were you able to get some sleep?" he asked, pulling back a chair for her in front of a table covered with a crisp white cloth and laden with food.

"Yes, thank you." Araminta eyed with pleasure the steaming coffee pot. "That smells good. May I have some?" Peering at him over her cup, she said, "You look in good spirits. Do you have any news of Odile?"

"Yes. I believe she left Dover with her captors at dawn this morning. The harbormaster reports that a party of 'foreign gentlemen' landed here two days ago in a two-masted French brig, a cargo boat, I believe. These men, 'dressed like ordinary English gents, do y'see, but *very* dark-complexioned, like,' had apparently chartered the boat in Calais. Immediately on landing, they inquired about hiring a carriage. They weren't seen again until early this morning, when they reboarded the brig and sailed for Calais. With them was a heavily veiled woman, who certainly hadn't been a member of the original party."

Araminta drew a deep breath. "That *must* have been Odile. All the pieces fit."

"Yes, I don't think there can be any doubt about it. Presumably the kidnappers stayed the night at some hotel in Dover, since they must have arrived here last evening."

"That sounds like Odile. Kidnapped or no, she would insist on spending a comfortable night in a real bed!" Araminta sobered. "You shouldn't have let me sleep. We should be boarding ship to follow them across the Channel."

"All in good time. I slept for several hours myself. After all, it wouldn't benefit Madame Lacoste if we were to begin the chase in a state of total exhaustion. I've reserved places for us on a packet leaving Dover at one o'clock. Meanwhile, I suggest we have some breakfast. I'm famished."

"What an excellent idea, Jason," said Araminta several minutes later. "I was near starvation myself. This is excellent ham. Will you have another glass of the claret?" She lifted a glass to her lips, and then, a startling thought occurring to her, she choked slightly as a swallow of wine went down the wrong way. "Jason! You said 'a party of foreigners.' Poor Roger mentioned only two dark-faced men. How many abductors are we dealing with, do you think?"

"The harbormaster wasn't paying strict attention, naturally, but he recalls seeing four or five men. He said one of them seemed to be very much in authority over the others. I've been wondering if . . ."

"If the Pasha himself is leading the group," finished Araminta. She gazed at Jason with a troubled frown. "That would make any attempt to rescue Odile much more difficult."

"We'll cross that bridge when we come to it." Jason put down his glass and leaned back in his chair, glancing around the parlor. "Do you recognize this room, Araminta?"

"Indeed I do." Her eyes glinted with laughter. "I recall having a bottle of champagne—actually, it was the best part of two bottles, wasn't it?—with a certain flirtatious rake in this very room."

"That was only a few months ago, but it's hard for me to remember a time when I didn't know you," Jason remarked wistfully. "On Lady Torrington's barge, sailing up the Thames to her *fête champêtre,* you said you wondered what would have happened if . . ."

Araminta hastily stood up. "I think we should be getting down to the harbor."

The chilly rain of the early morning had fortunately ceased by the time Araminta and Jason walked up the gangplank of the Channel packet, which was anchored next to the stone pier running into the sea from the western beach of the town, beneath the forbidding walls of the castle on the heights. They were among the first to board and counted themselves lucky to take possession of a pair of chairs on the deck. Araminta promptly settled back comfortably into her chair, closing her eyes and preparing to catch up on her sleep during the crossing. Shortly after they cleared the harbor, however, the sky turned a menacing gray and soon galelike winds were sweeping the ship. The crossing, which normally was accomplished in three hours in good weather, was obviously going to take longer than that. It would be, in fact, over six hours before the packet docked in Calais.

Araminta had never been troubled by seasickness. Today, as usual, she felt exhilarated rather than threatened by buffeting winds and tossing decks. It was only when she saw Jason making a frantic run for the railing that she realized he was in difficulties. She went over to him, placing her hand on his arm. "Is there anything I can do?"

He turned a ghastly face toward her. "Yes," he said bitterly. "You can ask the captain to fetch a gun and put me out of my misery. Tell me, Araminta, is there *nothing* that fazes you?"

She put her arm around him, supporting him as he moved unsteadily back to his chair. "I can't claim any credit for being a good sailor," she told him. "I was born that way. But I suspect that you knew, before you boarded the ship, that you'd be very ill if we hit rough seas. Am I right?"

"Yes," replied Jason morosely. "I get sick in a rowboat. Always have. My brother Rupert used to laugh himself silly at my sufferings."

"Then you're a real hero, and I admire you immensely."

"Thank you, my dear girl, but you do me too much honor," Jason said with a twisted grin. "Short of walking on the water, there's only one way for me to cross the English Channel, and that's by boat."

The winds had abated by late afternoon, and Jason was already feeling more himself when the packet neared Calais. Because of the low tide, however, the boat could not enter the harbor. The hapless passengers, many of whom had been very ill during the crossing, were required to climb into rowboats to be taken closer to shore, and were then ignominiously hoisted from the boats by watermen who carried them to the landing. Araminta scarcely had a moment to savor the expression of pure loathing on Jason's face as he was deposited on the quay by a brawny waterman before both of them were forced to cope with a

340

band of noisy, gesticulating porters, male and female, who insisted on carrying their portmanteaux to the Customs House for exorbitant fees.

Once arrived at the Customs House, the passengers' troubles were not over. The customs officers insisted on delving thoroughly into every writing case, purse, reticule, valise, and portmanteau, searching for contraband *marchandise anglaise*. The customs officials were more than thorough—they were intrusive and impertinent, insisting on personal searches of the passengers. Immediately ahead of Araminta in the slowly moving inspection line, a young woman, part of an English family group, suddenly screamed in horror, "Mama, that man reached down inside my *stays!*"

A low growl, deep in his throat, erupted from Jason. His lips were set in a rigid, uncompromising line as he and Araminta took their places in front of the customs officer. When the official emptied both of their portmanteaux on the counter and pawed through the contents, Jason said nothing, nor did he make any objection when the officer felt with rough hands along the ducal anatomy from the armpits to the ankles. However, when the official turned to Araminta and reached into the pocket of her pelisse, Jason acted. He put out his hand, squeezing the officer's shoulder in a sinewy grip that made the man wince, but before the officer could voice his anger at the affront, Jason remarked in strongly accented but perfectly comprehensible French: "My good man, I happen to be an intimate friend of *Monsieur le Comte* Decazes, your Minister of Police. I fancy Monsieur Decazes will be extremely happy to learn that you have extended every courtesy to my sister in her bereavement."

Slowly the customs officer's expression merged from outrage into complaisance. He even managed a difficult smile as he said, "Thank you, *monsieur.* My name, should you care to mention it to *Monsieur le Comte,* is Henri Lulac. *Madame,* my condolences on your loss. You

341

are free to proceed to the passport officer."

Outside the Customs House, Jason raised his hand to summon a *fiacre*. "Hôtel d'Angleterre," he told the driver. "We'll try the Angleterre first for news of the kidnappers," he explained to Araminta. "It's the hotel most patronized by foreigners. We can also hire a chaise there."

Calais was a small town, consisting of eight narrow streets converging on the central Place d'Armes, which was dominated by a tall medieval watchtower. Next to the Hôtel de la Ville in the square was the Hôtel d'Angleterre. Araminta waited in the cab while Jason went into the hotel to inquire about Odile. He returned with definite news. "The clerk reports that a party of five dark-complexioned men and one veiled woman hired a traveling carriage here just before noon and drove off along the Paris post road. I've hired a post chaise and we can be on our way as soon as we've had a meal."

Jason was standing at the open door of the *fiacre* as he spoke, with the late-afternoon sun shining directly on his face. Araminta was appalled to observe how exhausted he looked. "A meal, yes," she said firmly. "Resume our pursuit tonight, no. Both of us need at least a few hours' rest."

"We can't afford to let Madame Lacoste's captors get too far ahead of us," Jason fretted.

"If I know Odile, she'll throw a tantrum if the kidnappers attempt to make her travel too long and too fast. She's far too fond of her creature comforts!"

Jason capitulated without any further objection, proving, Araminta reflected, how close to collapse he was. However, after an excellent dinner in a well-appointed private parlor of the inn, served with a bottle of the establishment's justly famous champagne, he seemed to revive. "You know, it's fortunate for us that Madame Lacoste's kidnappers are keeping her veiled, I presume to prevent strange men from seeing her face," he commented at one point. "It makes it easy for us to keep on her trail. Every-

342

one—hotel keepers, porters, stable boys—remembers seeing a heavily veiled woman."

"Jason, I haven't really thanked you yet for coming with me. You've no obligation to Odile, I don't think you even like her . . ."

"I'm not doing this for your Odile," Jason interrupted. "You should know that."

Araminta looked away, trying frantically to think of something to say that would discharge the electric tension building up between them. At last she said, "It's just occurred to me that I have no idea what our plan of attack will be when we finally catch up with Odile."

"To tell the truth, neither have I. It will depend on circumstances."

"Well, I wanted you to know that I'll be of some help. I remembered to bring this." Araminta reached into her reticule.

Jason stared at the little pistol that she'd placed on the table between them. "No scimitars? No light artillery? You disappoint me, Araminta."

It was just beginning to grow light the next morning when Araminta stepped out into the pre-dawn chill to find Jason glumly surveying their postilion, an unprepossessing individual in a dirty sheepskin coat, greasy cap, and enormous jackboots rimmed with iron to protect his legs. Unlike his English counterparts, he would be accompanying the chaise astride his own shaggy pony instead of riding one of the horses in the team.

"I hope we won't have any trouble with this fellow," Jason remarked of the postilion as the post chaise lurched out of the courtyard, heading south through the dark deserted streets of Calais. "I hear that French postilions on the whole are a lazy, greedy, impertinent lot, as lief to cheat you or desert you as not." He suppressed a yawn. "Did you sleep well?"

"Well enough. I wonder, though, why the hotel puts so many mattresses on their beds. Mine was piled so high that if I had fallen out of bed during the night, I might have broken a limb! And what was that unpleasant odor I could smell throughout the building?"

"Drains. The drains of the military hospital run underneath the hotel. It's the one drawback of the Angleterre."

Fortunately for Jason and Araminta, the weather remained fine during the long, tiring day that followed. They were able to maintain a steady pace of roughly nine miles an hour, changing horses at every other post. At Montreuil, in late morning, Jason learned that the fugitives had stayed at an inn in the town the previous night.

"We're gaining on them," Jason said as they were leaving Montreuil. "We're only three, possibly four, hours behind them now."

"Perhaps they don't fear pursuit any longer. They know that Roger Craddock isn't a wealthy man; once they succeeded in getting Odile across the Channel, they may have concluded that Roger wouldn't attempt to follow them across Europe."

The wearying miles wore on. Nampont. The Forest of Crécy. Abbeville. Belloy-sur-Somme. And finally, at the end of the afternoon, they entered Amiens, where they ran their prey to earth at the Hôtel des Ambassadeurs.

"They've taken two bedchambers for the night," Jason reported to Araminta, waiting for him on the red stone floor of the foyer. "The man who appears to be the leader is supping with the veiled woman in a private parlor. The others are having a meal in the coffee room. This may be our best opportunity to catch the Pasha—if it is the Pasha—alone, without any of his henchmen to come to his assistance."

"How should we go about it, Jason?"

He paused for a moment, frowning in concentration. "What about this?" he said finally. "I'll knock on the door of the parlor and walk right in as if I were one of

344

the inn servants, shoot or tie up or otherwise incapacitate the Pasha, and rush Odile out of the hotel before the other kidnappers are even aware of what's happening. You'll be waiting in the carriage for us and we'll be able to get away immediately. Fortunately, I ordered a change of horses when we arrived here." He turned on his heel, his hand in the pocket of his greatcoat over the bulge that Araminta presumed was a pistol.

She followed him down the hallway, tugging at the skirt of his coat. "Now, look here, Jason, wait one moment. You make it sound entirely too easy," she hissed. "Shoot or otherwise incapacitate the Pasha, indeed! I'm not going to sit tamely outside in the carriage waiting for you. I'm coming with you. You may need my help."

Whirling to confront her, he cut back the words of protest on his lips as he noted the stubborn set of her head beneath the enveloping veil. "Just stay behind me, that's all I ask," he muttered. At the end of the hallway he paused, looking around him as if unsure of his way and extending his arm to Araminta with a solicitous smile for the benefit of the tall dark man who stood at attention in front of one of the closed doors in the side corridor to their left. "The Pasha's a cannier man than I thought," Jason muttered. "He's posted a guard. Drop your reticule when we draw abreast of him."

Araminta could feel her heart beating faster as she and Jason walked slowly toward the guard. Even through her heavy veil, she could see that the man was a typical Levantine, appearing ill at ease in his unfamiliar European coat and breeches. He kept an alert gaze on the approaching couple, but his attention was broken when Araminta, stumbling artistically, dropped her reticule at his feet. His eyes fell, and he made an instinctive move to pick up the reticule. At that moment Jason slammed a powerful fist into the man's jaw, sending him to the floor senseless. Almost in the same movement, Jason threw open the door and strode into the parlor. Snatching up her reticule,

Araminta followed close on his heels, closing the door behind her.

A man and a woman were seated at a table in front of a cozy fire. Odile, no longer veiled, gasped in fear as Jason erupted into the room. Her companion jumped up from the table, thrusting his hand inside his well-cut coat.

"Put your hands above your head," Araminta exclaimed in Arabic, motioning menacingly with the small pistol she had slipped out of her reticule. Switching to English, she said, "I think he was reaching for a knife, Jason. You'd best search him for a weapon." She threw back her widow's veil, training the pistol with a steady hand at Odile's kidnapper while Jason swiftly ran his hands down the man's sides and stepped back holding a long, wicked-looking knife.

"Araminta! Why—what are you doing here?" stammered Odile.

"We're rescuing you, of course. Come along, we haven't a moment to lose."

"I—I don't want to be rescued. I want to stay with Mirhan." While Araminta watched incredulously, Odile rushed to the Pasha's side, grasping his arm tightly.

Araminta turned her affronted eyes to the Pasha, whom she was seeing for the first time. He was a tall, lithe man with a handsome, swarthy face, considerably younger than she had imagined him. He stared back at her with an expression of mingled hauteur and anger. She suspected that he understood much of what she and Odile were saying in English.

"What do you mean, you don't want to be rescued? What about Roger and your plans to be married?" Araminta demanded.

Odile had the grace to look faintly ashamed of herself, but she clung even more tightly to Mirhan's arm, saying, "I don't think I ever really loved Roger. In any case, I couldn't bear the thought of living with his bourgeois parents, or in a tiny box of a house in Portsmouth, while he spent the next thirty years of his life at sea." She lifted her eyes to the Pasha and smiled angelically. "The moment I saw Mirhan again, I realized I loved *him*. He touched me so much when he told me he hadn't been able to get me out of his thoughts after I ran away, until finally he decided he must go all the way to England to fetch me back. And he's promised to divorce all his other wives and marry me, so I know we're going to be happy forever."

"Supposing he changes his mind again and takes back his other wives, or marries a completely new set of candidates? And what about his harem? *None* of those women was married to him."

"Oh." A tiny cloud flitted across Odile's brow and then disappeared. "Well, I don't think Mirhan will want to marry other wives, but the Koran does allow him to have four, you know. In fact, as he once explained it to me, it might be his *duty* to do so. One couldn't in conscience interfere with a man's practice of his religion, could one? As for the harem, that doesn't — won't — count."

"You're sure about this, Odile? This is your last chance to change your mind."

"I'm very sure. But thank you for caring about me. Perhaps someday we'll see each other again? You always said you'd like to go back to Syria."

Araminta spoke to the Pasha in Arabic. "I leave my friend with you, Your Excellency. I pray you will make her happy." A slight mile curved his mouth and he nodded.

"Then good-bye, Odile," Araminta said. "Let's go, Jason." Putting her veil down over her face, she turned to leave the room just as the door burst open and the room was invaded by four wild-eyed Levantines who rushed at Jason with drawn knives. Before they could reach the Duke, the Pasha raised his voice in a brief staccato command. The four men stopped in their tracks. Slowly Araminta and Jason walked out of the room.

In the hallway, Jason mopped his brow and said, "What would you say to a glass of champagne? Not here, of course. There must be another decent hotel in Amiens. I don't propose to travel another mile today, but I wouldn't fall asleep easily here, knowing that those Arabs, or Turks, or whatever you call 'em, were staying in the same hotel."

Le Lion d'Or was not, perhaps, quite as elegant a hostelry as the Hôtel des Ambassadeurs, but its bedchambers were adequate, and a supper, served by the landlord himself in his best parlor, was well prepared and delicious.

Araminta was unusually silent during the meal. She ate with her customary good appetite, but her mind was elsewhere. Jason forbore to interrupt her thoughts, merely leaning across the table from time to time to refill her champagne glass. At length she looked up, pounding her fist on the table. "Confound it, how could Odile turn her back on England and a life with Roger, who's a dear, kind soul even if he isn't a rich man, in order to become the Pasha's plaything? Mirhan says he loves her now, but you know he'll tire of her in a few years. She'll die an old lady in the harem."

"Not every female wants to be an independent woman, said Jason calmly. "It may be that Odile never really wanted to leave the harem. It wouldn't surprise me to learn that she never had a thought of escaping until you put the idea in her head."

"Don't be ridiculous," Araminta snapped. Then she fell silent again, biting her lip. "I remember now, the Pasha was about to take another wife at the time I located Odile in his harem. He said it was purely a marriage of convenience, a matter of local politics, but I think she probably had expected him to marry *her*. Perhaps you're right. Odile was feeling jealous and rejected, so when I came along, it was the easiest thing in the world to persuade her to run away." She drew a deep breath. "I swear, I will never attempt to interfere in anyone's life again."

"Not until the next time you encounter some unfortunate who badly needs taking in hand," grinned Jason. He stood up, walking around the table to pull Araminta to her feet. "Tell me something. Do independent women ever think of getting married?"

Araminta looked up at him, her breath coming a little faster. "Sometimes. But not to men who already have fiancées."

Jason said slowly, "I can't marry Damaris when I'm madly in love with you, Araminta. It wouldn't be fair to her. It would kill me. And if I cry off, I don't think Damaris would be hurt, except perhaps in her pride. I've suspected for a long time that she doesn't care for me deeply. Oh, I think she wanted to please her mother by making a grand marriage, I think she wanted to be a duchess, but . . ." He shook his head. "Once I wouldn't have cared about that. People in our class marry for a number of reasons, and love isn't necessarily one of them." He put his arms around her, drawing her close. "But now that I've met you, Araminta, I know that I don't want to live out the rest of my life without love. I'm not mistaken, am I? You do love me, just a little?"

"Oh, yes. A good deal, as a matter of fact. I've been restraining myself for some time from snatching you away from Damaris." Araminta reached up to trace the cleft in his chin with a gently probing finger. "That's all settled, then. Your betrothal to Damaris hasn't been announced, so neither of you will be embarrassed publicly. And you needn't fear that Damaris will go around wearing the willow for you and sink into a decline. Actually, I'm convinced that she loves Martin Corby. They were in love years ago, did you know that? Henrietta wouldn't countenance the match because Martin had no fortune. I don't think Damaris ever really stopped loving Martin. I know he's besotted about her! So let me see what I can do about promoting a match between them."

Jason looked alarmed. "Now, wait a moment." Then he

enveloped her in a crushing bear hug. "What a managing female you are. I should have known my fate from the first moment we met!"

Dear Reader,

Zebra Books welcomes your comments about this book or any other Zebra Regency you have read recently. Please address your comments to:

Zebra Books, Dept. WM
475 Park Avenue South
New York, NY 10016

Thank you for your interest.

Sincerely,
The Editorial Department
Zebra Books

REGENCIES BY JANICE BENNETT

TANGLED WEB   (2281, $3.95)

Miss Celia Marcombe's dark eyes flashed with righteous indignation. She was not a commodity to be traded or bartered to a man as insufferably arrogant as Trevor Ryde, despite what her high-handed grandfather decreed! If Lord Ryde thought she would let herself be married for any reason other than true love, he was sadly mistaken. He'd never get his hands on her fortune—let alone her person—no matter how disturbingly handsome he was . . .

MIDNIGHT MASQUE   (2512, $3.95)

It was nothing unusual for Lady Ashton to transport government documents to her father from the Home Office. But on this particular afternoon a gust of wind scattered the papers, and suddenly an important page was lost. A document desperately wanted by more than one determined gentleman—one of whom would murder to get his way . . .

AN INTRIGUING DESIRE   (2579, $3.95)

The British secret agent, Charles Marcombe, had done his bit against that blasted Bonaparte. Now it was time to nurse his wounds and come to terms with the fact that that part of his life was over. He certainly did not need the likes of Mademoiselle Therese de Bourgerre darkening his door, warning of dire emergencies and dread consequences, forcing him to remember things best forgotten. She was a delightful minx, to be sure, but it would take more than a pair of pleading emerald eyes and a woebegone smile to drag him back into the fray!